The Theatre of Tom Mac Intyre:

'Strays from the ether'

The Theatre of Tom Mac Intyre: 'Strays from the ether'

Edited by Bernadette Sweeney and Marie Kelly

Carysfort Press

A Carysfort Press Book

The Theatre of Tom Mac Intyre: 'Strays from the ether'
Edited by Bernadette Sweeney and Marie Kelly

First published as a paperback in Ireland in 2010 by
Carysfort Press Ltd
58 Woodfield
Scholarstown Road
Dublin 16
Ireland

ISBN 978-1-904505-46-4

Typeset by Carysfort Press Ltd

Printed and bound by eprint limited
Unit 35
Coolmine Industrial Estate
Dublin 15
Ireland
Cover design by eprint

This book is published with the financial assistance of
The Arts Council (An Chomhairle Ealaíon) Dublin, Ireland

For Bryan and Ruby Mae – BS

For Alan – MK

CONTENTS

Chapter 2: 'a conspirator's gleam'

Chapter 3: 'Down the ruckety pass'

Chapter 4: 'Warming to the fray'

Chapter 5: 'a gradle o' stories'

Chapter 6: 'between the worlds'

ILLUSTRATIONS

Front Cover

Actors: William Kennedy, Michael Grennell, Ciaran Grey, Dermod Moore, Vincent O'Neill and Tom Hickey (at rear) in *The Bearded Lady* (Peacock Theatre, 1984). Set design: Bronwen Casson. Photographer: Amelia Stein. Photograph courtesy of Amelia Stein.

Chapter Three

3.1   Actors: Tom Mac Intyre (and 3 others, names not recorded on file at National Library) in *Deer Crossing* by Tom Mac Intyre (Oberlin College, 1978). Photograph courtesy of Oberlin College. (Photographer unknown).

3.2   Centre pages from Peacock Theatre programme for *Snow White* by Tom Mac Intyre, 1988: Clockwise from top left: *The Great Hunger* (photograph), *The Bearded Lady* (photograph and poster image), *Rise Up Lovely Sweeney* (poster image and photograph), *Dance for your Daddy* (photograph and poster image), *The Great Hunger* (photograph), *The Great Hunger* (touring poster and programme cover). Illustration courtesy of the Abbey Theatre Archive.

3.3-   From *The Great Hunger* by Tom Mac Intyre.
3.6   Photographer Fergus Bourke. Set design: Bronwen Casson. Photographs courtesy of the Abbey Theatre Archive.

  3.3   Actors: (from left) Conal Kearney, Tom Hickey, Michele Forbes, Joan Sheehy

  3.4   Actors: (from left) Dermod Moore, Tom Hickey, Conal Kearney.

  3.5   Actors: (from left) Tom Hickey, Conal Kearney, Vincent O'Neill.

  3.6   Actors: (from left) Bríd Ní Neachtain, Tom Hickey.

3.7   *The Great Hunger* by Tom Mac Intyre. Bronwen Casson's drawing of the effigy (later realized by Frank Hallinan Flood). Illustration courtesy of Bronwen Casson.

3.8   Poster for *Rise Up Lovely Sweeney* by Tom Mac Intyre. Photographer: Fergus Bourke. Graphic design: Brendan Foreman. Poster courtesy of the Abbey Theatre Archive.

Chapter Four

4.1   Page 40 from *Rise Up Lovely Sweeney* (prompt script). Courtesy of Tom Mac Intyre and the Abbey Theatre Archive.

4.2   Unnumbered page from *Rise Up Lovely Sweeney* (prompt script). Courtesy of Tom Mac Intyre and the Abbey Theatre Archive.

Chapter Five

5.1-   From *Sheep's Milk on the Boil* by Tom Mac Intyre.
5.11   Photographer: Amelia Stein. Photographs courtesy of Amelia Stein. Set design: Monica Frawley.

5.1   (From left) Pat Kinevane and Olwen Fouéré.

5.2   (From left) Joan Sheehy, Deirdre Molloy, Owen Roe, Bongi MacDermott, Kathryn O'Boyle, Jasmine Russell.

5.3   (From left) Olwen Fouéré and Pat Kinevane.

5.4   Olwen Fouéré.

5.5   Pat Kinevane.

5.6   Olwen Fouéré.

5.7   Owen Roe and Joan Sheehy.

5.8   (From left) Jasmine Russell, Kathryn O'Boyle, Pat Kinevane and Olwen Fouéré.

5.9   (From left) Olwen Fouéré and Pat Kinevane.

5.10   (From left) Olwen Fouéré and Pat Kinevane.

5.11   Olwen Fouéré.

5.12   *The Chirpaun* by Tom Mac Intyre. Actor: Tom Hickey. Set design: Barbara Bradshaw. Photographer: Amelia Stein. Photograph courtesy of the Abbey Theatre Archive.

5.13   Poster *Good Evening, Mr Collins* by Tom Mac Intyre. Actor: Brían F. O'Byrne. Photographer: Amelia Stein. Poster courtesy of the Abbey Theatre Archive.

5.14   From *Good Evening, Mr Collins* by Tom Mac Intyre. Actors: Brían F. O'Byrne / Karen Ardiff (with backs to audience). Set design: Barbara Bradshaw. Photographer: Amelia Stein. Photograph courtesy of the Abbey Theatre Archive.

ACKNOWLEDGEMENTS

This anthology took a number of years to compile and began with Bernadette Sweeney's interest in the theatre of Tom Mac Intyre and a desire to fill a long-standing gap in the literature on this part of the canon. Marie Kelly is indebted to her co-editor for inviting her to take part in this project, for sharing her passion for this work and for mentoring her through her first experience of publication. Our journey together has been full of exciting and joyful discoveries; an archaeological dig into a very rich range of sources that will finally document, in pictures and words, Tom Mac Intyre's fascinating body of theatre work. On foot of thousands of emails and Skyped conversations between two continents, our project is now complete. Our final task is to say thank you to all of those who have given generously of their time and without whom this publication would have been impossible.

Firstly we would like to thank our commissioning editor Eamonn Jordan, as well as Dan Farrelly and Lilian Chambers of Carysfort Press, for all of their help, advice, and guidance through the process.

Grateful thanks also to the National University of Ireland for its generous financial support in bringing this book to publication.

We are indebted to all of our commissioned contributors for their articles and support for this project: Karen Ardiff, Selina Cartmell, Bronwen Casson, Finola Cronin, Ben Francombe, Fiach Mac Conghail, Dermod Moore, Bríd Ní Neachtain, Catriona Ryan, SarahJane Scaife, Daniel Shea, Amelia Stein, and Joe Vaněk.

We are also indebted to photographers Amelia Stein, Ros Kavanagh, Pat Redmond, and the late Fergus Bourke, with permission granted by the Abbey theatre, for their wonderful contribution to the collection of images which bring Mac Intyre's work to life in this book. Their work in archiving and documenting the theatricality of this extraordinary *oeuvre* is gratefully acknowledged.

We would also like to acknowledge with thanks permission to use material from a range of authors and their publishers: Marina Carr, Ciaran Carson, Paul Durcan, Olwen Fouéré, Michael Harding, Dermot Healy, Medbh McGuckian, Nuala Ní Dhomhnaill, Seamus Heaney, Tom Hickey, Kathryn Holmquist, Tom Mac Intyre, Christina Hunt Mahony, Patrick Mason, John Barrett, Deirdre Mulrooney, John Scott, Sean Rocks, Alan Titley, and Vincent Woods.

Theatre reviewers: Michael Billington, David Calvert, Jocelyn Clarke, Nicholas de Jongh, Diarmuid Johnson, Karen Fricker, Patrick Lonergan, Joseph McMinn, Helen Meany, the late David Nowlan, John O'Mahoney, Fintan O'Toole, Desmond Rushe, Michael Sheridan, Gerard Stembridge, Peter Thompson, Colm Tóibín, Victoria White.

Publishers: Abbey Theatre (for programme notes, and photographs), Patsy Horton at Blackstaff Press, Carysfort Press, Cengage Learning Inc, *Krino* Magazine, Jean Barry and Peter Fallon at Gallery Press, Eve Thompson at *Guardian* Newspapers, Antony Farrell at Lilliput Press, Adrienne Carolan at *Independent* Newspapers, Joan Hyland at *Irish Press* Plc, Helen Meany at *Irish Theatre Magazine*, Regina Dwyer and Eoin McVey at *The Irish Times*, Ruth Tellis at Palgrave MacMillan, Gretchen Oberfranc at Friends of the Library at Princeton University Press, *Prompts* Magazine, John Glennon of RTÉ Libraries and Archives, Paul Hadfield and Lynda Henderson at *Theatre Ireland* Archive, Celine Moran at *The Sunday Tribune*.

Very special thanks to the ever-helpful Mairéad Delaney and her assistant Mairéad Lynch at the Abbey Theatre Archives, and to Jennifer Traynor in the Literary Department for all their help in locating and obtaining permission to use a wide range of material sourced at the Abbey Theatre including images, programme notes, and prompt script extracts. Thanks also to Colette O'Daly, Bernadette Metcalf and Elizabeth M. Kirwan of the National Library of Ireland for their consistent helpfulness and for the Library's permission to use material sourced in the Tom Mac Intyre collection there. We also gratefully acknowledge the assistance of Roland M. Baumann, Archivist, Oberlin College Archives, in granting permission for use of photographic material relating to Tom Mac

Intyre's work at Calck Hook. Thanks also to translators Traolach O'Ríordáin and Micheál Ó Leidhin, and to others who helped along the way: Anna McMullan of Queen's University Belfast, Andrea Ainsworth, Holly Nic Chiardha, Barry Coyle, and Fiona Reynolds at the Abbey Theatre, Justin Binding, and Mark Lawlor.

We gratefully acknowledge the support of our colleagues: at the Drama and Theatre Studies Department in University College Cork: Ger FitzGibbon, Franc Chamberlain, Jools Gilson, Bernadette Cronin and Róisín O'Gorman.

At the School of English, Drama and Film in University College Dublin: Finola Cronin, Catherine Leeney and Eamonn Jordan.

At the University of Montana: Katie Kane and Traolach Ó Ríordáin of Irish Studies, and Clare Sutton.

Special thanks to Norma Shine, Terri Sweeney and Sean Meade, Mary and Dan Ferriter, and Mary Sweeney.

Finally, we thank our friends and families for their love, support and sustained encouragement throughout the process, most especially Ruby, Bryan and Alan.

Fiach Mac Conghail

Ó fhíorthosach aimsire, tá clú agus cáil bainte amach ag Amharclann na Mainistreach, ní hamháin mar amharclann liteartha ach mar amharclann ina dtriailtear an nua, de shíor ag lorg is ag cothú 'an nua.' Ó théatar iomlán agus drámaí rince Yeats go heispriseanachas O'Casey agus ardréalachas Synge, is é an claonadh seo chun teorainneacha a thástáil a samhlaítear le teist na Mainistreach mar amharclann náisiúnta. Ar an gcuma san, is í an cheapach a thugann, ní amháin téacsanna nua drámatúla le scríbhneoirí Éireannacha, ach slite nua amharclannaíochta agus seifteanna nua cur i láthair. Déanann saothar drámatúil Tom Mac Intyre na teorainneacha a phromhadh ag gach pointe fan an réimse úd. Is scríbhneoir gan eagla é, seaman, ceannródaí go smior, file muirneach de chuid ár n-amharclann náisiúnta. Ba í Amharclann na Péacóige ba mhó ba bhaile do Mac Intyre mar ar thug drámaí dúinn i mBéarla agus i nGaeilge, drámaí ina measctar an dá theanga go fiú drámaí gan aon fhocal in aon chor iontu.

Is díol mór iontais domsa i gcónaí mar a thumann Mac Intyre é féin i ngach urlabhra stáitse agus mar a choinníonn an Ghaeilge beo i ngach gné dá shaothar. Pé acu ag scríobh i nGaeilge nó i mBéarla nó i meascán den dá theanga, baineann Mac Intyre ceol as an miotas, an béaloideas, an meafar agus an tsiombail. Tá an urlabhra is dual dó fréamhaithe i gcaint dhúchais a mhuintire sa Chabhán thoir: Béarla mar a labhartar é de réir dul na Gaeilge. Is breá leis focail uilebhrí, focail a bhaineann macalla agus geit. Mar bharr air sin, is breá leis an fhuaim a dheineann focail, na rithimí agus na glórtha doimhne collaí a thugann cló tríd an gcorp don ráiteas labhartha. Ar ardán Mac Intyre, bíonn brí sna focail, bíonn cuisle iontu, anam a thagann i dtír ar spriorad an scríbhneora, an aisteora agus an luchta féachana in éineacht. Sin é fáth a chorraíonn urlabhra drámatúil Mac Intyre cuimhní a leanann de dhuine, a chuireann fé dhraíocht é, a dheineann gairdeas is mearbhall agus a théann i gcion ar lucht éisteachta ar go leor slite go héirimiúil is go fisiciúil dá ndeoin, ar uairibh, agus go glan ina n-ainneoin uaireanta eile. Ní haon ionadh go bhfuil go leor ama caite ag Mac Intyre sa seomra cleachtaidh leis an stiúrthóir, leis an aisteoir agus leis an dearthóir ag iarraidh a shaothar a thabhairt ar an saol.

D'fhiafraigh mé de Mhac Intyre tráth ar bhraith sé gur chuir a shaothar cor i gcúrsaí amharclainne in Éirinn. D'fhreagair sé go neamhbhalbh 'nár chuir dá laghad.' I mo thuairimse, tugann seo léiriú ar stíl gheanúil Mac Intyre, ag breith chuige i gcónaí roimh cháil a shaothair agus is tugann fianaise leis ar an luí is dual dó na himill a ghnáthú. Nuair a bhreithním ar amharclannaíocht na hÉireann sna déaga beaga anuas, ámh, is deacair gan na cosúlachtaí idir déantús Mac Intyre agus scríbhneoirí eile, leithéidí Marina Carr agus Michael Harding, a aithint. Is doiligh leis gan a anáil mhúnlaitheach a thabhairt fé ndeara ar scata de stiúrthóirí, aisteoirí agus de chleachtóirí amharclainne a d'oibrigh go dlúth leis síos tríd na blianta.

Dhein drámaí Tom Mac Intyre an cheist achrannach a chíoradh riamh, ag ceapadh plé is ag cothú conspóide. An déantús, go háirithe sna 1980aidí, áirítear é mar shlat tomhais i stair amharclannaíocht Éireann. I bhfairsingeacht agus i scóp dá urlabhra amharclannach a ghabhann thar ceithre dheaga, ámh, seans gur mó is ceart an díolaim ilghnéitheach seo a chur síos mar thomhas lena dtomhaistear amharclannaíocht na hÉireann féin. Tá an spleodar i gcanóin Éireann na linne seo go mór faoi chomaoin ag an scríbhneoireacht agus ag an amharclannaíocht dhúshlánach seo, fianaise ar ardchumhacht an scríbhneora ar leithligh seo atá ag saothrú laistigh d'amharclann neamhchoitianta náisiúnta.

From the very beginning the Abbey Theatre has distinguished itself not only as a literary theatre but a theatre of experimentation, continually seeking out and nurturing the 'new'. From Yeats's total theatre and dance plays into O'Casey's expressionism and Synge's higher realism, the ethos of testing boundaries is synonymous with the Abbey's reputation as a national theatre. As such it is the seedbed not only for new dramatic texts by Irish writers but also for new ways of theatre-making and new ways of performance. Tom Mac Intyre's dramatic work has always tested the limits at each point across this spectrum. He is a writer who knows no fear, a shaman, a true adventurer, a cherished poet of our national theatre. Mac Intyre's home has been predominantly at the Peacock where he has given us plays in English and in Irish, plays that intermingle both languages, and plays with no words at all.

I am continually fascinated by Mac Intyre's absorbtion in all dialects of the stage and his ability to keep the Irish language alive in all aspects of his work. Whether writing through Irish or English or a mixture of the two, Mac Intyre luxuriates in myth, folklore, metaphor and symbol. His predominant vernacular is based on his own east Cavan dialect: English spoken in the syntactical arrangement of the Irish. He loves words of multiple meaning, words that resonate and detonate. More than that, he loves the sounds that words make, the deep sensual rhythms and tones that give shape to verbal expression through the body. On Mac Intyre's stage words breathe, they have a pulse, a life that draws on the life force of the writer, the actor and the audience alike. This is why Mac Intyre's theatrical language touches memories, haunts, enchants, amuses and bemuses, reaching audiences in a million different ways, cerebrally and physically, sometimes intentionally and, at others, entirely unexpected and unforeseen. It is no wonder that Mac Intyre has spent so much of his time in the rehearsal room with the director, the actor, and the designer, bringing his theatre to life.

I once asked Mac Intyre if he felt that his work had influenced theatre-making in Ireland. Without any hesitation and with great conviction he replied, 'not [in] the slightest'. In my view this response is typical of Mac Intyre's self-effacing style, a life-long reticence in relation to his own successes, and evidence of a deliberate preference to occupy a position on the margins. When I look at Irish theatre over the last number of decades, however, it is difficult not to see parallels between Mac Intyre's work and writers such as Marina Carr and Michael Harding. It is also difficult not to see formative influences on a host of directors, actors, and theatre practitioners who have worked closely with him down through the years.

The plays of Tom Mac Intyre have continually posed awkward questions, provoked discussion and stimulated controversy. The work, particularly of the 1980s, has been described as a landmark in Irish theatre history. In the breadth and scope of its theatrical language spanning four decades, however, it is perhaps more appropriate to define this diverse *oeuvre* as a benchmark against which Irish theatre has defined itself. The vibrancy of the contemporary Irish canon is deeply indebted to this challenging writing and theatre-making, a testament to the powerful force of this extraordinary writer working within an extraordinary national theatre.

Introduction: 'Strays from the ether'[1]

Bernadette Sweeney and Marie Kelly

The title of this book 'Strays from the ether' is taken from Tom Mac Intyre's most recent play, *Only an Apple* (Peacock Theatre, April 2009). From the early 1970s to the present day Tom Mac Intyre's theatre has strayed from the ether of an anaesthetizing form of realism. His plays *are* strays, wandering in the margins of the dominant discourse, troublesome, hard to capture, to define or to pin down. Ether is considered the fifth and highest element after air, earth, fire and water – and each of these elements is invoked by Mac Intyre, as he works in the realm of the earthy, the fiery, but also beyond the worldly to the supernatural. Ether was once supposed to compose all of the heavenly bodies; strays from this substance are combustible things indeed.

Our cover image, beautifully captured by photographer Amelia Stein, shows the Houyhnhnms from Mac Intyre's *The Bearded Lady* (1984). Here the Houyhnhnms stray from theatrical record to illustrate for us the power of Mac Intyre's work and his use of image. Stein's photographs, and that of other photographers included in this book – Fergus Bourke, Ros Kavanagh, and Pat Redmond – preserve the theatricality, the physicality and the not-realness of Mac Intyre's imagery long after the productions themselves have closed. Their photographs do more than simply record production details, but document and often shape our memories of an elusive art form. These images remember for us, and we include them here not just as record, but as trace, fragment, haunting and revision.

In the preface Fiach Mac Conghail refers to Mac Intyre's plays of the 1980s as a 'landmark in Irish theatre' as well as a 'benchmark against which Irish theatre has defined itself.' Mac Conghail writes here particularly in his capacity as director of a national theatre which has championed Mac Intyre's work throughout his career. In this respect Mac Intyre occupies an anomalous position in the Irish theatre canon. Experimental by nature, most of his plays have been staged on the margins – at the Peacock Theatre (the Abbey's studio space). The greater proportion of Mac Intyre's canon is, therefore, part of the Abbey's repertoire or the repertoire of the institution of the National Theatre. Tom Mac Intyre's work has earned Mac Conghail's comments above and is set apart from many others in Irish theatre by the energy invested in the live performance and the interaction between performance and audience.

Despite such acclaim, Mac Intyre's canon of work has been largely overlooked in the literature on Irish theatre and it is only in recent years that articles and essays have begun to appear. The most significant of these include: Fiach Mac Conghail's interview with Mac Intyre in *Theatre Talk: Voices of Irish Theatre Practitioners* edited by Lilian Chambers, Ger FitzGibbon and Eamonn Jordan (Carysfort Press, 2001); Deirdre Mulrooney's 'Tom Mac Intyre Text-ure' in *Theatre Stuff: Critical Essays on Contemporary Irish Theatre* edited by Eamonn Jordan (Carysfort Press, 2000); Bernadette Sweeney's *Performing the Body in Irish Theatre* (Palgrave MacMillan, 2008), with chapter two dedicated to Mac Intyre's *The Great Hunger,* and most recently Charlotte Mc Ivor's 'Ghosting Bridgie Cleary: Tom Mac Intyre and Staging This Woman's Death' in *Crossroads: Performance Studies and Irish Culture* edited by Sara Brady and Fintan Walsh (Palgrave MacMillan, 2009). Tom Mac Intyre, Tom Hickey and Patrick Mason have also published articles on Mac Intyre's work in Deirdre Mulrooney's anthology *Nice Moves: An Illustrated History of Dance and Physical Theatre in Ireland* (The Liffey Press, 2006).

Mac Intyre's theatrical impulse derives predominantly from dance, dance theatre, and genres which resist 'fourth wall' or 'slice of life' drama. As Mac Conghail points out, Mac Intyre speaks in 'all dialects of the stage'. He writes movement and images with the same poetic impulse as he writes dialogue. So when Mac Intyre's plays are published it is no surprise that his stage directions are as exquisitely poetic as the dialogue, and that they have a 'liveness' that cries out for the human body, or human touch.

The Theatre of Tom Mac Intyre: 'Strays from the ether', then, intends to provide an insight into making, seeing and responding to Tom Mac Intyre's theatre as live performance framed by the conditions of its production and reception.

Commissioned recollections, academic articles and interviews sit here alongside republished articles, reviews and imagery. The collection includes an extensive range of retrospective contributions from practitioners involved directly in the making of this work, academic analyses, press reviews, and press articles generated at the time of production. The photographic images mentioned above, together with other sketches and illustrations, are central to this collection given the highly visual nature of Mac Intyre's plays. By offering this material we hope to capture the performance elements, and the performativity, of the work – elements which, it could be argued, defy capture and may be partly responsible for Mac Intyre's lack of visibility within the canon. We include an unusually high number of theatre reviews here, as these are often the only traces left behind by unpublished and long-since produced work.

Whilst we have endeavoured to cover as much of Mac Intyre's canon as possible in our selection of material, we are aware of the constraints involved in producing a first anthological publication on the work of such a prolific author, and therefore we have tried to achieve an appropriate balance between Mac Intyre's most well-known plays and work that has been less well documented.

Chapter 1: 'Someone opened a door ... And now the traffic's racin ...'[2]

Mac Intyre often uses the image of the open door or the 'creak in the door'[3] as a metaphor for an awakening into another reality. We have taken this as the theme of our first chapter, 'Someone opened a door ...', which presents a selection of overviews or commentaries offering a way into Mac Intyre's plays for those less well acquainted with the canon, or as reference for the more closer analyses of the work later in the book. In the first article of chapter one, 'A Vibrant Presence: A Biography of Tom Mac Intyre's Work', Bernadette Sweeney establishes the author's prolificacy in many literary genres; plays, short-stories, novels and poetry. Her article and accompanying biography of Mac Intyre's work includes the production details of each of Mac Intyre's plays together with commentary and analysis.[4]

Seamus Heaney's introduction to Mac Intyre's collection of short stories entitled, *The Harper's Turn* (1982), identifies Mac Intyre as a journey writer, 'following the star of some inner commitment'. In the interview that follows Mac Intyre talks to Vincent Woods about following this inner star. 'I knew I was here to be a writer' he says, 'I knew that that was my fate.' For Mac Intyre, however, the writer's journey demands 'constant blasts from the unconscious'. Mac Intyre's most long-term collaborator, actor Tom Hickey, gives a precise description of sharing such a journey and what it calls for in the actor: 'the determination of a rhinoceros', 'the courage of a lion', 'the physical grace of a panther', and 'the inner resources of a shaman', are but a few of the attributes that Hickey identifies here. The collaborative relationship between Mac Intyre and Hickey has spanned several decades and will, therefore, be of interest to many readers of this book. In his article Hickey gives an account of the working principles of his collaboration with Mac Intyre, as well as suggesting the roots of its success. 'It has to do with a mutuality that resides in the intuitive, in the unconscious', he says.

Chapter 2: 'a Conspirator's Gleam'[5]

In *What Happened Bridgie Cleary* Mac Intyre describes the main character smiling to herself as 'a conspirator's gleam comes over her'. This, for us, suggests the mischief and the determination of an earlier Mac Intyre, at the outset of his theatrical career. This phase of his work is inevitably harder to capture than later periods, and this chapter is necessarily shorter than others. We are all the happier, therefore, to include Ben Francombe's essay here.

To excavate the foundations of Mac Intyre's remarkable canon, Francombe goes all the way back to Mac Intyre's beginnings in Cavan and to his beginnings in the theatre in the 1970s. In 'The Long Surrender: Finding a Theatrical Voice Through the Plays of the 1970s', Francombe assesses the development of Mac Intyre's idiom as an apprenticeship that began with the cultural influences of his upbringing, an interest in the power of poetry and in unconventional narrative forms. The theatre's diverse range of physical, visual and aural languages provided the perfect vehicle for such beginnings. But, were Irish audiences ready for this new voice in Irish theatre in the late 1970s? As Francombe indicates, Mac

Intyre had developed a theatrical language of his own but not all of the critics and audience members could read that language, nor were they meant to.

Michael Sheridan noted the audience's receptiveness to the movement-only *Jack Be Nimble* at The Peacock in *The Evening Press* in 1976. '[T]he auditorium,' he says, 'reverberates with continual and consistent interest.' In the following year Desmond Rushe (*The Irish Independent*, 1977) praises the movement elements of *Find the Lady* which he sees as 'refreshing in its quality and newness.' When Mac Intyre brought *Doobally/Black Way* to Dublin in 1979, however, press reaction was more confused. David Nowlan's review, provided in this section, gives an indication of such confused responses to the work. Nowlan says, 'Someone should have told [Mac Intyre] that the theatrical experience is one which involves both intellect and emotion, ideally to the point of catharsis. Anti-intellectualism and bafflement is no substitute for drama, just as noise (verbal or musical) is no substitute for words. It's all as silly as thinking sad or feeling a great idea.'

Chapter 3: 'Down the ruckety pass'[6]

Whatever the confusion amongst reviewers and audience members, Mac Intyre was now heading 'Down the ruckety pass' towards *The Great Hunger*. In 1983 Mac Intyre's adaptation of Patrick Kavanagh's canonical poem *The Great Hunger* (first published in 1942) was staged at the Peacock Theatre. This production marked the start of an extremely fruitful collaboration, principally between Mac Intyre, director Patrick Mason and actor Tom Hickey. Other actors, such as Bríd Ní Neachtain, Dermod Moore and SarahJane Scaife were members of the collaborative team at different points throughout the 1980s, and their memories are recorded here and in chapter four. This chapter is dedicated to *The Great Hunger* as it is considered such a seminal production of its period, and a continuing influence on Irish theatre practice. We open with director Mason's thoughts on the process, taken from the Lilliput Press first publication of Mac Intyre's *The Great Hunger*.

The play's central image of The Mother as a wooden statue or effigy was imagined by Mac Intyre at the outset, but designer Bronwen Casson played a central role in the development and realization of the production's design. Her essay included here, 'Environmental Design and *The Great Hunger*', records her part in the process as well as providing a commentary from John Barrett. This essay includes some evocative images, including her early conceptual drawing for the mother effigy. Casson's contribution is an important one in documenting the role of the designer, as well as providing a unique insight into the processes of stage design. Barrett looks, meanwhile, at the origins of environmental design and gives examples of this kind of work on the Dublin theatre scene in the 1980s.

Press reaction to the original 1983 production of *The Great Hunger* and its subsequent revival and tour in 1986 varies greatly. We include four reviews of the piece to chart the passion of these reactions. Early reviewers of Mac Intyre's work, Gerard Stembridge ('A Great Poem without Words' *The Irish Press*, May 1983) and Colm Tóibín ('Images of a Fragmented Ireland', *The Sunday Independent*, July 1986) have since gone on to establish names for themselves as writers and directors of note – it is interesting to see these figures in dialogue with such compelling work as *The Great Hunger*. We also include two reviews from *The Guardian* newspaper to chart reactions to the piece in the UK. Following its triumph in Edinburgh in 1986, Michael Billington (*The Guardian*, August 1986) made a plea for the work to tour to London; Nicholas de Jongh ('People Hungering after Humanity', *The Guardian*, November 1986) was just one of a number of London reviewers who was nonplussed by the work. De Jongh, notably, references Kavanagh's source text here, considering the production to be 'hostile to the poem's great potential'.

In 1984 Kathryn Holmquist published 'In the Beginning Was the Image...' in the periodical *Theatre Ireland*. This essay is significant in that it places Mac Intyre's *The Great Hunger* within a tradition of 'Theatre of the Image'. Here Holmquist cites the work of Vsevolod Meyerhold and Peter Brook, Jerzy Grotowski and Antonin Artaud. This article is reproduced here as it is a contemporaneous consideration of Mac Intyre's *The Great Hunger* as belonging to an international theatre tradition, not based on the literary or the verbal, but not 'non-verbal' either. Holmquist's work also contextualizes Daniel Shea's article in chapter four, which considers Mac Intyre's plays throughout the 1980s in relation to a 'theatre of the image'.

We include two programme notes here, both from 1986: The first by Dermot Healy is a reworking of his note for the opening of *Rise Up Lovely Sweeney* (Peacock Theatre, 1985), but in this later version he includes an overview of that production too. Healy writes on the work of Mac Intyre, Mason, and the actors from the first production of *The Great Hunger* in 1983, to *The Bearded Lady* in 1984, to *Rise Up Lovely Sweeney* in 1985. Healy provides an overview of reactions to the work and its development throughout this period. He notes some ambivalence on the part of audiences and critics to *The Bearded Lady*: 'But questions were being asked. Was the play not more Mason's than Mac Intyre's? Why was Mac Intyre not composing an original script?' On *Rise Up Lovely Sweeney* he notes that 'the hurt mind came into its own', as greater risks had to be taken by the company to satisfy an audience growing familiar with their style. 'The Hurt Mind' is a recurring phrase during this phase of Mac Intyre's work and Healy sums it up in his programme note here: 'In the Aran Islands they say – "ta dearc im dearmad". There's hurt in my memory.'

Michael Harding's programme note, 'The Ghost, the Gate and the Go Beyant', (Peacock Theatre, 1986) offers an evocative reading of the context of *The Great Hunger*'s revival. Here Harding asks uncomfortable questions of theatre such as 'are we not ... touched with the uneasy suspicion that it has damn all to do with the nightmare of the world about us?' Of Ireland in the 1980s he writes: 'an island is like a solitary man; in danger of closing the gate and turning in on himself.' According to Harding, Mac Intyre confronted this danger by trusting his audience, then all that was needed was 'to hold hands, and open wide the gate'.

Catriona Ryan's 'Oedipal Desire in Mac Intyre's *The Great Hunger*: A Palaeo-Postmodern Perspective' provides us with a new way of seeing Mac Intyre's *The Great Hunger*. This extensive essay engages with the spoken and written languages of the piece, from Kavanagh's original poem to Mac Intyre's use of English and Irish as antithetical idioms. Ryan references W.B. Yeats's use of the supernatural and of mask as key influences on Mac Intyre at this time. She argues that the use of Irish is a subverting strategy in Mac Intyre's adaptation of this 'poem into play' and cites Lacan in her consideration of language here: 'Lacan's reference to the unconscious as being structured like language is relevant [...] in that it is the unconscious drives which highlight the arbitrary nature of language'. This essay invokes Jung too to wrestle with Mac Intyre's symbolic use of gesture, his extension of imagery from the poem and his 'palaeo-postmodern' use of Irish to articulate the lost voice of Maguire's subconscious.

Finally, in this chapter we have included Paul Durcan's 'What Shall I Wear, Darling, to *The Great Hunger*?' Again, this piece offers a contemporaneous view of the play, but through a different medium, giving the reader a wry and often cutting insight into the Ireland of that period. *The Great Hunger* is situated, socially and culturally, by Durcan's poem, as one art form engages with another.

Chapter 4: 'Warming to the fray'7

In a period of intense play, experimentation, and collaboration for Tom Mac Intyre and his ensemble at the Peacock Theatre, the 1980s is marked by the production of five extraordinary plays of which *The Great Hunger* is but one. *The Bearded Lady* (1984), *Rise Up Lovely Sweeney* (1985), *Dance for your Daddy* (1987) and *Snow White* (1988) are remarkable theatre pieces that are unpublished and largely undocumented in Irish theatre criticism. Yet the unique idiom developed over this period, both in rehearsal and in performance, broke new ground in Irish theatre.

In chapter four we have gathered together a selection of material which documents this outstanding but elusive period of Irish theatre history when Mac Intyre was really getting to grips with a new idiom; he was '[w]arming to the fray'. We have collated documentation from the period and place it here alongside commissioned essays, practitioner memoirs and an extract from Mac Intyre's own work, *Snow White*. We hope that this chapter will go some way towards documenting and recovering this part of Mac Intyre's canon, and the experience of making and seeing it on stage.

If *The Great Hunger* and *Rise Up Lovely Sweeney* evoke the 'hurt mind' through the channel of well-known literary or folkloric figures, the 1984 play *The Bearded Lady* utilizes this device as a means of delving into the source of the writer's imagination. The subject matter in this case is Jonathan Swift, a man of multiple and often conflicting identities. In Mac Intyre's staging, Swift the writer as a character in the play is at the mercy of his fictional character, Gulliver, and both the physical and creative instincts that Swift tries to repress. The action of the play surrounds Swift's dream world in which his illicit relationship with two much younger women overlap with the experience of Gulliver at prominent moments in *Gulliver's Travels*. In the dream, Swift takes on the guise of Gulliver. Mac Intyre's specific intention is to personify the creative imagination within which fictional characters are envisioned and out of which they emerge. The dilemma confronted by Gulliver, however, is that which creates or shapes Swift and not the other way around.

Although referencing Swift and his well-known text as highly misogynistic, however, this highly visual production constitutes a radical critique of absolute ideologies. The Houyhnhnms make a magnificent yet chilling entrance on to the stage in their black and white bodysuits and tall stilted shoes. The cover image of this book illustrates the extravagant theatricality of the presence of these figures on stage as does Dermod Moore's article (detailed below) 'Lunatics in the Basement: Madness in Mac Intyre': 'Sleek lycra and bronze makeup transforms us into highly strung stallions,' he says, 'Magnificent, fascist exemplars of reason'.

Looking at the press reaction to the play there is evidence of the kind of confusion that surrounded Mac Intyre's work of this period. Those with experience of theatre as a predominantly literary genre, for instance, found it difficult to reconcile the highly imagistic content with the textual elements of the piece. In his review for *Theatre Ireland* (September, 1984) Joseph Mc Minn notes that 'the language of the play is not very memorable. The allegory shows itself to us. It has no need of much talk'. Mc Minn, however, along with Peter Thompson (*The Irish Press*, September 1984) had no difficulty in drawing the psychological parallels between Gulliver's 'schizoid personality', Swift's love life and the popular myth that Swift was driven insane by self-control and the repression of his own desires. Thompson writes that Swift's sense of guilt over the women in this play becomes 'a deeper probing of our own fear of ourselves, our bodies, our smells, our excrement'.

Actor Bríd Ní Neachtain, who joined the ensemble in 1983 and appeared in *The Great Hunger, Rise Up Lovely Sweeney* and *Dance for your Daddy*, describes in interview with Marie Kelly the 'sense of playfulness' in the rehearsal room at this time and how this manifested itself in 'the sharing and exploring' of ideas where the actors were 'free to dig, explore and investigate the fabric of the play'. In all of this, the key for the actor was to 'express an emotional charge through physical activity'.

This 'emotional charge', meanwhile, is captured in the words of Dermod Moore, who joined the ensemble as a young Focus School trained actor in 1984 and stayed with the group until 1988. Moore's breathtaking day-in-the-life diary of rehearsing and performing in Mac Intyre's plays during this time exposes the physical sensations, the mental gymnastics, the playful antics, but most of all the waltz 'on the edge of sanity' that this theatre work demanded. 'Lunatics in the Basement: Madness in Mac Intyre' is an invitation into that experience and Ireland of the 1980s. Referring specifically to *Rise Up Lovely Sweeney*, Moore says, 'This was 1985. People were being regularly killed, tortured and disappeared on our poetic little island'. And, all the while, in the rehearsal room Mac Intyre's ensemble was creating (or 'recreating') a 'tortured psychic landscape,' building a simulated hallucination or dream of Irish folklore's most long-standing exiled figure.

In an era of heightened political conflict Mac Intyre was able to call on a powerful means of expression to stage the experience of these circumstances rather than the events themselves. Based on the twelfth-century text known as *Buile Suibhne* (or *The Frenzy of Sweeney*)[8] Mac Intyre's *Rise Up Lovely Sweeney* simulates the psychic experience of the hunted man, in this case an ex IRA man. In his review for *The Sunday Tribune* (September, 1985) Fintan O'Toole sees the play as a 'moment of extraordinary theatrical poetry' which 'burns with an unmistakable integrity and attempts a voyage that few in the modern theatre would venture.' In the 'shattering climax of images', he says, 'a sickness in the Irish mind, a condition of schizophrenia and deep disturbance' is laid bare.

For Mac Intyre, however, the playwright is the catalyst for play. '[T]he challenge for the writer now,' he says, 'is to somehow get into that space where the magic of play is readily accessible'.[9] Through a close analysis of the performance of *Rise Up Lovely Sweeney*, Marie Kelly focuses on Mac Intyre's theatre as a multi-dimensional space for play in which the audience is intrinsically implicated. In 'New Dimensions: Spaces for *Play* in *Rise Up Lovely Sweeney*', Kelly demonstrates how – despite the often dark nature of its subject matter – this element of play permeates everything from the casting of the actor to the use of text in rehearsal and performance, to the use of theatre space to movement of the body on stage. Illustrated with extracts from the Abbey Theatre's prompt script, this article takes a fascinating look at Mac Intyre's unpublished work and validates the extent to which these texts were played with during the rehearsal process.

Turning his attention from the masculine to the feminine perspective and a more personal reflection on relationships between daughters, their parents and their lovers, Mac Intyre's final two plays of the 1980s, *Dance for your Daddy* (Peacock Theatre, 1987) and *Snow White* (Peacock Theatre, 1988), implement what by this time was a tried and trusted idiom to extend existing themes. In his programme note for *Dance for your Daddy* Dermot Healy sees this play as an attempt to 'get beyond sexual prejudice' but 'without dispensing with all those games the sexes play'. There is, he says, a familiar 'kernel of grief', surrounding the loneliness of the separation between father and daughter. There is also a heightened sense of comedy which David Nowlan picks up on in a review for *The Irish Times* (March 1987). Nowlan's response reflects the warm reception of this play as 'the most ambitious and the most accomplished work yet from the team which started out a few years ago with *The Great Hunger*'.

Moving specifically into mother/daughter relationships through the medium of the much loved fairytale, meanwhile, *Snow White* marks the end of Mac Intyre's extended period of collaboration with Patrick Mason and the ensemble they had gathered together in the 1980s. We are delighted to (re)present here, with the kind permission of the author, an extract from *Snow White*. Originally published in *Krino* in 1988 this extract incorporates the first two scenes of the play along with the opening stage directions. The full script has not yet been published.

According to Nuala Ní Dhomhnaill in a programme note entitled 'Chomh geal le Sneachta', this subject matter is 'a minefield', a 'dangerous no-man's land in every sense including the literal, because here be more than dragons, here lie live and ticking all the undetonated timebombs of our girlhood'. Critical reception of the play, however, reflects a difference of opinion on the impact of its production. We include two reviews of *Snow White* here, one from David Calvert of *Theatre Ireland* (Summer 1988), and another, again from David Nowlan of the *Irish Times* (28 June 1988). Calvert is gripped by what he deems to be a 'wonderful play' in which, 'rather than characters of flesh and blood, the figures who appeared on the stage seemed like spectral remnants from a genteel and bygone world'. Nowlan, on the other hand, is less enthusiastic in a review which starts out with the marvellously provocative line: 'There has to be an air of presumption when men set out to try to delineate the relationship between mothers and daughters'. Nowlan was either reflecting or dictating a general response to a piece that did not complete its anticipated run – an ignominious end to a decade's worth of experimentation and theatrical risk by Mac Intyre and all those involved in the collaboration.

SarahJane Scaife addresses *Snow White* in detail in the following article of this chapter. As a performer in this final Mac Intyre production of the 1980s, Scaife returns to her experience of the rehearsal process with Mac Intyre and Mason in which the actors performed 'cyphers' or 'constructs' embodying Mac Intyre's idea of a mother, schoolgirl, wife, rather than playing characters in the conventional sense. We are given an insight into Mac Intyre's act of 'writing' a play through Scaife's voice from the rehearsal room. Scaife writes alongside memories of actor Michele Forbes (a member of the ensemble group from 1984 to 1988), and their chorused voices overlap and cross-reference here. The directness of their embodied memories offsets the analytical distance of Scaife's other register; she remembers the heat, sweat and confusion of the work in rehearsal and performance, but also analyses it from a cooler distance, speaking with reference to Laura Mulvey on the male gaze and Bruno Bettelheim's writing on the psychoanalytical.

To conclude this chapter Daniel Shea explores all five of Mac Intyre's plays of the 1980s in order to establish whether the term 'Theatre of the Image' is an appropriate way to categorize this work. His objective is 'to broach the matter of image as a vital element of theatre performance on a par with such radicals of the art of theatre as human performers and spectators, a place to perform, and proxemic and kinesic relations in the theatre space'. Adopting the theories of Alan Read and W.J.T. Mitchell, Shea finds these 'seldom researched' plays to be 'a wealth of material for the combined study of image and theatre'.

Chapter 5: 'a gradle o' stories'[10]

Between 1988 and 1990 Mac Intyre took a short break but it wasn't long before he came back to the theatre, his thirst for dramatic expression renewed by the potent theme of sex and death; a theme he had already begun to explore in the late 1980s, but which would be reinvigorated and probed more deeply over the next two decades. To varying degrees, then, the plays of the 1990s stage the power of the feminine and the male experience in confrontation with the *leannán sí,* or the spirit woman, and the *leannán lí,* or the flesh and blood lover. The transition from the 1980s into the 1990s not only heralds a renewed interest in this theme, however, but also a new approach to theatre form and process involving a selective refinement of the range of practices which underpinned the plays of previous decades. Part of this new approach emerged from a new working arrangement that Mac Intyre had with the Abbey after the end of the sustained ensemble work of the 1980s. Now creative teams were engaged according to the demands of each production and this had a knock-on effect, giving Mac Intyre the opportunity to work with and learn from a wider range of directors, designers, and actors, and returning him to a more traditional relationship within the theatre process. These developments also facilitated Mac Intyre's deepening interest in story throughout the plays of the 1990s and marked a greater emphasis on the text and the integration of narrative and mimetic techniques within a non-realist frame. Despite this increased emphasis, however, Mac Intyre continued to take liberties with his text, a text that had begun to shift, quite substantially at times, towards centre stage. Hence, our chapter covering this era of Mac Intyre's work is themed 'A gradle of stories'.

The first steps, as in any new departure, were tentatively placed. In his first play of the 1990s, *Kitty O'Shea* (Peacock Theatre, 1990), Mac Intyre shaped his drama around the female experience of desire, in this case the love affair between a married woman, Kitty O'Shea and a political leader, Charles Stewart Parnell. Our first entry for this chapter, Medbh McGuckian's programme note for the play, considers the appeal of iconic figure Parnell, and centres on Kitty living out her life after his death: 'the ageing, aged, long past childbearing figure, relives, re-enacts the walk of a young and pregnant self, a concept [...] both fragile and monstrous'. In our next entry, a review of the play for *Theatre Ireland*, Victoria White points to Mac Intyre's turn to monologue form as a medium of the theatre that is 'often as near to poetry and prose as to drama'. Whilst dramatizing subject matter from the past this play was, perhaps, too rooted in subjective reality to be of much interest to Mac Intyre. What it didn't have was that 'other' reality of which he is so deeply fond, the sublime 'wild crazy colours' of the zone of the unconscious.

In the early 1990s Mac Intyre brought his work west, with his play for young audiences, *The Mankeeper,* produced by Midas Theatre in Education company, in Limerick in 1991, and a series of one-acts, under the title *Go on Red,* produced by Galway's Punchbag theatre company the same year.[11] In 1992 Punchbag produced one of these, *Fine Day for a Hunt,* as a full-length production for that year's Galway Arts Festival. We include here

Jeff Connell's review of that production which appeared in *The Galway Advertiser*. This review documents the disturbing quality of the play's content but commends both playwright and company for tackling this 'powerful and unsettling hunt'. Aspects of the play as described here offer earlier, darker hints of material treated very differently in the 2009 *Only an Apple*, such as the presence of the 'Big House', the symbol of a braying pack of dogs, and an 'unsettling' mix of the real and the fantastical.

In *Chickadee* (Garter Lane Arts Centre, Waterford, 1993) Mac Intyre continued to reclaim the word but there is clear evidence of the author's need to develop a fresh form to match his new approach to the text and themes which preoccupy the plays of this period. Hence, in *Chickadee*, the theme of forbidden desire is once again broached – this time between an older man and much younger woman – but there is a sense of the author trying to find a balance between theatrical articulation and the word. In his review 'Love Lost and Love Eternal', included here, Jocelyn Clarke registers this as confusion between style and content. 'The style is the thing' he says, 'not the substance'.

By 1994, however, Mac Intyre was beginning to find a means of articulating his new theatre voice as highly theatrical, non-realist, but yet densely poetic. In a programme note entitled 'The Night Before the Morning After' Ciaran Carson picks up on this new emphasis of the word as he considers his experience of the 1994 play, *Sheep's Milk on the Boil* at the Peacock Theatre. The language brought Carson back to 'that time, of English coming from an underlying skein of Irish, becoming bright and new in its engagement with the old'. 'Mac Intyre's language' he says 'comes from the grit and rasp of speech and the backlog of stuff embedded in it: proverbs, spakes, pronouncements, jokes, tags, song-fragments, references, yarns'. In 'Between two languages ...', meanwhile, Olwen Fouéré, who performed in *Sheep's Milk on the Boil* (1994) and *Snow White* (1988), remarks on Mac Intyre's renewed enthusiasm 'towards spoken language and the written word'. Fouéré sees this as being informed by the power of his earlier work and his roots in ensemble theatre practice and 'the joint creative'.

If Mac Intyre was to bring the text centre stage again, however, it was not to the detriment of his sustained love of the imagistic. In her evocative photographic study, 'Images of *Sheep's Milk on the Boil*,' Amelia Stein's images support Fouéré's comments on the staging of archetypal energies in *Sheep's Milk on the Boil* as potently visual. Fouéré refers to the heightened sexuality and female energy invested in her character, 'The Inspector of Wrack' who, dressed like 'every female icon from the movie screen' made a magnificently memorable entrance through the kitchen wall of a remote island cottage. Stein captures this mood brilliantly in her selection of photographs in which Fouéré's character makes every effort to seduce the male householder, an implicit simulation of Synge's Christy Mahon. We include these images in this chapter alongside written contributions as another form of articulation. Mac Intyre's work is, even in this phase, rooted in the image and, therefore, Stein's entry here both describes and documents this production.

Of course, this was Ireland in the mid 1990s when the strait-jacket of repression had, for the most part, become undone, and there is no question but that Mac Intyre's impetus was pointed towards sensuality and the unconscious. Fintan O'Toole in his second opinion on the play published in *The Irish Times*, sees *Sheep's Milk on the Boil* as a backward glance, however: 'more a re-working of tradition than a piece of flagrant avant-gardism' and 'a very conscious turn towards the look and forms of the early Abbey.'

In 1995, putting Michael Collins under the same microscope in *Good Evening, Mr Collins* (Peacock Theatre, 1995, revived and toured nationally in 1996), Mac Intyre humanizes (but never sentimentalizes) perhaps the most iconic Irish political figure as a passionate lover of the opposite sex. Christina Hunt Mahony's overview of the play, republished here, shows how Mac Intyre, through the medium of dialogue and action, layers the dual worlds of Collins's private and public life in alternating scenes or cameos. These scenes or cameos contrast 'the political infighting of the day' with the 'sexually tinged exchange' between Collins and the three women in his life, Kitty Kiernan, Moya Llewelyn Davies and Hazel Lavery.

David Nowlan's review (*The Irish Times*, October 1995), describes the play as 'a vision of Collins driven primarily by his sexual drives' in which 'as usual, Mac Intyre is butting his head against the accepted means of theatrical communication'. The 'nation' seen in a new light by this reviewer is 'a tatty damaged Georgian Dublin room with holes in the walls and a piano in the corner'. Of course, the room is Collins's 'mind frame' and the characters who enter are the ghosts of this 'mind frame'. Marina

Carr in 'The Bandit Pen' (a programme note for the Peacock Theatre, 1995) sees these ghosts as the 'vital connection between Collins and his fate'. In this respect it is a haunted piece of theatre, what Mac Intyre calls a 'ghost sonata' in which 'the living man [is] trapped inside time and [...] outside time, watching himself, commenting on himself'. What Carr likes best about this play, however, is 'the abundance of storytelling in the script' – in particular, 'The Lap of Hay' story in which the whole of Collins's life and death is encapsulated. She sees this as writing out of 'Love' with a capital L.

Good Evening, Mr Collins has specific resonance for the actress and novelist Karen Ardiff who worked with Mac Intyre on several plays in the 1990s (*Good Evening, Mr Collins, Caoineadh Airt Uí Laoghaire* and *Cúirt an Mheán Oíche*). In 'Stories Happen to Storytellers' Ardiff shares recollections of this 'exhilarating' creative work as a kind of 'spirit journey' during which Mac Intyre imparted the phrase 'stories happen to storytellers'. 'Knowing a story does not make you a storyteller' she explains, 'it is the ability to experience and recognize stories that counts'. In Mac Intyre's theatre, however, it is not always the writer in the isolation of the subjective imagination, but the writer watching the actor at work in rehearsal that prompts such recognition.

Keeping in touch with 'story' as it occurs through the physical body, Mac Intyre embarked on a collaboration with the choreographer John Scott from which a theatre-dance piece, *You Must Tell the Bees* (Peacock Theatre, 1996) evolved. The piece is loosely based on Mac Intyre's poem *Widda*, where the theme once again is 'sex and death' but this time the story is told through fragmented use of text and movement of the body. The plot surrounds a reported episode from Mac Intyre's personal history in which a widow (Mac Intyre's grandmother) goes to tell the bees that her husband, the bee-keeper, is dead. The mood of the piece, then, as Mac Intyre says, is one of love as 'honey' but also love as the 'sting'. Helen Meany in 'The Magic of Dissonance' (*The Irish Times*, September 1996) dubs the performance a 'sensual meditation'.

In the next article in this chapter Deirdre Mulrooney speaks with the then dance critic Carolyn Swift, Mac Intyre, and John Scott about this collaborative work and its themes. Mac Intyre reiterates his theme here: '[I]t aims to be about love and the sensual', he says, 'and therefore death, and therefore about the only stories that are around us'. Scott describes their venture together, meanwhile, as a 'combination of pure dance, the performance of the text, the interpretation of [Mac Intyre's] images, and [the dancers' and choreographer's] own meditations on the whole thing'.

Surveying the last two plays of the 1980s and Mac Intyre's work of the 1990s one notices that the playwright's theme of sex and death is not solely focused on the physical presence of the body, its pleasuring, its ceasing to be, but about birth as a transcendental phenomenon in which the feminine power holds the dominant position in the creation of life. Invested in the feminine, therefore, is the writer's source as well as the life source. Towards the end of the 1990s Mac Intyre projects this powerful female energy on to an unmarried and pregnant teenager, Jacinta Concannon. In *The Chirpaun* (Peacock Theatre, 1997) the consistent question of the paternity of the unborn 'chirpaun' may suggest an anxiety over identity, but at a much deeper level the play reveals the stubborn reluctance of a young girl who, surrounded by judgmental peers and controlling men and women, breaks away from her innocence and the unspoken law of the collective. As Victoria White argues, in her theatre review included here (*The Irish Times*, December 1997) this play picks up on the themes of *Dance for your Daddy* (1987) but locates it in a more contemporary and recognizable setting. Jacinta, however, is also desired by her father's generation, imbued with mystical powers, and given 'iconic status', the combination of which leaves White feeling irritated. Outside the theatre Ireland was trying to come to terms with a plethora of institutional sexual abuse scandals against young people. Given the resonance of the subject matter of Mac Intyre's play in its contemporary context White's view is an entirely justifiable one.

Writing bilingually in the Irish and English languages Mac Intyre's last two plays of the 1990s *Caoineadh Airt Uí Laoghaire/The Lament of Art O'Leary* (Peacock Theatre and national tour, 1998) and *Cúirt an Mheán Oíche/The Midnight Court* (Peacock Theatre, 1999) dramatize what are often considered two of the greatest Irish poems of the eighteenth century. In the bilingual *Caoineadh* Eibhlín Dubh, the author of the poem, laments her murdered husband and seeks revenge. In a review for *The Irish Times* (April, 1998) Diarmuid Johnson says it is 'A play of strong women [...] an antithesis to feminist reading of Gaelic literature' which 'reminds us that notions of the subjugation of the matriarch may be coloured by Victorianism.' We also include Alan Titley's (Irish language) programme note on *Caoineadh Airt Uí Laoghaire* which opens by asking if there is in fact any need to dramatize *Caoineadh*, as it is dramatic enough already. Titley goes on, however, to identify Mac Intyre's deft touch in bringing his use of theatrical form to a poem that mere realism could not capture.

In *Cúirt an Mheán Oíche*, meanwhile, originally written by Brian Merriman, the women of Ireland put their husbands on trial. With dance and choreography as integral elements, Mac Intyre, with director Michael Harding, called on the choreographer, Finola Cronin, to develop, in movement, the play's 'rhythmical and bacchanalian sense of intoxication and excess'. Having worked as a dancer with Pina Bausch at Tanztheater Wuppertal, Cronin was well versed in Mac Intyre's working methods. In 'Choreographing *Cúirt an Mheán Oíche*', Cronin speaks about her first meeting with Mac Intyre in Germany when she was part of Bausch's company and gives a unique insight into the theatre process she developed with the company. Her article included in this section of the anthology documents the performance practice of *Cúirt an Mheán Oíche* through rehearsal notes, sketches and diagrams.

Chapter 6: 'between the worlds' [12]

Having developed an idiom that was unique to Irish theatre in the 1980s and then re-envisioning that style whilst consolidating his earlier themes in the 1990s, Mac Intyre found himself once again beginning a new decade with the monologue form. Always open to suggestion, Mac Intyre took another look at *The Chirpaun* following a conversation with Tom Hickey. What emerged was *The Gallant John-Joe*, a one-man play based on the character of John Joe Concannon. Fintan O'Toole's review for *The Irish Times* (November 2001), republished here, sees the play as a 'fierce vindication of a lingering uniqueness'. The play vindicates, for O'Toole, the extraordinarily productive and long-lasting collaboration between a prominent writer and an actor of high stature. Hickey's performance he says, is one of 'rare virtuosity, in which there is not a hair's breadth between author, actor and text'.

Next is an article on a production of *Giselle* choreographed by Michael Keegan-Dolan of Fabulous Beast Dance Theatre Company in 2003. We include 'Ballet in the Bog' by John O'Mahony (*Guardian* 23 February 2005) as an example of Mac Intyre's influence. Here O'Mahony links Keegan-Dolan's work with Mac Intyre's and acknowledges Mac Intyre as a seminal influence on a generation of theatre makers and, perhaps more significantly, audiences. Despite Keegan-Dolan's lack of familiarity with Mac Intyre's work, there were many points of comparison between Mac Intyre's *The Great Hunger* and Keegan-Dolan's *Giselle*, transplanted as it was to a rural Irish landscape.

After a five-year gap between *The Chirpaun* and his next outing at the Abbey,[13] Mac Intyre returned to the Peacock with Tom Hickey in a lead role, alongside actors Declan Conlon and Catherine Walker, in the award-winning *What Happened Bridgie Cleary* (2005). The play is loosely based on the Tipperary woman, Bridget Cleary, who was tortured and burned to death by her husband and neighbours in 1895 on suspicion of witchcraft: pure Mac Intyre territory, one might say. In 'Mapping the World of Bridgie Cleary' set and costume designer, Joe Vaněk gives us a unique insight into the designer's visualization of 'a place suspended somewhere between wakefulness and sleep'. In words and a selection of sketches, notes and images, Vaněk charts his journey through the imagining and build of this physical setting together with its objects, costuming and lighting. Echoing Marie Kelly's commentary on *Rise Up Lovely Sweeney* earlier in this book, Vaněk eloquently reveals Mac Intyre's precise vision of the stage image and how the script, through stage direction and dialogue, acts as a guide for the work of the designer.

The selection of key theatre reviews which follow Vaněk 's article here provide a hint of the intense reactions that this work evoked. Both Patrick Lonergan (*Irish Theatre Magazine*, May 2005) and Fintan O'Toole (*The Irish Times*, May 2005) highlight the strong resonances of Yeats's *Purgatory* and Beckett's *Play* in this work. O'Toole is particularly enthused: 'It is low-key, slow-burning, evocative,' he says, 'not a symphony but a strong quartet. And a rather lovely one too'. Also enthused is Karen Fricker (*The Guardian,* April 2005) who commends the '[e]xceptional production values', the 'superb ensemble acting' and 'Mac Intyre's dense and colloquial prose-poetry' which 'combine to create a haunting evening'. Patrick Lonergan is concerned, meanwhile, with the 'tragic brutality of [Mac Intyre's] source material' and the ethics of its use as a dramatic 'springboard for a celebration of female individualism, sexuality and love'. Here Lonergan's opinion echoes Victoria White's response to *The Chirpaun* (1997) several years earlier in which the character of Jacinta (and her predicament as a teenage unmarried mother) is given iconic status. Despite this varied criticism *What Happened Bridgie Cleary* was highly successful at box office and the play garnered two Irish Times Theatre Awards in 2006: Best Actress award going to Catherine Walker for her performance of Bridgie Cleary and Best New Play award to Tom Mac Intyre.

Mac Intyre's most recent play *Only an Apple* was produced by the Abbey Theatre in 2009 and directed by Selina Cartmell. The essay 'Anarchic and Strange: *Only an Apple*' by Sweeney and Kelly includes a recent short interview with Selina Cartmell on the production and also includes images by Ros Kavanagh. This article offers commentary on the production, its staging of two historical female figures in a contemporary setting, the play as indicative of Mac Intyre's recent output, and engages with some of the comments offered by Cartmell in her interview. We also reference some critical reactions and follow the article with a full review of the production by Patrick Lonergan (*Irish Theatre Magazine*, May 2009) indicating the kind of mixed response the play received. Lonergan's is an especially provocative review, praising the play for traits that would seem like flaws in any other production.

We conclude this chapter with a selection of 'letters to the editor' by other writers – Eilish Mac Curtain Pearse, Augustine Martin and Sebastian Barry – which documents a range of support for Mac Intyre's early theatre work.

With Mac Intyre's kind permission, we close this anthology with an End Note: 'The Hurt Mind', from the unpublished *Rise Up Lovely Sweeney* – some of Mac Intyre's most pivotal and memorable words for the Irish stage.

The selection of material collected here under the title *The Theatre of Tom Mac Intyre: 'Strays from the ether'* – from the journalistic to the academic, from photographs to actors' recollections and designers' sketches – emerged out of a desire to capture the immediacy, viscerality, and visual impact of this unique canon of plays in Irish theatre. We have great pleasure in presenting this long awaited anthology which is intended to fill a significant gap in the literature of Irish drama and theatre practice. We hope it will serve as a resource for other researchers and mark a new beginning in the discourse on the risk-taking, poetic, and compelling theatre of Tom Mac Intyre.

Works Cited

Mac Intyre, Tom, *Sheep's Milk on the Boil* in *New Plays From The Abbey Theatre 1993-1995* eds. C. FitzSimon and S. Sternlicht (USA: Syracuse University Press, 1996).

---, *The Great Hunger* and *The Gallant John Joe* (Dublin: Lilliput Press, 2002).

---, *What Happened Bridgie Cleary* (Dublin: New Island Books, 2005).

---, *Only an Apple* (Dublin: New Island Books, 2009).

Mac Conghail, Fiach, 'Tom Mac Intyre in Conversation with Fiach Mac Conghail' *Theatre Talk: Voices of Irish Theatre Practitioners* eds. Lilian Chambers, Ger FitzGibbon and Eamonn Jordan (Dublin: Carysfort Press, 2001), pp. 311-30.

Mulrooney, Deirdre, *Irish Moves: an Illustrated History of Dance and Physical Theatre in Ireland* (Dublin: The Liffey Press, 2006).

---

[1] Tom Mac Intyre, *Only an Apple* (Dublin: New Island Books, 2009), p. 22.

[2] Tom Mac Intyre, *Sheep's Milk on the Boil* in *New Plays From The Abbey Theatre 1993-1995* eds. C. FitzSimon and S. Sternlicht (USA: Syracuse University Press, 1996), p. 99.

[3] Mac Intyre speaks about this 'creak in the door' in Deirdre Mulrooney, *Irish Moves: an Illustrated History of Dance and Physical Theatre in Ireland* (Dublin: The Liffey Press, 2006), p. 180.

[4] For a detailed analysis of Mac Intyre's work, especially *The Great Hunger*, see also Sweeney's *Performing the Body in Irish Theatre* (Palgrave Macmillan, 2008).

[5] Tom Mac Intyre, *What Happened Bridgie Cleary* (Dublin: New Island Books, 2005) p. 99.

[6] Tom Mac Intyre, *The Great Hunger* (Dublin: Lilliput Press, 2002), p. 12.

[7] Tom Mac Intyre, *The Gallant John Joe* (Dublin: Lilliput Press, 2002), p. 86.

[8] Mac Intyre uses James G. O'Keeffe's 1913 edition of this twelfth century text.

[9] Tom Mac Intyre, 'Tom Mac Intyre in Conversation with Fiach Mac Conghail,' in *Theatre Talk: Voices of Irish Theatre Practitioners* eds. Lilian Chambers, Ger FitzGibbon and Eamonn Jordan (Dublin: Carysfort Press, 2001), p. 312.

[10] Tom Mac Intyre *Sheep's Milk on the Boil* in *New Plays From The Abbey Theatre 1993-1995* eds. C. FitzSimon and S. Sternlicht (USA: Syracuse University Press, 1996), p. 93.

[11] See Bernadette Sweeney's article 'A Vibrant Presence: A Biography of Tom Mac Intyre's work' in chapter one for more details.

[12] Tom Mac Intyre *Only an Apple* (Dublin: New Island Books, 2009), p. 25.

[13] Abbey and Peacock Theatres.

CHAPTER 1: 'SOMEONE OPENED A DOOR ... AND NOW THE TRAFFIC'S RACIN' ...'[1]

A Vibrant Presence: A Biography of Tom Mac Intyre's Work

Bernadette Sweeney

[This article was originally published in: *British and Irish Dramatists since World War II* ed. John Bull, (U.S.: Bruccoli Clark Layman, Inc., 2001) Revised and updated. Reprinted here by kind permission of Cengage Publications.]

Tom Mac Intyre has been a vibrant presence in Irish theatre since the early 1970s. In a country that treasures its literary tradition, particularly in the theatre, Mac Intyre has brought an element of play and of risk to the stage that has profoundly influenced recent theatrical developments. He has worked consistently and has had many of his plays produced at the Peacock Theatre, the smaller stage at the Abbey Theatre. Despite having worked within the establishment, however, Mac Intyre is a controversial figure who has somehow managed to remain outside the dominant discourse.

Born in Cavan on 10 October 1931, Mac Intyre, whose parents were teachers, studied English at University College Dublin and worked in the United States periodically from the mid 1960s until 1980. While in New York in the early 1970s he was deeply influenced by the developments in dance theatre, and his subsequent work throughout the 1970s and 1980s sought to marry his facility with words with a theatre of image, where his presence in the rehearsal process was central. Mac Intyre began to establish himself as a writer in the early 1970s; his first novel, *The Charollais*, was published by Dedalus Press in 1969; his first volume of poetry, *Dance The Dance*, was published by Faber and Faber in 1970; *Through The Bridewell Gate: A Diary of the Dublin Arms Trial* was published by Faber and Faber in 1971; and a volume of Mac Intyre's verse translations, *Blood Relations: Versions of Gaelic Poems of the 17th and 18th Centuries*, was published by New Writers' Press in 1972. Such diverse interests also came to include theatre, where he could combine language with the immediacy of movement, the potential of which he had come to appreciate in the work of Martha Graham, Pina Bausch and Merce Cunningham.

On 7 August 1972 Mac Intyre's *Eye-Winker, Tom-Tinker,* a two act political play set in Dublin in 'the modern era', was staged at the Peacock Theatre and directed by Lelia Doolan. *The Old Firm* was produced at the Project Arts Centre in September of 1975 and directed by Alan Stanford, and in August 1976 *Jack Be Nimble,* advertised as 'a new mime play by Tom Mac Intyre', was staged as a Peacock Workshop production, directed by Patrick Mason. Another Peacock Workshop production, *Find The Lady*, followed in May of 1977; based on the legend of Salomé the play was also directed by Mason. This association with Mason, who had initially joined the Abbey as a voice coach in 1972, would later prove fruitful for both playwright and director.

In 1978 Mac Intyre spent time working at Oberlin College in Ohio, collaborating with students and director Wendy Shankin on *Deer Crossing*, produced in the spring of that year. The Calck Hook Dance Theatre developed out of this project, and later in 1978 Mac Intyre was awarded a bursary by An Chomhairle Ealaíon/The Arts Council of Ireland, which enabled him to work with Calck Hook in Paris. Mac Intyre's *Doobally/Black Way* was produced by Calck Hook at Le Ranelagh, Paris in April 1979 and was received well by critics and public. In October *Doobally/Black Way* was staged at the Edmund Burke Theatre in Trinity College as part of the Dublin Theatre Festival. Reactions to the play in Dublin differed greatly from those of the Parisian audience, however, and on the second night of the run the performance was interrupted as irate members of the audience were removed by police. This controversy did not generate a bigger audience for the play; neither did its success in Paris endear Dublin audiences to it. Mac Intyre's experimentation with form, and his determination to explore alternative options for Irish theatre were, if anything, reinforced by this experience, however, as his stage adaptation of *The Great Hunger* proved four years later.

The Great Hunger, Patrick Kavanagh's 1942 poem, was shaped into a play by Tom Mac Intyre, in collaboration with Mason and actor Tom Hickey in 1983. To take an established work by a poet such as Kavanagh and transfer it onto the stage was in itself risky, but the creative nature of its staging further identifies *The Great Hunger* as a landmark in Irish theatre history. Mac Intyre's decision to rework one of the most celebrated of Irish poems was seen by some as foolish, if not irreverent. The original script comprises a selection of lines and images taken from the poem and reordered by the playwright. The language Mac Intyre used was sparse, and during the subsequent collaborative rehearsal process with Mason and the actors – including Hickey as the central character, Patrick Maguire – the physical nature of the piece became apparent.

Early reactions to Mac Intyre's *The Great Hunger* were guarded and some reviewers believed that the playwright would have been better served by a more rigid adherence to the text, staged in a more conventional way. The 1983 production of the play was a departure from theatrical practices in Ireland at that time, as the poem was a departure from conventional poetry when it was published in 1942. Maguire, the beleaguered small farmer of *The Great Hunger* is a lonely, frustrated man, living under the tyranny of the Catholic Church, the land, and, perhaps most interestingly, his mother. Kavanagh uses Maguire's mother to explore the combination of circumstances that have left Maguire trapped. The land, which provides Maguire's livelihood, offers little comfort. His life is an endless round of drudgery; the presence of fertility in nature joins with the presence of his mother to emphasize his impotent God-fearing existence.

Just as Kavanagh had dismantled the prevalent image of idyllic rural life, Mac Intyre used *The Great Hunger* to challenge the prevalent image of Irish theatre in the 1980s. He chose a vibrant, physical form of theatre to act as a vehicle for Kavanagh's masterpiece. The press release issued by the National Theatre prior to the opening of the play in 1983 described the poem as having 'evoked a unique and highly individualistic response from the playwright'. Mac Intyre created a nonlinear, image-driven text, (described by the playwright as a score) which evidences not only his 'individualistic response' to Kavanagh's poem, but also the playwright's exposure to the work of Meredith Monk and his discovery, as quoted by Mary Harron of *The Observer* (30 November 1986) of what he described as 'a gloriously contemporary idiom ... the fragmentation of narrative, the power of the image, the poetry of movement – these elements had an ability to reach the audience, to burn in a way that traditional narrative couldn't'.

The language of the performance score was taken directly from the poem but, through rhythm and chant, the lines became a fluid living part of the process rather than a faithful recitation of Kavanagh's work. These rhythms were developed for the production during the collaborative rehearsal period. Mac Intyre's constant presence facilitated the reworking of *The Great Hunger* both during the original run and to a greater extent for the subsequent production at the Edinburgh Festival in 1986. The 1986 production of the play differed considerably from the earlier one, in that there was less reliance on the soundtrack and more on the actors, and certain elements of the script were reworked or replaced. Discussions were held after the previews of the 1983 production in the Peacock Theatre, when Mac Intyre and Mason had the opportunity to assess the audiences' reactions to the play.

The choice of Kavanagh's poem was an initial play upon the general social frame of reference of the Peacock Theatre audiences, who were sufficiently distanced from the national image making of the 1940s to recognize it for what it was. Also, the audience of the 1980s recognized Kavanagh as an acknowledged and respected figure in Irish literature. Thus, Mac Intyre's play both included the intellectual expectations of the audience in the process and worked against them. Mac Intyre's aim was to connect with audiences on another level. He believed, as quoted by Kathryn Holmquist, that 'The immediacy of the pictorial, of the imagistic, by contrast with the verbal, relates essentially to what we call sensory impact: you *look*, you *see*. In the verbal theatre, the energy hasn't got that directness'.[2] Mason was also committed to the search for a means of communicating with an audience that would challenge any preconceived notions of theatre. *The Great Hunger* reached its audience through the staging of movement, image and association.

Maguire's life is depicted onstage in a space defined by a high farm gate upstage centre, a tabernacle downstage right, and a wooden effigy representing The Mother downstage left. From the beginning the audience is confronted by the three central forces on Maguire's life. The presence of The Mother on stage as an inanimate object resonates throughout the play. The decision to 'cast' The

Mother thus was one made by Mac Intyre at the outset. The object cleverly evokes the unfeeling driven creature of Kavanagh's poem, who is sketched as a seated woman. The Mother represents onstage the domestic hearth, the far-from-cozy domestic hearth. Maguire literally runs in circles around The Mother in scene 3 as he struggles to remove a cloth cover from the effigy. In scene 8 he poignantly strives to speak to her as he gently wipes her rigid face. The scene ends with Maguire slowly beating the unyielding breast of the effigy, encapsulating both his need for his mother and his frustration with her, without his speaking a word. The other women characters, Maguire's embittered sister Mary-Anne; the sexually vibrant neighbour Agnes; the innocent 'School-girl' – each offer insights into the frustrated potential of women in Kavanagh's rural Ireland.

In Mac Intyre's play Maguire is all too aware of his failure as he literally hits out against the controlling forces of the land, the church and his mother. Such a physical interpretation of Kavanagh's poem, which attempts to grasp all that the stage medium has to offer, was condemned by some, who felt that the form of the play had proven to be a poor vehicle for a poem of such literary weight. In 1988 the National Theatre toured to Russia for the first time with *The Great Hunger* and a production of John B. Keane's *The Field* (1965) directed by Ben Barnes. The decision to bring *The Great Hunger* was unpopular with many who believed that traditional Abbey fare would be more suitable for the debut of the National Theatre in Russia. Others believed that any success enjoyed by the play was ultimately because of the calibre of its source material. *The Great Hunger* also toured to London in 1986, Paris in 1987 and the United States in 1988. Kavanagh's genius was revealed in *The Great Hunger* through his fearless undermining of the preoccupations of the day. By shaping the play in such an uncompromising way Mac Intyre remained true to the iconoclastic nature of Kavanagh's poem; in their staging, the playwright, director and actors worked together to bring a broader awareness of theatre to Irish audiences.

As *The Great Hunger* toured throughout the mid 1980s, the collaborators continued to produce innovative work for the Peacock stage. Their 1984 production, *The Bearded Lady*, was a theatrical exploration of the mind of Jonathan Swift. Mac Intyre interpreted Swift through the author's own work, depicting him as Gulliver in the land of the Houyhnhnms and the Yahoos. The male Houyhnhnms and the female Yahoos are effectively portrayed – the rational Houyhnhnms as horses on high platform hoofs, the Yahoos as wild and primitive monkeys. Each group moved accordingly in the Peacock Theatre production, under movement direction by Vincent O'Neill, who also played the Master Houyhnhnm. Critical reaction favoured the performance of the piece over its text, but the collaborators furthered their explorations of the potential of physical theatre in this vivid production with Hickey as the conflicted Swift.

Rise Up Lovely Sweeney, the third collaborative production of Mac Intyre, Mason, and Hickey, was staged in September 1985. The play was a modern interpretation of the mythical story of Sweeney, *Buile Shuibhne*, who was cursed to wander Ireland as a bird. The myth has been explored by many, including Seamus Heaney in *Sweeney Astray* (1983), but Mac Intyre uses a modern idiom. Sweeney is politicized, a man on the run in contemporary Ireland. Again Hickey portrays a man with a damaged psyche, but the theatricality of the piece showed that Mason, Mac Intyre, and Hickey and their co-collaborators were not simply revisiting old territory but developing their work in an organic and challenging way. The design by Bronwen Casson created a clinical but disjointed environment where Sweeney realized the ambiguous anxieties of the age in a contemporary, broken Ireland. The 'mad' Sweeney could be in an asylum or a hospital – the setting is clinical but not realistic or definitive in its location – but the healing remains elusive. Mac Intyre's concern for the 'Hurt Mind' as noted by Dermot Healy in his programme notes for *Rise Up Lovely Sweeney*, quoting Sweeney – 'I'm talking of the hurt mind, hurt mind in wait and knowing as the hurt mind knows'[3] – can be recognized as central to Mac Intyre's plays of this period.

Dance for your Daddy was produced in March of 1987. In *The Great Hunger* Maguire's relationship with his mother was central; in the later play the playwright examines the relationship between father and daughter. In the original production Hickey played Daddy/Elderly Roué and Joan Sheehy played Daughter/Dark Daughter. In this instance, the 'Hurt Minds' are the split or damaged psyches of the main characters. Snatches of dialogue in Irish, French and English were combined in movement and dance with other stage languages in a way which had become synonymous with Mason's direction and the rehearsal process of the group. Other performances such as Vincent O'Neill as Homme Fatal/Dirty Old Man and Bríd Ní Neachtain as Wife/Liz Taylor highlighted the role of gender in society and the role-playing of the individual within that society. In *Dance for your Daddy* father and daughter are seen struggling to redefine their relationship.

On 27 June 1988 the final play of the collaboration opened. Mac Intyre's *Snow White* was directed by Mason, with Hickey as the Seventh Dwarf, Sheehy as Rose Red and Michele Forbes as Snow White. The absence of other actors who had performed in earlier plays and the participation of a new stage designer, Monica Frawley, signalled a change in direction for Mac Intyre. In *Snow White* the relationship of mother and daughter is central and, unlike in *The Great Hunger,* the mother is portrayed by an actor. Reminiscent of The Mother in *The Great Hunger*, however, is the presence of a dressmaker's dummy, and Snow White's interaction with it illustrates her perceived lack of physical affection. Mac Intyre uses Grimm's fairy tale, as told by the Seventh Dwarf in the prologue, as a point of departure from which he considers issues of recrimination and loss. By using a multitude of references and images Mac Intyre examines another injury to the hurt mind.

Kitty O'Shea was Mac Intyre's first play to be produced at the Peacock after *Snow White*. Mac Intyre has referred to the 'conservatism'[4] of *Kitty O'Shea* as representing a new beginning for him. The play was directed by Ben Barnes and opened on 8 October 1990. With its dense language, *Kitty O'Shea* examines the fate of a woman who played a pivotal role in Irish history, having been credited with the downfall of Charles Stewart Parnell. Mac Intyre concentrates on O'Shea and her experience; the form of the play, with its monologues and memories, contrasts her attitude towards life with that of her daughter Norah, and forces the women to re-evaluate their own self-images.

In the early 1990s Mac Intyre worked with the recently-formed Galway company Punchbag, who produced three of his one-act plays under the title *Go On Red* (1991); one of these one-acts, *Fine Day For a Hunt*, was produced separately by Punchbag the following year. Mac Intyre recalls having had a difficult working relationship with Punchbag, however. In 1993 he and Hickey reworked another of these one-acts, *Foggy Hair and Green Eyes* and presented it to an audience of ten people at the Clarence Hotel as a Project Arts Centre production for the Dublin Theatre Festival. Mac Intyre and Hickey also worked together earlier in 1993 on *Chickadee*, which Hickey directed for the Red Kettle Theatre Company of Waterford. Described on 19 May 1993 by *Irish Times* reviewer, David Nowlan, as a play that 'lies mid way between the lucid and the opaque',[5]

Chickadee was an unerring exploration of male sexuality through the relationship between the middle aged Hubert and his young lover Julie.

In 1991 Mac Intyre adapted his short story 'The Mankeeper' for a theatre-in-education project produced by Midas Theatre, a company set up under the auspices of Mary Immaculate College in Limerick. *The Mankeeper* was performed by professional actors,[6] directed by Paul Brennan, and toured primary schools around Limerick city and county.

Mac Intyre returned to the National Theatre in 1994 with a new play, *Sheep's Milk on the Boil*, which opened at the Peacock on 17 February. Elements of the collaboration of the 1980s were present; having successfully directed *Chickadee*, Hickey was once again working with Mac Intyre in the role of director; Mason, although not directly involved, was by this time Artistic Director of the Abbey. Mac Intyre identifies *Sheep's Milk on the Boil* as the beginning of a phase of work (including the successful 1995 production *Good Evening, Mr Collins*) which fuses the physicality of the earlier work with a poetic but at times prosaic use of language, an incisive and richly funny combination reflecting what the playwright referred to as 'a new excitement with the verbal in the theatre'.

Good Evening, Mr Collins was directed by Kathy McArdle and staged at the Peacock Theatre as part of the. 1995 Dublin Theatre Festival. A rich and irreverent exploration of the life of Michael Collins (played by Brían F. O'Byrne in the first production and Sean Rocks in the 1996 revival and national tour), the play combines dark comedy with an affection for its central character. Collins is depicted as a man of love and loyalty both personal and political. Shades of Mac Intyre's earlier work are present in the form of the play and also in the character of Collins, portrayed as another of Mac Intyre's hurt minds, an all-too-knowing victim.

Mac Intyre showed a biting political awareness in his portrayal of Eamon De Valera, a national figure who became, as the playwright Marina Carr noted in the programme for the 1995 production, 'the Court Jester who has his eye on the throne'.[7] De Valera assumes many guises in the course of the play. As a schoolteacher in cap and gown in scene 4, he addresses the audience directly as if he were speaking to a class, then instructs Collins on the work of Niccolò Machiavelli. As a concert pianist in scene 5 of act 2, he plays music by Frédéric François Chopin throughout a scene in which Collins expresses foreboding; then, after Collins leaves the stage, De Valera rises and accepts the applause of his rapturous public.

The audience was given theatrical insight into Collins through the women in his life, Moya Llewelyn-Davies, Kitty Kiernan and Hazel Lavery, played in the original production by the same actor, Karen Ardiff. While confusing at times, this casting decision underlines Collins's reputation as a ladies' man while drawing attention to the delimited role of women in the history of state politics. Mac Intyre developed a textured language of Irish, English and local idiom to identify each character and to play with notions of Irishness. Collins speaks plainly but tells of disturbing dreams that resonate with the audience's knowledge of the circumstances of the character's death. In Act 1 scene 6, Collins sits alone at a table, writing by candlelight. The intimacy of the scene grows as he speaks of his childhood, and tells how he fell through a trapdoor as a child, but was saved by 'a lap of hay'.[8] He recalled telling that story previously and how the listener had wished that the lap of hay 'always be there'[9] for him. This evocative blessing is immediately challenged as Collins was confronted by a vision of De Valera, Kitty Kiernan and the English Army captain, taunting him as they move about the stage.

In *Good Evening, Mr Collins* Mac Intyre presents his audience with an irreverent version of history, by turns hilarious, contentious and playful. The theatricality of the play was noted favourably by commentators, but its success with critics and audience implies a level of awareness that was fostered by Mac Intyre's earlier work. The comedy and subversiveness of the piece owe much to the many and varied references with which the audience could identify, but underneath was a softness towards Collins and what Mac Intyre described in an afterword for *The Dazzling Dark: New Irish Plays* (1996) as 'the man's courage, laughter, his fallible longings'.[10] The play was reworked and revived in 1996 at the Peacock Theatre before a successful national tour.

Mac Intyre again utilized dance in *You Must Tell the Bees,* devised by the playwright in collaboration with the Irish Modern Dance Theatre, known for its creative choreography and staging; the play was first performed in the Firkin Crane Arts Centre, Cork, on 26 September 1996. Although Mac Intyre's work was noted by this point for his use of image and movement onstage, his use of dance as the creative point of departure relates directly back to his work with the Calck Hook Dance Theatre in Paris in the late 1970s.

Identified by its collaborators as 'a dance theatre work' *You Must Tell the Bees* was choreographed by John Scott, with music composed by Rossa Ó Snodaigh. The piece is loosely based on Mac Intyre's poem *Widda*, in which a beekeeper's widow tries to come to terms with her husband's death. The imagery of bees and honey and of capture and release are central, with the dancers embodying the widow's memories. The play also includes poetry and fragments of dialogue spoken by the dancers. The dancers remained more comfortable with the language of movement rather than the word in performance, but, in its collaboration with as image-conscious a playwright as Mac Intyre, the company brought an awareness of the body to the stage which is often marginalized in Irish theatre. *You Must Tell the Bees* toured Ireland throughout September and October of 1996; it was then performed at the Peacock Theatre as part of the Dublin Theatre Festival and was well received. Mac Intyre's use of language and poetry is balanced by an appreciation of the visual, which places him outside the literary Irish theatre tradition; *You Must Tell the Bees* is a rich and evocative testimony to the playwright's vision.

The Chirpaun was first performed at the Peacock Theatre, Dublin, on 3 December 1997. This play was later revised as *The Gallant John-Joe* in 2001. Directed by Kathy McArdle, *The Chirpaun* staged the troubled relationship of John-Joe Concannon and his daughter Jacinta. The play featured Tom Hickey as John-Joe, Eva Birthistle as Jacinta, Pat Kinevane as The Hitmatist (Dallan Devine) Bosco Hogan as Boss-Man, Pauline Hutton as Clodagh, Renee Weldon as Dolores and Des Keogh as Gran-Pa; movement was directed by Finola Cronin. Jacinta, seventeen, is pregnant and John-Joe is tormented by this and the identity of the baby's father. He turns to hypnotist (Hitmatist) Devine for guidance. *The Chirpaun* follows on from Mac Intyre's 1980s body of work in identifying and interrogating a key familial relationship – here we have a father struggling to relate to his enigmatic teenage daughter. The play stages a heightened idiom of speech and discourse – Kinevane's Hitmatist was especially extreme in concept and delivery. Although the heightened text and theatricality sat uneasily at times with some more realist elements of the play, *The Chirpaun* offered some intriguing hints of what would become fully, and powerfully, realized in Mac Intyre's later work *The Gallant John-Joe.*

Caoineadh Airt Uí Laoghaire was first performed by the Abbey Theatre at Coláiste Chonnacht in An Spidéal, Co. Galway, on 16 April 1998. It was directed by Kathy McArdle and the cast included Karen Ardiff as Eibhlín Dubh, Liam Heffernan as Art/Brian, and Tom Hickey as Morris/Breitheamh. Music was by Steve Wickham. This play is based on the 1770s poem attributed to Eibhlín Dubh Ní Chonaill who is lamenting the death of her husband Airt. It is written in the tradition of the keen or *caoineadh* which, some have argued, is an oral rather than written poem, perhaps even sung. The original poem offered Mac Intyre strong female figures to work with, such as the widowed Eibhlín, Art's sister, Sorcha and the Old Woman. Mac Intyre's interplay of Irish and English here allowed him room to play with the stereotypes of the poetic native and prosaic occupier. *Irish Times* reviewer Diarmaid Johnson noted that this play's significance was especially due to its languages, '[t]his co-existence of the two national languages is too rarely met in dramatic writing, be it for stage, print or television'.[11] *Caoineadh Airt Uí Laoghaire* won the Stewart Parker Award in 1999.

Cúirt an Mheán Oíche was again produced by the Abbey Theatre but, like *Caoineadh Airt Uí Laoghaire,* opened in an Irish-language venue, Taibhdhearc na Gaillimhe, Galway, on 19 November 1999. It was directed by Michael Harding and among the cast were Bríd Ní Neachtain as Aoibheall, Peadar Cox as Merriman, Tomás Ó Súilleabháin as An File and Karen Ardiff as An Bhean. *Cúirt an Mheán Oíche* is a bi-lingual reworking of Brian Merriman's eighteenth-century poem of the same name, which means *The Midnight Court*. Here again we see Mac Intyre reworking or reimagining a canonical text, bringing to it his trademark theatricality and a playfulness with language, (or two languages here), character and space. The bawdiness of Merriman's original was sheltered behind its language, eluding censorship until Frank O'Connor's 1945 translation. Mac Intyre's version addresses both the play and its history. Here, he uses the theatrical device of framing the action of the Midnight Court with scenes of the Censor reacting to the publication of O'Connor's translation, and transporting the Censor to the world of the poem itself. As part of its national tour this production toured to Gaeltacht or Irish language-speaking areas, including the western island of Inishmaan. Ian Kilroy reported on the tour for *The Irish Times*, and commented on the audience's response: '[i]n a comic and lively performance, the unmentionables are boldly mentioned, taboos are flouted, and an identity is reinforced for a people who know that Irish is a living language'.[12]

The Gallant John-Joe, as mentioned above, is a reimagining of *The Chirpaun,* and premiered at McRory's Hotel, Culdaff, Co. Donegal on 23 January 2001. The direction of this one-man piece, performed by Tom Hickey, is attributed to Hickey and Mac Intyre. *The Gallant John-Joe* featured a widely-acclaimed performance by Hickey, reprising but also extending his performance as the same character in *The Chirpaun* four years earlier. The design as specified in the published script gives a clear indication of the sparseness of the stage; any gaps were more than filled by Hickey's performance:

> *Mangle upstage right, chair beside it ... story-telling chair stage left ... a shelf on the mangle provides room for a bottle of pills and two bottles of medicine ... hanging from above, just off centre, a Chinese lantern, lit. Dirty brown lino defines the playing area.*[13]

The Gallant John-Joe differs from *The Chirpaun* in that now all we hear is John-Joe's perspective on his relationship with his daughter. Other characters, such as Jacinta and the Hitmatist are related to the audience through John-Joe's partial viewpoint, interspersed with veiled references to the mental institution 'the Big House', the missing 'Chinee' (suspected by John-Joe of fathering Jacinta's child) and local lakes which, at Christmas time, become 'peculiar inviting'.

The Gallant John-Joe toured nationally and internationally from 2001 to 2007 and, when touring to New York, was enthusiastically reviewed by Lawrence Van Gelder of *The New York Times*: 'Mr. Hickey renders a rich portrait not only of Concannon, a widower, but also of a gallery of characters ... [Hickey is a] delight in the often unprintable humorous material and is deeply touching in his nostalgia for the days when he and his daughter were on better terms'.[14]

What Happened Bridgie Cleary premiered at Dublin's Peacock Theatre on 27 April 2005, directed by Alan Gilsenan, with Declan Conlon as William Simpson, Tom Hickey as Mikey Cleary and Catherine Walker as Bridgie Cleary. This play is based on the real, and horrific, story of the death of Bridgie Cleary, burned to death by her husband and neighbours in 1895 as they believed she was 'possessed'. Although the characters – Bridgie, her husband Michael, and her former lover William Simpson – share the stage, they address us and the other from a different world, an afterlife perhaps or, at least, a place of the dispossessed. As directed by Alan Gilsenan this production had a haunted and haunting quality. A dominance of physical stillness (relative to Mac Intyre's other work) contributed to the haunted or hushed nature of the piece; these characters are bound and constrained by their circumstances, the outcomes of their actions and actions acted upon them. This production was designed by Joe Vaněk , with lighting designed by Kevin McFadden and sound by Cormac Carroll. Together, they combined a ghostly other-ness with a scattering of mundane domesticity, to create a liminal setting for the piece, neither here in our world or in some idealized afterworld, but somewhere in-between, caught, lost and adrift. In February 2006 *What Happened Bridgie Cleary* won the Irish Times Theatre Awards Best New Play award and Catherine Walker won Best Actress award for her role as Bridgie Cleary.

Only an Apple is Mac Intyre's most recent play and it again was staged at Dublin's Peacock Theatre, on 21 April 2009. The premiere was directed by renowned young director Selina Cartmell, who has garnered a reputation for emphasis on the theatrical in all aspects of production, from movement to text, to image. This is a highly playful and at times surreal depiction of a beleaguered present-day Taoiseach (Prime Minister) who is visited by Queen Elizabeth I and sixteenth century Irish pirate Grace O'Malley. These are no fusty historical figures however, but vital and raunchy women, who bring a sexual voraciousness to their encounters with the Taoiseach, his side-kicks Arkins and Hislop, and pretender to his political throne, McPhrunty. *Only an Apple* encountered some criticism for its portrayal of these two female figures as archetypes but that was no doubt Mac Intyre's intention – these women mark a return to an overt theatricality on the part of Mac Intyre, matched by Cartmell's visceral engagement of the senses with sumptuous design and imagery. The first production featured Don Wycherley as Taoiseach, Fiona Bell as Elizabeth, Cathy Belton as Grace, Malcolm Adams as Sheridan, Steve Blount as McPhrunty, Tina Kellegher as The Wife, Michael McElhatton as Hislop, and Marty Rea as Arkins, with set design by Dick Bird.

The emergence of Mac Intyre as an innovative playwright with a deep commitment to the process of the play did not signal a departure from other writings. *The Harper's Turn*, a collection of short stories, was published in 1982, and other short story collections, *The Word For Yes: New and Collected Stories,* in 1991, and *Find the Lady* in 2008. He has published poetry collections, including *I Bailed out at Ardee* (1987), *Fleurs-du-lit* (1990), *A Glance Will Tell You and a Dream Confirm* (1994), *Stories of the Wandering Moon* (2000), and *ABC,* (2006). He has published Irish language poetry in *Ag Caint Leis an mBanríon* (1997), *Silenus na gcat,* (1999) and *Tamall Suirí,* (2004); and a novel, *Story of a Girl* (2003). He has also written articles, screenplays and a libretto for Opera North. There have also been radio productions of Mac Intyre's short stories and plays, including two versions of *Rise Up Lovely Sweeney,* in 1991 and 1993. In 1991 Mac Intyre became a member of Aosdána, the affiliation of Irish artists, writers and composers.

Mac Intyre's work and influence as a playwright have developed throughout his career. An early appreciation of modern dance and movement inspired his vision of a physical theatre of image. As poet, novelist and short story writer, Mac Intyre demonstrates an extraordinary command of language, and he has combined this quality with his interest in physical expression to produce some of the most challenging works of Irish theatre. These plays have not always been successful, some, such as *Doobally/Black Way* have antagonized audience members, while others, such as *Snow White,* have been considered too abstract. The importance of Mac Intyre's contribution was encapsulated by the reaction to *The Great Hunger,* however, especially national and international reactions to the reworked version of the play in 1986. The response highlighted not only international attitudes to Irish theatre, but also the reluctance of some Irish theatre practitioners to challenge those attitudes. With the end of the Mason-Mac Intyre-Hickey collaboration, which also included designer Bronwen Casson and a core group of actors, Mac Intyre's work took a new direction. His plays of the late 1980s and early 1990s represent a distancing on the part of the playwright from some of the extremes explored by the collaboration. By the mid 1990s, however, Mac Intyre's work had found a balance; word and image worked together with the playwright's imagination and sense of play. By the 2000s, Mac Intyre's work could be readily identified by the dominance of its theatricality, a recurring use of archetype and a skillful revelling in wordplay. Mac Intyre's influence can be seen in the work of other playwrights, including Michael Harding and Marina Carr.

An overview of Tom Mac Intyre's production history suggests that the National Theatre has offered him uncommon support. His work defies categorization. However, he writes with what fellow playwright Marina Carr describes – as quoted in the programme for *Good Evening, Mr Collins* – as 'the bandit pen'.[15] The risks he has taken have not always been successful, but he continues to take them nonetheless. Mac Intyre's presence within the Irish theatre tradition challenges actors and audiences alike to allow themselves to experience all of the potentials of theatre.

Tom Mac Intyre (10 October 1931–)

PLAY PRODUCTIONS:

Eye-Winker, Tom-Tinker, Dublin, Peacock Theatre, 7 August 1972, (director Lelia Doolan).

The Old Firm, Dublin, The Project Arts Centre, 25 September 1975, (director Alan Stanford).

Jack Be Nimble, Dublin, Peacock Theatre, 10 August 1976, (director Patrick Mason).

Find The Lady, Dublin, Peacock Theatre, 9 May 1977, (director Patrick Mason);

Deer Crossing, Oberlin Ohio, Oberlin College, Ohio, Spring 1978, (director Wendy Shankin).

Doobally/Black Way, Le Ranelagh, Paris, Calck Hook Dance Theatre, April 1979. Dublin, Edmund Burke Theatre, Trinity College, 8 October 1979, (director Wendy Shankin).

The Great Hunger, Dublin, Peacock Theatre, 9 May 1983, (director Patrick Mason).

The Bearded Lady, Dublin, Peacock Theatre, 10 September 1984, (director Patrick Mason).

Rise Up Lovely Sweeney, Dublin, Peacock Theatre, 9 September 1985, (director Patrick Mason).

Dance for your Daddy, Dublin, Peacock Theatre, 2 March 1987, (director Patrick Mason).

Snow White, Dublin, Peacock Theatre, 27 June 1988, (director Patrick Mason).

Ariane and Bluebeard, libretto by Mac Intyre, Leeds, Grand Theatre, Opera North, 17 September 1990, (director Patrick Mason).

Kitty O'Shea, Dublin, Peacock Theatre, 8 October 1990, (director Ben Barnes).

Go On Red, Galway, Punchbag Theatre Company, 14 February 1991– comprises *Fine Day For A Hunt, Foggy Hair and Green Eyes,* and *Jack Be Nimble,* (director David Quinn).

The Mankeeper, Limerick, Midas Theatre-in-Education Company, Mary Immaculate College, 30 September 1991 (director Paul Brennan).

Fine Day for a Hunt, Galway, Punchbag Theatre Company, 16 July 1992, (director Sean Evers).

Chickadee, Waterford, Red Kettle Theatre Company, 18 May 1993, (director Tom Hickey).

Foggy Hair and Green Eyes (revised), Dublin, Project Arts Centre Production, Clarence Hotel, 4 October 1993, (in association with Tom Hickey).

Sheep's Milk on the Boil, Dublin, Peacock Theatre, 23 February 1994, (director Tom Hickey).

Good Evening, Mr Collins, Dublin, Peacock Theatre, 11 October 1995, (director Kathy McArdle).

You Must Tell the Bees, Cork, Firkin Crane Arts Centre, 26 September 1996, (in collaboration with the Irish Modern Dance Theatre).

The Chirpaun, Dublin, Peacock Theatre, 3 December 1997, (director Kathy McArdle).

Caoineadh Airt Uí Laoghaire, An Spidéal, Co. Galway, Coláiste Chonnacht, 16 April 1998, (director Kathy McArdle).

Cúirt an Mheán Oíche, Galway, Taibhdhearc na Gaillimhe, 19 November 1999, (director Michael Harding).

The Gallant John-Joe, McRory's Hotel, Culdaff, Co. Donegal, 23 January 2001 (directors Tom Hickey & Tom Mac Intyre).

What Happened Bridgie Cleary, Dublin, Peacock Theatre, 27 April 2005, (director Alan Gilsenan).

Only an Apple, Dublin, Peacock Theatre, 21 April 2009, (director Selina Cartmell).

PLAYS PUBLISHED:

[& Patrick Kavanagh] *The Great Hunger: Poem into Play* (Westmeath, Ireland: The Lilliput Press, 1988).

Sheep's Milk on the Boil in *New Plays from the Abbey Theatre* Christopher Fitz-Simon and Sanford Sternlicht (eds) (Syracuse University Press, 1996).

Good Evening, Mr Collins in *The Dazzling Dark: New Irish Plays* selected and introduced by Frank McGuinness (London: Faber and Faber Limited, 1996).

Caoineadh Airt Uí Laoghaire (Baile Átha Cliath: Coiscéim, 1999).

Cúirt an Mheán Oíche (Baile Átha Cliath: Coiscéim, 1999).

The Great Hunger & *The Gallant John-Joe* (Dublin: The Lilliput Press, 2002).

What Happened Bridgie Cleary (Dublin: New Island 2005).

Only an Apple (Dublin: New Island 2009).

NOVELS:

The Charollais, (Dublin: Dedalus, 1969).
Story of a Girl, (Dublin: Lilliput, 2003).

POETRY:

Dance The Dance, (London: Faber & Faber, 1970).
Blood Relations: Versions of Gaelic poems of the 17th and 18th Centuries (Dublin: New Writers' Press, 1972).
I Bailed Out At Ardee (Dublin: Dedalus, 1987).
Fleurs-Du-Lit (Dublin: Dedalus, 1990).
A Glance Will Tell You and a Dream Confirm (Dublin: Dedalus, 1994).
Ag Caint Leis an mBanríon (Baile Átha Cliath: Coiscéim, 1997).
Silenus na gcat (Baile Átha Cliath: Coiscéim, 1999).
Stories of the Wandering Moon (Dublin: Lilliput, 2000).
Tamall Suirí (Baile Átha Cliath: Coiscéim, 2004).
ABC (Dublin: New Island, 2006).

SHORT STORIES:

The Harper's Turn, (Dublin: Gallery Press, 1982).
The Word For Yes: New and Selected Stories, (Oldcastle, Co. Meath: Gallery Books, 1991).
Find the Lady, (Dublin: New Island, 2008).

PRODUCED SCRIPTS:

The Visitant, radio, 60 minute play, RTÉ Radio, 22 October 1980, (director & producer Sean O'Briain).
Painted Out, television, one hour drama, RTÉ Television, 18 January 1983, (director Louis Lentin).
Green Sky Over White Bend, radio, short story, BBC Radio 4, 28 September 1981, (producer Cherry Cookson).
The Mirror, radio, play, RTÉ Radio, 1 January 1983.
Grace Notes, radio, 30 minute play, RTÉ Radio, 13 November 1983, (director & producer William Styles).
Fine Day for a Hunt, radio, 30 minute play, RTÉ Radio, 24 November 1985, (director & producer William Styles).
The Mankeeper, radio, 30 minute play, BBC Radio, 3 October 29 1988, (director & producer Jeremy Howe).
Stirabout, radio, 45 minute play, BBC Radio 3, 12 November 1988, repeated 16 June 1990, (director & producer Jeremy Howe).
Scruples, television, three part drama, RTÉ Television, 8, 15 & 22 June 1989 (director Peter Omerod).
Willy Wynne Con Motto, radio, short story, BBC Radio 4, 27 September 1989, (producer Eoin O Callaghan).

Fine Day For A Hunt, radio, 30 minute play, BBC Radio 3, 11
November 1989, (director & producer Peter Kavanagh).
Rise Up Lovely Sweeney, radio, 65 minute play, BBC Radio 3 (*Drama
Now* series), 13 November 1991, (director & producer Eoin
O'Callaghan).
Rise Up Lovely Sweeney, radio, 60 minute play, RTÉ Radio, 16
February 1993, (director & producer Garvan McGrath).

OTHER:

Through The Bridewell Gate: A Diary of The Dublin Arms Trial
(London: Faber & Faber, 1971).
Pádraic Ó Conaire, 'The Woman on Whom God Laid His Hand'
translated by Mac Intyre in *The Finest Stories of Pádraic Ó Conaire*
(Swords, Co. Dublin: Poolbeg Press, 1982) pp.11-24, (also in *The
Field Day Anthology III* (Derry: Field Day Publications 1991)
pp.827-837).

PERIODICALS AND OTHER PUBLICATIONS:

'The Bracelet' in Benedict Kiely (ed.) *The Penguin Book of Irish Short
Stories* (Harmondsworth: Penguin, 1981) pp.471-474.
'The Theatre of the Image' *Image Magazine* (Sept 1984).
'Pina Bausch in Manhattan' *The Irish Times* (Sept 1984).
'A Man, a Woman: a Woman a Man' *Cara Magazine* Vol., 19, No. 2
(Mar/Apr 1986).
'All the Lakes is Haunted' *Cara Magazine* Vol., 19. No. 6 (Nov/Dec
1986).
'On Sweet Killen Hill', 'The Yellow Bittern' and 'Drumlin Prayer' in
Anthony Bradley (ed.) *Contemporary Irish Poetry* (University of
California Press: 1988) pp.239-244.
'Snow White: Rehearsal Script One' *Krino 5* (Galway: Krino, Spring
1988) pp.51-56.
'No Young Bums: Why Don't Young People go to the Theatre?' in *Irish
Stage and Screen vol.1 no.5* (March 1989) p.26.
'Wing-Beat, Wing Feather', 'The Whisperer', 'The Dwarf', 'Birthday gift'
and 'Balaustra' in *Irish University Review* vol.19 no.2 (Autumn
1989) pp.264-268.
'Foggy Hair and Green Eyes' *Krino 13* (Dún Laoghaire, Dublin: Anna
Livia Press, 1992) pp.61-76.
'The State of Poetry' *Krino 14* (Winter 1993) pp.35-6.
'The Mankeeper' in Dermot Bolger (ed.) *The Picador Book of
Contemporary Irish Fiction* (London: Picador 1993) pp.9-13.
'An Hour with WCW (William Carlos Williams)' *Krino 18* (1995)
pp.16-19.

Works Cited

Byrne, Mairead, 'Two Men, A Poem, A Play. A Meeting Under Fire' *In Dublin* May 1983.

Carr, Marina, 'The Bandit Pen' Abbey Programme Note 1995.

Etherton, Michael, 'Patrick Mason at the Abbey: Theatre of the Image' *Contemporary Irish Dramatists* (London: Macmillan Publishers Ltd, 1989) pp.45-47.

Gelder, Lawrence van , 'Determining Paternity by Any Means Necessary' *The New York Times* 1 April 2003.

Hadfield, Paul, and Lynda Henderson, 'Plays in Performance: Ireland' *Drama: The Quarterly Review* Autumn 1983 pp.45-46.

Healy, Dermot , 'Let the Hare Sit' *Theatre Ireland 11* Autumn 1985 pp.9-10.

Holmquist, Kathryn , 'In The Beginning Was the Image' *Theatre Ireland 6* April-June 1984 pp. 150-152.

Hosey, Seamus , 'The Abbey in Russia' *Theatre Ireland* 15 May-August 1988 pp.14-17.

Johnson, Diarmuid , 'Caoineadh Airt Uí Laoghaire by Tom Mac Intyre' *The Irish Times* 20 April 1998.

Kennelly, Brendan , 'The Great Hunger For Experiment' *The Sunday Tribune* 20 September 1988.

Mac Intyre Tom [& Patrick Kavanagh] *The Great Hunger: Poem into Play* (Westmeath, Ireland: The Lilliput Press, 1988).

Mac Intyre, Tom, *The Great Hunger & The Gallant John-Joe,* (Dublin: The Lilliput Press, 2002).

Meany, Helen , 'The Magic of Dissonance' Dublin Theatre Festival Supplement *Irish Times* 24 September 1996.

Murray, Christopher , 'The Avant-garde' *Twentieth Century Irish Drama: Mirror Up to Nation* (Manchester University Press, 1997) pp.231-238.

Nowlan, David , *The Irish Times* 19 May 1993.

O'Toole, Fintan, 'Tom Mac Intyre taking away the Safety Net' *The Arts Tribune* supplement to *The Sunday Tribune* 8 May 1983.

---, 'Fire Brimstone and Sweeney' *Sunday Tribune* 15 September 1985.

Swift, Carolyn , 'You Must Tell the Bees' *Irish Times* 28 September 1996.

Sweeney, Bernadette , *Performing the Body in Irish Theatre* (Palgrave Macmillan, 2008) esp. pp.50-73.

---

[1] Tom Mac Intyre, *Sheep's Milk on the Boil* p. 99.

[2] Kathryn Holmquist, 'In The Beginning Was the Image' *Theatre Ireland 6* April-June 1984, pp. 151-152.

[3] Dermot Healy, 'The Hurt Mind' Abbey Programme Note 1986.

---

[4] Mac Intyre says, 'I'd call *Kitty O'Shea* [...] finding my way back into the room. Fun aspects to it but for Tom Mac Intyre incomprehensibly conservative'. 'Tom Mac Intyre in Conversation with Fiach Mac Conghail,' in *Theatre Talk: Voices of Irish Theatre Practitioners* eds. Lilian Chambers, Ger FitzGibbon and Eamonn Jordan (Dublin: Carysfort Press, 2001), p. 314.

[5] David Nowlan, *The Irish Times* 19 May 1993.

[6] The cast included the author of this article, Bernadette Sweeney, with Cathy Ryan, Catherine Walsh, Pat Shortt and Cathal O'Riordain.

[7] Marina Carr, 'The Bandit Pen' Abbey Programme Note 1995.

[8] Tom Mac Intyre, *Good Evening, Mr Collins* in *The Dazzling Dark: New Irish Plays*, (ed.) Frank McGuinness (London: Faber & Faber, 1996), p.193.

[9] Ibid.

[10] Tom Mac Intyre, 'Afterword' *The Dazzling Dark: New Irish Plays*, (ed.) Frank McGuinness, (London: Faber & Faber, 1996), p. 233.

[11] Diarmaid Johnson, *The Irish Times* 20 April 1998.

[12] Ian Kilroy, *The Irish Times* 13 November 1999.

[13] Tom Mac Intyre, *The Gallant John-Joe* (Dublin: Lilliput Press, 2002), p. 55.

[14] Lawrence Van Gelder, *New York Times* 1 April 2003.

[15] Marina Carr, 'The Bandit Pen' Abbey Programme Note 1995.

Introduction to *The Harper's Turn*

Seamus Heaney
(Gallery Books, 1982)

I have not grasped the full import and inner logic of all the stories in [*The Harper's Turn*] and cannot, indeed, be sure that 'stories' is the word to use about all of them. But that does not matter. With the publication of this selection of Tom Mac Intyre's shorter works, we are saluting a writer *nel mezzo del cammin*.

Yet he is not, after all, a middle of the road writer. He corners at speed, instinctively accelerating away from what Joseph Brodsky has called the 'aesthetic inertia' that is always threatening the professional writer of prose. There is a far thing, pierced and lonely, some crystal of hurt transmitting a pure signal. A few pieces reminded me of the hedged and elusive intensities of Eliot of *The Waste Land*, that sense of antic conjuring, a plot withheld but a probe going out. And what Eliot later sought as he struggled with *Little Gidding* seems to have been found in many places by Tom Mac Intyre, 'some acute personal reminiscence (never to be explicated, of course, but to give power from well below the surface)'.

Whoever it was defined writing as nervous energy translated into phrases might have been thinking of this writer's first talent. It was in the cell of the phrase that Mac Intyre's energy beat from the start. I remember my elation when '*Stallions*' first appeared almost twenty years ago in *The Dubliner* (it was then called '*At Twelve the Marketyard*') and though we can now see that story and the one that follows it, *Boarders*, in this collection as relatively conventional in the context of this writer's later work, we can also see, twenty years and a wilderness of short stories later, why his name figures in the very short list of Irish writers who have set out to make it new.

There is another exemplary feature of the career: a pursuit of impulse, an indifference to conventional literary success, a risk-taking. With *The Charollais* (1969) and *Dance the Dance* (1970) 'hailed', as they say, he could have 'followed up'. Instead he pitched *Through the Bridewell Gate* into the Dublin Arms Trial, then swerved into theatre, sailing close to the rocks of 'engagement' while following the star of some inner commitment. 'You know', said Frost, 'the real thing is that the sense of sacrifice and risk is one of the greatest stimuli in the world.' So next he went further and nearly abjured language altogether for the gesture of the dance, and it is from that stage and troupe-work that there springs some of the more elliptical (and still, to my mind, less persuasive) pieces in this book. But perhaps it was the exposure to the footlights which extended him beyond the burning-glass focus of the phrase; the new animating element at work here is the shape-shifting, submarine half-light of myth.

When Irish mythology began to become a literary currency at the end of the nineteenth century, it was used to vindicate a claim to national identity, historic culture, spiritual resource. A hundred years later the writer approaches it with less propagandist intent, with a primary hunger for form, in order to find structure for unstructured potential within himself. Thus, 'The Man-Keeper', while it could be said to demonstrate 'the riches of the folk tradition', should also be seen as a pure exultation in fluency and inventiveness *per se*; it is, in its modern way, distanced from itself by knowing what makes itself tick. Yet it is still free in an objective enjoyment of its own energies and is not niggardly with speech or incident in the way that some other pieces seem to be.

In fact, the drama we are witnessing in this book is a conflict between two strains of narrative, two contradictory imperatives. One says, 'Tell it all, let it run, enjoy the spill of words'; the other says, 'Withhold, cut back, condense'. In pieces like 'The Hurt Mind' and 'Occasion of Note', this tension between tale-telling and shape-making is just about held, but in many of the others it is the shape-making faculty that wins out strongest and the mythic lineaments insist on their presence as reminder – or projection – of the archetype. And this is why I wonder if 'story' is, after all, the term for everything here. Language left to play so autonomously is reaching for the condition of poetry.

A Conversation with Tom Mac Intyre

Vincent Woods
(*Rattlebag*, RTÉ Radio 1, 17 August 2006)

VW. 'By turns disenchanted and ecstatic, cantankerous and amorous, he resembles the solitary figure in the landscape whose unexpected presence somehow assembles the scene'. So says the poet, Michael Longley of his fellow Ulster writer, Tom Mac Intyre, poet, playwright, writer of prose, whose new collection of poetry *ABC* has just been published by New Island Books. I have been talking to Tom Mac Intyre about his work and this new collection. He began by telling me about one of the poems, 'Widda', in the new book.

TMacI. A lot of people are taken by a poem in the start of the book titled *Widda*. A relative told me that my grandfather, who died in 1916 and as I understand the matter in pacifist circumstances, had been a beekeeper and that on his death my grandmother a youngish woman was told: 'You must now go to the bees and tell them the beekeeper is dead'. Well, you've only to offer that material to a writer and all the bells start ringing! So here's the poem that emerged:

Widda

You must tell the bees
the bee-keeper is dead ...

She waited a few days
to catch breath, hold
while she might, his step,
Sunday, an ass's heat,
she approached the orchard,
found her way to the hives.

Low din of the business;
she watched the smart bundles
arrive loaded, enter, un-
load, leave on the wind
that was no wind, a wave,
suspended, knew again
the honey, comb, way
he'd present it – *Yours, Mary,*
let her taste-buds travel
heather-honey, clover-honey,
honey warbling the rose ...

She'd shut eyes to pray,
sip tea from a saucer,
bring word to the bees –

Thomas, your keeper, is dead.

She stood there, she looked,
was aware of the bees'
to-and-fro, and next
she saw him, head veiled,
move through the trees -
he moved bolder than life –
her chest thumped good-bye,
the light bee-keeper stride
became one with the haze.[1]

VW. Tom, I'm fascinated by the dedication on the book, dom leannán sí, is dom leannán luí. Is that the spiritual and the physical, the lovers who bring art and inspiration?

TMacI. Yes. *Dom leannán sí,* she would come first, the spirit woman, and then the flesh and blood lover.

VW. So these are the two elements that unite in the book because the poems are personal and then they are bigger, they are landscape, they are mythology, they are this wonderful combination of so many things, but coming back time and again are those two elements of the spiritual and the physical.

TMacI. Without a doubt. I'd see dom *leannán luí/leannán sí* nexus as the *raison d'etre* for writing poetry, for getting out of bed in the morning and for going to bed at night, because I have a powerful sense of writing as a journey.

VW. For you, where does this inspiration come from? In one of the poems, in 'Slieve Gullion', you conjure this image of the writer looking into the Oxford English Dictionary and finding a word to see what the powers will send. Is there that sense of being open to what the powers will send to you?

TMacI. Overwhelmingly, as far as I can push it. That is a major concern of mine, the theme you raise there. I think, not to be contentious and yet to be contentious, contemporary writing in Ireland, certainly for the last fifty years, has been wickedly divided between two camps. There's the ten percent camp, the Yeats/Kavanagh camp who believe in the transcendental and who listen all the time achingly for the creak of the door between the two worlds and their songs are intimately tied to that sound. And then there's the ninety percent battalion, we'll say Beckett and Joyce, who'd say 'please spare me that nonsense'. Joyce has a famous quote on the subject 'the only *esprit* that interests me is *l'esprit d'escalier*, thank you very much'.

VW. The bit of French reminds me that in these poems there are several languages happening, there's English, there's Irish, there's French and then there's the Irish/English of Cavan, of your own place, and what we might call your own language. Do you come back time and again to the word?

TMacI. You better believe it. The word is one of my primary weapons, but we are looking here at the problem of language and the magic of language and where it may take one. There's a major problem for the contemporary writer using the English language. English is exhausted, as Sam Beckett remarked in the thirties. He said it has been extracted to death and, not to make a song and dance about it, the Reformation, the Latinity of the King James I version of the Bible, the Industrial Revolution, really put the bankers in charge of the heart of the English language so that today what we have is a combination of Blair/Bush lingo. I believe Beckett was right when he said it was exhausted. So, if you are an Irish writer, what do you do about that? There are certain ways where we have an advantage in seeking to solve the problem and one of them is the huge resonating presence of the Irish language in our English. I really would advise any young person from Ireland interested in writing on a serious level to get hold of the Irish language fast. Because if you are writing in English to have Irish available to you is a huge help. It helps you to bust the syntax. It helps you musically. It helps you imagistically all the time. What else? The presence of everything short of Greek say, notably Latin and French. Well, in the long ago when I went to boarding school you were taught Greek and Latin and that was marvellous really so smidgens of that would still be with me. I did my starvation stint, not quite sleeping under the bridges, at Paris and it is easy to fall in love with the French language so you use whatever you have in your magic hat.

VW. Landscape is also crucial all the time and not just the landscape of language but your own landscapes and the landscapes of Cavan and into Ulster. 'Slieve Gullion', your poem about the great Ulster mountain, made me want to go back and read Michael J. Murphy again. But Tom maybe you'd read from the beginning of that poem and then we will talk about landscape and its importance to you.

Slieve Gullion

You've reached the summit, there's
the lake all the talk was about,
slap on top, an eye, it stares
back at you – 'Hello' – innocent.

The fawn, seems, led Fionn up here,
into the lake – her scut's a wand –
hero emerges 'three days later',
mop matt white that was blond,

should she meet you, the fawn
will say – 'Your hair's already white,'
and bockety three-score-and-ten
won't, for once, have answer pat.

Hellovan education already,
third-way up the mile climb
to the shabby cairn (just slid upsee-
Dutchy off it), I utter the crime

of looking back, ten counties
and a tranche of sea possess me,
suction plasmic, custody of the eyes
thereafter, Enclosed Order Custody,

that'll l'arn ye. Should mention,
caught the sound (same dunt)
of the mountain, feral, atropine,
felt – God's truth – arteries dilate,

o, one bonnie beaded clarion. Pass,
friend. Reconnoitre. From cairn
northward to the lake's a mess,
bog, bog hole, lake worn
now, lonesome, want *some*one,
asks – aches – for engagement,
'Gullion,' they say, from *Dhubh Linn*,
the black pool,' she'll stir, tantrum

threap recognizances
down your throat should you deny
her true regard, *Lá eile*, *Petals*,
and I mean that ...[2]

VW. Talk to me about that Tom, that great mountain and its place in the landscape of Ireland, in the mythology of Ireland and here in your work.

TMacI. Well, Gullion, and you do well to allude to Michael Murphy. I was brought up on Michael Murphy. He notably directed me to Gullion as the Holy Mountain in our stretch of territory. Gullion is visible from the heights of East Cavan and so it was easy for me to become intoxicated. I made a vow that I'm going to climb Gullion and this wasn't so very long ago. My knees shivered at that vow and people looked at me strangely but I walk a great deal and that was mini preparation for the physical end of the trip.

VW. I remember years ago Christopher FitzSimon saying to me that he felt there was something in the landscape of Cavan/Monaghan/Leitrim that brought this swathe of poetry and a kind of wild theatre that came from yourself, Michael Harding, Dermot Healy and others. Do you have that sense of your own local landscape as this constant source of both inspiration and challenge that the past is there both to remind us and to challenge us into the future?

TMacI. Overwhelmingly. Máire Mac Neill, in that wonderful book, *The Festival of Lughnasa*, speaks of three utterly haunted plateaux in the island of Ireland and one of the three is the mountainy area of East Cavan. It is utterly haunted. In what way is it haunted? Well, it's hard not to invoke the lakes and once you invoke the lakes ... It seems to me quality writing has access to what is called, fancily, symbolic thought and feeling. That is to say that a lake is not just a lake, it is the way into a world of magic and adventure. Those lakes of Cavan to me are haunted, perpetually haunted. They are so haunted that they persuade the population to walk into them, as anyone will tell you concerning Cavan. I waited a long day for an aeroplane journey over Cavan, and low over Cavan so I could inspect the landscape, and I looked at the lakes and I began to cry. I began to weep into the lakes. Fine. That shows the connection it seems to me.

VW. It's all connected. There's this huge sense of connectedness in all of your work. If you take a poem like 'A Sow Bends My Ear' we are into the world of mythology and the everyday, this kind of throwaway gloriously base world.

TMacI. The poem derives from a dream in which I met a sow. This sow was well able to inform me that she, for her part, took decided exception to my unwillingness to get into the clobber and the combat zone in the sense of the spirit combat zone; to stop being a little Lord Fauntleroy, in other words. I value her advice.

A Sow Bends My Ear

.... forget Hafners, never mind Olhausen,
she's the original Hairy Bacon
an' Only College of Higher Knowledge,
o, yes, and while I'm at it,
I'm aware you tickle the lore
of place-names from your sideline chair,
veranda hammock, Stylite's pillar,
anything to skip the glar, the glit,
okay, Mammy-Brat connoisseur
of sanitized toponymic bon-
bons, we'll spend our honeymoon
in *Muckanaghidirdháshâile* –
The Piggy Place between the Twin
Briny Inlets – riddle-me-randy,
riddle-me-ree, how's that for
a tidal, groined, pragmatical potpourri!'[3]

VW. You are described by Marina Carr as a 'Shaman', a kind of man of magic. Do you see yourself in this light?

TMacI. Yes. I think exciting writing demands constant blasts from the unconscious. I think, and it scarcely needs to be said, that getting access to the unconscious is a fearful undertaking. I think, as the Americans say, you have to give away an arm and a leg, and that is putting it mildly. I'd go scriptural and say you have to put down everything you have and follow that. But if you can get access to the unconscious and hold your nerve and begin to talk to the unconscious as a way of breathing and a very demanding way of breathing then you are in a zone where the magic and the shamanic are available to you at a constantly rising price. There's a wonderful law at issue. The law says, if you renege on this engagement we will destroy you, because having seen the magic you are not allowed ...

That's a particular kind of reneging and the punishment for it is swift and terrible. But it also says, now you are in here you must undertake the journey and the journey is constantly more demanding and there is no going back. And that is why access to the unconscious, deliberate or accidental, blows a lot of people off the planet. But any young person I talk to about writing, and lots who aren't young, but mostly young people I would say: 'So, you want to write wonderful stories or poems or plays? Then you are going to have to give away everything to get access to the unconscious and then you can begin to examine your extraordinary position'.

VW. Were there words there in your childhood? Where did this overwhelming love of the written word, of the creation of writing, come from?

TMacI. From when I was six, seven, eight, nine, people in my small town, not an especially literate small town, but literate enough to be able to say to me in the company of my parents, that child is going to be a writer, which is a tribute to the Irish literary tradition it seems to me. I believe in fate. That raises a wonderful question. Put it this way, I knew I was here to be a writer, I knew that that was my fate. My bother, everybody's bother, is to accept what your fate is. To contest it is fatal.

VW. You've made difficult choices along the way. You were a teacher for a while. You could have stayed with that but you chose to follow your own path. It's exactly what you have been talking about, facing up to the inevitability of following that fate that is there for you. Was that a hard decision to make in the mid 1960s?

TMacI. Frightening. I think it is hard anytime. John or Mary hears from within that this is what you are here to do in the world. That's scary for a start. If it has to do with being an artist it's especially scary. I was brought up in a world of magic, folklore and mythology but also a world of bigotry and lower middle class conservative attitudes. To sign my name on the document pushed me to the limit. But eventually I realized that if I didn't go with what I knew to be my fate I would be in the grave inside five or ten years. So, then I made my decision, and then my troubles were only beginning.

VW. Would you read us another poem, maybe Bridgie Cleary?

TMacI. Bridgie Cleary, as many listeners will know, was murdered because she insisted on being an independent woman, particularly in matters of the sensual and the sexual.

Bridgie Cleary

I love, love the stir o' company
ye can't see, it spakes of other
dominions, not that far
distant, men an' women tall
in silks an' sarsnets, organdie,
takin' the air or, come nightfall,
switchin' to their flaunty

daisybells, fondlin' other to a waft
o' notes, them notes audible, o, yes,
audible, be sure, to Bridgie Cleary,
aye, an' manys the Bridgie Cleary,
from 'ithin their Glens o' Quiet
or their ivy-walled demesnes.⁴

VW. Tom, many of us were delighted to see *The Gallant John-Joe* which Skehana did a few years ago, then last year *What Happened Bridgie Cleary* in the Peacock, and to see your work back on stage and being seen by a new generation of people. For me, and I'm sure for many others as well, *The Great Hunger*, was a pivotal moment in Irish theatre. I think I saw it around three times and I will never forget it. Do you distinguish beween poetry and theatre or do they run in together, are they caught up with each other for you?

TMacI. Not to give you too Irish an answer, they are and they aren't. Theatre is a wonderfully public art. Poetry, the kind of poetry I write certainly, is private, it's an exploration into the private dungeons and private galleries. They are two different voices. And I would say that writing short stories, which I enjoy doing too, that is a different notation again. The distinction I'd make is that the poetry is intricate and personal, while the stories are a move away from that. Lots of people would say, however, that there is a strange connection between the short story and the lyric poem. But the play is communal. It is communal art. You are there with ten or fifteen others hammering the piece together. It is seen by an audience. It has to work in a way quite other from the lyric poem, as actors will quickly remind you if you foist on them language that is not theatre language.

VW. What are you doing now? You are writing a play for the Peacock so we will see more of Tom Mac Intyre's theatre.

TMacI. Sure. The Dublin Theatre Festival will be doing a reading of a new play of mine, written for Tom Hickey and with Hickey standing with a whip in the vicinity to tell the truth, called *Don Murphy*. It is a Don Quixote play and we've had wonderful fun with it. Don Quixote is an irresistible theme.

VW. Tom, would you finish for us by reading a poem from the collection *ABC, The Clown*.

TMacI. Working with a genius can be very difficult and I decided at a certain point that I had to clarify my views on this topic and at some cost. Therefore I wrote a poem called 'The Clown' for Tom Hickey.

The Clown

Beware the clown, that portable
hatched grimace testament
to appetites unappeasable,
one taste worse than another,
you, you're worst of the lot,
get – *Basta!* – out of his sight.

But give him – *Merci, merci* –
the music, make-up, lights,
sweat, sawdust, razzmatazz,
and, font of voluptuary grace,
he ravishes you, you and yours,
with tender fingers lifts the veil,
most tenderly allows it fall.

You go home shriven, forsaken.
Where on earth have you been?
You've been to bed with the clown,
the huckster, hoaxer, shaman.
Don't ask him how it's done.
Himself again, he can't tell.
The veil, just. Lifted. Let fall.[5]

VW. Tom Mac Intyre, thanks very much indeed for talking to us on *Rattlebag*. Tom Mac Intyre's collection of poems, *ABC*, is published by New Island Books.

Works Cited

Tom Mac Intyre *ABC New Poems* (Dublin: New Island Books, 2006).

---

[1] Tom Mac Intyr,e *ABC new poems* (Dublin: New Island, 2006), p. 3.
[2] Ibid., pp. 25-26.
[3] Ibid.,pp. 38-39.
[4] Ibid., p. 21.
[5] Ibid., p. 22.

Tom Mac Intyre: Border Country Bandit

Tom Hickey

[This essay was first published in *Princeton University Library Chronicle* (Volume LXVIII, Numbers 1 and 2, Autumn 2006 – Winter 2007) pp. 632-639.]

First Meeting

My first meeting with Tom Mac Intyre took place in Houricans public house on Lower Leeson Street, Dublin, in March 1982. He approached me and asked me if I would be interested in performing in a play he had written about Paddy Kavanagh, which was to be staged by the Project Arts Centre, Dublin, as part of the Dublin Theatre Festival the following October. I told him I was not available because I was already scheduled to play in Neil Donnelly's *The Silver Dollar Boys* at the Abbey Theatre.

I had heard stories about Mac Intyre and his 'strange' and 'unorthodox' views about theatre, so I was disappointed to miss the opportunity of working with him, especially because his play was about the poet Paddy Kavanagh (1904-1967), a figure in whom I had more than a passing interest.

So, Mac Intyre went back to County Clare and I went back to the Abbey where I was working on a contract renewable every year. Bringing in freelance players on contract to work with members of the permanent company was an innovation and part of Artistic Director Joe Dowling's progressive agenda. Another major aspect of his artistic policy was encouraging and nourishing new writing. For example, by the end of 1982 I had appeared in nine new plays in the space of three years.

When in early 1983 the Artistic Director called me in to tell me what he had in mind for me in the coming year, he mentioned a play called *The Great Hunger* by one Tom Mac Intyre. He said Patrick Mason would direct it, and I would play the central character, Paddy Maguire. I was more than pleased not to have missed Mac Intyre's Kavanagh play after all!

As it turned out, the play wasn't about Paddy Kavanagh himself. Rather, it was a dramatization of his famous epic poem, *The Great Hunger*, and had been rejected by the Project Arts Centre, whereupon Mac Intyre submitted it to the Abbey. We started rehearsal on Monday, March 28, 1983.

The Great Hunger

On a first reading, the script was daunting, impossible to categorize, and yet thrilling. It was a spectral mélange of physical movement, extended stage directions, and visual imagery, punctuated by a measure of distorted and incantatory language. It was unlike anything I had encountered before. Nevertheless, I found I had an immediate rapport with its strange and beautiful demands.

In rehearsal, working with director Patrick Mason and the author, we, the actors, discovered that we were going nowhere unless we could create an original theatrical idiom to serve Mac Intyre's expressionistic vision of Kavanagh's epic poem. We discovered what the author described as a 'gestural' score as well as a 'verbal' score. We tried to make our bodies speak. Movement as dancing. Words as music. Repetition, the incantatory, strange distortions of words and sounds. And gradually the inner and exterior landscape of Patrick Maguire's world began to emerge, poised somewhere between the quotidian and the sacral.

The process was extremely demanding mentally and physically. The actor facing the cosmos of this play needs to have the determination of a rhinoceros, the courage of a lion, the physical grace of a panther, the delicacy of a butterfly, and the inner resources of a shaman. You are not just calling on the technical resources of voice and body, but you are forced, in a most substantial way, to look towards the inner life. In other words, you have to find out who you are before you can do it. It is this dimension that makes Mac Intyre's work so demanding and absolutely unique in Irish theatre of that time.

The Great Hunger opened on Monday, May 9, 1983, and was received with cautious approval by the critics. I didn't know then that *The Great Hunger* was the first leg of what was to become an extraordinary theatrical journey with Tom Mac Intyre, one that would last for more than twenty-five years.

It was not long before we were regarded by many in the Abbey as 'the lunatics in the basement.' With this production and others that followed, the 'lunatics' emerged into the sunshine and blew gusts of fresh air into every corner of the Abbey Theatre and elsewhere during the 1980s.

During the early rehearsals of *The Great Hunger* I had a line that surfaced several times in the proceedings. I didn't know what to do with it, how to play it. I'd only known the author for a week at this point, and it was the first major question I asked him. How should I deliver this line? A pause. Then he said, 'Pitch it somewhere between the quotidian and the enigmatic'. Perhaps that was the moment when our collaboration really began.

The Great Hunger was original, powerful, and surreal, and it made severe demands on an audience that came expecting conventional, naturalistic drama. At the opening performance in the Assembly Rooms at the Edinburgh Festival (1986), we were fifteen, maybe twenty minutes into the show when the seats started to go clack, clack, clack as the audience began to leave. By the time we reached the interval, I would say we had a third of the audience we started with. It was a tough and unnerving experience, a vote of no confidence in what we were doing. I remember saying to myself: 'We must keep going. We must continue to play with concentration and passion and not to be intimidated'. And we did. And the audience that stayed until the end gave it a tumultuous reception. It played to full houses for the rest of the run, got rave reviews, and won a Fringe First Award.

Inspiration

The Isabella Gardner Museum, Boston, 1980. A Pissarro exhibition. Mac Intyre in attendance. He didn't have anything else to do. Unemployed, he had lots of time to consider the how of putting Kavanagh's poem on the stage. Part of his conscious and unconscious preparation was to immerse himself in modern dance theatre – Pina Bausch, the Mabou Mines Company, Richard Foreman, the Wooster Street Group, Tadeusz Kantor, Merce Cunningham, Trish Brown, Meredith Monk.

He walks into the exhibition in Boston. Looks up at a drama of men and women in a hayfield making hay. Pitchforks and hay – and *pa-ching*! Lightning struck! He'd found the way! Now he could go and write the script of *The Great Hunger*.

And ask him how long it took to write *The Great Hunger*, Mac Intyre's answer is two to three weeks, and there's no problem with that if you have spent the previous fifteen years considering your options.

Vocation

A three-year-old Mac Intyre in a red *geansaí* [jersey] in the kitchen of the grandmother's farm. She's pounding spuds. She looks up. The child is gone. She hares to the door. Looks out. The red *geansaí* is dizappearing round the first bend of the lane. She heads after the child, pursues the child. Next bend of the lane, no sign of the child. She keeps going. The child must be gone into a field. She comes to an open gate. Halfway up the slope of the hill the child is to be seen entranced, holding a white calf by the tail. The initiation of the poet.

Mac Intyre's Credo: Origins

The writer's task is to tell the truth and tell it beautifully. Assume he has the gift to tell the truth beautifully. Now the larger question, What is the truth? The truth is what silences the room. The living room, the bedroom, the bed...

If that's the writer's position, there will be problems for everybody, including the writer. For the writer to be candid with the problem of the truth, he has to have been born and reared in a haunted zone.

Máire Mac Neill, the daughter of the man who sent the telegrams that almost stopped the 1916 Rising and the author of a marvellous book on the Lughnasa Festival, describes the highlands of East Cavan as one of the three super-haunted plateaus of the island of Ireland. The other two, needless to say, are in the province of Munster.

The language available in that zone is an English wonderfully varied. Words and syntax available from Middle English to Chaucer to the Elizabethans to the eighteenth century. And that English riddled with an enormous, vital contribution from the Irish language. That's the mixture.

The next crucial dimension was happily present for Tom Mac Intyre in his upbringing, and indeed exists in the Cavan Hills to this day. That is, a willingness on the part of the local population to play with that fierce linguistic inheritance. *Divilment* is the key word. For the Greeks, the god Hermes; for the Romans, Mercury. For we Irish, the god Lugh. That's the spirit of adventure, discovery of the unforeseen, the unforecastable, the magical.

Implicit in Mac Intyre's work is a battle against mainstream Irish theatre in which the erotic and the sensual are for the most part nowhere to be found. An unfortunate state of affairs.

So it is no surprise that the central thrust of the work from *The Great Hunger* to *Only an Apple* (Peacock Theatre, 2009) has to do with forcing the intransigent male dominant energy to confront the suppressed female. In many ways *What Happened Bridgie Cleary* (Peacock Theatre, 2005) and *Only an Apple* represent the natural development of Mac Intyre's plays on this trajectory. The argument has moved from the blatant suppression of the female in *The Great Hunger* to the indomitable female rebel energy addressed in Bridget Cleary, a woman who never wore bloomers and regarded that as her right if it so pleased her. In the recently staged *Only an Apple* this female energy escalates yet again taking the form of Queen Elizabeth (I) and the legendary pirate queen, Grace O'Malley, who haunt an incumbent *Taoiseach* [Prime Minister] as he broaches both the physical and spiritual worlds.

Collaboration with Mac Intyre

Collaboration may not be the right word. Mac Intyre is the writer. I am the actor (although I have directed two of Mac Intyre's plays). Our process: He sends the first draft to me in Dublin. Then we meet in Kilnahard, Cavan. I contribute what might be called a director energy. The writer listens. Accepts. Rejects. Makes notes. He writes another draft. We meet again. And so on. And eventually there emerges what we call a rehearsal script. Next stop, the adventure of the rehearsal room.

Mac Intyre describes the rehearsal procedure as follows: 'There's the script. Instantly tear it to bits. Throw the pile of bits in the air. They will fall as they please. Now take a close look at what you've got. The magic is the aleatory'.[1]

This has been the pattern since our early work together in the 1980s. After the premiere of *The Great Hunger* we did a revival and then national and international tours between 1983 and 1988. And in the same period, *The Bearded Lady* (1984), *Rise Up Lovely Sweeney* (1985), *Dance for your Daddy* (1987), and *Snow White* (1988): by all accounts, a hectic time.

I think of all of these plays we worked on together in the 1980s the most difficult, the most demanding and the most underrated, was *Rise Up Lovely Sweeney* (1985). To this day people who have seen the play, and even some who haven't, talk about its explosive language, the powerful imagery and its playfulness. And that pivotal speech at the end: Sweeney's desperate search for his 'nayshun' that goes in leaps and bounds from the 'busted telly in the bog hole' to the arcades that 'spit and stutter like a sea of tranquility inside a poxy equinoctal [sic] moon'.[2]

In 1993 it was decided that I would direct *Chickadee* for Red Kettle Theatre Company and in the following year I directed *Sheep's Milk on the Boil* at the Peacock. *Sheep's Milk* is effectively Mac Intyre's *Midsummer Night's Dream*. We had fantastic fun with it and like all of our collaborations it motored on the fuel of 'play'. Mac Intyre sees this as the essence of collaboration and I suppose I do too.

In 1997 I played the role of John-Joe Concannon in *The Chirpaun* (Peacock Theatre). The production didn't quite hit the mark but I became very interested in the character of John-Joe who expressed himself from time to time in several beautifully written soliloquys. Some time later I asked Tom if he would write a one man play about John-Joe which he agreed to do. He proceeded to write several drafts which we worked on over the course of a year or so, and eventually it had its world premiere in Culdaff, Co. Donegal on 3 January 2001.

The *Gallant John-Joe* tells the story of John-Joe Concannon who lives in a council cottage on the outskirts of a small town somewhere in rural Cavan. His unmarried daughter Jacinta is pregnant and she won't tell him who the father is. John-Joe suspects the *Chinee* who runs the local chipper. From time to time he drinks from a medicine bottle which he carries around with him. He has troubles coming from everywhere but what keeps him on his feet is his capacity to make a story of anything that occurs to him. He uses language as crutch, ointment, talisman.

The play is a tour de force of storytelling, swinging from the tragic to the richly comic. A Lear-like figure, John-Joe, too, is circled by phantoms. With the relish of the afflicted he brings them before us, beguiles them, and us, by sheer word magic.

In a programme note for a run at the Everyman Theatre, Cork, the author wrote as follows:

> Composing the play was a great joy, not least the collaborative engagement with Tom Hickey. Constantly developing the play, adding, subtracting, refining, is a great joy ... The vital common ingredient is the quality of *play*. Without the mercurial spirit, the space won't sing.[3]

The *Gallant John-Joe* is one of the great one-man plays in Irish theatre. It has been a huge success and has toured Ireland almost every year since it was written. It played at the Edinburgh Fringe Festival in 2002 and at the Irish Arts Centre in New York in 2003.

In *What Happened Bridgie Cleary* (2005) I played the ghost of Mikey Cleary who is suspended in the afterlife with his wife Bridgie and her lover, William Simpson. The play is based on real events, the tragic murder of Bridget Cleary in Tipperary in 1895. A trip to the area where Bridget lived and died had a huge impact on how I approached the role of Mikey. Standing outside that cottage where they lived with Slievenamon right in front of me. To know that she saw this beautiful mountain when she looked out her front door, to know that was hugely beneficial as an actor. We did a six week run in the Peacock and then took the play out on national tour where rural audiences immediately tapped into the language of the piece.

Whatever the circumstances during this long and varied period of work with Mac Intyre our collaboration has always been a mystery, beyond rational explanation or definition. It has to do with a mutuality that resides in the intuitive, in the unconscious. Such collaborations cannot be arranged. They happen or they don't.

Mac Intyre's Well

The mark of Mac Intyre's writing is the presence of the mythic note. That is to say, the presence of symbolic thought and feeling.

The well in Mac Intyre is never just a well – it's the well that contains the magic fish or magic frog in some guise or other. We're talking here of a way of breathing, a way of seeing the world, a way of storytelling permeated by the spirit dimension. That line of energy in our modern literature is the Yeats/Kavanagh line of energy. And Mac Intyre's deference to it is total. How does the writer get into that meadow? The only access to it is through the unconscious. How do you get across to the unconscious? By giving away everything you have. To get gold you must pay gold. It's no wonder most writers prefer the secular mode.

A Dream

Mac Intyre once resided in a house in Quilca, County Cavan, which at one time belonged to Dr. Thomas Sheridan. Jonathan Swift frequently visited Sheridan and in the summer of 1724 he revised *Gulliver's Travels* while staying there.

One midsummer day, Swift came to Mac Intyre in a dream, the Swift we all know from the pictures – indescribable grief in the eyes and face. Swift looked at Mac Intyre gravely. Mac Intyre looked back. A wordless conversation. Concerning? Women, the only topic. And the outcome of this parley? 'Better get it right.' Mac Intyre's play *The Bearded Lady* was staged in the Peacock Theatre in 1984. The central theme dealt with Swift's troubled relationship with the female and in particular his ill-fated relationships with Stella and Vanessa.

You might say that Swift came to Mac Intyre in a dream; and, indeed, the play opens with Swift's dream, which then goes on to become Gulliver's dream.

Mac Intyre and the Image

Mac Intyre is a storyteller. One way of telling stories is through the image. Language pushed to the incantatory takes on the force of the imagistic. What is that force? It's the force of the image jumping the cerebral and going direct to the visceral. There is a gain in immediacy that can be terrifying. When Mikey says in *What Happened Bridgie Cleary*, 'There's only two sounds in the world. Sound of the scythe singin' ripe in the meadow, sound of the scythe hittin' stone'.[4] The aim is to hit the audience in the visceral. Likewise with Bridgie's 'Don't go makin' a herring o' Bridgie Cleary',[5] you have the same incantatory thrust.

Contemporary English/English and American/English are bereft of the possibility of that incantatory note. Irish/English and for sure Cavan/English still have it, and crucial to its survival is the seething presence of the *as Gaeilge* [the Irish language] texture. Never forget that Irish is a spirit language and so remains. English was thus in Will Shakespeare's time, but the King James Bible and the Industrial Revolution banished it. Mac Intyre's storytelling is haunted by the imagistic and is constantly playing with Irish/English and Cavan/English.

The Last Word

The plays of Tom Mac Intyre cannot be classified as mainstream theatre, and there is little appetite for his work in the commercial sector. Since we met in 1983, the Abbey has staged, quite properly, the bulk of his output. But even there, acceptance or rejection can depend on the theatrical taste buds of any given artistic director. The Abbey, for instance, rejected *Don Murphy* (an unpublished work, 2006), Mac Intyre's take on *Don Quixote*, which in my view is vintage Mac Intyre, but went on to commission the recently staged *Only an Apple*.

So, at seventy years plus, Mac Intyre remains undiminished in energy and output. This poet, this outlaw 'down from the hills,' provoking support and vituperation in equal measure, constantly testing the magic, even if it's a minority art for a minority audience. But then Mac Intyre's nature is to be on the outside. There's nothing he won't dare, from the haunted image about to explode, to strange and beautiful language. You pray for the hour when his theatre will have the impact it deserves.

I will leave the last word to the poet himself:

> A writer is one condemned to tell a story. You want to make it – there's only one story – as if it's never been told before. You want to disturb and entertain. You want to gather people together and move them communally as well as individually. Your response to the traffic of the living and the dead is to sing grief rather than cry it. Your response to the verboten (you're Irish!) spill of the sensual is to make bodies speak on the stage. What are you anyway? A child with the killer instinct. And pictures galore. Just let them be hot, wild mother of dreams, just let them be on fire![6]

Works Cited

Tom Mac Intyre *What Happened Bridgie Cleary* (Dublin: New Island, 2005).

---, 'Theatre of the Image' *Image Magazine* (September 1984).

---, 'The Hurt Mind' in *Rise Up Lovely Sweeney* (1985) pp. 88-90. Also published as 'Appalachia' in *I Bailed Out at Ardee*, (Dublin: Dedalus Press, 1987).

---

[1] Tom Mac Intyre, unpublished interview by Tom Hickey, 2007.

[2] Tom Mac Intyre, 'The Hurt Mind' in *Rise Up Lovely Sweeney* (1985) pp. 88-90. Also published as 'Appalachia' in *I Bailed Out at Ardee*, (Dublin: Dedalus Press, 1987).

[3] Tom Mac Intyre Programme Note *The Gallant John-Joe* (Everyman Palace Theatre, Cork, 2003).

[4] Tom Mac Intyre, *What Happened Bridgie Cleary* (Dublin: New Island, 2005), p. 51. Note: line as quoted above comes from performance which differs slightly from published text.

---

[5] Tom Mac Intyre, *What Happened Bridgie Cleary,* p. 76.

[6] Tom Mac Intyre, 'Theatre of the Image' *Image Magazine* (September 1984).

CHAPTER 2: 'A CONSPIRATOR'S GLEAM'[1]

Long Surrender: Finding a Theatrical Voice Through the Plays of the 1970s

Ben Francombe

At a performance at the Peacock, the Abbey Theatre's studio stage, of Tom Mac Intyre's 2009 play *Only an Apple*, a member of the audience, glancing through the brief biography of the author in the programme, was heard to say, 'I'll say this for Mac Intyre: he's no Johnnie-come-lately ...'. Mac Intyre has been writing for Irish theatre audiences for nearly forty years and has emerged in very different circumstances to other defining writers of the contemporary Irish theatre scene. *The Great Hunger* (1983), seen to this day as his most important contribution to theatre and certainly the point at which he gained a significant profile and reputation as a playwright, was not a 'bombshell' of a first play: Mac Intyre had had six theatre pieces produced before this point, representing an extensive apprenticeship, and this apprenticeship emerged in turn from a hinterland of an early life spent in obscurity in his native County Cavan.

Cavan, cited by many, not least himself, as a cultural influence on his work, was also his home up until he married and moved to Kildare in the 1960s: married with children, clinging to his 'mammy's skirt'[2], and working as a teacher in Clongowes until he was 'as near 40 as makes no difference, which is Cavan timidity at its worst'.[3] When he finally reached his 'midlife crisis', therefore, turning his back on his non-creative hinterland, he approached the whole process of being a writer, not only with an intensity and urgency that came to be reflected in all his work, but with an equally resonating experimentation which has made his theatre, in Mick Heaney's words, 'restlessly innovative'.⁴ Thus, before the ultimate recognition of *The Great Hunger*, there were a significant number of productions and unpublished texts that reveal at times a confused, isolated, frustrated, incomplete, and under-recognized dramatist, but one, ultimately, that shaped demonstrably a series of styles, forms, and cultural contexts that can contribute to an understanding of his more recognized latter career.

This essay serves as a brief, critical overview of Mac Intyre's early theatre career in the 1970s. By drawing on four key plays, produced in Dublin during the 1970s – *Eye-Winker, Tom-Tinker* (1972), *The Old Firm* (1975), *Jack Be Nimble* (1976), and *Find the Lady* (1977) – and concluding with a brief look at two works that emerge at the very end of the decade – *Deer Crossing* (1978) and *Doobally/Black Way* (1979) – produced away from Ireland and reflecting a final exploration of an interdisciplinary collaboration, one can clearly recognize fragments that help define Mac Intyre's theatre work. In a review of *Doobally/Black Way*, the last of these pieces, David Stevens was to identify a unity of these fragments that reflect a culmination of exploration.

> [The Production's] goal clearly is a theater of gesture and movement for which the strongest influence has probably been Meredith Monk, and in which music and words surrender their independence in a remarkably cohesive attempt at that elusive goal – total theater. ⁵

But, as this paper identifies, it was a long surrender: Mac Intyre wrote a number of structural and demarked theatre works in the early stages of his career. But, gradually, tentative – yet, at times, exciting – steps into a now familiar visual theatre were taken: theatrical moments informed by language and movement in a variety of interesting ways; an understanding of theatrical methodology that had collaboration at its centre; and thematic preoccupations that recur in his later work.

Before *The Great Hunger*, Mac Intyre's writing is recognized more in non-theatre forms, at least in terms of publication. *The Charollais* (1969), a comic novel; *Through the Bridewell Gate: A Diary of the Dublin Arms Trial* (1971), an irreverent attempt at reportage; *Blood Relations* (1972), a collection of Irish poems in translation, all reflect Mac Intyre's determination to try his hand at a range of defined writing styles: a disparate approach that might have slowed a drive towards theatre. Two further key texts, however, published before producing *The Great Hunger* and defined as short stories (a description that Sean Dunne found 'too much and too little'[6]), show signs of an experimentation and interdisciplinarity that reflects his emerging theatre work. In *Dance the Dance* (1970) and *The Harper's Turn* (1982), Mac Intyre uses a combination of prose and poetry in 'stories' that each last a few pages. The economy and eclectic selection of vocabulary tends to relieve the reader of the enthusiastic rush of words popular with other Irish writers, drawing one into a world of personal and stark understanding of a blend between myth and fact. It is this economy of language, together with the whole notion of crossing over in terms of content that seems to provide a parallel for understanding his theatre work. And while no theatre text was published at the time, there was certainly recognition of his commitment to this form. Writing at the time of *The Great Hunger*, Vincent Hurley attempts an early reflection of Mac Intyre's dramatic approach:

> Theatre has been a liberation for him. Here he found a medium which could encompass the range of his talents and interests, accommodating both the verbal and the visual, admitting the exhilarating possibilities of experiment while remaining rooted in concrete reality.[7]

Through theatre, Hurley suggests, Mac Intyre found a method of communication that served a commitment to diversity, as well as needing less explanation, suiting an antipathy for over-statement. And, in his discovery of a diverse theatre form, Mac Intyre was responding to what he saw as a dry and inert form of theatre, leading-the-line in Ireland at the time. Reflecting, in conversation with Fiach Mac Conghail in 2001, upon his early career, Mac Intyre suggests that – embracing his Cavan-Presbyterian roots – he adopted an 'adversarial stance ... starting out' and that he 'was surrounded by tame, boring, verbal theatre. A play [was] three or four people standing on a stage talking platitudes to each other'. Mac Intyre suggests that, when he decided to do something about what he terms 'daddy theatre' within 'daddy-society', embracing a 'female energy' that mitigated against 'the patriarchal goosestep', he had already 'done a certain amount of homework' in preparation. Mac Intyre cites Meyerhold: 'look if you want to learn how to write plays, write a play without words'. It is from this reading (and from the ideas of Appia, Grotowski, and Pina Bausch), Mac Intyre suggests, that 'he was on his way' to discovering his particular form of theatre'.[8]

It took some time, however, to develop this understanding. Mac Intyre's first attempts at writing for the theatre had seen little of this extreme use of the image and his first two plays, as D.E.S. Maxwell points out, 'kept language at [their] centre'.[9] *Eye-Winker, Tom-Tinker* is a full-length, two act (fourteen scene), play produced by the Abbey Theatre, with Lelia Doolan as director, Brian Collins as designer, and, remarkably, a full cast of sixteen actors, with Frank Grimes in the leading role.

In this first play, Mac Intyre writes of a revolutionary group and its passionate, dynamic, but ultimately inert leader, Shooks. The Irish Playography provides a pertinent synopsis: 'Having reorganized the revolutionary movement and hypnotized the masses to the edge of action, action doesn't come ...'.[10] The entanglement of the empty rhetoric, the improbability of commitment, and the confused psychology of the central character, tends to reflect certain themes of frustration and procrastination that emerge as recurring themes seen throughout Mac Intyre's work. Indeed, in an interview discussing his 1978 play, *Deer Crossing*, Mac Intyre describes his work, in general terms, to be about 'the hunger many of us have for intense living – and the reluctance many of us have to pay the price for that elusive goal'.[11] Whether Shooks's outlook can be described as a hunger for intense living, there is certainly a frustrating reluctance to push for an ultimate price: Act Two of *Eye-Winker, Tom Tinker* is a litany of deflected rhetoric, with each scene a series of empty promises, reluctant alliances, and moments of inaction. But the play's value on these terms is undermined by an equally frustrating absence of political contextualization. In Act One Mac Intyre aims for a social (and political) realism, but the audience does not know the political cause or its historical context. Within the first scene it becomes clear that we are in Ireland and it appears that this 'Ireland' is perceived – or *conceived* – as a Police State. In scene 2, a great political meeting takes place: the First Revolutionary shouts '[T]he Country's a corpse', and there is a general contempt for the weak-willed people, particularly from Shooks, but there is also a remarkable absence of the detailed political rhetoric or historical positioning that would be expected at a political meeting of this type, at this time: as Maxwell states, '[T]he play's debates barely touch upon the morality, the demands, and the tactics, of violence as a political expedient'.[12]

Certainly, the vagueness of this political movement's (and, correspondingly, this play's) context could reveal something of the author's emerging suspicion of the literal and explicit constructs of a 'daddy society': the absolutes of doctrine, which one Revolutionary in the play suggests, are understood 'to a degree not achieved by many' (Act 1, scene 7). But, in truth, this play tends to reflect rather than refute Mac Intyre's 'daddy theatre', or what Dan Rebellato describes as 'the repressive hypothesis' of post-1956 modern drama.[13] Certainly, there lacks, here, any evidence of a 'female energy', with its one female character, Anne Reilly, determined to make a stand against the propaganda-machine of the movement, but ultimately serving as an over-easy target for Shooks's sexual seduction. Indeed, this is a clear example of a play with 'three or four people standing on a stage talking platitudes to each other'. *Eye-Winker, Tom-Tinker* appears to have been written before Mac Intyre had read Meyerhold or Appia, or had heard Grotowski speak, or had seen Pina Bausch dance: it is committed to a literal theatre and a politic more readily identified in his non-fiction book *Through the Bridewell Gate: A Diary of the Dublin Arms Trial* – an irreverent and charged documentary on a moment of high drama (or farce) in the political history of the 'Cabbage Republic'[14] – rather than a poetic fiction identified in *Dance the Dance*.

The relationship between the literal and the poetic is critical when considering the evolution in thinking from *Eye-Winker, Tom-Tinker* to his second play, *The Old Firm*. It becomes clear that while language is, if anything, more central to Mac Intyre's second theatrical attempt, there is a poetic exploration that takes us beyond a literal and linear narrative, so that, while there is a similar lack of defined ideology, the linguistic construction of this play transforms the emptiness-of-intent into a Kafkaesque nightmare. Indeed, Mac Intyre is critiquing the absolutes of ideology through very deliberately drawing attention to an overbearing and punishing sense of violence that has no political root or through-line.

Reminiscent of Pinter, both at the very start and very end of his career, *The Old Firm* introduces us to the unfortunate character of Sloper, who, tied to a chair and blindfolded, is interrogated by Burns, and his sidekicks Bill and Charlie, three representatives of an undetermined authority, or 'firm'. The three men accuse Sloper of what they describe as 'filthy work' (scene 2). What does this mean? What are Sloper's crimes? In an unnerving representation of societal indifference, nothing is ever revealed. Burns asks the rhetorical question: 'what does it all add up to? Call it the calendar of treachery and leave it at that' (scene 7), and that seems to be enough for everyone: as the highly representational character of the Elder suggests in a scene of metaphorical hand washing, 'these things are best wound up quickly' (scene 4). But, in a return to *Eye-Winker, Tom-Tinker's* theme of procrastination, the final action of 'finishing Sloper off' seems to be a step too far for Burns, much to the frustration of Charlie and Bill, who, representing an inevitable shift in power and authority, turn against Burns with their own menacing, yet vague accusations: 'You've given us failure, failure and more failure. Any time you don't give us failure you give us farce' (scene 8). Ultimately Burns replaces Sloper in the chair and the aggression resumes: the mindless and motiveless acts of cyclical violence, seen as the compelling determinant of power. For all the talking – and there are lots of words in this play – it appears that words are beginning to lose their power for Mac Intyre: there is a palpable feeling of waste in all the talk – a not seeing-the-wood-for-the-trees – and this idea is given compelling resonance in a prologue delivered by The Woman:

> There's a window high in the gable, large, warm with light, always there – but they won't look, they are otherwise occupied. There's the hope that they'll see it by chance – and be gripped. That could happen. There's the consideration also that any sudden seeing, however, gained – or bestowed, would blind, and what then? Some say: in the unseeing eyes the instant is remembered, held and to have seen sustains (Prologue).

This opening speech serves as an overarching challenge to the emptiness that follows: an ambiguous yet confident response to a cold secular world; a world afraid of 'any sudden seeing', unlikely ever to see anything by chance, and charges the litany of violent interrogation that follows with a sharp sense of tragic frustration.

The Old Firm, receiving a public production directed by Alan Stanford at the Project Arts Centre, Dublin on 25 September 1975, is hardly referred to today, either by Mac Intyre or by his commentators: the inference is that the play shares a similar simplistic narrative and inert form as *Eye-Winker, Tom-Tinker*, and therefore has little more to offer in terms of understanding Mac Intyre's theatrical development. But it is far more sophisticated than its predecessor, not least in the way it leaves things unsaid, allowing, in this respect, a greater regard for and demand upon its audience.

Also, there is, in The Woman – still the only female character but one liberated from the repressive obedience of Anne Reilly in the previous play – a sense of 'female energy' that serves as a quiet yet compelling counterpoint to the 'patriarchal goosestep' of closed meanings and absolute rhetoric. There is, of course, a parallel frustration borne out by the relentless language, the heavy verbose and entrenched dialogue that serves as a heavy-handed way to demonstrate a spiritual emptiness and, not for the last time, Mac Intyre's abstraction can leave a sense of confusion and a desire for a more direct literal purpose. The Old Firm is not an easy play, nor need it be, but with this comes a lack of playfulness and simplicity that Mac Intyre professes as key to his emerging work.

Living now away from his native Cavan, in resonating isolation on the Island of Inishbofin, off County Galway, it was at this point that he started to do a 'certain amount of homework', reading Meyerhold and Appia and Grotowski, and discovered – possibly as much through the silence of his geographical position as through reading Meyerhold – the idea that 'if you want to learn how to write plays, write a play without words'. This is, literally, what he did.

One year on, and the transformation from The Old Firm – not to mention from Eye-Winker, Tom-Tinker – to Mac Intyre's third play Jack Be Nimble was total. Gone was the verbal rhetoric of his first play or the verbal poetic of his second, to be replaced by an all-embracing use of mime. Jack Be Nimble is a forty-minute mime play, first presented as a lunchtime workshop production at the Peacock on 10 August 1976. It brushes away the (quite literal) clutter of early plays, to be left with a simple bare stage and a cast of four who, using simple representational masks, deliver a series of nine visual motifs. These motifs explore in whimsical fashion the complacency of Jack, in his effortless flexibility and quickness, and the consequential regret and anger as his youthful energy deserts him and life passes him by.

There is, in the simplicity of this piece, an undoubted cautiousness and a diminished authorial authority: this is a very literal interpretation of 'a play with no words', and the writer has not yet moved beyond the over-obvious in theatre: the visual references, identified by watching critics,[15] are Marcel Marceau and Chaplin, rather than Pina Bausch or Meredith Monk. Only in the last scene, when a final enigmatic figure enters with two masks pressed hard against his/her face, and there is a more ritualistic process of revealing a cyclical inevitability, does the play move beyond the

explicit representation of images: elsewhere, the use of mime is a
literal non-verbal device that replaces 'lost' words. In these terms,
Jack Be Nimble is a clear step backwards from *The Old Firm*. But
there is also a cathartic sense of starting again, and, in its simplicity,
a clear departure from the kind of self-consciousness that informs
his previous plays. *Jack Be Nimble* may be derivative and over
literal, but it is genuinely fresh, funny, and, while its treatment by
the Abbey Theatre (through its status as a lunch-time workshop
production) was cautious and speculative, it was welcomed as a
refreshing, if safe, break from the norm. David Nowlan, in *The Irish
Times* commented that the 'young players show more command of
movement than is generally evident in the Abbey'[16] and it was seen,
certainly, as an opportunity for young actors and a young team to
emerge in a 'young' play. The most significant member of the young
team was to become one of the most significant directors in
contemporary Irish theatre and the director most associated with
Mac Intyre's work: Patrick Mason.

Jack Be Nimble was Mason's first professional production. Born
and educated in London, of Irish descent, Mason trained as a voice
tutor at the Central School of Speech and Drama before joining the
Abbey as a voice and movement coach in 1972.

Mason had the qualifications to assist in the development of an
image and movement based theatre project. Further to his early
work in movement, both at the Abbey and Manchester University,
Mason trained in the Graham technique with Irene Dilkes of
London Contemporary Dance Theatre. He followed this, in 1975, by
becoming a visiting observer to Peter Brook's International Centre
of Theatre Research in Paris. Mason's interests in theatre reflected
those of Mac Intyre. Further to this, it could be suggested that
Mason provided Mac Intyre with a defined bridge to the Abbey: as a
young staff director, Mason would have been anxious to make this
project work on the Abbey's terms and the knock-on effect of this
would be to give Mac Intyre a sense of a theatrical home. By *Jack Be
Nimble*, therefore, there are embryonic signs of the level of
commitment shown by the Irish National Theatre to Mac Intyre's
work in the 1980s. Often described by in-house cynics as the
'lunatics in the basement', the Abbey nonetheless showed
remarkable commitment to allowing these lunatics free-run.

The Abbey's contribution to allowing the development of Mac
Intyre's work is underlined by the fact that, within a year, another
project by the same author, directed by the same director, was

presented in the Peacock. *Find the Lady*, opening on 9 May 1977, was a far more ambitious production, with an increased production team and a cast that had more than doubled. In certain respects, *Find the Lady* is a follow up to *The Old Firm* rather than *Jack Be Nimble* in that its meaning and intention is somewhat opaque and its ambition and cultural reach is designed to stretch its audience (not to mention its cast) rather than gently divert them. But in other ways *Find the Lady* is a respectful development of key artistic thinking that produced *Jack Be Nimble* and, as such, a deliberate reaction to the privileging of literal dialogue found in the first two plays.

Find the Lady is a big, disjointed play, with fragments of colour and mimetic spectacle clinically placed upon verbal motifs that are clear precursors to the work Mac Intyre produced in collaboration with Mason in the 1980s. Based on the biblical legend of Salome and John the Baptist the play retains the playfulness discovered in *Jack Be Nimble* but exploits the idea of game-playing in a more deliberate and unnerving fashion. The four central characters of John, Salome, Herod, and Herodias are fixated with one another, sometimes feigning indifference, sometimes lustfully attentive, but always in constant awareness of each other to the point where nothing else seems to matter. Naturally, it is Salome who motivates the obsessions: the play starts with a highly seductive scene in which she playfully sings 'I Know Where I'm Going', but this is somewhat ironic as there remains, for the other characters at least, a culture of procrastination that again takes us right back to *Eye-Winker, Tom-Tinker*. But the processes of avoidance employed by the characters, here, represent a huge advance in Mac Intyre's imagination and sense of humour: taking a cue from *Jack Be Nimble*, there is a preoccupation with nursery rhymes, folk songs, and folk sayings that serve as a jolt to the formality of the biblical setting and stimulate an ironic *dance macabre* or burlesque; incongruous objects arrive from nowhere – a camera, a nail-file, a gilded hairbrush, a pair of slippers – serving, at times, as deflecting imagery, denying a consistency or a uniformity of genre. Indeed, the only consistent form within this play is mimetic dance, at first as part of a neo-narrative concerning Salome, but ultimately as a rhythmic development away from order and control: all the characters *have* to dance and their movements, together with the sudden shifts of focus and visual motifs, suggest a deliberate confusion of authority – a contempt and exposure of authority.

More than in any previous play, Mac Intyre draws a picture of intense living – of rich indulgence – countered by a hesitation and 'the reluctance many of us have to pay the price for that elusive goal'.[17] There is also a terrible, casual, violence that returns in a number of his later plays: the head of John the Baptist, brought on as a final piece of show-stopping burlesque, is a vicious confirmation of the fragmented and off-hand power of the play. Any backward step, in terms of authorial deliberation in the writing of *Jack Be Nimble*, is regained here in a strident move towards the thematic demands that inform his work from *The Great Hunger* onwards.

There are clear steps forward, in this work, towards a theatre form and content associated with Mac Intyre in the next decade. *Find the Lady* is, of course, an interpretation of an established story: the Salome story. In much of the work that was to follow, Mac Intyre used familiar fable and myth as the root of the work, not only to develop a political subversion of perceptions, but also to give structured foundation to very eclectic experimentation. Also, in critical reception to the work, there are the beginnings of a methodological and dramaturgical inter-changeability: a confusing of roles, which brought into relief a fundamental sense of collaboration. Kevin O'Connor in *The Stage* commented that 'on balance the achievement may be that of the director, such is the chemistry involved,'[18] and John Finegan, in *The Evening Herald*, suggested that early signals are that 'this is to be a director's night out'.[19] More measured, David Nowlan in *The Irish Times* commented that '[I]t is hard to know where Tom Mac Intyre's script leaves off and where Patrick Mason's directorial imagination takes over'.[20] The critics' observations reflected a growing intrigue, tempered by a confused unease, in the critical response to Mac Intyre's work. Previously, with *Jack Be Nimble,* the essential simplicity of the mimetic form allowed easy understanding and consequential acceptance in the press; now there was greater suspicion. Finegan comments: 'As a poet's play there isn't, surprisingly, any memorable lines to stir the imagination; it is a strong play, struggling in vain to get out of the bonds of modernity'. To Frances O'Rourke in *The Sunday Press*, the company 'brings us a meticulous production which includes much that is baffling'.[21] Again, the most measured and, ultimately, pertinent criticism comes from Nowlan who suggested that Mac Intyre had few equals in knowing how to say something in the theatre, 'but leaves us very uncertain just what it is that he has to say ... he seems to be getting to the nub of something [and then] he changes tack and leaves us either without a question or an answer'.

While it is quite clear, therefore, that Mac Intyre's work was developing, there remained a number of unresolved problems with the play. *Find the Lady* uses many dramatic forms and yet these forms are seen, rather self consciously, in isolation, detached from a fused totality. There are individual scenes in which gesture and mime are used, a clear example being scene 3, where a camera is used as focus for a rather obvious non-verbal interaction between Herod, Herodias and Salome. The intention is to show the tensions that underlie the image of happy families. The games that are presented seem similar to the most basic 'high/low status' games, and the discoveries made about the relationships within the scene hardly represent a sophisticated or challenging understanding of the characters. But, ultimately, what weakens the effectiveness of these non-verbal scenes is that they are punctuated with scenes in which traditional dialogue is the major method of communication. The verbal language in these scenes tries to be complex – there is a lot left unsaid – but, because a traditional form of communication has been defined, the language seems hollow and rather self-conscious. Because of the fragmentation of the differing methods of communication used in *Find the Lady*, it becomes clear that, at this stage, David Nowlan's incisive criticism is correct: Mac Intyre is less concerned with the message and more concerned with the medium. It also tends to demonstrate how no one involved with the creation of the play could let go of the consciousness of verbal theatre. Non-verbal image scenes are adopted, but isolated: as if to underline the separate nature of the communication. The result, while interesting, is disjointed with only the most simple of underlying relationships communicated.

The disjointed nature of the piece seemed to parallel the wider reaction of the Abbey to the work. At this point the cast consisted of regular members of the wider company, who were more concerned with the repertoire as a whole. The Abbey saw this work as an isolated experiment: valuable but irrelevant to the development of Irish drama. Mason comments:

> We were working in a theatre that was geared to fairly traditional scripts and you were trying to find, within the company, the odd one or two who might have been interested in this kind of work. We were reduced to scraping around: 'So-

and-so's good at moving; such-and-such seems interested,' that sort of thing.

The most valuable lesson learnt from *Find The Lady*, therefore, was that if such drama was to work and a totality of communion be attempted, then the process would have to remove itself from a conventional programme-then-cast method of staging drama. Mason continues:

> After *Find The Lady*, it became clear that if the work was to continue, we would need a different kind of actor: someone who actually had a strong movement background; was interested in this kind of work and was prepared to do it.[22]

What was needed was a company that was defined by a unified sense of purpose.

By the time Tom Mac Intyre and Patrick Mason got together again, the available pool of actors had changed. What Mason suggests is that around the turn of the 1980s, there were, on the scene, several actors who had returned to Dublin after studying mime and dance in Paris and London, who were 'quite physical and quite visually aware'. Others, who had remained in Dublin, were becoming 'increasingly aware of the wider possibilities of drama'.[23]

What is interesting about Mason's comments, here, is the impression of an art-form evolving (quite literally) in exile and that the embryonic exploration experienced in *Find the Lady* could only sustain itself with outside influence. Indeed, during the final two years of the 1970s, Mac Intyre himself worked extensively away from Ireland, both in America and France, predominately with Wendy Shankin and Doris Seiden of Calck Hook Dance Theater who, during 1978, were based in Oberlin College, Ohio, before spending time in Paris in 1979. In this period Mac Intyre produced two further performance works, *Deer Crossing* (1978) and *Doobally/Black Way* (1979), which were as much dance as they were drama. Wendy Shankin, in particular, had a clear background in the New York avant-garde performance-art scene that would have provided further introduction to the works of such artists as Pina Bausch and Meredith Monk.[24]

Perhaps more pertinent, however, was that, through working with people whose artistic practice had evolved in a medium that was removed from the conventions of theatre, a greater notion of collaboration evolved, to the point where, in *Doobally/Black Way*, Mac Intyre was prepared to perform himself. [Mac Intyre also appeared in *Deer Crossing*, see fig. 3.1]. So, while in *Deer Crossing*, there are similar starting points and content connections with *Find the Lady* there is a greater sense of a blending of form: to Ron Weiskind, a local critic, there was a strong foundation in dance theatre, 'stylized movements, and body language [which] take on a universal meaning beyond words and play with your emotions'.[25] There is also a commitment to continuing collaboration, from one project to another, with the same group of artists that has few parallels in established theatre practice. So why did Mac Intyre return to resume his work with Mason? Why not remain in communities more suited to, and respectful of, an avant-garde approach that now provided Mac Intyre with a compelling focus for his theatre work? A clue to the answer comes in *Doobally/Black Way*, the last of Mac Intyre's theatre pieces before *The* Great *Hunger*. More than in any previous theatre work, Mac Intyre started to explore particular cultural tones and language that resonated from his very particular Irish identity, with the title referring to thoroughfares found in Cavan and the blending of different languages, including Irish, a possible representation of what he has identified in recent years as the 'extravagances of language ... in East Cavan, with our version of English riddled with Gaeilge'.[26]

Mac Intyre's work needed an Irish soul, or at least *his* Irish soul, as much as it needed American/European dramaturgy. *The Great Hunger*, while the seventh theatre production Mac Intyre had been involved in, was the first (of many) that drew on a very deliberate and definable Irish iconography, so, while he had previously played with universal stories and myths, he now embarked on 'explorations of a hidden Ireland [using], as starting points, Irish stories, folklore and myth to provide on stage ... ventures into dream territory'.[27] Perhaps there remained a little of the 'adversarial stance' in his direct use of Irish imagery, as it is clear that, with *Doobally/Black Way*, Irish criticism of his experimentation was becoming more pronounced.[28] It is clear, however, that, with a certain amount of homework having already taken place, Mac Intyre was ready to stretch understanding of Irish theatre with a confidence that comes from depth of experience, insight, experimentation, and opportunity.

Works Cited

Byrne, P.F., *Evening Herald* 11 August 1976.

Dowling, Noeleen, *The Irish Examiner* 11 August 1976.

Dunne, Sean, *The Harper's Turn* by Tom Mac Intyre (Dublin: Gallery Books, 1982): inside page.

Finegan, John, 'Way-out Look at a Very Old Story', *Evening Herald* 11 May 1977.

Francombe, Ben, Interview with Patrick Mason, 30 July 1992.

Heaney, Mick, 'Theatre: Keeping Sight of his Goals' (an interview with Tom Mac Intyre), *The Sunday Times* 24 April 2005.

Hurley, Vincent, '*The Great Hunger*: a reading', Patrick Kavanagh and Tom Mac Intyre, *The Great Hunger: Poem into Play* (Dublin: Lilliput, 1988).

Keating, Sara, 'Born with Storytelling in his Blood', *The Irish Times* 25 April 2009.

Mac Conghail, Fiach, 'Tom Mac Intyre in Conversation with Fiach Mac Conghail', *Theatre Talk: Voices of Irish Theatre Practitioners,* eds. Lilian Chambers, Ger FitzGibbon and Eamonn Jordan (Dublin: Carysfort Press, 2001), pp. 309-310.

Mac Intyre, Tom, *Through the Bridewell Gate: A Diary of the Dublin Arms Trial* (London: Faber, 1971).

Maxwell, D.E.S., *A Critical History of Modern Irish Drama 1891-1980* (Cambridge: CUP, 1984).

Murray, Christopher, *Twentieth-Century Irish Drama: Mirror up to Nation* (Manchester: Manchester University Press, 1997).

Nowlan, David, *The Irish Times* 11 August 1976.

---, *The Irish Times* 10 May 1977.

O'Connor, Kevin, *The Stage* 16 June 1977.

O'Rourke, Frances, 'Salome Gets the Modern Treatment', *Irish Independent* 10 May 1977.

Rebellato, Dan, *1956 And All That: the Making of Modern British Drama* (London: Routledge, 1999).

Salisbury, Wilma, 'Space to Step in', *The Sunday Plain Dealer*, Cleveland 5 September 1976.

Sheridan, Michael, *Evening Press*, 11 August 1976.

Stevens, David , 'Dance in Paris: Calck Hook Collective Provides Surreal Images', *International Herald Tribune* 1 April 1979.

Sweeney, Bernadette, 'Tom Mac Intyre', *British and Irish Dramatists Since World War Two, Third Series,* ed. John Bull (Woodbridge: Bruccoli, Clark, Layman, 2001), pp. 251-258.

Weiskind, Ron, '"Deer Crossing": Abstract, Stylised', *The Journal, Lorain Ohio* 5 May 1978: 10.

www.irishplayography.com/search/print_play.asp?play_id=1354 *Eye-Winker, Tom Tinker*', *Irish Playography,* 29 October 2008.

[1] Tom Mac Intyre, *What Happened Bridgie Cleary* p. 4.

[2] Mick Heaney, 'Theatre: Keeping sight of his goals' (an interview with Tom Mac Intyre), *The Sunday Times* 24 April 2005.

[3] Ibid.

[4] Ibid.

[5] David Stevens, 'Dance in Paris: Calck Hook Collective Provides Surreal Images', *International Herald Tribune* 1 April 1979.

[6] Sean Dunne, The Harper's Turn by Tom Mac Intyre (Dublin: Gallery Books, 1982), inside page.

[7] Vincent Hurley, '*The Great Hunger*: A Reading', Patrick Kavanagh and Tom Mac Intyre, *The Great Hunger: Poem into Play* (Dublin: Lilliput, 1988), pp. 78-79.

[8] Fiach Mac Conghail, 'Tom Mac Intyre in Conversation with Fiach Mac Conghail, *Theatre Talk: Voices of Irish Theatre Practitioners,* eds. Lilian Chambers, Ger FitzGibbon and Eamonn Jordan (Dublin: Carysfort Press, 2001), pp. 309-310.

[9] D.E.S. Maxwell, *A Critical History of Modern Irish Drama 1891-1980* (Cambridge: CUP, 1984), p. 182.

[10] '*Eye-Winker, Tom-Tinker*', *Irish Playography,* 29 October 2008 www.irishplayography.com/search/print_play.asp?play_id=1354

[11] Ron Weiskind, '"Deer Crossing": Abstract, Stylised', *The Journal,* Lorain Ohio 5 May 1978 p. 10.

[12] Maxwell p. 182.

[13] Dan Rebellato, *1956 And All That: the Making of Modern British Drama* (London: Routeledge, 1999), p. 6. As the title suggests, Rebellato's concern is for British drama, but a certain theory of colonial discourse is appropriate for Irish theatre at the time.

[14] Tom Mac Intyre, *Through the Bridewell Gate: A Diary of the Dublin Arms Trial* (London: Faber, 1971), p. 209.

[15] See Noeleen Dowling, *The Irish Examiner* 11 August 1976; P.F. Byrne, *Evening Herald* 11 August 1976; Michael Sheridan *Evening Press*, 11 August 1976, David Nowlan, *The Irish Times* 11 August 1976.

[16] David Nowlan, *The Irish Times* 10 May 1977.

[17] Mick Heaney, 'Theatre: Keeping Sight of his Goals' (an interview with Tom Mac Intyre), *The Sunday Times* 24 April 2005.

[18] Kevin O'Connor, *The Stage* 16 June 1977.

[19] John Finegan, 'Way-out Look at a Very Old Story', *Evening Herald* 11 May 1977.

[20] David Nowlan, *The Irish Times* 10 May 1977.

[21] Frances O'Rourke, 'Salome Gets the Modern Treatment', *Irish Independent* 10 May 1977.

[22] Mason. Interview with the author, 30 July 1992.

[23] Ibid. The group of actors, who came to the attention of Mac Intyre and Mason, was led by Tom Hickey, an established actor with a recognised record in traditional theatre and television, but there was also a group of

young and enthusiastic actors at the beginning of their careers and they, as well as Hickey, were to become involved closely with all, or nearly all, of the Mac Intyre productions during the 1980's: Vincent O'Neill, Conal Kearney, Bríd Ní Neachtain, Dermod Moore, and Michele Forbes.

[24] See Wilma Salisbury, 'Space to Step in', *The Sunday Plain Dealer*, Cleveland 5 September 1976. An article to mark the arrival of Wendy Shankin Metzker as Director of Dance at Oberlin College. Not only does the article outline Shankin's pedigree (having working in New York with Meredith Monk), but also a similar adversarial stance as Mac Intyre, as she moves away from the cosmopolitan heartland. 'At this point Ms Metzker has no idea what response her work will draw from Ohio audiences. She does know, however, that for those who have never before seen her performances, the initial experience could be mind-boggling'.

[25] Weiskind p. 10.

[26] Sara Keating, 'Born with Storytelling in his Blood', *The Irish Times* 25 April 2009.

[27] Christopher Murray, *Twentieth-Century Irish Drama: Mirror up to Nation* (Manchester: Manchester University Press, 1997), p. 232.

[28] See Bernadette Sweeney, 'Tom Mac Intyre', *British and Irish Dramatists Since World War Two, Third Series,* ed. John Bull (Woodbridge: Bruccoli, Clark, Layman, 2001), pp. 251-258.

**Theatre Review: *Find the Lady* by Tom Mac Intyre.
'*Salome* Gets Modern Treatment'**

Desmond Rushe
(*The Irish Independent*, 10 May 1977)

The most interesting of the languages employed in a stylized, disciplined and imaginative production of *Find the Lady* by Tom Mac Intyre at the Peacock theatre are mime and movement, particularly movement. Music, song and words are also used in a modern treatment of the Salome theme, but the words are, by and large, undistinguishable though they occasionally have a dry and wry humour.

The play lends itself to the workshop presentation it gets. It deals with the inter-relationship between John the Baptist, Herod, Herodias and Salome, and there is a somewhat obscure exploration of attitudes and motivations. Without the mime and movement, excellently orchestrated by Patrick Mason, there would really be little of interest here.

The production is in-the-round and the acting area scope is utilized to its limit. The approach has a strong sense of ritualistic burlesque, and there are several fine performances, with Martina Stanley a hauntingly waif-like Salome. The disciplined team-work of the company is of the highest order, and is refreshing in its quality and newness.

Individual performances of much strength are given by Desmond Cave (Herod), Raymond Hardie (John), Billie Morton (Herodias) and Phillip O'Sullivan as a ringmaster-type.

Theatre Review: *Doobally/Black Way* by Tom Mac Intyre

David Nowlan
(*The Irish Times*, 9 October 1979)

Music, painting, sculpture, dance and other arts have all enjoyed abstract forms of their works and I suppose that, in theory, there is no reason drama should not try the abstract too. That is what Tom Mac Intyre seems to be attempting in *Doobally/Black Way*, which opened as part of the Dublin Theatre Festival in the Edmund Burke Hall in Trinity last night.

He has proved his dramatic skill before now and, on the evidence of their technique last night, his collaborators in this enterprise also appear to be accomplished.

With Eric Watson's music, Wendy Shankin's and Doris Seiden's choreography and direction and the members of the Calck Hook Dance Theatre, the purpose seems to be bafflement of the intellect and an attempt to engage the emotions alone. It is done in a series of images, conflicting and complementary, of sounds, dissonant and consonant and of moves, fluid and fractured.

A glimpse of Chinese martial arts dissolves into sequences of boot-changing. Sinuous moves of trunk and arms merge into the clip of tap dance. Children and corpses, birth, death and decadence are all evoked and hurled aside in a bedlam of disorder as the short evening ambles its way through its author's dissociated vision.

It might be all right if its audiences could be persuaded to leave their minds at home. As things went, however, last night's audience starting taking their minds and their bodies out of the place within twenty minutes of the start and the trickle to the exit continued in ones, twos, and fours, pretty well throughout.

I can't say I blamed them, although some of them might have got some small satisfaction had they waited until the point where the author was hauled across the stage, strait-jacketed and seemingly dead.

Someone should have told him that the theatrical experience is one which involves both intellect and emotion, ideally to the point of catharsis. Anti-intellectualism and bafflement is no substitute for drama, just as noise (verbal or musical) is no substitute for words. It's all as silly as thinking sad or feeling a great idea.

But never mind: few avant garde experiments work and perhaps Mr Mac Intyre's next attempt to seek new stage forms will meet with more success.

Theatre Review: *Jack Be Nimble* by Tom Mac Intyre. 'A Nimble Mime at the Peacock'

Michael Sheridan
(*The Evening Press*, Aug 1976)

The Peacock maintains an excellent impetus in its lunchtime offerings this week with a finely drawn interpretation of a new mime play by Tom Mac Intyre.

The author punctuates the rhyme of *Jack Be Nimble* in his title and this production by Patrick Mason suggests that slick could well be substituted for a nick.

Imagination and execution are not only nimble in this work-shop expression but also intensely accurate in their simplicity. Anybody that might be lulled into thinking that mime is an easy medium should be reminded that it is probably the most difficult mode of theatrical communication.

The fact that the mimic appears so much at ease in action belies the painstaking process of definition needed to make a play work without words. Mac Intyre's vehicle never renders the silence stunning, but the auditorium reverberates with continual and consistent interest.

The central figure is of course Chaplinesque, always at physical odds with the world, and Stephen Brennan's achievement is that he makes his beanstalk body equal to a task better tailored to the psychological physique of the Arab dwarf.

His awkward angularity provides a poignant counterpoint to the twinkling toes of Ingrid Craigie and Martina Stanley and the electrically elephantine presence of Ronan Patterson.

CHAPTER 3: 'DOWN THE RUCKETY PASS'[1]

The Great Hunger: A Director's Note

Patrick Mason

> [The following director's note was first published in Patrick Kavanagh and Tom Mac Intyre *The Great Hunger*: Poem into Play (Westmeath, Ireland: Lilliput Press Limited, 1988).]

The production history of *The Great Hunger* is one of inspirations and transformations that began in the spring of 1983 with the meeting of a writer, a director, and a player. These three became the nucleus of a theatre group that collaborated over five years (from 1983 to 1988) on five productions, including a re-working of *The Great Hunger* in 1986. The published script is the most recent version of the play. It contains not only the best features of the original production, but many innovations and insights achieved through working on *The Bearded Lady* (1984), *Rise Up Lovely Sweeney* (1985) and *Dance for your Daddy* (1987). *The Great Hunger* thus represents the beginning and the continuation of this work. It is an initial revelation of Tom Mac Intyre's unique theatrical vision subsequently revealed more fully in other plays.

The realization of any artistic vision is a tortuous process. In the performing arts it is especially so, as the performers themselves have first to see that vision clearly, then assimilate it and make it their own. Only by bringing something into the light of consciousness can we begin to see what it is. To effect this we first go down into the dark unconscious to fetch it up. Tom Mac Intyre is a sure guide. We begin to look about and point out features along the way that the guide himself may not have noticed. He in turn is able to relate our observations to what he knows lies ahead. Sometimes the leader becomes the led, and he trusts to those around him. Eventually he brings the travelers back to the starting point, but now they know the place for the first time, transformed by their journey. Now they have the power to transform others in the alchemy of theatre.

In practical terms the steps of the journey were marked by the writing of an initial draft script which was passed between writer, director and player, until a first draft rehearsal script was composed. Then, in rehearsals with the company, that script developed into a performance script. In the case of *The Great Hunger* this grew into a second performance script.

The transformations were both major and minor, affecting all aspects of the play. So a green baize table in the draft script became a golden tabernacle in the rehearsal script, which in turn became a locked door and a glittery mirror in performance. A bifurcated manifestation of Maguire and Maguire Poet was reduced to pure Patrick Maguire, hanging upside down on a wooden gate. A spectral youth on the fringes of the Heifer Romp took flesh and blood as the wandering Packy, weaving his way in and out of Maguire's days and nights, a holy fool holding the world in a rusty can. A Sacrament of Clay was suppressed and re-emerged as a dream of stiffened limbs and swaying headstones, where the 'men and wimen' go down into the ground, to be raised again by the priest's Lenten rattle.

The workplace is the shifting floor of the imagination. In every theatre that we played, we adapted and re-shaped our play: Edinburgh, Annaghmakerrig, Paris, Moscow, Manhattan, each setting inspired and transformed the work because the work was alive. The published script is a description of that life, not a definition. Like all such descriptions it must animate and be animated, inspire and transform in turn, if it is to live again as theatre.

---

[1] Tom Mac Intyre, *The Great Hunger,* p. 12.

On Design

[The following articles are included as a pair; firstly Bronwen Casson's recollections of her work as designer for Mac Intyre's *The Great Hunger* and other works, followed by an article by John Barrett, which Casson references as elaborating on her recollections. Barrett's article 'Environmental Design in the Dublin Theatre' first appeared in the June 1983 edition of *Prompts* (a bulletin of the Irish Theatre Archive).]

'Environmental Design' and the plays of Tom Mac Intyre

Bronwen Casson

The set design for *The Great Hunger* (1983) did not emerge until after the first or perhaps even the second week of rehearsals. After my first reading of a draft of the play (not the finished version) I had pre-rehearsal discussions with the director, Patrick Mason, so I had some kind of general idea – but only very general – of where the design was going. In rehearsal, the actors, together with Tom Mac Intyre, discussed the visual as well as the textual format of the piece, while remaining under the guidance of the director. I attended, and indeed participated in, these discussions.

The figure of The Mother, for instance, was conceived during these discussions as being a cross between a bog oak Madonna and a piece of kitchen furniture. It was also decided that the object would have to incorporate a drawer. I firstly did a rough sketch (see fig 3.8) and the piece was then realized by another designer, Frank Hallinan-Flood, who had some experience in crafting such objects. Frank built the piece on the framework of a square metal chair. So, this is an example of the kind of collaboration that took place and how we worked together to realize the final design. Through this process I provided my own input as the designer but, in the end, the main credit for building the iconic Mother figure should belong to Frank Hallinan-Flood.

With all four plays I designed, *The Great Hunger* (1983), *The Bearded Lady* (1984), *Rise Up Lovely Sweeney* (1985) and *Dance for your Daddy* (1987), there was certainly a script, but that script was not fixed in stone, aspects were open to discussion. While the director, the designer, and the actors had their own roles or responsibilities, these roles were not as rigidly adhered to as is common in theatre practice here in Ireland. Rehearsals were, to a certain extent, a forum for discussion in which all participated.

The costume design evolved in much the same way as this. There was a general idea to begin with, then the cast tried on various found or bought garments until the right look was achieved. Some actors had a lot of input into their costume. Tom Hickey, for example, was happy to be left alone with a large heap of fairly suitable clothing and would build his own character's look by assembling various pieces together.

The design brief for the costumes of *The Bearded Lady* was slightly different than the other plays. Since this was more or less a period piece there was a specific look to adhere to. Swift wore a frock coat and collar of the period, for example. The specific movements and physique of the characters of the Houyhnhnms and the Yahoos, meanwhile, had an impact on how the costumes were designed. This required some adaptation from the preconceived design and evolved through the kind of collaborative process I have just described.

Working on Tom Mac Intyre's plays at the Peacock with the director Patrick Mason in this group or open situation gave me the opportunity to work as a designer in the manner in which I felt most comfortable and most truly creative theatrically. That is, I did not work in isolation or in some separate artistic limbo, but as part of a team, a cooperative. I felt involved in the totality of the creative process. Of course, there were others in Irish theatre working in this way during the period: I had a similar experience, for instance, when designing other productions at the Peacock and Project Arts Centre with the director Michael Scott: for example, *Bent* by Martin Sherman (Project Theatre, 1981) and the dramatization of Seamus Murphy's book *Stone Mad* (Peacock Theatre, 1982) adapted by Fergus Linehan and Sean McCarthy.

The following article by John Barrett elaborates on the idea of 'environmental design' and gives more detail on some of the productions mentioned above. Barrett echoes many of my own feelings, not just in relation to the environmental idea of design and production, but also on the concept of working with an ensemble company where a production evolves through a process of collaboration. This exemplifies the kind of cooperative effort I experienced when working with Tom Mac Intyre and the ensemble group at the Peacock in the 1980s.

Environmental Design in the Dublin Theatre

John Barrett

[The following article originally appeared in the journal, *Prompts* (a bulletin of the Irish Theatre Archives) in June 1983. It outlines the beginnings of 'environmental design' in the USA and London and gives examples of this kind of work happening in Irish theatre in the 1980s, including that of Brownen Casson in designing *The Great Hunger*.]

Environmental design can perhaps best be defined as a type of design that aims to create an atmosphere of authenticity in the theatre, and this often, but not necessarily, involves the use of natural objects and materials. Not that this is a new form of expression by any means – a wish for this type of design is expressed by Strindberg and by Brecht, for example. And the idea of using natural objects is not confined to the theatre; it is found in many art forms today – perhaps a reaction against the hard-edged office blocks and the artificial textures of modern living.

In its modern manifestation the movement can be traced to the off-Broadway scene of the 1950s which eventually propagated to become the London Fringe of the 1960s – mainly through the efforts of American emigrés – and found homes in the Open Space Theatre in the Tottenham Court Road, under the direction of Charles Marowitz, and the Almost Free Theatre in Rupert Street, London W1.

Ronald Hayman, in his work on contemporary English theatre, points out how our receptivity to a play is conditioned by the way in which we enter the theatre:

> ...moving from the crowded pavements of Shaftesbury Avenue into a foyer which looks rather like a party where everyone has an overcoat on and no one has a drink, being directed to one of several entrances according to what kind of ticket we have, giving the ticket up to be torn by a man in uniform, buying a glossy programme and following an elderly usherette into an auditorium where people in other seats are talking in low expectant voices – all this is doing more than we realize to programme our expectations.

Those who believed in environmental design were determined to challenge this comfortable predictability.

The people who arrived at the Open Space in July 1968 to see its first production, *Fortune and Men's Eyes* by John Herbert, had to clamber down an iron fire escape under surveillance of a prison guard with a machine gun. After having their fingerprints taken and waiting outside a cell door, listening to an impersonal official voice over a loudspeaker, they were led through the set, which consisted of four prison bunks, on their way to their seats.

For the December 1971 production of Picasso's play, *The Four Little Girls*, the whole interior of the Open Space was elaborately restructured by Marowitz:

> On the way in you had to duck your head to pass through the small toyland doorway, and the whole interior was transformed into a childhood fairyland. You sat down on uneven spangled banks and the spangles stuck to your clothes.

Another fringe director, Ed Berman, has conceived a play for performance in a swimming pool, with part of the audience in the water.

As the London Fringe follows belatedly in the footsteps of off-Broadway (now off-off-Broadway), so the Dublin theatre scene lags considerably behind the London. But in the last couple of years there has been a spate of plays incorporating environmental design, mainly through the work of Bronwen Casson, scene designer at the Abbey, Michael Scott, who is theatre director at the Project Arts Centre, and the freelance director Patrick Mason, perhaps best known in this country for his close association with the work of Tom Mac Intyre and Thomas Kilroy. To cite some recent examples on the Dublin stage: in August 1981 the Project Arts Centre presented *Bent* by Martin Sherman, directed by Michael Scott, design by Michael Scott and Brownen Casson. In May 1982 we saw the Project Arts Centre's production of Sam Shepard's *Curse of the Starving Class*, directed by Michael Scott and design (significantly listed in the programme as Setting and Environment) again by Michael Scott and Bronwen Casson. In July 1982 the Peacock Theatre presented *Stone Mad* from the book by Seamus Murphy adapted by Fergus Linehan and directed by Sean McCarthy. The design was by Bronwen Casson and for this she received one of the 1983 Harvey's Bristol Awards. April 1983 saw a production of Tom Murphy's *The Morning After Optimism* at the Project Arts Centre, directed by Michael Scott, and the setting a cooperation between Michael Scott, Brian Power and Barbara Bradshaw. At the Peacock in May 1983 there opened Tom Mac Intyre's *The Great Hunger*, based on Patrick

Kavanagh's poem, directed by Patrick Mason, with design by Bronwen Casson. It would appear that this philosophy of design is pretty well confined to these two venues. Of the two the Project Arts Centre is the better suited because the seating and acting areas are flexible and adaptable without limit.

But why go to all this trouble? Why go to the bother of creating an authentic stonemason's yard with dust and dirt and real stone (*Stone Mad*)? Why cover the stage with ten tons of washed gravel and piles of real rocks and surround the acting area with barbed wire (*Bent*)? Why go to the trouble of burying the floor of the entire auditorium in four tons of washed sand and involve yourself in the anxiety and frustration of nurturing a pet lamb (*Curse of the Starving Class*)? Or why introduce silver birch trees and cover the floor with tons of peat moss (*The Morning After Optimism*)? Why drag a quarter of a ton of clay onto the stage of the Peacock and laboriously work it into potato drills (*The Great Hunger*)?

After all, the audience is not likely to be deceived by some sods of earth and a bucketful of potatoes when the entire evening's transaction in the theatre is itself essentially an artifice. But, of course, it is not realism that is aimed at, but an aspect of authenticity. The potatoes clanging in the metal buckets, the clouds of dust rising, the sound of chisel on stone, of boots moving slowly and monotonously across gravel, the slap of a hand on the bark of a real tree – these all heighten the audience's awareness and the level of their responses, so that the actor in turn can respond and heighten his performance.

The potential of the medium of the theatre is being properly exploited. In *Curse of the Starving Class* the audience have to walk across the floor covered with gritty sand to get to their seats, feeling it underfoot, rising puffs of dust as they walk. For *The Morning After Optimism* similarly the audience have to walk between the tress of the forest – the impulse to touch the trees irresistible – their feet sinking into layers of moss. In both cases they come immediately into contact with the physical texture of the play.

To add to the textural quality, the physicality, would it not be logical to invoke also the sense of smell? It is present to a degree in the smell of clay and sand and the dampness of peat moss, which is watered before each production. And Michael Scott had planned to use pine trees, the barks of which he had intended to score so that the resinous smell of pine would permeate the auditorium. As it turned out, however, it was silver poplars that the Department of

Forestries provided him with. But why not introduce the wholesome smell of farmyard manure to the fields of *The Great Hunger*? Aesthetically it would be perfectly appropriate, though it might present aesthetic problems of another sort.

Bronwen Casson is a dedicated exponent of environmental design, believing that it greatly enchances the actors' performance. She says,

> They get more of the feel of the play than they could otherwise hope for. All their movements are conditioned by the feel of the texture.

The set of hers that she is happiest with is *Stone Mad*, a stoneyard with an earthen floor, containing a shed open on two sides. The earth had to be kept damp but this presented no technical problems, as it was on a concrete floor. There was, however, considerable difficulty for the actor, Eamon Kelly, in that he was affected by the dust, not only the dust from the floor but also the dust from the piece of stone on which he was working. This can be a very real problem with environmental design, and it is one which Bronwen Casson is much aware of. In *The Great Hunger* the cast are walking on clay and lying on damp patches of mud.

One of the actresses said to me that she does find it difficult and uncomfortable but she wouldn't dream of complaining about it because she feels that it is in the nature of the play. I wonder to what degree one can make actors uncomfortable. I think only so far as they're prepared to accept it without losing their performance.

These natural materials, too – earth, sand, peat moss – all have to be sterilized. Otherwise the actors would be faced with unwelcome competition from the floor.

The Great Hunger is a most interesting set; upstage centre a wooden five-barred gate, beyond that a red and rusted barn structure, to the right potato drills, in the foreground loose soil and the set is supported by props – buckets, baskets, potatoes, rope etc. Certainly it gives rise to some highly effective moments. One such would be where the characters reject the pleas and threats of religion and, all in a row, prostrate themselves on the ground, scooping up the soil reverently in their hands and kissing it, while the priest intones the first line of the poem.

> Clay is the word and clay is the flesh.

Then the priest kisses the soil and eats it and gives it to the mother to eat, in the sacramental procedure.

But, if it has some effective moments, the play overall is a sad example of the misuse of environmental design. Because it seems to be used for its own sake, without any reference to the needs of the audience. It is so esoteric, so self-consciously clever in its use of setting and mime and sound effects and the bewildering multiplicity of symbol and suggestion, that the audience feel that they are excluded from the meaning. They may admire the clever set and the fine acting but they are not engaged in any act of theatre. It is strange, moreover, that the play is not done in the round. To have environmental design in proscenium-type setting with the old rigid separation between actors and audience makes no sense at all. What it gives with the right hand is taken away with the left.

Bronwen Casson is particularly interested in the effects of nature on certain textures, on wood and metal especially. The original design for *The Great Hunger* called for a backcloth of neutral sky, but it was felt that this was conflicting with the earth and it would be better to have something that had the texture of a barn or cowshed: 'I went looking everywhere for sheets of rusty metal. I was delighted when I found them – I thought I'd have to rust them myself.'

There were technical problems with the set as well:

> The lines of the drills caused a problem – the difficulty of having to preserve the drills. And we had terrible trouble with the floor. I worked with earth before on *Stone Mad*, so I thought I knew, but that was on a concrete floor. Here the earth dries out under the lights and, if you wet the earth, the underlay starts to lift. I'm obsessed with the problems of the floor.

Patrick Mason has declared that he would love to tour with this play, presenting it outdoors in an actual field – the ultimate in environmental design and the solution to Ms Casson's problems.

Theatre Review: *The Great Hunger* by Tom Mac Intyre. 'A Great Poem without Words'

Gerard Stembridge
(*The Irish Press*, 11 May 1983)

The production of *The Great Hunger* which opened on Monday at the Peacock has a marvellous sense of teamwork about it. Writer, director, and actors have collaborated to produce a fairly rare visual feast for Dublin audiences.

If most of Patrick Kavanagh's words are not heard during the play, nevertheless the essence of this original poem has been retained by Tom Mac Intyre's dramatically sensitive text and Patrick Mason's meticulous direction.

In what is virtually a wordless production, a marvellous cast, in which Tom Hickey, Conal Kearney, and Vincent O'Neill are outstanding, presents us with a series of striking images, which attempt to recreate the pain, innocence and repression of Irish rural life as Kavanagh saw it.

Certainly some of the images were too opaque for me, while others seemed a shade outdated and obvious, but for the most part it was quite riveting.

Tom Hickey's Paddy Maguire is played in an almost Beckettian style: fear and pain permanently etched across his face, haunted by dreams of escape, which are doomed to fade into the country night, with only the red glow of a cigarette to light his way home.

His homage to priest and mother are the real parameters of his existence and even at the end of the play when the gates are opened, he does not pass through. Around him idle games, idle drinking, idle wishes, form a bleak landscape, perfectly mirrored in the beautiful set and daring lighting.

This production is decidedly different, and daringly well done. It is the sort of chance the Peacock can afford to take, and should take more often. I certainly hope they do.

Theatre Review: *The Great Hunger* by Tom Mac Intyre. 'Images of Fragmented Ireland'

Colm Tóibín
(*The Sunday Independent*, 20 July 1986)

If the plight of the male sex is much emphasized in [Sean O'Casey's *Juno and the Paycock*], it is still nothing to the plight of the hero of *The Great Hunger*, a play by Tom Mac Intyre based on the poem by Patrick Kavanagh, back at the Peacock. (Tread softly, Tom Mac Intyre, you tread on our masterpieces.)

The production is a bit like the state of the nation itself: sometimes highly inventive, full of energy, then funny, confusing, impenetrable, boring, dark, and often seeming to chance its arm.

The image of the mother and tabernacle stand covered on the stage, and when the covers are removed they remain there, implacable throughout, keeping Patrick Maguire in his place.

The countryside is full of midges, small noises, irritants. Man and beast live in uncertain harmony. Humility becomes servility.

It is Ireland: the fragmented world we have come to know and love, a lost language bearing down on us, the victors gone, the vanquished left behind, the ghosts of the famine dead thickening the air, the church and the squires having moved in to take over.

What this production has tried to do is to catch all that cultural fall-out, these fragments of our ruin, and present them as images. As with the other efforts of this team to present the world of Swift, and Sweeney, the images are of being haunted and hunted, from within and without.

Certain scenes are really funny such as the attendance at Mass and the lads fighting with their caps.

But Patrick Mason's production can move with ease to other, more difficult, more hard-won moments such as Maguire, played by Tom Hickey, putting his face up against the tabernacle, or his sister, played by Bríd Ní Neachtain, rubbing up against the statue of the mother.

There are, however, other scenes, which seem merely gratuitous with the characters prancing about without much aim or much effect, filling time, if nothing else. These are in the minority, but they still affect the production.

The experiment which this writer, director and group of actors are conducting is probably at its most successful in *The Great Hunger*. It is, for the most part, entertaining and intriguing. It has also established itself as a matter of vital importance in shifting theatre here away from the verbal towards a more visual and suggestive way of trying to deal with the fragmentary nature of our culture.

Theatre Review: *The Great Hunger* by Tom Mac Intyre

Michael Billington
(*The Guardian*, 13 August 1986)

The Fringe provides a towering example of how drama can work through image and gesture as well as speech. The piece is *The Great Hunger* and [it] represents a collaboration between the writer, Tom

Mac Intyre, the director, Patrick Mason, and the actor, Tom Hickey, with a first-rate company based [at] Dublin's Abbey Theatre.

The key figures are Maguire (Mr Hickey) and his spinster sister. They worship a squat stone image which is simultaneously their own dead mother, Mother Ireland, and Mother Church. And the barrenness of their lives is evoked in myriad ways. At one point Maguire extracts a pair of bellows from a bottom drawer set into the statue and fans them vigorously over a sack in a symbol of masturbation: at another, a girl tempts him with a book of sweepstake tickets which he nicks and rustles in her face in a mad, taunting, sexual game. Most movingly the villagers also seize fronds of palm and beat themselves in an instinctive pagan rite which is stamped out and converted into religious orthodoxy by the local priest with his portable altar.

Everything conspires to the same end: to re-create the loneliness, hardship, and guilt of isolated Roman Catholic Ireland. Mason's production (first seen in Dublin's Peacock in 1983) is an eloquent departure from the literary tradition of Irish theatre. And in a company of seven Tom Hickey is outstanding.

At one point, driven insane with desire, he hangs upside down on a gate: at another he rocks frenziedly on the ground uttering cries of 'Mother' [...]. *The Great Hunger* shows how mother worship can also warp and stifle human nature. I hope that someone has the courage to bring it to London.

Theatre Review: *The Great Hunger* by Tom Mac Intyre 'People Hungering After Humanity'

Nicholas de Jongh
(*The Guardian*, 27 November 1986)

Tom Mac Intyre's *Great Hunger*, which aspires to bring a new delicacy to the theatrical menu, has already been delightedly consumed in Ireland and Edinburgh. But this Abbey Theatre production does not strike me as much more than an artful old hors d'oeuvre, very cleverly dressed.

The piece, based upon Patrick Kavanagh's 1942 poem, *The Great Hunger*, amplifies the poet's portrait of Irish peasantry dolefully petrified in ancient, childish rituals, lives stunted. And it principally abandons the methods of narrative theatre, in exchange for the techniques and manners of modern abstract dance, while words are put at a rare premium. Litanies of sound, both animal and inexplicable grunts and howls, underscore episodes of rural life.

Bronwen Casson's stage design, with a corrugated iron backcloth, a furrowed field with farmyard gate, and lines of excavated potatoes is appropriately dark, and bleak.

To one side of the set there stands a bound statue, which, when undraped, turns out to be both a kind of Mummy and mummy – a graven image, Virgin Mary or idol or mother-figure. It is this figure, pummelled in child-like rage by Maguire, the middle-aged, unmarried peasant who shares his life with his sister, and which, reverently washed and adored, becomes the play's focal figure.

It inspires both the emotional hunger and angry regressive impotence which defines Maguire's character, and indeed the whole of the community. Maguire, part village idiot, part put-upon labourer and springtime gamboller, is conceived as a perpetual youth stranded in adolescence. He is forever fighting with his cloth cap as weapon, jovially cheating in a game of shove penny, jerking his legs in the air while his sister repeats an arid domestic ritual of pouring water from pail to vast kettle.

The still set-points of this community are priestly authority and sexual desire, each inspiring frightened awe. The trio of girls who bring on the top of a soup tureen under which repose scent bottles and lipstick plaster their mouths with red as if they were excited children. But they become sexually predatory and threatening.

When sex puts on its winning face, it disguises itself as a juvenile farmyard prank, the woman in control, the youth, trousers down, finally whimpering for 'mummy' before he shuffles off shame-faced to the one-word, taunting accompaniment of 'soft'.

The grotesque, abruptly oscillating gestures of Patrick Mason's production are best realized in a sequence where springtime breaks out in a frenzy of green branches held aloft. The scene dissolves into a mass where the congregation as if in mockery of Catholic unquestioning submission to the church become a troop of neighing horses. The techniques on display here strike me as grotesquely reductive of human personality and imagination.

But that is the effect intended. The actors over-project with intentional enthusiasm. The sense of over-pitched extremity becomes both reiterative and dull, hostile to the poem's great potential. Tom Hickey's Maguire has the kind of spontaneous physical grace of a clown, shifting his limbs and his voices as if to tread the full gamut from village idiot to despairing peasant was no large mission.

In the Beginning Was ... the Image ...

Kathryn Holmquist
(*Theatre Ireland Magazine*, April/June 1984)

Hearing the theatre of the image described in Ireland as 'non-verbal' and 'trendy' invites one to scrutinize the relevance of those terms. The theatre of the image, in fact, is rarely 'non-verbal'. Meredith Monk, Robert Wilson, Richard Foreman, and the Mabou Mines collective – all of whom have made international reputations since the early 1970s – use words. Their focus is not anti-verbal, the verbal simply takes its place as a mode of communication beside other equally important modes, primarily visual and musical. In their work, significantly, words are freed from the narrative mooring and images from the literal.

These 'play-makers' have sought ways to rediscover the language of theatre which is, and always has been, far more than words.

'Trendy'? Far from being a 'trend', the rescusitation of the image has been the single most important current in the twentieth-century theatre. Meyerhold was the first director whose major preoccupation was to create powerful images to make statements in their own right rather than merely to illustrate the text with the realization that the image could communicate a complexity of thought and feeling not available to the word alone. Meyerhold opened up the entire concept of the interpretation of text in his productions of Blok's *The Fairground Booth* (1906), Crommelynck's *The Magnanimous Cuckold* (1922), Gogol's *The Government Inspector* (1929). He demonstrated that images could forcefully portray aspects of the human condition which tended towards the abstract when expressed through the literary. In searching for the most effective means of creating images he revolutionized the concept of the actor's function. They no longer portrayed characters but rather presented images, often through stylized movement. Costume and décor were elevated to an active role making, as well as aiding thematic statements. The audience were moved closer to the performance area and were encouraged to feel a part of the action, as in circus or fairground. The significance of these innovations to the development of the theatre this century should not be underestimated.

The acknowledgment of the growing power of the image has been accompanied by a corresponding deteriorization of language. As director Patrick Mason states:

> People are getting weary of the word and the way the word has operated an extraordinary tyranny over theatre, reducing it simply to the kind of political debating society that's been inflicted on the theatre over the last ten to fifteen years ... Words have become sterile, they've been debased, over-used, partly through the PR business of 'hype'... If you thirst for some kind of emotional – psychic, if you like – or spiritual communion, image, sound and gesture are all that are left.

The image, then, may have come to dominate theatre through default but it has in its own right unparalleled properties of communication, a power to penetrate and to move the spectator that is rivalled only by music. Perhaps it is really the dance – which is physicalized music, music to be seen – and the dance visionaries that have finally convinced us that the image has an extraordinary resonance and regenerative power. Dance has freed us from the intellectual bind which prevented us from perceiving intuitively, and which locked us into a literal mode of interpretation. The late George Balanchine, one of the foremost creators of the new dance, stated:

> I'm not doing anything in particular, I simply dance. Why must everything be defined by words? When you place flowers on a table, are you affirming or denying or disproving anything? You like flowers because they're beautiful. Well, I like flowers, too. I plant them without considering them articulately. I'm no physicist, no mathematician, no botanist. I know nothing about anything. I just see and hear.

Dance, and its appeal to our senses through music and movement, has reminded us that seeing is the key to theatrical expression. The word 'theatre' derives from the Greek *teatron* or 'seeing place'. The same Greek root leads to 'spectator', which the Oxford English Dictionary defines as 'One who is present at and has a view or sight of anything in the nature of a show or spectacle'. By contrast, 'audience' is defined as 'The persons within hearing, an assembly of listeners', and as 'The readers of a book'. The literary tradition post-Shakespeare has transformed the theatre from a 'seeing place' to a 'hearing place'. Spectators have become audience;

those who see have become those who hear. Since the beginning of the century, certain men and women of the theatre have been making the theatre again a 'seeing place'. Today's audience, with few exceptions, is schooled in the literary and sees the theatre essentially as a text illustrator and, in their capacity as play-readers and interpreters, as a 'reading place'. The imagistic theatre is a reaffirmation inviting 'hearing' audiences to become 'seeing' spectators. Hearing is not done away with but enhanced through music and through new approaches to the use of language. This is the first challenge to the spectator.

The movement to create a theatre based on the image was continued by Eisenstein, Artaud, Grotowski and Brook, among others. The major work of the director, in the development of the image, initially centred on the interpretation of text: in other words, the creation of imagistic theatre from literary sources. But for instance, in Brook's landmark productions of Shakespeare's *A Midsummer Night's Dream* and *Timon of Athens* the creation of the image through the interpretation of text reached its climax. What was then needed for the theatre of the image to move ahead was a completely new approach to the creation of theatre which dispensed with the literary intermediary. Thus, in the early 1970s, a new generation of 'play-makers', rather than playwrights, began to create a theatre which centred on the image. Words, dialogue, verbal narrative, receded decisively, and became, simply, ingredients, and often, lesser ingredients.

The second demand that the theatre of the image makes on those who see and hear it, is that they should perceive intuitively, rather than intellectually, allowing the image to resonate within themselves rather than trying to interpret it literally. The play-makers, of course, must create images that are compelling so that the spectator feels this resonance and which are accessible without being literal.

In Ireland, leading play-makers in the theatre of the image are writer, Tom Mac Intyre, director, Patrick Mason, and actor, Tom Hickey. *The Great Hunger* (Peacock Theatre, 1983) was, for many in the Irish audience, a new kind of theatre experience. When asked what appeals to him about the theatre of the image, Mac Intyre outlines one of its essential qualities:

> You can say it in a split-second in the image. In the verbal theatre it would take you a paragraph and you couldn't come anywhere near making the same weight of statement ... You're seeking to work in the same leaping way as the best poetry.

Mac Intyre also points to the fact that we experience the world primarily in terms of image and action so that, naturally, the imagistic theatre can come closest to expressing our lives. He states:

> I conceive of theatre as action, first, and the verbal dimension deriving from that. But that's the high-voltage truth of our experience of the world, in any case. In all of the searing memories I have, I immediately think of a picture or an action, and a long time afterwards of words. So there's a truth to life in the idea of the image as fundamental theatre, that is to say, it's really the conservative theatre.

Patrick Mason, as a director, is aware of the importance of the image in all theatre. He states:

> I do feel that the theatre in the beginning was the image rather than the world of sound and sense that belongs to the word. So it's really nothing new. It's going back, if you like, to something very fundamental about the theatre, that the first thing that happened was the image. Take Murphy's play *The Gigli Concert*, for instance – its major medium is language, *dramatic* language, and because it's *dramatic* language the words have to be accompanied by images ... What the imagistic playmakers are doing is simply trying to right a balance, to explore, to kind of banish the words, as far as possible, in order to make people more and more aware of images ... The image is enormously seductive in a way the word just isn't.

The 'seductive' quality of the image is probably one of its most powerful attributes. Mac Intyre expands on this: 'The immediacy of the pictorial, of the imagistic, by contrast with the verbal, relates essentially to what we call sensory impact: you *look*, you *see*. In the verbal theatre, the energy hasn't got that directness, it has to come through the cerebellum, if you like, and then down to the solar plexus'. The theatre of the image aims to encourage in the spectator this kind of intuitive and emotional perception, as does ritual. In ritual, an image becomes potent when the participant, responding to the image's associations, imbues it with the power to communicate directly. It is much the same in the imagistic theatre. Each image attains its potency when – informed by the experience of the viewer – it is vulnerably absorbed and allowed to resonate at leisure. This makes fresh demands and offers fresh joys. The difference, for the spectator, between the literary theatre and imagistic theatre is essentially one of perception. Mason elaborates:

The specific problem of the Irish audience is to get them to trust their own responses. The image is primal and people's responses to it – provided it's compelling – is instinctive ... We're all so predominantly verbal – our education is geared to the word – that there is a moment of panic when the word is not present ... If you're going to sit there saying 'What does it mean?', this is a totally inhibiting response. Unfortunately, it's one that people are conditioned to – and this, perhaps, is the biggest problem: how do you get people to stop saying 'What does it mean?' and simply say to them, 'Look, forget about what it means, what does it feel like? What does it do to you?

Each image is made up of gestures, signals, objects, sounds, spatial relationships, pacing and other elements. The spectator's perception of these elements and their position in the overall design of time and space is crucial to the communication of the piece. Therefore, the actor must physicalize, be keenly aware of timing, of shaping the space, and communicate through these means in a way which places exceptional demands. Tom Hickey puts it this way:

In the literary theatre, you're carrying the audience along on the literal, on ideas, the literary is intellect-dominated. The inner life or the inner forces at work in the actor need not necessarily be as strong in – for want of a better word – the conventional theatre, because the words are there ... It's possible with a less active inner life, using words, to stay in a communicative disposition with the audience. Now remove the means of the words and you definitely have to be about your business. To me the essence of it is that it requires the performer – and this would be my own actor's language now – to 'live through' an experience which communicates itself to the audience, first of all, by almost psychic perceptions. In *The Great Hunger* it's a day in the life of Patrick Maguire which is a special day – there's nothing routine, there's nothing 'by-the-way', it's very specific. It is essential that the spectator should feel a deep sense of recognition, and that the image should draw the spectator into the experience of the play. The actor must enable the spectator, to some degree, to see the experience of the play as his own experience.

Mason also touches on this:

If the direct impact is missing, there's simply confusion, and this seems to me to be the difficulty. On the one hand you can end up with almost semaphore images which are easily read, that have nothing more to them; on the other hand, you can have images of sometimes great beauty and breadth which are totally obscure because they are not focused. One of the great lessons I've learned working in this particular kind of theatre is that it's very often the accessibility to an audience of the elements that create the image that allows new meaning, a new dimension to be revealed. Let's give people an 'in', so that they're not perplexed, bewildered by the image.

This 'in' that Mason talks about has a lot to do with the image being 'rooted in the familiar'. According to Mac Intyre: 'I have to be able to find images that are at once fresh and shocking and disturbing and entertaining and – and this is very important – *rooted in the familiar experience for them.* Otherwise, I'm left without an audience. The images must be of a world that's inside the viewer, maybe *far* inside the viewer, but there'. In other words, an image must be concrete in order to lead the audience towards the spiritual dimension, towards – as in the case of *The Great Hunger* – a recognition of their own constriction. This mixture of the concrete and the spiritual – of the vulgar and the holy – is something that the image, when properly constructed, conveys comprehensively. Mac Intyre gives an example of this:

> Tom Hickey upside down on the gate, a wooden gate – Patrick Maguire upside down on the wooden gate – that's pretty concrete, that's pretty physical. The associations of that image bring in more than a whiff of the metaphysical. It's the crucifixion image, and like all images of any richness – in our dreams or in that film or a stage piece – it's multifaceted. Every slightly altered angle the viewer gives it sets new reverberations loose. That is maybe, centrally, why the image, as opposed to the verbal, has such power of communication in the theatre.

Another aspect of giving the audience an 'in' is to provide moments of release through comic episodes. In *The Great Hunger*, for example, Agnes comes upon Malone in a field. A game ensues. Agnes lifts her skirts higher and higher as she repeatedly crosses a fence. Malone is drawn into the game, is ensnared, is pounced on by Agnes, who nearly rapes him before he escapes and scurries off, his pants around his ankles. This scene conveys the sexual dilemma central to the play, while at the same time providing the release of laughter in the spectator. Mac Intyre terms this 'the element of *jeu d'esprit*', and considers it to be vital. The unique quality of the non-literal, flexible image is that the spectator can be enlivened through comedy while perceiving instinctively the tragedy of the play.

The alchemy between performance and spectator is constantly shifting, however, and it is not a matter of pressing buttons in the spectator for a facile response. Hickey describes the performance/spectator relationship as 'mysterious'. 'What was going to be done had been decided clearly during rehearsal. There it was for the audience and when they added their contribution it brought more into a psychic area. It didn't change it, it heightened it, it consolidated it. In terms of nuance, it's different every night'. Hickey feels that there was an intimate exchange between the audience and the performance, enhancing the spiritual dimension.

Vivid images, such as the masturbation scene in *The Great Hunger*, in which Hickey conveyed Maguire's spiritual and emotional isolation through the image of working a bellows, challenge the audience differently from night to night in ways that the performer can best describe. 'The masturbation sequence – some nights men would laugh out of nervousness, some nights you could hear people holding their breath. Another night you could feel a wave in the audience, the way crows fly off a tree'. If presented literally, this image would be pornographic and would stop at that. But because it is presented ritually, it arouses in the spectator tenderness, shame, excitement, embarrassment, in short, the same emotions Maguire is feeling. Thus the spectators look inward, and are able to identify with Maguire's hunger.

Hickey, Mason and Mac Intyre have found that the Irish audience is sensitive and eager for challenge. In response to the suggestion that the Irish audience has problems with the imagistic theatre, Mac Intyre stressed:

> I think that the problems are grossly exaggerated. I've met innumerable audience members who went in there never having experienced that kind of theatre before and who came out disturbed, excited, thrilled, shaken, pleased to have been challenged by it – audience members ranging from the 'rude', if you like, to the sophisticated. In short, I think we don't give the audience half enough credit for their capacity to be challenged. I think that's an Irish *faiblesse*, to assume laziness.

Programme Note: *The Great Hunger* by Tom Mac Intyre

(Peacock Theatre, October 1986)
'The Hurt Mind'

Dermot Healy

'I'm talking of the hurt mind, hurt mind in wait and knowing as the hurt mind knows ...'[1] *The Great Hunger*, written by Tom Mac Intyre from Patrick Kavanagh's poem of the same name, was first performed in the Peacock Theatre, Dublin on May 9th, 1983. It was directed by Patrick Mason, design was by Bronwen Casson and lighting by Tony Wakefield. Tom Hickey played Maguire. With some changes this team have remained together for two other productions, *The Bearded Lady* and *Rise Up Lovely Sweeney*, both also performed in the Peacock Theatre in 1984 and 1985.

At the core of the group are Tom Mac Intyre, Patrick Mason and Tom Hickey. *The Great Hunger* brought them all together (though Mason had directed earlier work of Mac Intyre's) for the first time, and the company reached extraordinary heights in what was cautiously referred to as 'experimental theatre'. The key word since then has been collaboration, and allied with that – image, gesture, rapport and fragmentary dialogue. If they seek out the bizarre or frenzied, the company is also capable of immense poetic tenderness and a sure lightness of touch. Mac Intyre had been watching the French and the Americans at play, Hickey the Russians, Mason, European and English theatre, but their themes together have always been Irish, hence the introductory title 'the hurt mind' which is a condition Mac Intyre feels he inherited, but for hurt mind you can also read 'the joyous senses', or at another remove, 'The Great Hunger'.

The Great Hunger as a poem records the terrible isolation of a male individual tied to husbandry of poor soil. Yet, despite its hero's absence from world affairs and sexual pleasure, the work succeeded in being both celebratory and spiritual. It still remains one of the masterpieces of twentieth-century Irish poetry. Its proposed adaptation by Mac Intyre was greeted with a certain amount of disbelief. But as a play *The Great Hunger*, as well as renewing the strengths of the poem, smashed open a mirror in Irish theatre. No longer was an audience looking at themselves in a way to which they were accustomed. The poetry accrued from image and gesture. Farmers spoke the words of the Mass in ordinary conversation. The priest from the pulpit sold land. Dialogue was not undermined by subscribing to the progression of plot or character. Mac Intyre used the repetition of telling lines of speech in the poem as a pivot round which the play would turn, and the rest was left unsaid.

This demanded supreme accuracy from the players. For behind what was visually happening was another text – the poem itself, and yet the play must work for those who never read the poem, yet satisfy those that had. And it must entertain. The company succeeded. Ritual was heavily disguised in natural colours. The humour immediate. The accents exact. There were some unforgettable moments. Those audiences from the country, having a certain empathy with the condition, started laughing from the first curtain. The urban folk were inclined to find the play tragic. At the previews talk centred round the masturbatory scene, in which Tom Hickey, his face gone puce and withered with his vigorous exertions, on his knees worked a bellows into the auditorium.

But other things were happening besides the scandalous and the obvious. The sister would stiffen in pent-up silence, and hold it and hold it. Maguire, driven mad with desire, went upside down on a gate. The mother became a chair in whose bottom drawer the bellows rested. The priest turned into a crow. Tom Hickey was in his element, and unforgettable, as were the rest of the cast, for as they went about their repetitive chores, each gesture and slip of dialogue was being re-affirmed and re-echoed below the minds of the audience, without benefit of plot or naturalism.

Some people felt the epic poem had been trivialized. If they agreed the acting was great, others bewailed the absurdity of the piece. But the critics were not all hostile. Slowly the relentless craftsmanship of the play was realized. People returned again and again. Then came the question – could such a work be repeated? Was this only a one-off? A year later came *The Bearded Lady*. The tendency here was towards sustained, often ghostly spectacle. The psyche was extended into darker terrain – to worry away at the constraints of the intellect. *The Bearded Lady* was ostensibly about Swift, but Swift as a vehicle meant the collaborators, with Mason to the fore, had to draw on all their resources. The cast was big. There were magnificent costumes and design from Bronwen Casson. The gestures were more enigmatic. Perhaps it might have been better to stay with a named text of the Dean's rather than take the man entire, but the enterprise was justified, for *The Bearded Lady* gave up some fine performances, eerie moments and subtle buffoonery.

But questions were being asked. Was the play not more Mason's than Mac Intyre's? Why was Mac Intyre not composing an original script? *The Great Hunger* grew in stature as the fracas continued, albeit muted. But others saw *The Bearded Lady*, despite its flaws, as an important step forward for the company. The collaborators had entered into a new area, the hatred of women, wonder at the primitive, and the sense of the physical. We were in the realm of self-disgust. And also narcissism, which was captured brilliantly by the appearances of the horse-folk, the Houyhnhnms. If Swift himself had vanished somewhat during the enterprise, still the audience were given a rich insight into his creativity.

Then came *Rise Up Lovely Sweeney*, which, though using as its source material O'Keefe's edition of *Buile Shuibhne*, was considered by many Mac Intyre's most original text to date. Because the company's work was now familiar to Irish audiences the risks taken had to be greater. 'The hurt mind' came into its own. The story of Sweeney concerns itself with the travails of a man turned into a bird for a crime in his past. The themes of guilt and expiation were what Mac Intyre was after.

His Sweeney sets off to seek a safe house in the maelstrom of Irish history – not the most linear place in the world – only to find himself ousted each time. Yet he does not shirk the insults thrown from both sides –

> **INTERROGATOR.** Are you not a congenital liar and breeder of congenital liars, congenital killer and breeder of congenital killers, and when not thus occupied – in your teeming and congenital spare time, so to speak – isn't your main occupation the howl and the whinge in the dark of the day for the paps of the world you never had the moral courage to put your mouth to?[2]

A question which is answered elsewhere by the following –

> **SWEENEY.** My nation is the howl – but not the black howl. Some say the whinge. I say the howl – but not the black howl.[3]

Tall steel walls, as doors slammed shut, buckled between scenes. There was swift disorientating activity. A terrifying interrogation between Sweeney on stage and Sweeney on video whose simple subject matter was a litany of Irish trees. A hospital scene turned from fragmentary spectacle into a comfortable Irish 'Tennessee Waltz'. Instead of bees, helicopters. Then finally the piece climaxed with Sweeney's direct speech to the audience. 'The Hurt Mind' was exposed – with all its self-importance, melodrama and magical intent, in a few riveting minutes of superb acting by Tom Hickey –

SWEENEY. It's too long a war, it's too long.[4]

What is 'the hurt mind?' It can be construed as National Paranoia. Words, in capital letters that shouldn't be. Something emanating from people who conceptualize in one language and relinquish their ideas in another. Yet there is a certain satisfaction in that back-log of bitterness; for everything is not as it appears. In the Aran Islands they say – 'tá dearc im dearmad' – there's hurt in my memory. And that condition provides for a form of communication that treads dangerous ground, while meanwhile, the players, with breath held watch their backs.

Works Cited

Mac Intyre, Tom, *Rise Up Lovely Sweeney* (unpublished rehearsal draft, 1985).

---

[1] Tom Mac Intyre, *Rise Up Lovely Sweeney* (unpublished rehearsal draft, 1985), p. 89.

[2] Ibid., p. 91.

[3] Ibid., p. 7. [This is also a reference by Mac Intyre to MacMorris's 'What ish my nation?' in Shakespeare's *Henry V* (Act III scene ii)].

[4] Tom Mac Intyre, *Rise Up Lovely Sweeney* (unpublished rehearsal draft, 1985), p. 89.

Programme Note: *The Great Hunger* by Tom Mac Intyre

(Peacock Theatre, July 1986)
'The Ghost, The Gate, and The Go Beyant'

Michael Harding

The collaborators of playwright Tom Mac Intyre, director Patrick Mason, and an exquisitely disciplined and committed troupe led by actor Tom Hickey, is a story which began some years ago, and is marked by sustained success at the Peacock Theatre in Dublin, bringing a new idiom of the theatre to a new Irish audience. Any initial unease of audience or critic in the face of an arcane show has given way to pleasure and acclaim. What the argumentative mind might have resisted some years ago as irrational or obscure, is now accepted as a gate into a wider mystery and magic of the Imagination.

Of course the formal theatre of psychological narrative, discourse and argument continues to endure and to hold the centre stage. But it is now arguable that such an idiom is caught in the hermeneutic of its time, and that the times, as the man said, have changed utterly.

It can be difficult sometimes to lose oneself in a play full of small provincial tragedies argued out in domestic discourse and rhetoric, forty years after you know what. In a world polluted with helicopters and secret police, where the innocent imagination has been murdered a thousand times in a thousand silent ditches, it is occasionally difficult to listen with equanimity to another character in a play talking himself towards the final insight. Even on good evenings, when we go home elated by a fine 'performance' or the grace of a 'classic' brought to life, are we not also touched with the uneasy suspicion that it has damn all to do with the nightmare of the world about us?

Mid-way through the twentieth century the Character had begun to escape from the novel, the syntax of painting has collapsed under the strain of a new experience, and everywhere, Certitude was flaking like the walls of unused Italian churches. In theatre the moment was marked by Beckett to assert that the silence in Godot's ear would never again be broken.

Leaving aside the more commercial flippery of the 'Sixties, the past three decades have been marked with a new seriousness to discover a fresh theatrical moment or event that might adequately concur with the power, or powerlessness of our time.

In Poland Grotowski was establishing the actor, not as player of his part, but as 'holy' actor; finding in the idiom of his total movement and expression the hope of a new encounter with the world; calling the audience to be more than spectators; to partake in an event which might resonate in their ordinary lives.

In Wuppertal in the 'Seventies Pina Bausch began to take the clothes off the old arguments and the old polarities – 'the man the woman, the woman the man,' as the man said.

And in New York, Merce Cunningham was dancing his dancers against the music, reaching a contra-puntal idiom which widened perception and did something to the eye of the beholder akin to tearing canvas.

Random examples – but the point is that modern anxiety was beginning to haunt the stage, and those in the house were alive to the fright.

An island is like a solitary man; in danger of closing the gate and turning in on himself. In theatre, like politics, or the human heart, there can be good cause to kick the gate open again. Two factors made the success of *The Great Hunger* a probability when it first opened in Dublin in 1983. Firstly, Mac Intyre trusted his audience. That was critical. And secondly, nothing was dragged in from outside.

Kavanagh, like MacDiarmuid or Maclean is always in danger of being put to the margin in a British tradition – hough seen in their own territory, they are great poets of this century. The territory of Kavanagh's life, and poetry, is south Ulster; a shifting ground; a buffer zone between north and south; a place unsure of itself. It is also an interior landscape; a townland of the imagination; a mudwalled space, unknown and unknowing, where a man noses about like an animal for a clean place to die.

In the uneasy solitude of Patrick Maguire, the poem's central figure, Kavanagh was touching the stone of a peculiarly Irish anxiety; alone, seedless – a quiet lingering death in a field of its own making.

There was a fierce truth to the poem, particularly for a society where identity often means isolation; a society which had closed the gate against the stranger, and gander-stepped through its own special solitary version of the twentieth century.

For Tom Mac Intyre the poem was a standing stone in the corner field. All that was needed was to hold hands, and open wide the gate.

Oedipal Desire in Mac Intyre's
The Great Hunger: A Palaeo-Postmodern Perspective
Catriona Ryan

Tom Mac Intyre's play *The Great Hunger*[1] is an adaptation of Patrick Kavanagh's long poem of the same name. It represents the life and dreams of Patrick Maguire, a Monaghan small farmer who suffers from sexual and spiritual starvation. The play is a fusion of image, language and movement and represents a significant moment in Irish theatrical history. First performed in 1983 in the Peacock Theatre, Mac Intyre's *The Great Hunger* adopts an experimental approach which has many influences including European and American avant garde innovators such as Grotowski and John Cage. Mac Intyre's aesthetics in this play place an emphasis on the language of the body which at the time challenged conventional Irish theatrical practices. In this article I define Tom Mac Intyre's aesthetic as palaeo-postmodern[2] in that it combines traditional Irish themes with an experimental format. Whilst dealing with complex and inter-related ideas of the unconscious, the feminine principle and Oedipal desire, this aesthetic utilizes the Irish language as a means of deconstructing the language of English. Mac Intyre's point is that authenticity of art and Irish identity – as symbolized by Maguire's experience in *The Great Hunger* – can only be found in the feminine space of the unconscious and the defamiliarization of English via the subversive presence of the Irish language is a powerful aesthetic pathway into that unconscious space.

In *The Great Hunger*, Mac Intyre marries the traditional with the experimental in what I term as a palaeo-postmodern approach to a classical Irish poem. The term 'palaeo-postmodern' is used here as a means of describing Mac Intyre's disruption of Yeats's palaeo-modernist interest in mysticism, which Mac Intyre extends to his interest in the subversive potential of the Irish language. The author's strategy involves the deconstruction of the English language through theatrical silences and language play. My analysis of Mac Intyre's palaeo-postmodern disruption of the English language in *The Great Hunger*, is reflective of the experimental and traditional aspects of his aesthetic. I will explore the experimental aspect of Mac Intyre's play in terms of his deconstructive approach to language using Lacan's concept of Freud's Oedipus Complex and how that relates to Mac Intyre's disruption of Yeats's palaeo-modernist representation of the mask.

Mac Intyre uses the Irish language as a deconstructive device. In a radio interview with Vincent Woods concerning the publication of Mac Intyre's poetry collection *ABC* (2006) the author refers to the 'exhausted' nature of English due to its overuse and – in the context of Irish cultural usage of English – it's only the 'huge resonating presence of the Irish language in English' which helps the Irish writer to 'bust the syntax'.[3] Mac Intyre's defamiliarizing approach to the English language to 'bust the syntax' through the Irish language is one of the most interesting aspects of his work. Mac Intyre's deconstruction of English in the play is related to Lacan's Oedipal concept of the Symbolic. The classic Freudian idea of the child renouncing his Oedipal desire represents the point of the child's acceptance of paternal authority and in a Lacanian context this imposition of patriarchal authority is rendered in terms of Symbolic language. In *Literary Theory: An Introduction* Terry Eagleton defines the Symbolic order as

> the pre-given structure of social and sexual roles and relations which make up the family and society. In Freud's own terms, it (the symbolic order) has successfully negotiated the painful passage through the Oedipus complex.[4]

The Symbolic phase of childhood is the beginning of the child's socialization process which incorporates a rejection of the pre-linguistic Oedipal desire for the maternal body in favour of the paternalistic route of language acquisition. In the play there is a correlation between the Symbolic and the English language, which may be interpreted in a Symbolic paternalistic context, which Mac Intyre constantly deconstructs throughout the play. Patrick Maguire, the main protagonist in *The Great Hunger*, seems to reflect this Lacanian idea through what may be interpreted as his failure to renounce his Oedipal desires for his mother and therefore his inability to articulate the paternalistic representation of the Symbolic language of English. Therefore Maguire is stuck in a pre-

Oedipal phase of pre-symbolic desire which is manifested in the play through his lack of speech.

Mac Intyre's deconstruction of language in a Lacanian context can be related to Yeats's palaeo-modernist metaphysics. Yeats's palaeo-modernism is defined by Frank Kermode as an aesthetic of 'formal desperation' and a Romantic vision that was typical of Yeats's Celtic and apocalyptic literature.[5] Palaeo-modernism is related to early modernism which at the end of the nineteenth century was influenced by aesthetic reactionary movements such as the Symbolists, where the metaphysical was valued above the physical. In Kermode's terms palaeo-modernism is 'devoted to the theme of crisis' and is 'apocalyptic' in its response to the breakdown of Victorian ideals due to advances in science and the growth of philosophical skepticism.[6] Yeats responded to this existential 'crisis' through his development of a trans-rational aesthetic of Celtic spiritualism, which was rooted in the occult. Mac Intyre is very influenced by Yeats and Mac Intyre's palaeo-postmodernism is both a continuation and a defamiliarization of Yeats's aesthetic. Where Yeats's palaeo-modernist concerns in mysticism are rooted in Irish mythology, Mac Intyre's spiritual aesthetics are also palaeo-modernist in that they are rooted in a mystical Irish ideological framework in the context of the Irish language and identity. However, Mac Intyre deconstructs Yeats's ideas through the former's deconstructive experimentation which introduces a unique kind of postmodern (which normally negates meaning) 'play' with language where meaning is displaced through neological statements: the purpose of which is to reveal a kind of totalizing, transcendent, unconscious, feminine space endowed by the Irish language. In Mac Intyre's play *The Great Hunger* I interpret the author's palaeo-postmodern aesthetic in terms of Lacan's Oedipus complex. Lacan's theory of the symbolic phase of language in an Oedipal context sees language as a relative body of signifiers which contain logical gaps linked to repressed Oedipal drives. Lacan's reference to the unconscious as being structured like language is relevant here in that it is the unconscious drives which highlight the arbitrary nature of language. This relates to the Oedipal theme in the play which I interpret in terms of Mac Intyre's deconstruction of English. Mac Intyre's palaeo-postmodernism is based on the unconscious power of the Irish language which acts as a subversive force on the language of English in the play. Therefore Mac Intyre's methodology in this play is very Lacanian in terms of emphasizing the arbitrary nature of English language signification.

In Mac Intyre's *The Great Hunger* the Oedipal narrative may be read in terms of Yeats's concept of the mask. In his mystical work *A Vision* (1942) Yeats explores man's unconscious nature in terms of the self and anti-self and states that 'All unity comes from the mask',[7] and the antithetical mask is described as a 'form created by passion to unite us to ourselves'. In the play the main protagonist, Patrick Maguire, is portrayed as struggling to dissolve the patriarchal mask of socialized masculinity in the face of his tabooed desire for a feminine Oedipal apotheosis in the form of his mother.

Kavanagh's poem, from which the play is adapted, is centred on the character Patrick Maguire who lives a depressive rural existence where he is controlled by his mother and married to the land. Mac Intyre refers to the theatrical nature of Kavanagh's poem which suited his own experimental theatre:

> *The Great Hunger* (1942) is an extraordinary poem, working essentially in charged images and when that's around, you've got to be on for it ... A piece like *The Great Hunger* is dying to find expression on the Irish stage. The material is so charged before one goes to it, one is aiming to match that charge ... that means a lot of people are going to be disturbed.[8]

In relation to Kavanagh's concept of the theatrical nature of his poem, Antoinette Quinn observes that:

> Kavanagh refers to his narrative enterprise in theatrical metaphors, yet fictional technique in *The Great Hunger* is really cinematic, rather than dramatic, short on dialogue, highly visual and scenically mobile.[9]

Mac Intyre recognized this minimalist quality in Kavanagh's poem by creating a play where the visual performance takes precedence over the written form. Mac Intyre's advocation of the theatre of cruelty device where the audience is 'disturbed' is very much influenced by his colleague Patrick Mason who collaborated with the playwright on *The Great Hunger* on its first production in 1983 and subsequent reworking and production from 1986 to 1988. Mason was a disciple of Peter Brook whose development of theatre of cruelty – which is a term created by Artaud[10] – was very influential.[11] Brook's influence on the form of Mac Intyre's *The Great Hunger* is evident in terms of the impact it had on the audience. The audiences' reactions to the play were often negative.

Nicholas Shakespeare highlights the impact of Mac Intyre's theatre of disturbance on London audiences: 'Midway through one of the performances, a man walked up to the stage to protest against "this travesty of religion"'. His walkout was not an isolated incident.'[12]

The disturbing imagery in Mac Intyre's *The Great Hunger* is immediately reflected at the beginning of the play by the mother who appears as a 'wooden effigy' and whose deathly presence is a dominant force (9). This dominance is reflected in the first scene of the play:

> *The kitchen and the chapel areas: place downstage left and right, respectively.* THE MOTHER *will usually be found in the kitchen area; place there, also, a large black kettle and a bucket. The chapel is distinguished by a tabernacle resting on its pedestal* (9).

The dominance of The Mother in this scene manifests itself in her position in the kitchen, '*the kitchen and chapel areas: place downstage left and right, respectively*' as being on a par with the symbol of God, the 'chapel'. Yet, in the written context of these stage directions, in this scene, the lack of a patriarchal representative of God is deliberate in that the upper-cased citation of the mother's presence as The Mother in contrast to the lower-cased words of 'tabernacle' and 'chapel' serves as a symbol for her quiet authority which Mac Intyre uses as a deconstructive force throughout the play.

In Kavanagh's *The Great Hunger* (1942) The Mother is portrayed as a controlling figure. Edna Longley makes the point:

> Maguire's purgatorial entrapment, from which the narrative voice cannot or does not wholly extricate itself, resembles the hero's failure to deliver himself from the mother archetype (and from the infantile unconsciousness that the hero's bondage to her authority represents for the conscious personality).[13]

Kavanagh's portrayal of the mother's relationship with her son, in the sense that it involves nothing more than 'purgatorial entrapment' for Maguire, differs radically from Mac Intyre's approach to the poem where Maguire's unconscious Oedipal desire for the mother is made conscious. This is illustrated in scene 8 of the play:

> *As she exits,* MAGUIRE *rouses himself. He clutches* THE MOTHER, *leans his head on her shoulder. With his fist he*

beats her breast, slowly, mechanically, the fist beats on the breast of THE MOTHER (32).

Maguire's Oedipal desire in scene 8 reinforces what Edna Longley refers to in 'Jungian terms' as an attempt to reunite the 'male anima with maternal origins' as Maguire's unconscious Oedipal desire has been made conscious. Jung is significant in Mac Intyre's work in that the author is influenced by Jung's archetypal perspective on the unconscious and therefore is an important aspect of my interpretative analysis of the palaeo-postmodern nature of Mac Intyre's work. According to Mac Intyre, in a personal interview (2005), Jung's autobiography *Memories, Dreams and Reflections* (1965) has had a major impact on Mac Intyre's aesthetics of the unconscious. The male anima in Jungian terms refers to the female aspect of masculinity and in scene 8, as outlined in the action above, Maguire is seeking fulfilment of his Oedipal desires by attempting to seek a sexual oneness with his mother. Jung is quite Yeatsian in terms of his ideas on the unconscious; what Jung calls the collective unconscious, Yeats refers to as the anima mundi. In a palaeo-modernist context Yeats's idea of the mask as the space of the self and anti-self is rooted in the unconscious as a 'form created by passion to unite us to ourselves'.[14] Scene 8 of the *Great Hunger* is therefore Yeatsian as Maguire is attempting to conjoin his patriarchal mask of the male self with his Jungian anima self in order to achieve an Oedipal union with his mother. However, Mac Intyre also disrupts Yeats's concept of the mask in that Maguire's conflict of self in the play is extended into the palaeo-postmodern deconstructed space of language.

Maguire's Oedipal desire in scene 8 of Mac Intyre's play is notable in that it transcends Kavanagh's use of words to describe Maguire's mindset. In a Lacanian context language acquisition is related to renouncing Oedipal desires as the child enters the socialized world of patriarchal Symbolic language. Maguire seems to reflect this Lacanian idea through what I interpret as his failure to renounce his Oedipal desires, hence his inability to articulate language adequately. This is demonstrated dramatically through the emphasis on physical gestures. The author's attention to physical theatre in the play reflects his advocation of the theatre of the image aesthetic. The ideology of the theatre of the image was developed by Antonin Artaud who believed the function of theatre was to make the unconscious conscious by placing a visual emphasis on theatre which is 'why it was so important to him that the word also speak to the body'.[15] Artaud's ideology of theatre of cruelty had the intended effect of shocking audiences through the power of raw visual imagery as he says, 'Words mean little to the mind; expanded areas and objects speak ... But spatial, thundering images replete with sound also speak'.[16] Mac Intyre praises the artistic vision of Artaud whom he describes as a 'wonderful madman'.[17] Like Artaud, Mac Intyre also believes in making the unconscious aspect of theatre available to an audience.

Mac Intyre adopts the modernist theoretical concerns of Meyerhold into his theatrical experimentation, where, like Artaud and Grotowski, Meyerhold advocates an imagistic non-naturalistic theatre and where the importance of the text becomes secondary to the visual impression of the play in terms of body language. Mac Intyre cites Meyerhold's influence:

> I had read Meyerhold and Appia and Grotowski and the whole bunch. I came on a wonderful sentence in Meyerhold in the long ago when I was living, not unexpectedly, on a remote island off the west coast of Ireland and Meyerhold says 'if you want to learn how to write a play, write a play without words'.[18]

Through his concept of bio-mechanics Meyerhold advocates 'centering attention on the principal material resource of the theatre, the actor's body'.[19] In other words Meyerhold placed an emphasis on the physical gestures of the body to express emotions. Similarly, Mac Intyre's play *The Great Hunger* uses Meyerhold's technique in the sense that the physicality of the play's stagecraft carries all the weight of the play's presentation. A good example of this aspect of *The Great Hunger* is scene 8 where Maguire's Oedipal desire transcends the use of words, 'the fist beats on the breast of the mother' (32). Maguire's violent physical action is designed to create an intense visual impact on an audience. This scene also highlights the essential difference between the visual and the written word in that Mac Intyre's portrayal of the mother is a potent and effective symbol whose silence is a postmodern interpretation of the verbal language Kavanagh bestows on her in his poem. Mac Intyre's palaeo-postmodern approach is very unique as the traditional theme of Irish rural sexual repression is more forcefully evoked through language deconstruction. Maguire's unconscious Oedipal Yeatsian mask has been disrupted in a disturbing conscious physical theatrical display of desire; a desire expressed through a defamiliarized English language signification.

In his adaptation of *The Great Hunger* Mac Intyre places the power of unconscious language in the context of the anima. According to Jung, the anima is

> a factor of the utmost importance in the psychology of man wherever emotions and affects are at work. She ... intensifies and mythologizes all emotional relations with his work and with other people of both sexes. The resultant fantasies and entanglements are all her own doing.[20]

Jung relates the anima in an Oedipal context in terms of the archetype of the mother figure when he says: 'The growing youth must be able to free himself from the anima fascination of the mother'.[21] Antoinette Quinn highlights this point in relation to Maguire in Kavanagh's poem when she says:

> Patrick Maguire has fallen victim to the stereotypical Irish mother/son relationship that precludes all other relationships, a grotesque Oedipal parody in which she is 'wife and mother in one' and he upholds their marriage contract.[22]

The problem for Patrick Maguire is that he is unable to free himself from the 'anima fascination' with his mother and this becomes his downfall. In Mac Intyre's play the anima is represented by The School-Girl who becomes an externalization of Maguire's repressed emotions and a focus of his own unconscious desire for his mother. Kavanagh's reference to The School-Girl in his poem is less complex than Mac Intyre's and becomes a mere lustful projection:

> The schoolgirls passed his house laughing every morning/ and sometimes they spoke to him familiarly-/ he had an idea. Schoolgirls of thirteen would see no political intrigue in an old man's friendship/ love/the heifer waiting to be nosed by the old bull.[23]

Kavanagh objectifies The School-Girl as a source of lustful desire for Maguire who is portrayed as the 'old bull' fantasizing about the schoolgirl's passive innocence; from Maguire's perspective she lacks 'political intrigue' and is simply waiting to be unburdened of her virginity.

Mac Intyre's portrayal of The School-Girl is more complex than Kavanagh's. For Mac Intyre the schoolgirl is also Maguire's object of desire, but she transcends this objectification in scene 15 of *The Great Hunger* and becomes a powerful feminine unconscious force which embodies the Irish language in the play:

She sits now beside the basin. Empties her schoolbag of its books. Carefully she makes a pyramid of the books on the flat of the upturned basin, counting in Irish - 'doing her lesson' - the while.

As she starts building the pyramid, MAGUIRE *enters upstage left, rattling coins. He halts, focuses on* THE SCHOOL-GIRL *and watches her silently from his upstage position. In the same breath* MARY ANNE *has come on downstage left. She, in turn, focuses on* THE SCHOOL-GIRL. *Eyes on* THE SCHOOL-GIRL. *She drifts to* THE MOTHER, *and, arms about* THE MOTHER, *head resting on* THE MOTHER's *downstage shoulder, watches, watches ...*

The pyramid of books either collapses or is collapsed and THE SCHOOL-GIRL *becomes a barking terrier, picks up her schoolbag, and runs off upstage right, working a reprise [sic]24 of her counting in-Irish verbal score* (46).

The significance of the Irish language in the play takes a mystical perspective when The School-Girl builds her books into a pyramid. In his book *Memories, Dreams and Reflections* (1965) Jung talks about the significance of the symbol of the pyramid in relation to his own experiences of submitting himself to the 'impulses of the unconscious':[25]

preoccupied with the question of how I could approach this task, I was walking along the lake as usual one day, picking stones out of the gravel on the shore; suddenly I caught sight of a red stone, a four-sided pyramid ... I placed it in the middle under the dome, and as I did so, I recalled the underground phallus of my childhood dream ... I had no answer to my question, only the inner certainty that I was on my way to discovering my own myth. For the building game was only the beginning. It released a stream of fantasies which I later carefully wrote down.[26]

Jung's building game was the key to his unconscious self. It brought him face to face with his own unconscious Oedipal desires. The girl's building game is symbolic of a Jungian journey into the unconscious and she is preparing her own journey to an unconscious space which is the unconscious anima of Maguire's self. As opposed to Kavanagh's portrayal of the girl who lacks 'political intrigue', Mac Intyre sees her as a source of wisdom, an underworld Goddess whose wisdom is beyond Maguire's understanding. In scene 15 of the play when Mary Anne, Maguire's sister, shows affection to The Mother and they are both 'watching, watching ...'

(46) the mystical vision of The School-Girl building her pyramid, they are united in that moment in a triangulated stance of feminine power. Maguire is at the same time alienated from the scene as he is alienated from the fulfilment of his Oedipal desire to be the phallus for The Mother.

The symbol of the pyramid is very relevant to the concept of the triangular nature of the Oedipus complex. In a Lacanian context the child must renounce the desire for the mother and leave the Imaginary phase to the maturation process of the patriarchal Symbolic sign system. In Mac Intyre's context Maguire fails to renounce his desire for The Mother and the Symbolic language of English which he speaks is constantly deconstructed into empty phrases and repetitions: 'The tubs is white ... The tubs is white ... The tubs is white ...' (11). Maguire's inarticulation takes an ironic swipe at the patriarchal symbolization of English as the mystical power of the girl's presence is reinforced by her verbal fluency of 'counting in Irish verbal score'. The language of Irish is the unconscious language of the other and in order to fulfill his unconscious Oedipal desire for the mother, Maguire must acquire the Irish language. Mac Intyre's emphasis on the Irish language as possessing a powerful unconscious force is also referred to by the author as 'the furious subtext of Irish'.[27] Mac Intyre associates the unconscious power of Irish with a feminine impulse:

> the truth we're talking about for me brought up in Gestapo Ireland of the 'Thirties and 'Forties where you were told you had no permission to think, and women don't exist by the way ... the Catholic Church was leading the Gestapo attack ... if you are interested in quality story-telling you have to shed everything you have and follow the star that is your star and you will come back to the Goddess really, the aisling figure or put it another way to the conversation with the form interior'.[28]

The core of Mac Intyre's aesthetics is based on the unconscious power of the feminine which he feels is a necessary pre-requisite to creativity, but which had been repressed through the patriarchal power of the Catholic Church. In this context the Catholic symbolism of the 'tabernacle' in the first scene of the play is set against the figure of The Mother whose silent presence subverts the Catholic symbol of patriarchal power; a power whose ineptness is reflected in the weak male persona of Maguire. The term 'aisling' is the Irish for dream, and Mac Intyre's aesthetics of the unconscious is bound up with the symbolism of the Irish language and its relationship to the feminine. The writer's concept of 'the furious subtext of Irish' acts as an unconscious, anti-Christian, feminine subversive force in the play where Mac Intyre has strategically placed Irish linguistic terms to disturb the patriarchal nature of the English language.

In Jung's terms the anima is 'hidden in the dominating power of the mother'[29] and in scene 15 of Mac Intyre's play the girl's and The Mother's language is bound up in the mystical presence of death which becomes an Irish verbal score.

Jung writes:

> On the negative side the mother archetype may connote anything secret, hidden, dark: the abyss, the world of the dead, anything that devours, seduces, and poisons, that is terrifying and inescapable like death.[30]

Jung's reference to the negative aspect of the maternal image may be seen in the play as Maguire's primal fear – as well as desire – of his mother's dying presence.

Kavanagh's form of innovatory shock was what Alex Davis refers to as 'the poem which most successfully imports the techniques of *The Wasteland* into Irish poetry'.[31] Formally Kavanagh's *The Great Hunger* (1942) consists of a montage of different sequences, which mirrors aspects of Eliot's free-verse technique. Mac Intyre takes the experimental qualities of Kavanagh's *The Great Hunger* (1942) and invokes a variety of different modernisms – Yeats's palaeo-modernism, Grotowski's experimental theatre and other modernist techniques – are left to play in this theatrical piece where the central underlying themes are enmeshed in the play's formal fragmentary nature. This study of Mac Intyre's adaptation of Patrick Kavanagh's poem highlights the uniqueness of Tom Mac Intyre's palaeo-postmodern aesthetic which involves the disruption and extension of Yeats's palaeo-modernist perspective of the self. Mac Intyre's aesthetic involves a unique combination of traditional themes and experimental influences in order to create a palaeo-postmodern vision of the tragic artist embodied in Maguire, whose inability to connect with his own feminine side incurs a loss not only of his feminine identity but that of his own language, the mystical form of which remains elusive.

Works Cited

Anon., *Irish Press*, 'Looking for a new theatre Language', 6 May 1983.

Artaud, Antonin, *The Theatre and Its Double*, Trans. Victor Corti (London: Calder & Boyars, 1970).

Bosmajian, Hamida, 'Looking Glasses and Neverlands: Lacan, Desire and Subjectivity in Children's Literature', *The Lion and the Unicorn* 29 (April, 2005).

Brook, Peter, *The Empty Space* (London: Penguin, 1990).

Byrne, Mairead, 'Two Men, a Poem, a Play. A Meeting Under Fire.' *In Dublin* (6 May 1983).

Davis, Alex, *Introduction, Modernism and Ireland: The Poetry of the 1930s*, eds Alex Davis and Patricia Coughlan (Cork: CUP, 1995).

Derrida, Jacques, 'Of an Apocalyptic Tone Recently Adopted in Philosophy'. Trans. John P. Leavey, Jr. *Semeia* 23 (1982).

Eagleton, Terry, *Literary Theory: An Introduction*, 2nd edn. (Oxford: Blackwell Publishers, 1996).

Esslin, Martin, *The Theatre of the Absurd* (London: Penguin Books, 1961).

Fink, Bruce, *The Lacanian Subject: Between Language and Jouissance* (New Jersey: Princeton University Press, 1997).

Fink, Joel, *Theatre Journal*, 40.4 (December, 1988), pp. 550-552.

Finter, Helga, 'Antonin Artaud and the Impossible Theatre: The Legacy of the Theatre of Cruelty', *TDR* 41. 4 (Winter 1997), pp. 15-40.

Franklin, Ann and Paul Mason, *Lammas: Celebrating Fruits of the Harvest* (Minnesota: Llewellyn Publications, 2001).

Goldman, Arnold, 'Yeats, Spiritualism and Psychical Research': *Yeats and the Occult*, eds Robert O'Driscoll and Lorna Reynolds (London: Macmillan, 1975), pp. 108-29.

Goodby, John, *From History into Stillness: Irish Poetry Since the 1950s* (Manchester: Manchester UP, 2000).

Grene, Nicholas, 'Tom Murphy: Famine and Dearth' *Hungry Words: Images of Famine in the Irish Canon*, eds George Cusack and Sarah Goss (Dublin: Irish Academic Press, 2006), pp. 245-62.

Jung, Carl, *The Archetypes of the Collective Unconscious* (London: Routledge, 2nd edn., 1999).

---, *Memories, Dreams, Reflections* ed. Aniela Jaffe, Trans. Richard and Clara Winston (NY: Vintage books, 1989).

---, 'On The Relation of Analytical Psychology to Poetry' *The Norton Anthology of Theory and Criticism* (NY and London: WW. Norton & Co., 2001), pp. 990-1000.

---, *Psychology of the Unconscious: A Study of Transformations and Symbolisms of the Libido, a contribution to the Evolution of Thought* (London: Kegan Paul Trench Truber, 1912).

Kavanagh, Patrick, *The Complete Poems,* ed. Peter Kavanagh (New York: Peter Kavanagh Hard Press/Goldsmith Press, 1984).

Kelly, John S. and George Mills Harper, 'Preliminary Examination of the Script of Elizabeth Radcliffe' *Yeats and the Occult*, eds Robert

O'Driscoll and Lorna Reynolds (London: Macmillan, 1975), pp. 130-71.

Kermode, Frank, *Continuities* (London: Routledge and Kegan Paul, 1968).

Longley, Edna, *The Living Stream: Literature and Revisionism in Ireland* (Belfast: Bloodaxe Books, 1994).

McGuinness, Frank, ed. *The Dazzling Dark: New Irish Plays* (London: Faber and Faber, 1988).

Mac Intyre, Tom, *ABC* (Dublin: New Island Press, 2006).

---, *Fleurs Du Lit* (Dublin: Daedalus, 1990).

---, *The Great Hunger/The Gallant John-Joe* (Dublin: Lilliput Press, 2002).

---, *Story of a Girl* (Dublin: Lilliput Press, 2003).

Mac Conghail, Fiach, 'Tom Mac Intyre in Conversation with Fiach Mac Conghail' *Theatre Talk: Voices of Irish Theatre Practitioners* eds. Lilian Chambers, Ger FitzGibbon and Eamonn Jordan (Dublin: Carysfort Press, 2001), pp. 311-30.

Piette, Adam, *Remembering the Sound of Words: Mallarme, Proust, Joyce, Beckett* (Oxford: Clarendon Press, 1996).

Pitches, Jonathan, *Vsevolod Meyerhold* (London: Routledge, 2003).

Ryan, Catriona, Interview with Tom Mac Intyre (2005).

Shakespeare, Nicholas, 'Irish Incantations' *The Times* (22 November 1986).

Soanes, Catherine and Angus Stevenson, (ed.s) 2nd edn. *Oxford Dictionary of English* Revised (Oxford: OUP, 2005).

Quinn, Antoinette, *Patrick Kavanagh: Born-Again Romantic* (Dublin: Gill and MacMillan, 2003).

Woods, Vincent, Interview with Tom Mac Intyre *Rattlebag* (RTÉ Radio 1, Dublin) 17 August 2006.

Yeats, W.B, *A Vision.* 2nd edn. (London: MacMillan, 1937).

---

[1] Tom Mac Intyre, *The Great Hunger* in *The Great Hunger/The Gallant John-Joe* (Dublin: Lilliput Press, 2002). All quotations in this essay are taken from the 2002 edition of the play. References to this play will be incorporated in parenthesis in the text.

[2] This is a term I have created to describe Mac Intyre's disruption of Yeats's palaeo-modernist aesthetics.

[3] Tom Mac Intyre interviewed by Vincent Woods *Rattlebag* (Dublin: RTE Radio 1, 17 August 2006).

[4] Terry Eagleton, *Literary Theory: An Introduction* 2nd edn. (Oxford: Blackwell Publishers, 1996), p. 145.

[5] Kermode Frank, *Continuities* (London: Routledge and Kegan Paul, 1968), p. 10.

[6] Ibid. p. 8.

[7] W. B. Yeats, *A Vision* 2nd edn. (London: MacMillan, 1937), p. 82.

[8] Tom Mac Intyre in Mairead Byrne 'Two Men, a Poem, a Play. A Meeting Under Fire.' *In Dublin* (6 May 1983), p. 17.

[9] Antoinette Quinn, *Patrick Kavanagh: Born-Again Romantic* (Dublin: Gill and MacMillan, 2003), p. 130.

[10] Artaud states that 'everything that acts is cruelty. Theatre must rebuild itself on a concept of this drastic action pushed to the limit' in his classic text *The Theatre and Its Double,* Trans. Victor Corti (London: Calder & Boyars, 1970), p. 65.

[11] '[O]ther influences Patrick Mason admits to are ... Peter Brook, with whose company he toured and who he visits in Paris, pilgrim like, each year'. (*Irish Press*, 6 May 1983).

[12] Nicholas Shakespeare, 'Irish Incantations' (*The Times,* 22 November 1986), p. 16.

[13] Edna Longley, *The Living Stream: Literature and Revisionism in Ireland,* (Belfast: Bloodaxe Books, 1994), p. 210.

[14] Yeats, W.B, *A Vision*, p.82.

[15] Helga Finter, 'Antonin Artaud and the Impossible Theatre: The Legacy of the Theatre of Cruelty', *TDR* 41. 4 (Winter 1997), p. 15.

[16] Finter, p. 66.

[17] Tom Mac Intyre interviewed by Catriona Ryan (2005).

[18] Tom Mac Intyre in Fiach Mac Conghail, 'Tom Mac Intyre in Conversation with Fiach Mac Conghail,' in *Theatre Talk: The Voices of Irish Theatre Practitioners,* eds. Lilian Chambers, Ger FitzGibbon and Eamonn Jordan (Dublin: Carysfort Press, 2001), p. 310.

[19] Jonathan Pitches, *Vsevolod Meyerhold* (London: Routledge, 2003), p. 34.

[20] Carl Jung, *The Archetypes of the Collective Unconscious* 2nd edn., (London: Routledge, 1999), p. 70.

[21] Ibid. p. 71.

[22] Quinn, p. 127.

[23] Patrick Kavanagh, *The Complete Poems* (ed.) Peter Kavanagh (New York: Peter Kavanagh Hard Press/Goldsmith Press, 1984), p. 95.

[24] In the the 1988 version of the text, this word is 'reprise'. See Tom Mac Intyre *The Great Hunger: Poem Into Play* (Westmeath, Ireland: Lilliput Press, 1988), p. 63.

[25] Carl Jung, *Memories, Dreams, Reflections* ed Aniela Jaffe, Trans. Richard and Clara Winston (New York: Vintage Books, 1989), p. 173.

[26] Ibid pp. 174-175.

[27] Tom Mac Intyre interviewed by Catriona Ryan 2005.

[28] Ibid.

[29] Carl Jung, *The Archetypes of the Collective Unconscious* 2nd edn. (London: Routledge, 1999), p.71.

[30] Ibid. p.15

[31] Alex Davis, Introduction, *Modernism and Ireland: The Poetry of the 1930s,* eds Alex Davis, and Patricia Coughlan (Cork: CUP, 1995), p. 12.

'What Shall I Wear, Darling, to *The Great Hunger*?'

Paul Durcan

> [This poem was first published in *Going Home to Russia* by
> Paul Durcan, published by Blackstaff Press, in 1987.]

What shall I wear, darling, to *The Great Hunger*?
She shrieked at me helplessly from the east bedroom
Where the west wind does be blowing betimes.
I did not hesitate to hazard a spontaneous response:
'Your green evening gown –
Your see-through, sleeveless, backless, green evening gown.'
We arrived at the Peacock
In good time for everybody to have a good gawk at her
Before the curtain went up on *The Great Hunger*.
At the interval everybody was clucking about, cooing
That it was simply stunning – her dress –
'Darling, you look like Mother Divinity in your see-through,
Sleeveless, backless, green evening gown – it's so visual!'
At the party after the show – simply everybody was there –
Winston   Lenihan,   Consolata   O'Carroll-Riviera,   Yves   St
Kirkegaard –
She was so busy being admired that she forgot to get drunk.
But the next morning it was business as usual –
Grey serge pants, blue donkey jacket – driving around Dolphin's
Barn
In her Opel Kadett hatchback
Checking up on the rents. 'All these unmarried young mothers
And their frogspawn, living on the welfare –
You would think that it never occurs to them
That it's their rents that pay for the outfits I have to wear
Whenever *The Great Hunger* is playing at the Peacock.
No, it never occurs to them that in Ireland Today
It is not easy to be a landlord and a patron of the arts.
It is not for nothing that we in Fine Gael have a social conscience:
Either you pay the shagging rent or you get out on the street.
Next week I have to attend three-and-a-half *Great Hungers*,
Not to mention a half-dozen *Juno and the Paycocks*.'

Fig 3.1 *Deer Crossing* (Oberlin College, 1978). Actors: Tom Mac Intyre (and 3 others). Courtesy of Oberlin College. (Photographer unknown).

Fig 3.2 *Snow White* programme pages. Clockwise from top left: *The Great Hunger* (photograph); *The Bearded Lady* (photograph and poster image); *Rise Up Lovely Sweeney* (poster image and photograph); *Dance For Your Daddy* (photograph and poster image); *The Great Hunger* (photograph); *The Great Hunger* (touring poster and programme cover). Courtesy of the Abbey Theatre Archive.

Fig 3.3 *The Great Hunger*. Actors: (from left) Conal Kearney, Tom Hickey, Michele Forbes, Joan Sheehy. Set design: Brownen Casson. Photographer: Fergus Bourke. Courtesy of the Abbey Theatre Archive.

Fig 3.4 *The Great Hunger*. Actors: (from left) Dermod Moore, Tom Hickey, Conal Kearney. Set design: Bronwen Casson. Photographer: Fergus Bourke. Courtesy of the Abbey Theatre Archive.

Fig 3.5 *The Great Hunger*. Actors: (from left) Tom Hickey, Conal Kearney, Vincent O'Neill. Set design: Bronwen Casson. Photographer: Fergus Bourke. Courtesy of the Abbey Theatre Archive.

Fig 3.6 *The Great Hunger*. Actors: (from left) Bríd Ní Neachtain, Tom Hickey. Courtesy of the Abbey Theatre Archive. Set design: Bronwen Casson. Photographer Fergus Bourke.

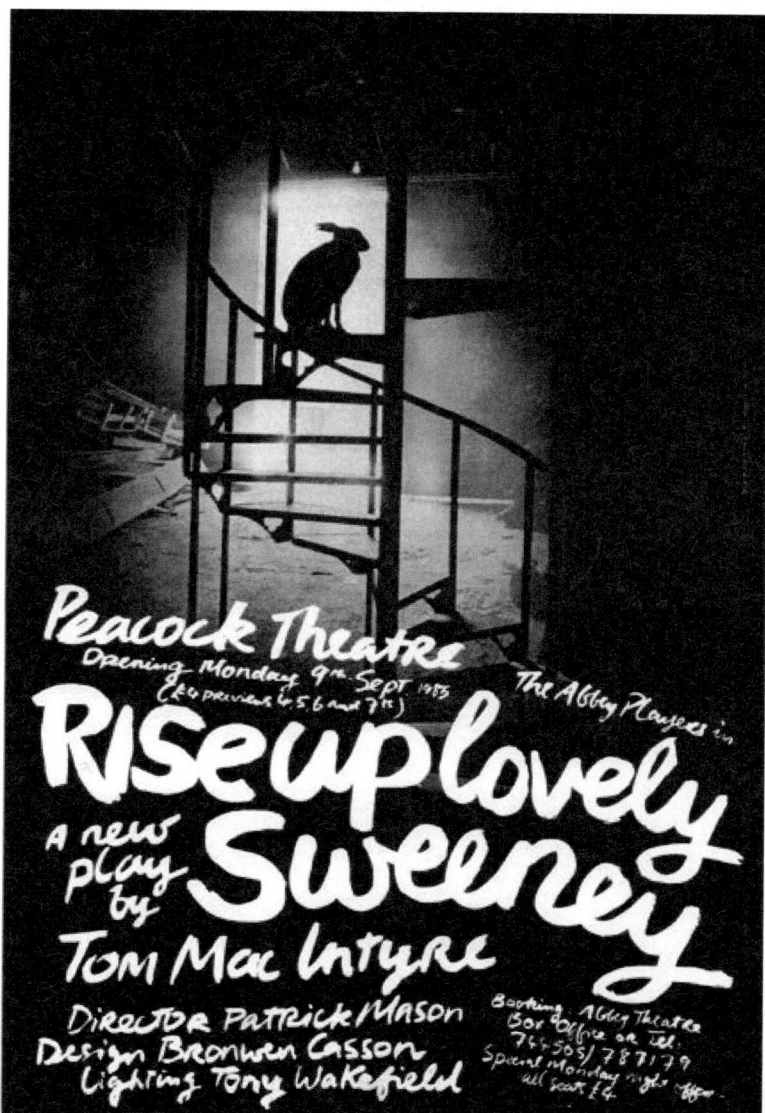

Fig 3.7 *Rise Up Lovely Sweeney* (poster). Poster: Abbey Theatre Archive. Photographer: Fergus Bourke. Graphic design: Brendan Foreman. Courtesy of the Abbey Theatre Archive.

Fig 3.8 *The Great Hunger:* Bronwen Casson's drawing of the effigy (later realized by Frank Hallinan Flood). Courtesy of Bronwen Casson.

CHAPTER 4: 'WARMING TO THE FRAY'[1]

Theatre Review: *The Bearded Lady* by Tom Mac Intyre

Joseph McMinn
(*Theatre Ireland*, Autumn 1984)

Tom Mac Intyre's latest piece of theatre, The Bearded Lady, *exploring the psyche of Jonathan Swift and realized in collaboration with the director Patrick Mason and the company of actors led by Tom Hickey and Vincent O'Neill, has just had its premiere at the Peacock Theatre. Joe McMinn, himself the author of a series of articles on Swift, reviews the production and considers its relation to the Dean of St Patrick's.*

Freud suggested that normal people have a lot to learn from the abnormal. Tom Mac Intyre's play about Swift accepts the theory but damns the reasoning. He dramatizes Swift's supposed personality – torn between the forces of reason and the urgings of primitivism. The 'bearded lady' of the title refers to those parts of a woman which reason cannot touch. We are shown Swift as a street rationalist and a house neurotic, desperate for Stella and Vanessa, but denying his sexual desires in the interests of reason and manners. The rest is madness and misery.

Yet the play does not stay with Swift and his two women. It is almost entirely a dramatization of the central allegory of *Gulliver's Travels*, especially Book IV, where Gulliver is guest of the Houyhnhnms, and discovers, to his horror, that he is nothing more than a Yahoo. His life-long held belief is reason was a waste of energy. He was always an animal. By moving from the biographical to the literary, Mac Intyre converts Swift into Gulliver, while retaining a token connection with the historical Swift. The real play centres on

Gulliver and the Houyhnhnms. This is the clearest and most theatrically effective dimension of the production. The bewildered and tormented Gulliver, performed with great power and clarity by Tom Hickey, endures the tyrannical company of the rational Houyhnhnms. He is desperate to please and imitate them, equally desperate to indulge his animal lust for a female Yahoo. All aspects of Gulliver's schizoid personality are played out here with great force. Reason in the form of the horses – with the male actors in shining leotards, elevated on theatrical hooves, ferocious punk-like features, swishing tails easily convertible into ships of submission, circling Gulliver in imperious, measured movements. Primitivism in the form of the monkeys – with the actresses revealing abundant flesh and hair, crawling about the stage, grunting and making rude gestures at tormented homo sapiens who would secretly love to escape from the control of the Houyhnhnms into the anarchic world of the Yahoos. Everything about these sequences is well-combined, the movements, the costuming, the exchanges, and the chess-like co-ordination of the horses, to produce an episode of really entertaining theatre. (The whole scene is identical in structure and feeling to the Night-town episode in *Ulysses*; even more, the bewildered innocence of Hickey's Gulliver recalls Milo O'Shea's Bloom in the mortifying and nightmarish predicament). After several sessions with the horses of reason, which alternate between sneering advice and physical humiliation, Gulliver is rejected and eventually washed up home. He has nothing left to say.

At the risk of sounding rational, what is this play about? It is, in my opinion, certainly not about Swift. At least not the Swift in history. It is about a particular and popular myth which surrounds Swift – that he was driven insane by self-control. (Historically, this could be explained as readily in political as in sexual terms). It dramatizes the myth through the imagery of *Gulliver's Travels*, and links this with those two women we know Swift loved. The mythology and the biography do not mix well, for the purposes of theatre. The former gives the play its force and meaning, the latter becomes irrelevant. I think this is why the language of the play is not very memorable. The allegory shows itself to us. It has no need of much talk. Also, the play may be the victim of its own ideology. If, as the play suggests, the rationalist is the false Swift, then what is there to say? An anti-rational theatre needs to be very good with words to show their emptiness.

---

[1] Tom Mac Intyre, *The Gallant John-Joe*, p.86

Theatre Review: *The Bearded Lady*
    by Tom Mac Intyre

Peter Thompson
(*The Irish Press,* 12 September 1984)

True enough, there has been a big hullaballoo about Tom Mac Intyre's new play, *The Bearded Lady*, which has opened at the Peacock Theatre. But it would be impossible, nonetheless, for anyone who has seen this not to recommend it wholeheartedly to everyone they meet. It's given this writer food for conversation for weeks ahead.

On one level, this is theatre, a play about Dean Swift, and the conflict of flesh and mind within the great writer. But it is also circus, a cartoon strip, a cinema in technicolour of ideas of haunted dreams and neurotic fantasy, brilliantly realized by the director Patrick Mason. It is presented by designer Bronwen Casson in a set and with costumes which vividly, and ingeniously, serve the script.

'I think, therefore I am,' said Descartes early in the seventeenth century. 'Happiness is the amusement of those who cannot think', counters Mac Intyre, in this play, late in the twentieth.

We have come full circle in our civilization to realize that body and mind live apart at their peril, or so it may seem. Mac Intyre's examination of Swift's sense of guilt about Vanessa and Stella become here, in images of marvelously dramatized fantasy, a deeper probing of our own fear of ourselves, our bodies, our smells, our excrement.

Tom Hickey is Swift here – a typhoon of controlled and concentrated power, excellently supported by John Olohan as the narrating Anatomist. Vincent O'Neill's horsemen of reason and screaming Yahoos are perfectly drilled and suitably frightening.

You must see this: it's extraordinary.

A Conversation with Bríd Ní Neachtain

Marie Kelly

MK. Your first appearance in Mac Intyre's work was in *The Great Hunger* in 1983. What was your experience in Irish theatre up to this point?

BNíN. In 1983 I was a member of the Abbey Theatre company and therefore I had the good fortune to work with and to observe some of our great Irish actors and directors.

MK. How much of Mac Intyre's theatre had you seen before being cast in *The Great Hunger*? What interested you about the work?

BNíN. I had never met Tom Mac Intyre but I had seen *Eye-Winker, Tom-Tinker* in The Peacock in 1972 and I was familiar with his poetry and his prose. I was not cast in *The Great Hunger* from the outset. I was playing the lead in a musical (*Mary Makebelieve*) in the Abbey and I got a call from the Artistic Director (Joe Dowling). He told me that I would be taking over from Máire Ní Ghráinne in the play – she had had an accident on her bicycle. He said there would be a script at the stage door and that I was to join the rehearsals in the morning. I found the play very challenging. The first draft of the rehearsal script was very loose, a couple of lines of dialogue here and there with the emphasis on 'exploration in the rehearsal room'.

MK. So you became part of the ensemble playing in *The Great Hunger* (1983), *Rise Up Lovely Sweeney* (1984) and *Dance for your Daddy* (1987). Can you describe the experience of being part of this ensemble and how your work as an actor developed in this particular environment?

BNíN. I can remember being very nervous on my first morning in rehearsals. I felt a strong collaboration between the actors even at that early stage. By this stage the rest of the cast had been in rehearsals for two weeks. Following on from *The Great Hunger*, I felt that as a group of actors we had developed a sort of shorthand where we could pick up on a gesture, or a look, or a sound from each other and develop it into something else – grasping the ball, holding on to it and then passing it on but changing its direction in doing so. This was very exciting for me as an actor, but it was also very challenging. I began to see the text as having a beginning, middle and an end but not necessarily in that order, that this could work for an audience.

MK. One of the striking things about Mac Intyre's drama is its sense of playfulness. Do you have anything to say about how this manifested itself in rehearsals?

BNíN. This sense of playfulness manifested itself in the sharing and exploring of our ideas, trusting each other, and leaving our egos outside the rehearsal room door (which posed a problem from time to time!). We were working towards a fresh and vibrant form of theatre that served the playwright and challenged the audience.

MK. Given the emphasis on collaboration here can you talk about the way in which rehearsals proceeded? Did you begin, for example, with a reading of a rehearsal script? How did the process unfold and what kinds of rehearsal room activities led up to performance?

BNíN. Rehearsals started with some limbering exercises and then we went on to improvise. Tom Mac Intyre was a very strong presence in the room. He would pick up on our improvisations to change different aspects of the work, putting our discoveries to the test, constantly stimulating, provoking, and challenging us as actors, and guiding us on our collaborative journey. For me this was a completely different approach to a text. I had been used to the traditional form – the first reading, blocking, etc. Under Patrick Mason's direction nothing was imposed, we were free to dig, explore and investigate the fabric of the play until we came to an organic form where we were free to invent even in performance.

MK. What happened once the play was in performance? Would you say, for instance, that the dramatic process continued to the end of the run? Were there any changes to the performance script during performance? Can you recall how these might have arisen and how the changes were effected?

BNíN. As I have said the dramatic process continued during the performance. It might be a different look, a bit of business, or a different way of playing a line that might prompt a different response. We made no changes to the performance script, as that would confuse the technical staff and indeed the other actors. Within our framework there was a discipline and a precision but we were also aware of keeping the work fresh and vital.

MK. Bearing this in mind, do you think it is possible to say that there is a different relationship between audience and actor in the context of this kind of work?

BNíN. Yes, I think that there is a different relationship between audience and actor in the context of this type of work. We felt that our audiences were at times very hostile. We had walkouts in the Peacock during the run of *The Great Hunger* and *Rise Up Lovely Sweeney*. People said that they did not understand what was going on, and yet when we played it in a cowshed in Annaghmakerrig the locals understood every nuance of the piece. What was very interesting, though, was that audiences were never bored. There was frustration, anger and confusion, but never boredom.

MK. Do you think Mac Intyre's immersion in the Irish language feeds into his dramatic work in English?

BNíN. Tom Mac Intyre's relationship with the Irish language is a very healthy one. He is respectful of it but not precious about it. This can be seen in his adaptations of *Caoineadh Airt Uí Laoghaire* and *Cúirt an Mheán Oíche*. He was aware of my ability to speak the language and he used that to incorporate into the work. For example the use of the word 'Féirín' in *Rise Up Lovely Sweeney*.

MK. Can you say a little about how you arrived at your performance of Mary Anne?

BNíN. This is a difficult question for me as an actor as I do not like to analyze that mental, physical or emotional process. I was very aware of the fact that Mary Anne was much older than I was at the time so that presented a challenge in itself. I didn't want to use make up and I wouldn't have had time anyway because I was also playing a village girl in a later scene. In rehearsals I was encouraged by Patrick to produce everything good and bad and as the weeks went on I began to strip away the excesses until I could visualize her. I tried to keep the physical side simple so that I could place more emphasis on her inner side.

MK. In *Rise Up Lovely Sweeney* and *Dance for your Daddy* you played more than one role. What was the experience of embodying several different characters and what challenges did this present to you as an actor?

BNíN. Playing different characters didn't present any problems for me. All of our exercises and our improvisations involved different characters in different situations. In fact I found it a welcome relief in *The Great Hunger*. You have to remember that as an actor you must be prepared for all eventualities in a Mac Intyre play!

MK. Mac Intyre's plays are visually rich yet intensely poetic. Gesture, movement of the body and stage image are prominent features and each and every word delivered by the actor is carefully scripted by the dramatist. Can you describe how the combination of movement and text was dealt with in rehearsal? Were there any specific views on whether the word prompted movement or vice versa? I'm asking this question with specific reference to Mac Intyre's influences (Pina Bausch, Grotowski, Meyerhold and so on) and the range of skills amongst the ensemble group.

BNíN. Tom was always interested in a form of theatre that could express an emotional charge through physical activity. I remember asking him about a particular scene in *The Great Hunger;* his reply was, 'to pitch it somewhere between the enigmatic and the quotidian'. There were constant shifts between movement and text but in a subconscious way.

MK. How would you say that Mac Intyre's work has influenced you as an actor?

BNíN. Being part of a group of actors that I admired in a close relationship with a playwright who was not afraid of pushing the boundaries, challenging theatrical conventions, marrying opposites and breaking rules was very exiting for me as an actor. I learnt so much from that experience – not to be afraid to take risks as an actor, not to stand still and, to trust your inner voice.

The Lunatics in the Basement: Madness in Mac Intyre

Dermod Moore

My body still resonates with the sounds and sensations of my Mac Intyre years. A clench of the gut, a raising of the hackles, goosebumps. A physical ache, an infinite sadness. A sick, youthful attraction to pain, to loss, the giddy foolish exhilaration of rushing in where angels fear to tread. The cost of putting Shadow on stage, the only safe space for it to be. Or, perhaps, merely the safest. The endorphin rush after a marathon of physical and emotional catharsis, night after night. We waltzed on the edge of sanity, on an iceshelf shifting and tilting under our feet, slippery, the black magic waters of the cold and empty bog lapping against our toes. Disturbing. Inviting.

Pagan, animal ecstasy, the body stretched beyond its limits. My first outing in those Mac Intyre-Mason-Hickey plays of the 1980s, fresh out of drama school, completely at sea: I'm a Houyhnhnm, one of Swift's imagined races, in *The Bearded Lady.* Sleek lycra and bronze makeup transform us into highly-strung prize stallions, with alarming six-inch metallic hooves, on loan from the National's [Royal National Theatre London] production of *Equus.* Magnificent, fascist exemplars of reason, we stomp around on the terrifyingly steep

wooden rake, down to whinny and snort in unison at the intimidated
audience, and turn on a sixpence. Physically, the most taxing, precise
thing I've ever required my body to do, requiring every ounce of agility
and nimbleness I could muster. On opening night, the buckle snaps on
my hoof. Dressage curtailed, I shuffle off in panic: emergency repair,
no harm done, but never as sure-footed again. Cold sweat of pure
terror under the baking lights. They shoot horses, don't they?

⊰⊱⊰

We're rehearsing, off Talbot Street. Violence, destruction, pain.
Concrete floors, grimy windows, wire mesh, florescent hum. We're
workshopping, creating, inventing, collaborating to create a tortured
psychic landscape. Correction: to *recreate* it. This was 1985. People
were being regularly killed, tortured and disappeared on our poetic
little island.

Exercise: We're to play a scene as if we're specifically wounded,
secretly hurt, concealing, covering up. My wound, groin-located, does
not leave me afterwards. I'm in tears. Some wounds should never be
evoked, conjured up, wished into reality. They run too deep.

We watch, with horror, as Willie Kennedy sits on the ground and
meticulously mimes the construction of a bomb inside his skull.
Fiddly wires, twisted. Explosives packed. Detonator connected. Button
pushed. Head explodes, neck breaks, torso flops. Then, he sits up, a
clockwork mannequin. Repeats the procedure. *Exactly* as before. And
again. And again. And again.

The door bursts open, a little tyke storms in and with a passionate
swagger kills us all with his wooden stick of a machine gun, 'eh-eh-eh-
eh-eh-eh-eh!' he rattles, jeering at the playactors doing their
playactin'. Bang, bang, we're dead. We stand there, dumbfounded.
Poltergeists follow us. Synchronous, insistent, ghosts in the machine.
Headlines of insane violence assail us. Mysterious glitches in the
technical equipment. We're haunted.

We take a trip to the well. The healing well. You know. The *real*
one. Wet stone and incantations, damp jeans, a coke can relic. The
silence on the bus home afterwards.

The previews: The cast, having hurriedly stepped out of our rags,
tiptoes backstage and hunkers in the darkened wings, listening to the
audience vent their feelings about what they've just experienced to
Patrick Mason and Tom Mac Intyre, at their bravest. Their anger,
their shock, their dismay. One heavy silence is broken, electrifyingly,
by someone wailing at the chairs, the fucking *perfect* chairs, enamel-

chipped metal tubing and veneered oxblood hardboard, institutional totems. Designer Bronwen Casson's genius, experience and woundedness on display.

'We'll find you, because you want to be found!'[1] We're in the gantry, helicopters battering our ears from above, accelerating our heartbeats, searchlights probing the detritus below, yelling that inescapable truth. The safety curtain, the iron, cranks mechanically up. So opens another show, the lunatics in the basement doing our thing, again. Sweeney on the run, adrenaline-shocked, bursts from the floor. Ireland as madhouse. The hunt is on. *Rise Up, Lovely Sweeney.*

The late, lamented, Joan O'Hara, Nurse Ratched-like, grins with silvery braces on the TV screen, as she advocates on a loop the benefits of 'Happy Brain Chemicals'.

'The Tennessee Waltz'. That mournful genteel tune, an elegy to a lost *Radio Éireann* world. The melody wafts in, like the soundtrack to Blanche DuBois' fragile, crumpled psyche. The inhabitants of the madhouse wander on stage, clutching life-sized dummies for dear life, rocking back and forth, the Largactil shuffle. My damp cheek presses to a battered foam-filled chest, a cold-comfort blanket, desperate for a heart-beat, for life, for love. The song ends. We slip behind the doors of the white-tiled box of a set, and shut them silently behind us. Our dancing partners are unceremoniously piled backstage, a heap of canvas corpses, our alter-egos. We run around and take our places for the next scene. But, every night, I leave something behind with mine, in him, on him, in the dark. Every night.

Bríd Ní Neachtain: 'Ashamed! Ashamed! Ashamed!'[2] she roars, broken, defiant, tormented. And shame, her shame, my shame, our shame, seeps down to the auditorium, that toxic black ooze.

⋖⋗⋖⋗⋖⋗

The Great Hunger: Benjamin Britten's *Sanctus* from the *War Requiem*, the triumphant soundtrack to our elevation of the Madonna, Mother, the turf-brown tyrant, over our heads. I can't hear it now without a thrill, as the trumpeting climax is reached – joy unleashed like no other, lepping as high as I've ever lepped. Animals, again: birds, screeching. Nightmare cattle, stampeding, invading. As a gurning adolescent acolyte, overtaken by the surge of my rising sap, I freeze one night, as the audience revolts. *Opus Dei* members, stand up, bear dignified witness to our sacrilege, the mocking of the Mass, and leave the house.

Then, we go on tour, across the world, our insanity on display for all to see, *that* dirty laundry. The Moscow Art Theatre, the actor's Mecca. A bear-hatted Hajj in the snow. Perestroika. Gorbachev. Chekhov. Audiences laughing at the instant translation, before or after the line was delivered. The formal reverence of the Parisians, the giddiness of being the hot ticket at the Edinburgh Festival. The American audiences are insulted, affronted, disgusted at our refusal to give in one inch to American-Irish sentimentality or nostalgia – the brutality of the piece alienates, and, truth be told, we are misunderstood. The respect to us shown by the New York crew, who believe us to be world-class in our professionalism and dedication. Despite Hickey and I becoming ill, we do not miss a night. I am brought to a Manhattan clinic, and all around me I see men dying with AIDS. We march in the St Patrick's Day Parade, and meet Mayor Koch. In London, we have an astonishing experience, more than once: we leave the stage to a desultory round of applause, which is followed by a weird silence – no one leaves their seat. Then, to goose-bumps, in our dressing rooms, we hear them start applauding again, having allowed the experience to sink in, and we come back, dazed and delighted, to take a last bow.

The most sacred performance of all: the staging of the piece in a cowshed in Annaghmakerrig, Co. Monaghan. The set was bare bones: the gate, the tabernacle, and, of course, The Mother. *The Great Hunger* came home, for two nights. The first night, for glitterati, came and went pleasurably enough, but the second night, for the locals, was the one we knew was the acid test. If there was one false note, one step too far straying from the spirit of Kavanagh's original piece, one fancy Jackeen pretension too far, they would be sure to let us know. As one, they all rose in tumultuous cheers at the end, instantly. I believe that we all had a profound sense that night that the characters we played were, indeed, well known in those parts. Rooted. Real.

ఆ్ఆ్ఆ్

Moving on: away from the muck, the dirt, the straitjackets, the bombs, to more contemporary craziness. The inspired absurdity of the cross-dressing tango in *Dance for your Daddy* – a crazy quick change backstage, we men slip into sequins, white gloves and high heels, the women await us in tuxedos, and before we know it we're being marched and thrown around by the women, to giddy delight. I am my alter ego, again. Another one.

I'm a cat in *Snow White*. The cat. The dancing cat. The cunt-struck cat. It seeps into my unconscious, like no other role. My most important dream, ever: I am searching for fish, the symbols of my Piscean self. I can't find them in the supermarket basement. I am sent out to a battered cage in the car park, and there's an old cat inside. *The* cat. My cat. There are no fish here, I complain, to the great big woman in white. She takes the cat and slices him in two, and in an instant the two halves become gleaming mackerel, diving and glittering in the sea. Being a cat is not for me. My last Mac Intyre play, my last true adventure as an actor.

⋘⋙

As long as I live, every cell in my body will remember one repeated moment, one repetitive, ritualistic dip into the Styx, one searing *pieta*, in which I played a part.

Under the spiral staircase going nowhere, towards the end of *Rise Up Lovely Sweeney,* in response to an intensely disturbed *cri de coeur* from me, Tom Hickey shoots me, repeatedly. Another needless casualty of war. Another young man lost. My limp body is gathered up in Hickey's arms, down centre stage, and he begins his aria, his lament, his exorcism of his beloved land. One of the greatest speeches I know, on woundedness. On Ireland.

> **SWEENEY.** My nation is Appalachia, Appalachia,
> worn rail of eye for hand, tooth
> for claw, scalp for cup and saucer,
> busted telly in the bog-hole,
> washing machine sneezing rust
> on the uninsurable bargain-line –
> listen for the wind
> through the nuts and bolts[3]

I have stilled my breath to near nothing. There is no air. I am beyond awareness, I enter some dissociated state. Hickey grieves over my corpse; I am pawed and wept over. Time and time again, that magic of theatre makes itself felt, when an actor and audience connect so fully that there is no room for anything but rapt, silent attention. *Awe.* There is no other word.

> **SWEENEY.** she's cratered, the scenic route,
> she's cratered, all the bridges
> smithereen'd – Christ I love this country...

And at that moment I feel something shift and melt, for the madness we've been portraying as actors is, indeed, done from love.

The grief we've been feeling is our own way of expressing the dementia of our troubled island, the hatreds and the losses and the endless cruel tit-for-tat rigmarole of death and destruction. *It did not make sense but it could not have made sense. It never did. It never does.*

> **SWEENEY.** I ask, why have they hidden trust?
> Where may I find it?
> White of an egg? The shoe-
> box smell? Under the ash-tray?
> You tell me.

Each night, in my coma, I do not know the answer to that question. I try to float above myself and Hickey, see what is happening, to see what the audience is seeing, to try to make sense of it. Each night, I lose sight of it. I knew the answer once. Didn't I? Am I not *supposed* to know? Who knows? Is Hickey asking *me*? No, Dermod, he's not. You are an actor in a play, and he is an actor speaking a poem over your dead body. You played dead before, didn't you, Romeo? It'll be over soon. Shower, fresh air, pints, home to bed. Someone to hold me alive, if I'm lucky. If I'm very lucky.

Someone hold me alive.

> **SWEENEY.** You do not perhaps
> credit the hurt mind?
> I remember one morning
> a disc in the sky
> Is that sun or moon?
> I can't tell sun from moon,
> can't tell sun from moon.

Works Cited

Mac Intyre, Tom, *Rise Up Lovely Sweeney* (Rehearsal draft, 1985).
---, *I Bailed Out at Ardee*, (Dublin: Dedalus Press, 1987).

---

[1] Tom Mac Intyre, *Rise Up Lovely Sweeney* Abbey Theatre prompt script, denoted by the author as Rehearsal Draft 2, September 1985 p. 3. All quotations in this essay are taken from this version of the play. References to this play will be incorporated with relevant page number in parenthesis in the text.

[2] Ibid. p. 73.

[3] Tom Mac Intyre 'The Hurt Mind, in *Rise Up Lovely Sweeney* (1985) pp. 88-90. Also published as 'Appalachia' in *I Bailed Out at Ardee*, (Dublin: Dedalus Press, 1987).

New Dimensions: Spaces for *Play* in *Rise Up Lovely Sweeney*

Marie Kelly

[With the kind permission of Tom Mac Intyre and the Abbey Theatre this illustrated article refers to examples from the working prompt script of the 1985 play *Rise Up Lovely Sweeney*.]

In Tom Mac Intyre's theatre the playwright is the catalyst of the activity of *play*. '[T]he challenge for the writer now,' he says, 'is to somehow get into that space where the magic of *play* is readily accessible [my italics]'.[1] From writing to rehearsing and right through into the run of performances, Mac Intyre cultivates a range of spaces for *play* to be shared by artist and audience alike. His text is never set in stone, but rather a blueprint for *play*-making; the rehearsal room, a dynamic *play*ground of exploration and experimentation; the staged performance, a shared space for creative *play* between actors and audience alike. This interest in theatre as a space for *play* came from a seminar Mac Intyre attended in Kent State University in the mid-1970s where Grotowski talked about theatre and *play*. He recalls: 'We speak of going to a *play*, never lose sight of a *play*, never lose sight of the noun to *play*, to *play*, to *play*' [my italics].[2]

At home Mac Intyre's main influences come from the symbolism, dream states and physicality of W.B. Yeats and the high theatricality of George Fitzmaurice. Further afield his interests lie in the choreography of modern dance and dance theatre, in particular the work of Pina Bausch. Influences also come from modern theatre practices (most notably Antonin Artaud, Jerzy Grotowski, Vsevolod Meyerhold, Peter Brook, and Tadeusz Kantor) as well as the cinema of, amongst others, Federico Fellini, Jean Cocteau, and Werner Herzog. With the insights of these artists and practitioners under his belt in the late 1970s, Mac Intyre began to play with stage image and gesture, and to test new ways of working against the conventions of linear narrative and mimetic representation. Some of the most ground-breaking moments of his dramatic work occurred in the 1980s during a period of close collaboration or intense creative play with the director Patrick

Mason, actor Tom Hickey, designer Bronwen Casson and a variety of other theatre artists[3] at the Peacock Theatre.[4] The group staged five new plays between 1983 and 1988, the most acclaimed and well documented of which is Mac Intyre's well-known stage version of Patrick Kavanagh's *The Great Hunger*.[5]

Up to now, however, much of the literature on Irish theatre tends to focus on *The Great Hunger* and overlooks the four other plays staged by the company in this period: *The Bearded Lady* (1984), *Rise Up Lovely Sweeney* (1985), *Dance for your Daddy* (1987) and *Snow White* (1988). These plays were not revived and remain unpublished and largely undocumented, yet their significance in the development of Mac Intyre's unique theatrical idiom and in the Irish theatrical canon should not be underestimated.

This article will attempt to redress this gap in the literature by exploring *Rise Up Lovely Sweeney* (1985) and the way in which this *play* aspect of Mac Intyre's work permeates everything from the overall concept, to content, into all stages of the theatre process and performance and involves theatre artist (playwright, actor, designer, director) and audience in equal measure. The discussion will be structured around Mac Intyre's various spaces for play beginning with the writer's concept and then moving into the casting of the actor, scenic design, language and, finally, the movement of the body on stage.

The article is compiled from a larger piece of post-graduate research conducted in 2004/2005 at The School of English, Drama and Film, University College Dublin, which involved the analysis of a production prompt script and VHS recording of the play made during its run at the Peacock Theatre in 1985.[6] Both prompt script and VHS recording are held on file at the Abbey Theatre's archive. The VHS recording was filmed from the control room at the rear of the Peacock's auditorium and, while the quality of this recording is poor at times, most of the performance is captured intact. The prompt script is a different matter entirely, however. Held together in a ring-bound booklet, or folder, this text was originally the author's second typed rehearsal draft of the play. It became the theatre's 'prompt script' once stage management had inserted their own handwritten notes and any other amendments implemented during rehearsals and in performance. These notes include a variety of cues; or the sequence of various components of the performance (stage action, lighting changes, sounds, entrances, exits etc).[7]

The stage manager's notes are lengthy at times, evidence of frequent alterations made to the piece during rehearsals as well as highly complex and often simultaneous stage action. To accommodate these notes many additional handwritten pages have been inserted into the prompt script by stage management. Many of these are unnumbered and pasted into the prompt script on the flipside of the preceding page so that the dialogue and notes appear together on opposite sides of the book. On occasion sections of text have been cut from one part of the play and either sticky-taped over another or inserted on separate pages without adjusting page numbers. Pages are periodically out of sequence and there are instances where completely new sections of text have been inserted into the script on separate pages and in a different typeface. This is a clear example of the writer and ensemble company working on the hoof, producing new elements of dialogue when necessary in rehearsal.

The prompt script also provides evidence of the extent to which the text was played with beyond the rehearsal process. The script shows a range of changes made to the text during the run of performance. On page thirty-three, for instance, stage management make a note that Sweeney's line, 'The heart's needle is an only daughter' was dropped from the performance on 23 September 1985 and reinstated on September 26. On page seventy-seven, meanwhile, the line 'Jesus stabs Ireland in the epididymal canal' is crossed out on 12 September and amended in handwriting to read, 'Jesus stabs Ireland in the North, South, and South, South East by South'.

The prompt script in its original form as the rehearsal draft of the play has a structure of sixteen scenes over two acts. Each scene is provided with a number and a title determining the main action to take place: Scene 1, for instance, is called 'The Freak Out', scene 2, 'The Casualties' and so on. In the performance, however, it is difficult to distinguish any division between scenes as the action overlaps completely from one scene to the other. A comparison between prompt script and performance also shows that an entire scene, 'Scene 9: The Whipping' has been cut from the end of the first act with the interval taking place after the eighth scene and not the ninth as set out in Mac Intyre's rehearsal draft. The performance, therefore, has fifteen scenes and not sixteen as originally envisaged by the playwright. Elements of this cut scene, meanwhile, have been implemented elsewhere in the performance of the play.[8]

The exceptional number of alterations and notes to the text as well as problems with page sequencing, however, make it difficult, if not impossible, to read and analyze the text as it exists in prompt script form. Figs 4.1 -4.2 illustrate the condition of the script and how these notes were recorded. A detailed record of the performance through viewing of the video recording had to be made and then compared with the text before any form of analysis could begin.

This methodological process, however, has proved to be an invaluable exercise in reclaiming an otherwise overlooked but extraordinarily rich part of Irish theatre history. *Rise Up Lovely Sweeney* marks the point at which Mac Intyre, Mason, Hickey and the ensemble group of the 1980s had really found their feet with their new idiom, when they could test this way of working to its absolute limit. Thus, this production represents a key moment in the development of Mac Intyre's repertoire and in the Irish canon as a whole. It is a privilege to interact with this kind of material, to be in a position to document the development of the work and to experience – even at second remove – this strange yet wonderful performance which, even by today's standards, challenges all sorts of theatre conventions. Even from a poor quality production video and sometimes illegible script the impact of this performance is extremely powerful. It is important to say, however, that the commentary provided in this article does not intend to speak for audiences of the play during its 1985 run of play, but to provide my own personal response to the material available to me.

Mac Intyre's theatre work began in a period of renaissance in philosophical thinking in Ireland with the subject of the 'Irish mind' at the centre of much debate. In the late 1970s and into the 1980s writers and artists tried to find new ways of expression during a time of heightened political crises and social uncertainty. As Terence Brown points out, 'the lack of a satisfactory, workable self-image after the economic and social change of the 1960s and 1970s had destroyed the once serviceable version of the national identity of Ireland as Gaelic, Catholic, and republican'.[9] In the late 1970s a 'fifth province' of mind was proposed by the literary journal, *The Crane Bag*. This 'fifth province'[10] was intended as an imaginary space, a no man's land, a neutral ground where things [could] detach themselves from all partisan and prejudiced connection.[11]

It is against this precise background that Mac Intyre developed his own language of the theatre and his most predominant theme of the 1980s, that of the 'hurt mind'. As a metaphor for a whole range of conflicting psychological states – suppressed sexuality, pain, joy, fear, bitterness, aggression, jealousy, regret[12] – the 'hurt mind' epitomizes the self, damaged by centuries of hostility, repression and war. *Rise Up Lovely Sweeney* is perhaps the most poignant example of this theme. The play is based on a twelfth-century text known as *Buile Suibhne* (or *The Frenzy of Sweeney*).[13] The folkloric character of Suibhne is the victim of religious conflict, a man in exile. Evicted from his land and cursed to a journey without rest, Suibhne is stricken by shame, homesickness and mistrust for others. Thus he takes off 'like any bird of the air, in madness and imbecility'.[14] In Mac Intyre's play the central character lives through much the same levels of hardship, mistrust, loneliness, and guilt as O'Keeffe's Suibhne. But Mac Intyre's Sweeney is an ex-IRA[15] man on the run, a metaphorical simulation of the contemporary Irish male psyche damaged by a history of violence and repression.

The play's opening stage direction reveals the author's intentions:

> Rise Up Lovely Sweeney *conceives of Sweeney as an avatar of eternal Irish troubles. Sweeney is warrior, he's on the run, he's afflicted by a sense of grievance, the clinging flavour of defeat, remorse for violent deeds, desire for vengeance, fear of vengeance upon himself, death wishes. Domestic hankerings intrude. And his tie to the land, motherland, is symbiotic.*

> *For theatrical impact, the events have been given a twentieth-century nightmare context.* Rise Up Lovely Sweeney *aims to disturb/entertain the viewer by way of pictorial reflections on tribal violence, violence as old as the hills – and fresh as dung.*[16]

Like other major writers who revived the character of Sweeney – Seamus Heaney, T.S. Eliot, and Flann O'Brien to name but a few – Mac Intyre adopts stories and myths of the accepted past as a means of dealing with highly charged contemporary issues.[17] In framing the dramatic work around such stories, myths and characters, Mac Intyre relies on an audience who come to the theatre with a particular story, or even the residue of that story or archetype already existing in their own minds. He is then free to concentrate on the staging of experience rather than a rigidly structured linear narrative. By digging into the audience's store of stories of the past, however, Mac Intyre calls on the psychological power of myth, a power endemic to that of narrative, fairytale and creative play.

According to Richard Courtney in his book, *Play, Drama and Thought*, myth and fairytale offer a space for creative play by providing archetypal situations where the individual can confront anxieties and fears from the safe perspective of the story form.[18] In this sense, it is possible to consider the audience's experience of Sweeney as a process of coming to terms with some of the most sensitive aspects of their own lived experience. In his choice of mythological figure, therefore, Mac Intyre creates a space for play. The Sweeney myth provides a safe distance between implied events on stage and that of the audience's world. At the same time, however, the audience is sufficiently close to the performance to experience at first hand the character's disturbed state of mind, perhaps as an aspect of their own state of mind.

In this regard, the casting of Tom Hickey in the role of Sweeney was of extreme importance. In the mid 1980s Tom Hickey's enactment of the role of 'Benjy', the male lead in the popular Irish television soap opera, *The Riordans*, was still fresh in the minds of Irish theatre audiences. *The Riordans* was broadcast once weekly on RTÉ for fourteen years between 1965 and 1979 and is described by a recent newspaper columnist as having 'dominated Irish life like no other TV drama before or since'.[19] The serial, set on a farm in the midlands, captivated audiences with 'controversial moral and social issues' of the period: divorce, contraception, and illegitimacy.[20] It challenged De Valera's romanticized view of rural life by bringing modern concerns into the everyday world of the Riordan family. At the centre of this Benjy represented a young, modern, educated, rural man, up to date with the latest agricultural developments and embracing the onset of a sexual revolution taking place around him. 'In the case of Benjy' says Luke Gibbons, 'the mothers of Ireland have to some extent looked on him as a foster-son. And like Mary [Riordan], they think nobody is good enough for him'.[21] As a consequence, Tom Hickey was probably the most high profile Irish actor working on the stage in Ireland, recognized everywhere he went as Benjy Riordan'.[22] Hickey acts, in this respect, as the simulacrum of the rural Irish man and, just as his casting was central to the realization of Maguire in *The Great Hunger*, Hickey's playing of Sweeney is key to the representation of masculinity in *Rise Up Lovely Sweeney*.[23] In other words, Hickey's previous work as an actor, both on TV and on stage in *The Great Hunger*, had a significant impact on Sweeney's identity as a character for at least a large proportion of the 1985 Peacock Theatre audience.

Before setting foot on the stage, the identity of Mac Intyre's Sweeney is already proportionally determined through the casting of the actor. As such, this character comes closest to full realization when he is perceived by the individual spectator and that individual spectator's knowledge and experience of Maguire and Benjy Riordan aka Tom Hickey. But who exactly is this Sweeney on the stage? Tom Hickey is not entirely Sweeney, he is an actor playing Sweeney. At the same time, Sweeney is not entirely Tom Hickey, he is a fictional character enacted by the performer. More precisely, Hickey as an actor playing Sweeney operates as a double negative: he is not not Sweeney, and Sweeney is not not Hickey.[24] The character's existence, then, is perhaps more virtual and open-ended than that of the text in *Death of the Author* because the fictitious theatrical character can never solely belong to the actor, audience or playwright.[25] It is only the individual actor's enactment that brings a given character to life, and that enactment can never be the same or repeated in exactly the same manner in each consecutive performance. In this regard, Sweeney, like any other character in a play, does not concretely exist in the text, rehearsal room, nor on the stage, but floats ephemerally in the imagination of the playwright, actor and spectator and is best described as just one instrument of play shared among many in the theatre space. As a consequence of this Sweeney is most appropriately described as sign, symbol, metaphor and subjective 'experience' all in one.

In the opening moments of *Rise Up Lovely Sweeney* the audience firstly experiences what it is like to be in Sweeney's nightmare and co-creates that same nightmare via the imagination. To this extent, the stage space resembles Nietzsche's 'mobile army of metaphors,'[26] a wide range of locations that can only fully exist in the imagination of the spectator through abstract association between signifiers and signifieds. As a response to the impossibility of the true horrors of the 'hurt mind', the metaphorical, the 'proposed conditional' or the 'what if' provide the only truth that can reasonably exist in the context of Mac Intyre's theme.

The stage space is deliberately designed as a site of several simultaneous universes: the literal and the metaphoric, the real, the liminal, the conscious and unconscious. The prompt script shows that Mac Intyre has a very specific vision in terms of how the stage will look. A stage direction in scene 1, 'The Freak Out' reads,

> Lights up on space. It's bare, just a few objects to be seen. A fridge (down right, say), a small white box (shoe-box size) prominently positioned in the same zone. Elsewhere, a television set and a tape-recorder. Upstage mid, a spiral staircase that leads nowhere. On the bare back wall, daubed in huge letters, UP DOWN WHATEVER. Also on the back wall, a metal stairway, rickety fire-escape style ... And it does lead somewhere (Act 1, scene 1, unnumbered page).

The video recording verifies that several of these ideas were fully realized in performance. The playing area has been stripped back to the outer theatre walls and then covered in grubby off-white functional tiles. There is a ladder up against the back wall stage right. A bulky 1950s style refrigerator stands downstage left while a television is placed downstage right. The spiral staircase which leads to nowhere provides a focal point centre stage. The disparity between text and video recording indicates the subsequent design choices of institutional tiling along the wall surfaces and replacement of the 'metal stairway' with a more simple ladder. The absence of the small white box, the tape-recorder, and the words 'UP DOWN WHATEVER' across the back wall, meanwhile, signify some of the writer's ideas that have been discarded altogether or used elsewhere in the play (Act 1, scene 1, unnumbered page).

A comparison between prompt script and performance provides a taste of the depth of Mac Intyre's vision in relation to the images created on stage. It also exposes developments during the design process and provides evidence of the way in which the group played around with ideas in creating the visual aspects of Sweeney's world. The full extent of this vision and the divergence between text and performance, and therefore the extent to which that text was played with in rehearsal and beyond, becomes even more apparent as the action of the play begins.

The video recording shows that the stage is in complete darkness in the opening moments. The sound of helicopters and walkie-talkies reverberate overhead. Under dim lighting, dark shadowy figures can be seen scurrying over and back across the space, trampling on crumpled up newspapers strewn around the floor area. The sound is like autumn leaves crunching underfoot. An explosion of images and sounds fills the stage: Distorted voices shout, 'We'll find you [...] Because you want to be found'(1), dogs growl and bark. There are two gunshots, feathers float downwards, but there is no sign of the kill. A door slams somewhere off-stage and footsteps walk away into the distance. A male figure, The Interrogator, comes on with two actors on all-fours playing sniffer dogs. On the TV monitor a 'wanted' photo of Sweeney flashes up while torches shine down on the action below. From under a pile of crumpled newspapers Sweeney pops up like a jack-in-the-box. He roots around beneath the newspapers and pulls out an armalite gun.[27] In the background children's voices sing the playground song, 'The Big Ship Sails on the Alley Alley O'.[28]

In the design of setting, choice of objects, and in the action of the opening moments the stage space may be regarded as the site of both interior and exterior which co-exist in the realm of Sweeney's unconscious mind. The tiled walls and the slamming of the door in the distance give the impression of an asylum or prison cell, yet the activity and sounds onstage suggest woodland, playground or a more open space. The fridge symbolizes the feminine and the domestic; the TV, the public and patriarchal. The spiral staircase flanked by these two objects symbolizes Sweeney's eternal flight between inside and outside, consciousness and the unconscious.

The atmosphere onstage, meanwhile, is oppressive, threatening, and surreal. There is a stark contrast between the playfulness of Sweeney's sudden appearance from beneath the scattered newspapers, the innocence of the schoolyard song, and his brandishing of the gun. These absurdly contrasting elements of the opening moments bring the performance into a kind of *dark play* where the harmless or innocent co-exists with the sinister and destructive.[29]

In the liminality of the auditorium, meanwhile, the mind is free to imagine and to explore a range of possibilities. The more invested the performance is in the 'metaphorical' the more the audience must submit to another reality or another consciousness, becoming complicit in the fiction performed onstage. In other words, the predominance of theatrical metaphor forces the spectator towards what Bert O. States describes as a 'transaction between consciousness and thickness of existence'.[30] The woodland or asylum is 'sensed' and 'felt' before it is fully realized in the imagination. The lack of a fixed location or meaning presents a space of endless possibility or play. In this sense, what Mac Intyre and his co-collaborators present on stage is primarily a theatre of experience and a virtual playground of continuous transformation.

As the prompt script shows, Mac Intyre has very precise ideas about stage design and the, but this is not always set in stone. The first paragraph of the opening stage direction reads, for instance:

> Din of battle, explosions, gun-fire, gashes of flame ... we glimpse Sweeney, armed ... we lose him, glimpse him again: He's calmly/inquisitively knocking on his left fist – as he might knock on a door – and the fist opens ... we lose him, we find him again: this time he's serenely ripping buttons from his jacket and throwing them away ... then we lose him (unnumbered page).

The initial stage direction is crossed out, however, in the prompt script. As outlined above and, according to the video and stage manager's cues, the stage is in complete darkness during the opening moments of the performance, Sweeney is hidden under the scattered newspapers at this stage and he does not appear until well after the entrance of the sniffer dogs. Sweeney's knocking gesture does not take place, meanwhile, at this point in the play but is taken from here and used later in scene 2.

Here Mac Intyre is the originator of the overall concept or rehearsal script. In the theatre-making process, however, aspects of that concept are played with until an agreed performance is settled upon. 'I have no possessiveness in reference to the text', Mac Intyre says, 'What we all wanted was what would work ... I slapped [the text] down and then it would be torn up, played with and put back together'. [31]

Moving through the prompt script, instances of alteration and change become more and more prolific. The rehearsal script also shows how Mac Intyre uses language and popular song as a means of accessing the unconscious and how play and collaboration facilitated this access.

In scene 7, entitled 'The Prison Hospital', Sweeney is subjected to a series of medical treatments. He is firstly forced into the space by a nurse pointing a torch. A second nurse, The Probationer, enters with a trolley and, in a rough manner, begins to apply a bandage to Sweeney's head, obscuring his face. A loofah is used, bubbles float in the air, but there is no sign of water. The language used by the The Nurse and The Probationer is comical, fragmented, and peppered with cliché and popular song:

NURSE. Appetite?
PROBATIONER. He'd ate the head of a horse, nurse –
NURSE. Pulse?
PROBATIONER. Ate a farmer's arse [through] a bush, nurse –
NURSE. <u>Pulse?</u>
PROBATIONER. Oh – hoppin' up and down like an egg in a [porringer], nurse –
NURSE. Stool?
PROBATIONER. Not a gig, nurse –
NURSE. Sleep?
PROBATIONER. Like a thrush, nurse –
NURSE. Thank *you* – (36-37).

The action surrounding this dialogue involves the blinded Sweeney being pushed around by the physically aggressive Nurse and Probationer who sings:

PROBATIONER. And she'll have fun, fun, fun / Till her daddy takes the t.bird away / And she'll cool her jets / Cool her jets / Cool her jets / When her daddy takes the t.bird away (35A).

Sweeney's reaction is to revert to infantile behaviour. He leaps up and down like a disturbed child while The Nurse and Probationer attack him with the loofah. Sweeney desperately pleads, 'I want to be the man with no skin' (35A), but this is completely ignored by The Nurse and Probationer, who goes up into the spiral staircase where she dangles her legs before the audience and loses herself in song and thought:

PROBATIONER. Eatin' another man's bread, climbin' another man's stairs (37A).

The combination of popular song and the unnatural language of the dialogue between The Nurse and The Probationer, together with their unconventional behaviour, contributes to a nightmarish atmosphere where the audience may imagine themselves inside Sweeney's fragmented and disconnected mind. The Probationer's rendition of the song lacks melody and rhythm, and her eerie toneless voice enhances this surreal atmosphere. All three appear to be submerged in their own thoughts, speaking at but not listening to each other. The powerful culmination of the action, in which all the characters dance together in the dimly lit stage to the song of 'Tennessee Waltz', unites sound, light, image, and movement in a space that is far from the natural. The Probationer dances with a trolley, a man in mourning dress dances with a coathanger on which a gossamer veil has been pinned, Sweeney waltzes with The Nurse but separates from her and embarks on a series of jerky frenzied movements.

Several sections of the original stage directions and text for this scene are shown in the prompt script as either having been removed completely or placed in an alternative sequence. One of the scored out sections includes a detailed description of three phases of action involving The Nurse and Sweeney squaring up to each other as if in battle and then turning away as if in terror. Phase One is reproduced here as an example:

Phase One

> SWEENEY *bowling along (play first time in slow or slowish motion?) sees coming towards him an evident mad one,* NURSE *in her best lunatic vein.* SWEENEY *scared, turns on his track, gets outa there, retreat, retreat* ...(40).

What looks like the word 'eating' is handwritten above the phrase 'bowling along' in the prompt script; an indication, perhaps, of the development of ideas surrounding Sweeney's action in the rehearsal room. A sound-track to accompany the action, originally using Sweeney's voice, is also amended on the same page with The Probationer's voice replacing Sweeney's. Again, this example shows how, through collaboration and play, the playwright's script is worked and reworked until a final performance is agreed upon. In this instance, several ideas have been worked through and then the material is abandoned altogether (see fig. 4.1).

If the stage provides a space in which the artist and audience co-create through the imagination, then the body of the actor reveals the performative nature of play. As he darts across the stage expelling energy through absurd movements Mac Intyre's Sweeney – as embodied by Tom Hickey – conveys an inability to curb spontaneous action. This Sweeney moves like a child who is deeply disturbed. At other times his gestures are slowly measured to the point of obsession.[32] This carefully choreographed physical action – which shifts from the wildly spontaneous to obsessively observant – mirrors a range of childish behaviours normally suppressed in the course of adulthood. Once again, this vulnerable out of control body is not just *any* body; but, to borrow Luke Gibbon's words, the infamous 'foster son' of 'the mothers of Ireland'. In this regard, the body on stage reveals what speech cannot. This is fertile ground in a play which seeks to dramatize the 'hurt mind'. It allows, in this context, for the staging of actions or situations that cannot be represented in any conventional sense, and where experimentation with absurdity and spontaneity can take place through playing with the human body in the safety of the theatre space.

By foregrounding image and gesture in *Rise Up Lovely Sweeney*, Mac Intyre writes both movement and verbal scores with the powerful impact of the visual ensuring that the verbal cannot dominate. In his theatre work Mac Intyre channels play towards the active, physical and visual where playing with the moving body means inventing new ways of approaching that body. Central to this objective is the body as used to arouse feeling rather than relay meaning.

Patrick Mason speaks of the way in which Mac Intyre's theatre of the 1980s created a theatrical language which brought its audiences, 'into another dimension'.[33] In cultivating an ethos of play Mac Intyre provided a means of accessing such a dimension, or another province of consciousness, which merged with his central theme of the 'hurt mind'. Sifting through the remnants of *Rise Up Lovely Sweeney* it is clear to see that at no point in the making, watching, or researching of this magical piece of theatre can anyone lose sight of Mac Intyre's mission to play, to play, to play … .

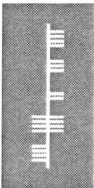

Research funded by The Irish Research Council for the Humanities and Social Sciences

IRCHSS

Works Cited

Anonymous, 'Get Up the Aisle There, Benjy' *The Sunday Tribune* 8 February 2009.

Barthes, Roland, 'The Death of the Author' in *Image, Music, Text: Essays Selected and Translated by Stephen Heath* (London: Fontana Press, 1977).

Brown, Terence, *Ireland: A Social and Cultural History* (London: Harper Perennial, 2004).

Chambers, Lilian, Ger FitzGibbon and Eamonn Jordan, eds, *Theatre Talk: Voices of Irish Theatre Practitioners* (Dublin: Carysfort Press, 2001).

Courtney, Richard, *Play, Drama and Thought* (London: Cassell & Collier MacMillan, 1968).

Gibbons, Luke, 'From Kitchen Sink to Soap: Drama and the Serial Form on Irish Television', *Transformations in Irish Culture* (Cork: Cork University Press, 1996), pp. 44-69.

Healy, Dermot, 'Rise Up Lovely Sweeney' Programme Note: *Rise Up Lovely Sweeney* (Abbey Theatre, 1985).

Healy, Dermot, 'The Hurt Mind' Programme Note: *The Great Hunger* (Abbey Theatre, 1986).

Heaney, Mick, 'Keeping Sight of his Goals' *The Sunday Times* (24 April 2005).

Hederman, Mark Patrick and Richard Kearney, eds, *The Crane Bag Book of Irish Studies* Vol. 1, 1977-1981 (Dublin: Blackwater Press, 1982).

Hickey, Tom 'A Farm Drama That Gripped The Nation' *The Irish Times* (7 February 2009).

Jung, Carl, *The Archetypes and the Collective Unconscious* 2nd edn (London and New York: Routledge, 1968).

Kelly, Marie, unpublished interview with Tom Mac Intyre (2005).

Mac Intyre, Tom, *Rise Up Lovely Sweeney* prompt script, denoted by the author as Rehearsal Draft 2 (Abbey Theatre, 1985).

Murray, Christopher, *Twentieth Century Irish Drama: Mirror Up To Nation* (UK: Cambridge University Press, 1998).

O'Keeffe, James, G., ed., (1913) *Buile Suibhne (The Frenzy of Suibhne) being The Adventures of Suibhne Geilt: A Middle Irish Romance* in School of Celtic Studies *DIAS* (1999). Accessed April 2004 http://www.celt.dias.ie/publications

Orlick, Terry, *Cooperative Games and Sports* (USA: Human Kinetics Publishers, 2006).

Schechner, Richard, *Performance Studies: An Introduction,* 2nd edn, (London: Routledge, 1996).

– *The Future of Ritual* (London and New York: Routledge, 1993).

Smith, Peter, K., and Helen Cowie eds, *Understanding Children's Development* (Oxford and Cambridge: Blackwell, 1988).

States, Bert O., 'The Phenomenological Attitude', Janelle G. Reinelt and Joseph R. Roche, *Critical Theory and Performance* (Revised edition) (Ann Arbor: University of Michigan Press, 2007).

Sweeney, Bernadette, *Performing the Body in Irish Theatre* (Basingstoke: Palgrave Macmillan, 2008) formerly *Wooden, Wounded, Defaced – Performing the Body in Irish Theatre 1983 – 1993* (Doctoral Thesis – The School of Drama, Trinity College Dublin, 2002).

Zarrilli, Phillip, *Acting (Re) Considered: Theories and Practices* (London and New York: Routledge, 1995).

Video Recording:

Rise Up Lovely Sweeney by Tom Mac Intyre (Peacock Theatre 1985) courtesy of the Abbey Theatre Archives.

---

[1] Tom Mac Intyre, 'Tom Mac Intyre in Conversation with Fiach Mac Conghail,' in *Theatre Talk: Voices of Irish Theatre Practitioners* eds. Lilian Chambers, Ger FitzGibbon and Eamonn Jordan (Dublin: Carysfort Press, 2001), p. 312.

[2] Tom Mac Intyre citing Grotowski in *Theatre Talk: Voices of Irish Theatre Practitioners*, p. 311.

[3] The main company of actors included: Michele Forbes, Tom Hickey, Conal Kearney, William Kennedy, Dermod Moore, Fiona Mac Anna, Bríd Ní Neachtain, Vincent O'Neill, Joan Sheehy, and Martina Stanley. A number of other actors joined the company at various stages during the five year period: Graham Boland, Catherine Byrne, Olwen Fouéré, Geoffrey Golden, Michael Grennell, Ciaran Grey, Sian Maguire, Joan O'Hara, SarahJane Scaife.

[4] Studio space of the Abbey Theatre (Ireland's national theatre).

[5] *The Great Hunger* was revived and toured nationally and internationally during this period.

[6] Marie Kelly 'Busted Telly in the Bog Hole' and 'Galactic Zippity-dooh-dah': Elements of Play in the Theatre of Tom Mac Intyre (MA Thesis: University College Dublin, 2005).

[7] The stage management team included Ailish McBride (Stage Director), John Kells (Stage Manager) and Linda Collins (Assistant Stage Manager).

[8] A section of dialogue, for instance, is taken from the main action of this ninth scene and used as an interview on the television monitor in 'Scene 7: The Prison Hospital'.

[9] Terence Brown, *Ireland: A Social and Cultural History* (London: Harper Perennial, 2004), p. 319.

[10] This 'fifth province' was later appropriated by Field Day Theatre Company, with the intention of providing new ways of 'looking at Ireland, or another possible Ireland – an Ireland that first must be articulated, spoken, written, painted, [or] sung' Brian Friel cited in Terence Brown *Ireland: A Social and Cultural History*, p. 349.

[11] Mark Patrick Hederman and Richard Kearney eds., *The Crane Bag Book of Irish Studies Vol. 1, 1977-1981* (Dublin: Blackwater Press, 1982), p. 3.

[12] Dermot Healy defines what this means: 'What is "the hurt mind?" It can be construed as National Paranoia. Words in capital letters that shouldn't be. Something emanating from people who conceptualise in one language and relinquish their ideas in another. Yet there is a certain satisfaction in that

back-log of bitterness; for everything is not as it appears. In the Aran Islands they say – "ta dearc im dearmad". There's hurt in my memory [...] for hurt mind you can also read "the joyous senses", or at another remove, "The Great Hunger"'. Abbey Theatre Programme Note 1986.

[13] Mac Intyre uses James G. O'Keeffe's 1913 edition of this twelfth century text.

[14] James, G. O'Keeffe ed., (1913) *Buile Suibhne (The Frenzy of Sweeney) being The Adventures of Suibhne Geilt: A Middle Irish Romance* in School of Celtic Studies DIAS (1999), p. 15. www.celt.dias.ie/publications accessed April 2004.

[15] The Provisional IRA (Irish Republican Army) stepped up violence against British military occupation in Northern Ireland from the late 1960s. The 1980s was a time of unprecedented violence with hundreds of soldiers and civilians being killed and injured on both sides of the divide.

[16] Tom Mac Intyre, *Rise Up Lovely Sweeney* Abbey Theatre prompt script, denoted by the author as Rehearsal Draft 2, September 1985 (Unnumbered page). All quotations in this essay are taken from this version of the play. References to this play will be incorporated with relevant page number in parenthesis in the text.

[17] I refer here to Seamus Heaney's *Sweeney Astray* (1983), Flann O'Brien's *At Swim-Two-Birds* (1939), T.S. Eliot's play *Sweeney Agonistes* (1932) and his poems, 'Sweeney among the Nightingales' and 'Sweeney Erect' (1920).

[18] Richard Courtney, *Play, Drama and Thought* (London: Cassell & Collier MacMillan, 1968), p. 75.

[19] Anonymous 'Get up the Aisle There, Benjy' *The Sunday Tribune* 8 February 2009.

[20] Luke Gibbons 'From Kitchen Sink to Soap: Drama and the Serial Form on Irish Television', *Transformations in Irish Culture* (Cork: Cork University Press, 1996), pp. 44-69.

[21] Ibid. p.61.

[22] 'My big problem' says Hickey, 'was simply getting down the street as I was recognised everywhere I went, so I developed a quick walk.' 'A Farm Drama that Gripped the Nation', *The Irish Times* (7 February 2009).

[23] It should be noted here, however, that Mac Intyre was not familiar himself with Tom Hickey's work prior to his initial casting in *The Great Hunger*, but Hickey had been working extensively at the Abbey Theatre and was well known to Patrick Mason who was Staff Director there and, indeed, Joe Dowling, the incumbent Artistic Director. Mac Intyre says, ' ... I was asking my friends: "Who in hell can I find, where do I get a company, where do we get a player to carry Paddy Maguire?" and everybody said, "There's only one player in Ireland to do that and it's Hickey." And I said, "Who's that now?" (because I had been living a lot abroad and on remote islands) and they said: "That's Tom Hickey – you've got to meet him".

Tom Mac Intyre in Conversation with Fiach Mac Conghail' in Lilian Chambers et al., p. 312.

[24] I am guided here by Richard Schechner who says, 'While performing, he [the performer] no longer has a "me" but a "not me," and this double negative relationship also shows how restored behaviour is simultaneously private and social. A person performing recovers his own self only by going out of himself and meeting others – by entering a social field. The way in which "me" and "not me," the performer and the thing to be performed, are transformed into "not me ... not not me" is through the workshop-rehearsal/ritual process'. Richard Schechner cited in Phillip Zarrilli, *Acting (Re) Considered: Theories and Practices* 2nd edn. (London and New York: Routledge, 1995), pp. 298-299.

[25] I refer here to Roland Barthes' assertion that 'a text is made of multiple writings, drawn from many cultures and entering into mutual relations of dialogue, parody, contestation, but there is one place where this multiplicity is focused and that place is the reader, not, as was hitherto said, the author. The reader is the *space* on which all the quotations that make up a writing are inscribed without any of them being lost; a text's unity lies not in its origin but in its destination.' Roland Barthes, 'The Death of the Author' in *Image, Music, Text: Essays Selected and Translated by Stephen Heath* (London: Fontana Press, 1977), pp. 147-153.

[26] Nietzsche called attention to the problem of claims of implicit truth in language by saying, 'What therefore is truth? A mobile army of metaphors, metonymies, anthromorphisms ... truth are illusions of which one has forgotten that they are illusions'. Friedrich Nietzsche cited in Phillip Zarrilli, p. 9.

[27] The 'armalite gun'; weapon synonymous with the IRA.

[28] This song derives from a nursery rhyme which traditionally accompanies a schoolyard game where children form a human chain. Terry Orlick *Cooperative Games and Sports* (USA: Human Kinetics Publishers, 2006), p. 63.

[29] This is *play* in Nietzschean terms as a 'coming-to-be and passing away, structuring and destroying, without moral additive, in forever equal innocence'. Friedrich Nietzsche *Philosophy in the Tragic Age of the Greeks* in Richard Schechner *Performance Studies: An Introduction* 2nd edn. (London: Routledge, 1996), p. 109.

[30] Bert O. States 'The Phenomenological Attitude' in Janelle G. Reinelt and Joseph R. Roche, *Critical Theory and Performance* (Revised edition) (Ann Arbor: University of Michigan Press, 2007), pp. 26-35.

[31] Tom Mac Intyre, interviewed by Marie Kelly, July 2005.

[32] This happens at the beginning of Scene 6 where Sweeney hops around like a madman in the company of The Interrogator and his sidekicks; and again later on in the same scene when Sweeney approaches the prison cell area of the set and slowly extends his right leg over the space as if avoiding an invisible obstruction.

---

[33] Patrick Mason cited in Bernadette Sweeney *Wooden, Wounded, Defaced – Performing the Body in Irish Theatre 1983 – 1993* (Doctoral Thesis – The School of Drama, Trinity College Dublin, 2002) p. 249. An expanded and revised version of this text was published as *Performing the Body in Irish Theatre* (Basingstoke: Palgrave Macmillan, 2008).

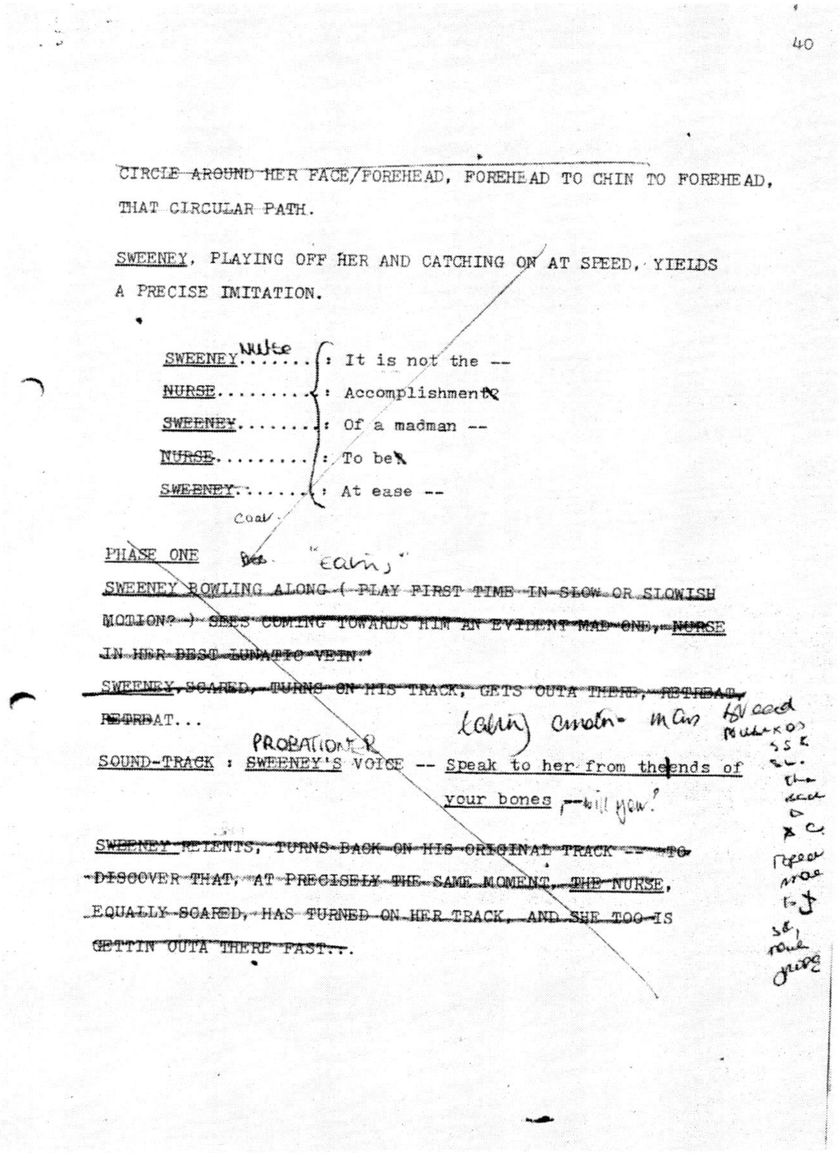

40

~~CIRCLE AROUND HER FACE/FOREHEAD~~, FOREHEAD TO CHIN TO FOREHEAD,

~~THAT CIRCULAR PATH.~~

SWEENEY, PLAYING OFF HER AND CATCHING ON AT SPEED, YIELDS A PRECISE IMITATION.

SWEENEY Nurse....... : It is not the --

NURSE......... : Accomplishment

SWEENEY....... : Of a madman --

NURSE......... : To be

SWEENEY....... : At ease --

PHASE ONE "Eating"

~~SWEENEY BOWLING ALONG (PLAY FIRST TIME IN SLOW OR SLOWISH MOTION?) SEES COMING TOWARDS HIM AN EVIDENT MAD ONE, NURSE IN HER BEST LUNATIC VEIN.~~

~~SWEENEY, SCARED, TURNS ON HIS TRACK, GETS OUTA THERE, RETREAT, RETREAT...~~

SOUND-TRACK : PROBATIONER SWEENEY'S VOICE -- Speak to her from the ends of your bones — will you?

~~SWEENEY RELENTS, TURNS BACK ON HIS ORIGINAL TRACK -- TO DISCOVER THAT, AT PRECISELY THE SAME MOMENT, THE NURSE, EQUALLY SCARED, HAS TURNED ON HER TRACK, AND SHE TOO IS GETTIN OUTA THERE FAST...~~

Fig 4.1 *Rise Up Lovely Sweeney:* prompt page 40. Courtesy of Tom Mac Intyre and the Abbey Theatre Archive.

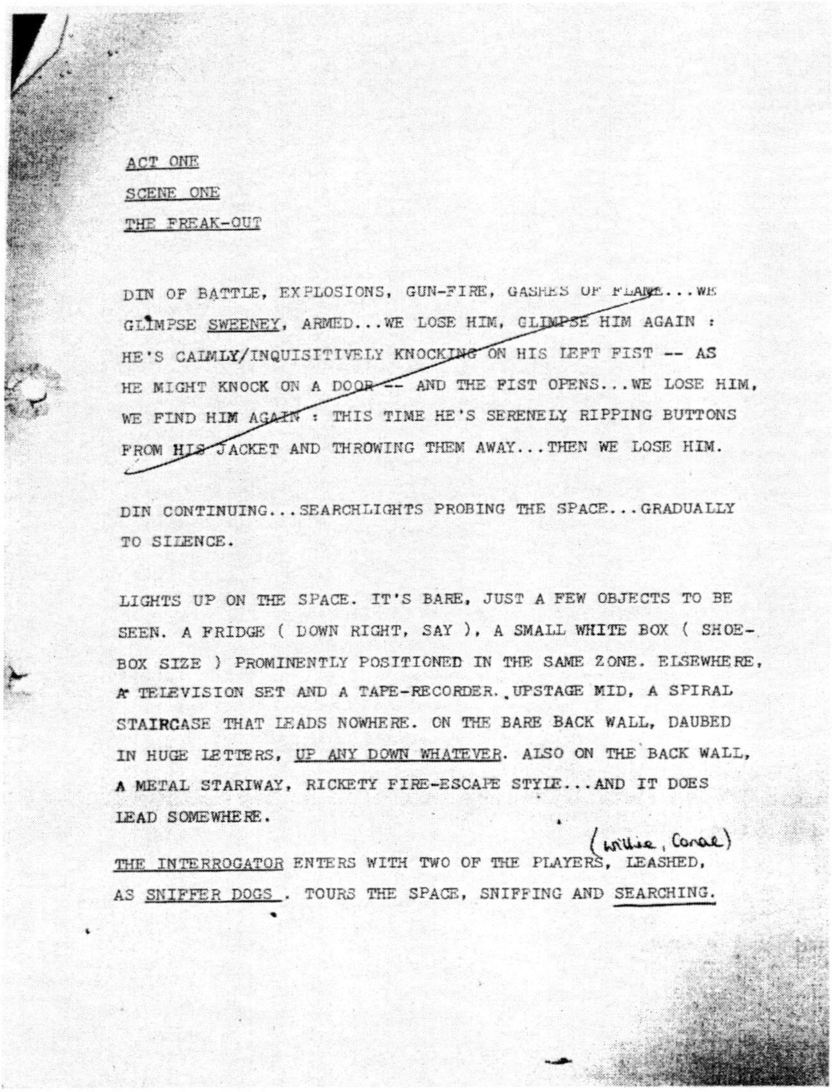

ACT ONE

SCENE ONE

THE FREAK-OUT

DIN OF BATTLE, EXPLOSIONS, GUN-FIRE, GASHES OF FLAME...WE
GLIMPSE SWEENEY, ARMED...WE LOSE HIM, GLIMPSE HIM AGAIN :
HE'S CALMLY/INQUISITIVELY KNOCKING ON HIS LEFT FIST -- AS
HE MIGHT KNOCK ON A DOOR -- AND THE FIST OPENS...WE LOSE HIM,
WE FIND HIM AGAIN : THIS TIME HE'S SERENELY RIPPING BUTTONS
FROM HIS JACKET AND THROWING THEM AWAY...THEN WE LOSE HIM.

DIN CONTINUING...SEARCHLIGHTS PROBING THE SPACE...GRADUALLY
TO SILENCE.

LIGHTS UP ON THE SPACE. IT'S BARE, JUST A FEW OBJECTS TO BE
SEEN. A FRIDGE (DOWN RIGHT, SAY), A SMALL WHITE BOX (SHOE-
BOX SIZE) PROMINENTLY POSITIONED IN THE SAME ZONE. ELSEWHERE,
A TELEVISION SET AND A TAPE-RECORDER. UPSTAGE MID, A SPIRAL
STAIRCASE THAT LEADS NOWHERE. ON THE BARE BACK WALL, DAUBED
IN HUGE LETTERS, UP ANY DOWN WHATEVER. ALSO ON THE BACK WALL,
A METAL STAIRWAY, RICKETY FIRE-ESCAPE STYLE...AND IT DOES
LEAD SOMEWHERE.

(willie, Conal)
THE INTERROGATOR ENTERS WITH TWO OF THE PLAYERS, LEASHED,
AS SNIFFER DOGS . TOURS THE SPACE, SNIFFING AND SEARCHING.

Fig 4.2 *Rise Up Lovely Sweeney:* unnumbered prompt page. Courtesy of Tom
Mac Intyre and the Abbey Theatre Archive.

Theatre Review: *Rise Up Lovely Sweeney* by Tom Mac Intyre

Fintan O'Toole
(*The Sunday Tribune*, 15 September 1985)

Out on the borderlines, the critic's simple distinctions between success and failure begin to break down. Half way through Tom Mac Intyre's new play at the Peacock, *Rise Up Lovely Sweeney*, you think: 'This is either great stuff or rubbish'. By the end, you begin to feel that it's both. There are plays that are born onto the stage like sparrows' eggs, small, neat, perfectly formed and delivered with a self-satisfied cheep. There are others that explode like volcanoes, releasing a blaze of fire and a few tons of rubbish. *Rise Up Lovely Sweeney* is one of these, a dangerous and enlightening play whose burning core is often obscured by seemingly arbitrary distractions. It is not easily judged or summed up, but it burns with an unmistakable integrity and attempts a voyage that few in the modern theatre would venture.

Tom Mac Intyre's theatre draws on two main sources in modern drama. The first is Beckett's economy of language, the whittling away of words until they approach, as nearly as possible, silence. Mac Intyre's continuation of Beckett's approach was brought to mind last week by the coincidence of Chris O'Neill's performance in Beckett's *Krapp's Last Tape* at the Gaiety Dress Circle Bar, an accurate and entertaining performance of the play.

As well as the economy of language, *Krapp's Last Tape* shares with *Rise Up Lovely Sweeney* the same sense of memory and regret, the same sense of isolation, the same pining for a lost woman and a similar use of the devices of modern technology as part of the action. And the second source of Mac Intyre's theatre is contemporary American theatre [and] dance, the trend towards a language of movement on the stage. In *Rise Up Lovely Sweeney*, these two impulses, the economy of verbal language and the use of a language of gesture and movement, seem to be working at times in opposite directions.

The irony of Mac Intyre's play, created with director Patrick Mason and actor Tom Hickey, is that while the dialogue uses words in a way which is as cryptic and as terse as a set of crossword clues, the visual language of movement and action is often profligate, arbitrary and anything but economical. While the words are precise and poetic, the visual images are jumbled and often incoherent, with a television screen competing for attention with the live action and a general air of fussiness preventing the formation of a single, stark image.

Again ironically, it is the narrative, the literal story of Sweeney rather than the images, which holds the piece together. The story of Sweeney, the king who is driven mad and turned into a bird-man for his transgression against a saint, has had a particular meaning for our century and we can see it now as a precursor of the many images of man turned into animal which occur in modern writing from Kafka to Neil Jordan. It is thus ideal for the conflation of history which Mac Intyre attempts, bringing together an ancient and modern consciousness.

Mac Intyre's Sweeney, played by Tom Hickey, is a modern man on the run, seeking forgiveness for his violent deeds, pining for the women from whom his madness has separated him, seeking solace in nature, trying to evade at once the embrace of a repressive stage and the embrace of a medicine that seeks, not to heal, but to control his madness.

The play's political resonances are all drawn from contemporary Northern Ireland, its nightmarish quality a deliberate reflection of Irish reality. That reality is defined in images of threatening authoritarian power and a pervasive media consumerism.

Tom Hickey's Sweeney, like his Gaelic original, is placed in a military society. The play opens to the sound of helicopters and the search of tracker dogs for the escaped man. There is a literal story of the chase, of the gradual intertwining of the hunted man and his interrogator, played by Vincent O'Neill, until Sweeney becomes his own interrogator, questioning himself from the television screen.

But there is also a symbolic story, as Sweeney becomes a kind of representative historical Irishman, asking the question which the first stage Irishman (In Shakespeare's *Henry V*) asks: 'What is my nation?', seeking that elusive identity and finding an answer only in the whirl of history and nature: 'My nation is the howl, some say the whinge, I say the howl, but not the black howl'.

This story is told essentially through words, both in English and in Irish, and through the interplay of Hickey and O'Neill, who represent two faces of madness. Hickey's madness is shameless, calling out and crumpling up in pain and anger. O'Neill's is the madness of official terror, cold, sharp and blind as a knife.

The verbal images work cumulatively, by repetition, becoming clearer and more potent as they reach towards the end, taking on new meanings and deeper echoes. The visual images, on the other hand, largely fail to establish any kind of cumulative coherence, working on a hit-and-miss basis and often missing. The most potent visual images are the ones which are allowed to develop without the bombardment of the eyes and ears: the eating of watercress, the drinking of milk, the simple gestures between lovers. Too often, however, there is a sense of mere bustle, of actors and actions doing nothing other than adding to the impenetrability.

That so much integrity should survive the seemingly arbitrary and indulgent play of some of the action is a mark of the seriousness and courage that lie at the heart of the piece. *Rise Up Lovely Sweeney* builds up to a shattering climax of images that represents a moment of extraordinary theatrical poetry. By laying bare a sickness in the Irish mind, a condition of schizophrenia and deep disturbance, Mac Intyre, Mason and Hickey have made it possible to touch on a nerve that is still raw, as they do at the end of this play. What they touch is a longing for wholeness and forgiveness. *Rise Up Lovely Sweeney* ultimately manages to suggest that, to lay aside the confusions it has created and to reach some kind of clarity. For that it is worth sticking with.

Programme Note: *Dance for your Daddy* by Tom Mac Intyre

(Peacock Theatre, February 1987)
'Must you play the piano in your nightgown?'

Dermot Healy

The usual story concerns the Mother and the Son. If there is a dance there at all, it might be the Old Time Waltz. In that relationship, it is deemed appropriate to see her as domineering, him as pathetic. But in the other relationship – that between the Daughter and the Daddy, the dance has speeded up. In the play tonight, sometimes it's the Tango. And the relationship is fraught with unspeakable and ambivalent tensions. It is right therefore that the group which has given us such memorable theatre as *The Great Hunger*, where the mother is immobilized into a wooden effigy, should turn their attention towards this dangerous pairing of male and female, where, by virtue of the family's social traditions, the male would appear to have the custodial position, and the female, the more passive role.

But Mac Intyre, always on the look out for a new way home, has other, more subversive routes at hand. First, to avoid any puritanical or declarative approach, the playwright has chosen to present the clash mainly through the medium of cartoon. Each page of the script contains variations on the sexes' stock responses to each other. Here it is the machismo and the exhibitionist are being lampooned, there the vulnerable and those in need of minding are being gently gratified. On the first page Daddy is described as being 'the very picture of stricken tolerance'. But Daughter is gay and impulsive. While he keeps all Romeos at bay, daughters mock him endlessly. He is a cheerful old cod, constantly harping on, forgetting himself, then switching to the maimed, the overwrought.

To keep pace with his daughter he will have to undergo gender reversals, become the dirty old man, find that he is an inveterate ass-patter. He becomes all that the female abhors in the male, yet blunders on, resignedly, and not without panache. Even when his very private sexual fantasies are being aired, he stands aloof, keeping his bad ear in the direction of any notion of blame. Sometimes quiet familial scenes ensue. There is touching, understanding, but you know it can't last.

For one day his daughter will be leaving him. And so before she goes, could she dance, just the once, please? But daughter has a variety of tests and puzzles and games ready for her father, which he must first fathom. Daddy has to be constantly mollified, and daughter does sometimes stand up for him, and even play with him. There are set rituals they both go through. 'Loving father and daughter' is one of their cameos. As is the exchange of goodbyes in a number of languages. They even go parading at restaurants and race-courses. But the haste grows. The liaisons become more frantic. She is leaving him, and he is sorely tried.

This then is the general theme. Much is presented in terms of body language. The actors are involved in showing us the various ways of doing things. Of kissing. Walking. Dancing. Everyone is on display. One odd partial personality they may select, hold it, drop it, pass on. Rather than seeking to enter character, they will be involved in trying to release themselves from the constraints of character, and yet remain instantly recognisable. This is the medium. The attempt is to get beyond sexual prejudice, yet without dispensing with all those games the sexes play, for they are the life blood coursing between those intimates, Daddy and Daughter, and are their secret assertion against the roles society has made for them.

Sometimes we are at toilet, sometimes in an office. Father has his set of conspirators, *Homme Fatal*, *Romeo* and *Hubby*. Daughter has the *Dark Daughter*, the *Girl Child* and *The Wife*. But none of these are true types. They are possibilities. Try-outs. Though in time it is the women who prove victorious, the men, though perturbed and confused as the ground is swept away from beneath them, are not without a certain vexed dignity. It is in the Daughter's favour that she is generous in victory. And in the Daddy's favour that he partnered her in the dance, and did not remain only as voyeur.

The dialogue, as in previous productions, can be both haphazard and finely wrought. The Irish language is for recrimination and love-making. The French for classical lover's aside. Proper English endorses the whimsical and lofty fraternal. Clipped dialogue catches the ritual games. But again, as in Mac Intyre's *Rise Up Lovely Sweeney*, certain lucid speeches point towards the kernel of grief that hovers in the background ...

> **DAUGHTER.** I'm ready for three kinds of tears, three kinds there, and I have to be ... I'm ready for the ice tears, the ones that freeze as they fall, they're the hard cold tears, I know, I know.

It is a play this group will revel in, stepping lightly from enchantment to despair, the bestial to the tender, laughing as they frighten themselves. The test they've undertaken is not to shun the exotic in the everyday. Their means are sense of touch, cartoon humour, and such words as have been tried over and over till they re-echo with a multiplicity of meanings. Where Daddy and Daughter will go from here is not known. It is always a gamble. It is just as difficult to leave the family as to stay. But something has to give way before long.

Theatre Review: *Dance for your Daddy*
by Tom Mac Intyre

David Nowlan
(*The Irish Times*, 3 March 1987)

Dance for your Daddy which opened in the Peacock Theatre in Dublin last night, is the most ambitious and the most accomplished work yet from the team which started out a few years ago with *The Great Hunger*. To Tom Mac Intyre (author), Patrick Mason (director), Bronwen Casson (designer) and a company of players who can combine thought, utterance, movement and conjoint imaginations into a vision of the world as she is, congratulations are the order of the night.

Here is high comedy, base terror and mundane reality mixed into a kind of theatrical cartoon strip of a father's relationship with daughter and, by extrapolation, man's relationship with woman.

Those who would pause during the performance to try to understand consciously what is before them will be lost. This is one of those theatrical occasions when only the eyes and the ears should be open so that the sights and the sounds can be allowed to impinge, *sans censor*, on the mind and the feelings. Each person will come out with different perceptions of what the entertainment was about; and it is, above all, a dazzling entertainment.

It is a succession of fleeting images. Father is distracted from contact with daughter by pressure of business or recreation. Father is distracted from concern for daughter by recreational proclivities, only to be awoken to possessive jealousy by precisely those proclivities. Yet there is a fire alarm whenever father becomes too sexually close to daughter. And when father has a specific worry in relation to daughter, there is instant amplification into how man thinks about woman – whether by way of race track analogy or dance hall observance.

One of the more theatrically dazzling of the images offered is that in which the male members of the cast come on in drag to become the victims of the tuxedoed females, strutting their way to dominance. Yet as the daughter removes her male garb after the ball, she becomes visibly the more vulnerable of the species all over again. It is an unforgettable moment of pure theatre. There are other such moments scattered through the night, and each member of the audience will find his own, or her own, to treasure or just to make each of us aware of how we have rendered this relationship between father and daughter, between man and woman.

To all concerned must go thanks for one of the most exciting, most vibrant and most challenging evenings of theatre in years. In addition to those already mentioned, Tony Wakefield has provided an almost perfect lighting design and the players are Joan Sheehy, Michele Forbes, Hilary Fannin, Tom Hickey, Vincent O'Neill, Dermod Moore, Bríd Ní Neachtain and Conal Kearney, while David Nolan provided the soundest of soundtracks to accompany the telling dance of reality with imagination. Absolutely not to be missed.

Snow White

Tom Mac Intyre

> [The following extract from *Snow White* (1988) was originally published in *Krino* (Vol. 5. Spring 1988). Republished here with kind permission of Tom Mac Intyre]

Rehearsal (Script One)

SETTING:

On an arc from downstage right to downstage left:
A Cradle, largish, on rockers.
A Swing.
A Weighing-Scales: A la *The Shop Scales (old style) from weighing the bacon, ham, so on.*
An Armchair, style constricted, 'Mother's Chair'.
A Shop Window Mannequin, female, on which a transparent plastic raincoat, matching hat, and matching umbrella may potently rest. The stand from which the mannequin grows to be on castors. And the mannequin, in turn, should be capable of spinning freely on its axis. The mannequin, bare or garbed, will be alluded to in the script as SW2.

PARTICIPANTS:
MOTHER
SNOW WHITE
THE SEVENTH DWARF

RED ROSE
BRIAR ROSE
GOOSE GIRL
THAT FELLA
For RED ROSE, BRIAR ROSE, GOOSE GIRL and THAT FELLA,
a degree of doubling and tripling.

SCENE 1: INTRODUCTION

>MOTHER, *acting younger than she is, is seated on the*
>*motionless swing. She sets it in motion. In a dubious way, she's*
>*losing decades as the speed of the swing increases. Skirts are*
>*flying. Legs splayed. The light is post-card sunshine. MOTHER is*
>*breathless with vertigo. The swing, pendulum of the swing,*
>*reaches zenith. MOTHER screams: exuberance, sort of. Cue for*
>*the* SEVENTH DWARF *who appears, observer/ambiguous, in*
>*evening dress. He watches unobserved.*

SEVENTH DWARF. Beautiful.

MOTHER, *caught in the whirl of the swing, tries, coyly/vainly, to*
acknowledge this interpolation from a stranger. She had not
anticipated a viewer. Perhaps she had. The swing will take time to
sober.

SEVENTH DWARF. How does it feel to be a pendant?
Pendulous? A pendulum incarnate? A body suspended?

The questions are rattled off dangerously, and, at once, The
SEVENTH DWARF *– as* MOTHER *stares/frowns – wipes the*
questions out using his cancellation 'geste': right hand briskly across
the chest and back on the same track. He resumes –

SEVENTH DWARF. That is *really* beautiful –

MOTHER. Flatterer –

SEVENTH DWARF. No –

MOTHER. Yes –

SEVENTH DWARF. No, no, no –

MOTHER. Yes, yes, yes –

SEVENTH DWARF. Keep it going –

MOTHER. What do you mean?

SEVENTH DWARF. Keep it going –

MOTHER. The gab?

SEVENTH DWARF. The motion, emotion, commotion, the
lotion, dee-votion –

MOTHER. Oh –

SEVENTH DWARF. It is quite – quite simply – simply quite – quite quite beautiful.

The swing has now slowed to the easily controllable. Lacuna. MOTHER stares at this interloper who's – unrebuffable. The SEVENTH DWARF, brazen – stares at MOTHER.

MOTHER, coolly, stops the swing. Sits there. Looks at the ground. Pensive, plus. Possible she's about to throw a tantrum. A stratagem – MOTHER looks up to find the SEVENTH DWARF has gone to sleep. There on his feet. Rocking back-and-forth as he sleeps. MOTHER scrutinizes this development.

SEVENTH DWARF. *(wide awake)* You know it too –

MOTHER. Know what?

SEVENTH DWARF. Keep it going – keep it going – keep it going –

They lock energies. She refuses to take him on. He acts boldly, advances, propels the swing towards fresh exhibitionistic vertigo. She doesn't look at him anymore. The swing whirls, skirts fly, she blossoms feverishly.

The SEVENTH DWARF watches from a remove again. Ambiguous, hand on chin, one finger keeping time, he could be on Mars. The swing careers towards zenith. At zenith, again, that giddy hysterical sound from MOTHER. The SEVENTH DWARF joins in.

Cue for abrupt change of atmosphere. Snowfall, gentle, clouding the space ... clouding the swing, MOTHER, the SEVENTH DWARF – who, high on the twist to the weather, kicks into his celebratory 'Dancing in the Snow' routine (but muted, there's an hour-and-a-half to go). He has a geste as prelude to his dance – a shoe-shine twirl: right foot against left calf and vice versa. The SEVENTH DWARF spins about the space, greeting the figures who are now drifting on in transparent plastic raincoats and hats and cocooned in those matching umbrellas ... we have SNOW WHITE, ROSE RED, BRIAR ROSE, GOOSE GIRL, and THAT FELLA. The latter's guise here (under the wrappings) is that of presentable young male suitor.

The SEVENTH DWARF has no hesitation in taking over as enigmatic orchestrator of the scenelet forming. Explore the choreography. There are meetings. No doubt there's a huddle. An identification parade? Individual scores: SNOW WHITE – face pressing against the plastic at regular intervals. RED ROSE – palm fluttering against the interior of the umbrella cocoon. BRIAR ROSE – constantly rubbing the interior of the cocoon with a rag (as in cleaning the car window). GOOSE GIRL – spasmodically cutting loose with a fly-swatter inside the cocoon. THAT FELLA – *rubbing his umbrella wooingly against other umbrellas.*

Note the availability of SW2, *in particular re* THAT FELLA.

MOTHER *wanders among the figures, peering at faces, at events. She will respond variously, the* SEVENTH DWARF *consistently at her elbow or in her slipstream. For climax, she'll meet* SNOW WHITE *in the throng. (The other figures dissolve.)*

MOTHER *stares at* SNOW WHITE – SNOW WHITE *with face pressed against cocoon. They stare at each other. 'Geste' for* MOTHER – *finger pensively to lips/mouth.*

SNOW WHITE, *before exiting, endows* SW2 *with open umbrella, raincoat, and hat. Make of that cameo a textured conversation involving* MOTHER, SNOW WHITE, *and* SW2.

SCENE 2: THE WEIGHING OF THE INFANTS

MOTHER *alone in the space. She goes to* SW2 *fusses playfully/possessively, adjusts this and that. Next, she takes an infant from the cradle. Swaddled (pink) but plainly an infant. She holds the infant as one might hold a strange object for inspection. She applies the infant to her left breast ... pause ... now to* THAT FELLA – *wearing overalls, his service man guise – may appropriately brush the 'snow' clear of the space. Her right breast ... now to each in turn until she creates a tick-tock motion, bizarre in its contours. She stops. Jolt-stop. Humanely, embraces the infant.*

MOTHER. I can see her – summer day, summer day – sprawled on grass, I can see her grown, so grown ungrown, I can see her bride at the altar, see her child to her breast and when I look into her eyes I see ... What do I see? When I look into her eyes I see what everyone sees, everyone says, I see *my* eyes ...

MOTHER *works on the infant again. She has an array of spectacularly elongated Q-Tips. Manipulating these like a sophisticated drummer, she cleans one ear, the other ear, navel: work well done.*

Three female figures cross the space upstage of MOTHER. *A* GRANDMA *in wheel-chair who's holding her hat vehemently in place, A* MOM *who's irritably pushing the wheel-chair, and a* SCHOOL GIRL *who's on one of those baby leashes.*

MOM. But Grandma –

GRANDMA. But me no buts –

SCHOOL GIRL. But Mom –

MOM. But Grandma –

SCHOOL GIRL. But Mom –

GRANDMA *removes hands from the hat, fretfully. The hands return at once to clamp the hat more securely than ever.*

GRANDMA. But me no buts!

The three exit. Back to MOTHER *and the Q-Tips.* MOTHER *has noticed something else, the nostrils, one of them, some of them. Yes, undoubtedly. The contest here is fraught. Q-Tips come and go, varying in length and pliability. The contest ends in a draw, say.*

THAT FELLA, SNOW WHITE *cared for, has come back on and is tenderly polishing the seat of the swing, oiling the metal sections, gauging the alignment of the swing vis-à-vis the stanchions, so on.* MOTHER *pays no heed. She speaks to the ambient air, someone may be listening.*

MOTHER. My father named a boat after me when I was nine. Called the boat after me. I was nine at the time –

THAT FELLA. What was it called?

MOTHER. My father died when I was ten.

A hint of chastisement there. MOTHER *views him as he works. He's aware of her watching. There's an odd current between the two, a sexual tinge – and yet it's awry. For climax to his serene fussings,* THAT FELLA *almost sits on the swing. Exit* THAT FELLA.

MOTHER. I find the young – young per-sons – of late … It was called *The Alma Maria*. That boat was a jewel, a jewel of the ocean.

She studies the infant upside-down. The action is playful/tender/déraciné. She shakes the infant upside-down. Same colour to the action.

Radio pips signal the hour. MOTHER *to action – fretful/compulsive. To the scales, carefully places the infant on the scales, adjusts – very carefully – the lie of the infant on the scales. Takes the reading. Disconcerted. Takes the reading again. Fretfully, notes reading in her black notebook. Back to the scales. Lifts the infant. Feels the weight of the infant in her own hands. Moves about the space 'weighing' the infant in her own hands. Tone is one of frustration. She halts. Stands there stiffly. Flips back to the right breast/left breast tick-tock movement score with the infant.*

The pips again. Flip again. Flies to the scales. Weighs the infant. Checks reading. Checks it again. Notes reading – evident fret – in the notebook. Tears out the page, dumps it. Back to the scales. Collects the infant. Turns away. Pips sound. Turns back. Resumes ritual as the space becomes populated, and the note is mayhem.

The SEVENTH DWARF *will distribute infants from the cradle.* ROSE RED, BRIAR ROSE, GOOSE GIRL, *all in nurses' uniforms.* SNOW WHITE *in ordinary dress.* THAT FELLA *as doctor on duty. Suddenly we have a fair day of figures with infants, with notebooks, with makeshift scales – the swing, the cradle, two hands – and the weighing of the infants is madly spiralling.*

The SEVENTH DWARF *is in the elements of his glory. Note: There's a din – deriving from the various unrestrained responses to the 'readings' obtained: grief, joy, bafflement, and so on.* MOTHER *is sucked hopelessly into the furore … Eruption is brief but explosive. Space clears.*

SNOW WHITE *and* MOTHER *alone there.* SNOW WHITE *circling* MOTHER. *For* MOTHER *a reprise of that hand/finger to the mouth 'geste'.*

SW2 *a spectral spectator from stage left.* SNOW WHITE *circling* MOTHER *coolly, dispassionately … next the two circling each other like animals who love each other, and, also, don't. The radio pips – ghostly. The two approach each other, eyes locked. Within a metre of each other, beside each other, neutral amiability, say. They say 'hello' by pressing extended finger (right hand) against extended index finger at an angle of 45°. Flavour of the salutation: caution.*

Programme Note: *Snow White*
   by Tom Mac Intyre.
   'Chomh geal le Sneachta …'
   (Peacock Theatre, 1988)

   Nuala Ní Dhomhnaill

Tom Mac Intyre's *Snow White* is a chancy romp through a minefield, the territory bounded by the mother/daughter relationship. It is a dangerous no-man's-land in every sense including the literal, because here be more than dragons, here lie live and ticking all the undetonated timebombs of our girlhood. You are well warned beforehand. A sign says 'Trespassers will be persecuted'. And in the language of childhood that means one thing and one thing only; you will be thrown to the lions. What? You mean to tell me that for just putting my big toe in that circumscribed space I will be eaten by carnivores? The emotional tenor of the piece says yes, this is so. For isn't this the very field where a man was ploughing on a Sunday long ago when ignoring the taboo on 'Obair Dhomhnaigh' he heard the first bell for Mass chime from the Franciscan Friary behind him. And then the second bell sounded and he took no more notice and just when he was ignoring the third and final bell didn't the ground open up and swallow him, horses and plough and all. Yes, awful strict, I admit, but true because as soon as we violate the 'geasa droma draíochta', the unspoken and for the major part unspeakable taboos with which our lives are hedged about by the tribe, believe you me, the ground *does* open up and swallow us.

And the witch-mother complex is at the solar plexus of the body social and politic. Nail it and a shiver runs down through the whole system. How central it is to our existence, to use a buzz-word, how crucial. It is hardly coincidental that when Walt Disney's *Snow White* was first screened in the Capitol Cinema in Dublin, in the thirties, its greatest fan was no less exalted a personage than, wait for it, the dearly beloved and late lamented Dev himself, who went to see it no less than thirteen times. Picture it. The great man takes time off from gainful and important employ and mitches in the afternoon in order to catch the matinee, allowing himself the pleasures of schoolboy truancy that he could never have allowed himself in his real schooldays. Thirteen times. And to what do we owe this conspicuous excursion out of character? To the fact that the animated moving-picture depiction of his own inner reality gripped him to his soul. A childhood bereft of a real flesh and blood mother left him with nothing to buffer him from the witch archetype. We can further picture him, catharsis taken neatly (thirteen times), being driven back home where he proceeded forthwith to work, penning that outward manifestation of the concentration camp of his inner reality, writ large, which has come down to us as The Irish Constitution. Just goes to show that everything is confessional, especially constitutions, though not in the sense that is usually meant by the word.

Nor does it stop at that. Next door at the moment an iron-corsetted, never-let-bulge-in-the-belly-be-said châtelaine holds a whole country up to ransom. 'Mirror, mirror, on the wall' she says 'Who is the greatest leader of us all?' 'Thou, O Margaret', answers the mirror in every cabinet minister's eye. Meanwhile all the gains of the twentieth century, the right to strike, the National Health, go down the castle's tubes like the disobedient huntsman and never a whit taken out of her. She offers us her dear mother's sweet lullaby;

'I packed myself in ice/a long time ago'. Everywhere she sees her eyes, her nose, her chin, her witch's mark left for posterity. And everything she ever did she did it, yes ring out the chorus, FOR OUR OWN GOOD.

But to return to the piece which sparked off such ruminations. Of the four little would-be women in the early scenes, the four little eggs, the embryos of potential womanhood, only Snow White is destined to make it. With a mixture of bloodymindedness and just sheer good luck she manages to break free of the witchmother's spell. The other poor unfortunates perish, sealed forever in the clingfilm of motherly love and filial devotion; 'we're both incredibly close, I mean I can tell her next move before she can herself'. Snow White is different, more guts there, more sheer personality. Chronic cradle-defiance the mother calls it, predictably. But Snow White, no glass coffins for her, mind, she's not on display. Waterbeds, solaria are more her style. She wants to be touched. Good, you say, at last. Speed up the action. Edit the dreary old hundred years sleep down to about two minutes. Then bring on Prince Charming on a white charger .... breá bog, not so fast, hold yer horses now, will ye? An attack of the witchmother erupts at the very last minute 'Out,' she says to the unfortunate princeling, 'out out out'. The by now self-imposed hedge of thorns is so daunting that few, if any, attempt it and those who do, perish. Finally.

Exeunt, to the kind of music RTÉ plays due to circumstances beyond its control. Do not adjust your sets. This is reality. Riddle me why?

> Cad tá chomh geal le sneachta,
> cad tá chomh milis le mil
> as buidéilín órga
> nách bhfuil rí ná prionnsa
> nár ól deor as.

> Freagra.   Bainne cín.

Theatre Review: *Snow White* by Tom Mac Intyre

David Calvert
(*Theatre Ireland*, Summer 1988)

Tom Hickey's prologue, which provided us with the unexpurgated version of Grimm's most-loved fairy-tale, anticipated in miniature the key devices and effects of Patrick Mason's gripping and disconcertingly vivid production of Tom Mac Intyre's *Snow White*. Our attention was alerted by the slightly absurd punctilio in the telling of the story, a compulsively precise articulation which was punctuated with spasms of frustration at the story's formulaic progress. The arbitrarily vengeful cruelty of the ending, (excised in Disney's sanitized animation) was told with a gothic relish – sinister shadow cast across the actor's face as he moved with blatantly melodramatic timing towards the solitary footlight – but left us with a feeling that, as with the Ancient Mariner, the story controlled the teller.

A summons of clangorous bells immediately followed the prologue and a young woman was revealed on a swing in a bright lemon dress and singing in almost maniacally discordant accompaniment to an operatic sound-track. From this disturbing similitude of youthful abandon Olwen Fouéré's 'Mother' appeared in various fractured and extreme states, as the play spun-off from Grimm's fairy-tale which was thereafter only glimpsed at as if through some distorted glass. On a stage, bare except for a swing and a dressmaker's female dummy on castors, the eerie world of some old deserted country house was conjured up. Fragments of sound – a distant susurrating sea, running water and peacock cries, the ticking of a pendulum clock in a nursery, the sound of musical scales played on a piano in a distant room, a decorous ballroom waltz – hinted at the setting and, rather than characters of flesh and blood, the figures who appeared on the stage seemed like spectral remnants from a genteel and bygone world.

In this setting the Mother seemed about to shatter into atoms at any instant. The shreds of her being were held together with speeches of manic exactitude, the words swelling up from some unconscious turbulence and seeming to just find a mouth. We see her propelled onto the stage in a rhapsodic waltz that has the energy and danger of a dervish while speaking to an absent interlocutor about her love for her daughter, in a hysterical syncopated exchange with her daughter that sends white hot shards of recrimination all around them; and in her most chilling appearance as a dried-up, exhausted figure making her somnambulant way across the stage in a narrow passage of light, an image of tightly corseted repression.

Tom Hickey's Seventh Dwarf was both the decrepit and demented retainer and simultaneously an enigmatic playmaker or animator who seemed to offer dangerous possibilities through cryptic signs and trigger off explosive forces in those near him. Michele Forbes was the tormented daughter, Snow White, brazen enough to fart in the face of the audience, but so brittle that a nod of her head would distort into a convulsive threshing until she lay supine on the floor of her nursery mumbling repetitively and abstractedly touching her pudendum. At times she looked to the dummy and caressed it with the longing of one hoping to connect with some disembodied and unattainable true self, a child crippled by the anxiety and hysteria of her mother's love. And Joan Sheehy must, I suspect, wait for a revival of this excellent production to equal her riveting entrance as the viperous grandmother in a motorized wheelchair careering round the stage spitting vituperative and obscene barbs into the dark recesses of this wonderful play.

Theatre Review: *Snow White* by Tom Mac Intyre

David Nowlan
(*The Irish Times*, 28 June 1988)

There has to be an air of presumption when men set out to try to delineate the relationship between mothers and daughters. The current Abbey triumvirate of Tom Mac Intyre, Patrick Mason, and Tom Hickey, who have done so much to inject new visions and new techniques into the national theatre in their previous collaborations, set out last night in *Snow White* to depict a relationship in which mother and daughter live in a cocoon of mutual resentment, jealousy, and guilt.

Mr Hickey starts the evening by reciting, with some elaboration, the fairy tale of how Snow White, done down by her mother, finally having made loving adult contact with the outside world, gets her own back. But dramatically the tale is already told right there and what happens thereafter is merely hung, with little further elaboration, on that Grimm tale.

There are verbal references to how women grow older – from pert to pendant to pendulous to pendulum, a body suspended – and to pop psychology about cradle-defiant relationships between mother and daughter. But they do not provide further insights into that small slice of female relationships, symbolized by the Brothers Grimm, which in real life are far more subtle and complex and far-reaching.

With images of snow and umbrellas and swings and female tailor's dummies, the narrative – such as it is – goes on repeating its message in arbitrary words and visions. But few of the repetitions add much to what has previously been stated. And the techniques which this collective has made very much its own, while more assured than in earlier productions, are somehow less inventive than in previous manifestations.

Michele Forbes's Snow White is the most extended and effective performance of the night, now cowed and uncertain, next cheeky yet never quite assured. Olwen Fouéré's Mother embodies statuesque uncaring arrogance, followed by collapse and compromise. The rest are cyphers, and misleadingly titled on the programme. And the whole, in Monica Frawley's plain but effectively dark setting and Tony Wakefield's sometimes errant lighting, is – in a word – trite.

Performing Women in Tom Mac Intyre's Drama

SarahJane Scaife

[This article includes substantial contributions from the actress Michele Forbes who appeared in all five of Tom Mac Intyre's plays during the 1980s including *The Bearded Lady* (1984), *Rise Up Lovely Sweeney* (1985), *The Great Hunger* (1986), *Dance for your Daddy* (1987) and *Snow White* (1988).]

In 1988 I was asked to perform in Tom Mac Intyre's new play, *Snow White* at the Peacock Theatre. Unfortunately this was to be the last play in a series of collaborations between Mac Intyre, the actor Tom Hickey and director Patrick Mason. I studied and performed in physical theatre in New York in the 1980s but managed to see a performance of Mac Intyre's adaptation of Patrick Kavanagh's *The Great Hunger* at the Abbey Theatre before I left Ireland for the US. This play left an indelible impression on me. It burnt an image on the retina of the imagination that I have never forgotten. I have such a strong image of Vincent O'Neill, Conal

Kearney and Tom Hickey playing old country characters that could have walked out of my childhood from summers spent with relatives in County Clare.

There is one specific image where they were leaning into a country gate; the gate moved with them as they embodied the actions and physicality of the rural characters. These were not the realistic rural characters that one saw in John B. Keane's work or even the highly poetic ones in J.M. Synge's, but rather they lurked in my subconscious and operated in an almost embarrassing, inexplicable way; a way that I could not at the time put into words but knew that it represented the 'feeling' of the Ireland of my youth or even of the time. The girls were boisterous and loud and physical, again not the characters that I would have associated with Irish drama. Later the actress Michele Forbes drew my attention to a quote from Mary Harron in *The Observer* that said 'a procession of images that seem to come from Ireland's subconscious onto the stage ... The girls are Dionysian, the men are cowards'.[1] There was a definite animalism about the images, again nothing I could articulate in any specific way at that time. In a very literary and language-based tradition Mac Intyre seemed to be one, if not the only, writer looking to performers and to the visual and physical side of theatre when exploring his use of form. It was the kind of theatre I went to New York to study.

Snow White was my first professional production and the process was an extremely intense one for me. There were two particular areas of difficulty that I encountered during the rehearsal process. The first one was the group's different approach to the notion of improvisation and the creation of physical imagery and gesture. The second one related to the significance of the role of the Seventh Dwarf within the text itself. The signification of this character, for instance, affected the reading of the play both from my view as a female performer and audience members' views as spectators whether male or female.

In writing this article, I asked the actress Michele Forbes, who was involved in *Snow White* as well as other Mac Intyre plays, to contribute her recollections on performing in this work. Michele's input is important and much welcomed because my own memory of what occurred during *Snow White* provides just one point of view rather than a balanced account of the overall artistic journey. Michele's knowledge, like my own, comes from experience and in writing this piece I aim to look at the problems of staging *Snow*

White from an experiential angle. Michele and I have found it very interesting and have immensely enjoyed revisiting our individual memories and experiences of the process involved in this production, which took place nineteen years ago!

In order to help tease out what I consider the thematic problems of this play I am drawing on Bruno Bettelheim's writing on the psychoanalytical basis for fairy tales and Laura Mulvey's analysis of the *male gaze* within cinema.[2]

In Ireland of the 1980s the terms 'physical theatre' or 'image based' theatre covered a multitude of styles, basically anything that didn't have the primacy of words as a starting point. The idea of physical theatre, of mixing genres of movement and theatre, was only in its infancy. In 1980, Vincent O'Neill, Conal Kearney and the late Jonathan Lambert had come back from studying mime with Marceau in Paris. They formed the Irish Mime Group, which presented their only show *Silent Conflicts* for the Dublin Theatre Festival that year. O'Neill in turn formed the Oscar Mime Company. Both Kearney and O'Neill went on to work with the Mac Intyre group and were an integral part of the creative process for the original production of *The Great Hunger*.[3]

Having studied with Kearney at the old Project Theatre I was encouraged by him to go to New York in 1983, to enlarge my movement vocabulary and study with Polish mime Stephan Niedzialkowski. Whilst there, I also studied with the modern dancer Eric Hawkins, and Butoh artist Maureen Odo.

For an actress like myself, having just returned from studying physical theatre, to be asked to be part of what I felt was the cutting edge of Irish theatre, with such a strong cast, in a play that was not only *about* women but featured *five women*, was sheer fantasy. As I had been away from Ireland between the first production of *The Great Hunger* in 1983 and the rehearsals for *Snow White* in 1988, I talked to Michele Forbes about the group that had been together for the intervening years and how they had approached the work. I wanted to interrogate my memories of the process and try to understand why I had had problems with it.

Michele was introduced to Mac Intyre's work in 1984. Patrick Mason had approached O'Neill in an effort to find actors with movement skills for the parts of the 'Yahoos' in *The Bearded Lady* (1984) which was based on the works of Jonathan Swift. Michele had been training at both the Oscar School of Acting and the Oscar Mime Company. She then went on to work with Mac Intyre in *Rise*

Up Lovely Sweeney (1985), the revival of *The Great Hunger* (1986), *Dance for your Daddy* (1987) and *Snow White* (1988).

Mac Intyre used the imagery and, to a certain extent, the underlying psychoanalytic structure of the fairytale *Snow White*, as a framework from which to analyze his theatrical reading of the mother/daughter relationship. Olwen Fouéré played the mother and Michele Forbes the daughter, Snow White. Joan Sheehy, Sian Maguire and I played her sisters, Briar Rose, Rose Red and Goose Girl. Dermod Moore played the part of the young man, or the 'love interest', and Tom Hickey played the part of the Seventh Dwarf. In this case the Seventh Dwarf embodied the notion of the dwarves collectively within the traditional fairy-tale. As with the other Mac Intyre scripts in this series of collaborations, the *Snow White* script was composed of words, gestures and images. It did not read like other texts I had been used to working with up until that point in my career. It appeared to be more like a piece of performance art, far removed from what I considered to be a conventional script for the theatre. On reading the script again for this article I was struck by one thing, how little had actually changed from what was actually texted or written on the page to what ended up on the stage. In fact, when I began rehearsals on the play I was surprised at how my experience of improvisation differed from the way in which the group was actually working. I asked Michele how this process had worked in regard to the other Mac Intyre plays that she had worked on, how the script was approached in these instances and how much the performance had actually been changed in response to the input of the actors:

MF[4]. As a company, hired in the traditional way as actors by the National Theatre to interpret a new Irish play, we were presented on the first day of rehearsals with what was termed the rehearsal script. This was always a malleable and flexible transcript, and understood as such from the beginning, but was very clearly a draft based on the vision and ideas of Tom Mac Intyre. He would write a draft, show it first to Tom Hickey and Patrick Mason who would discuss it with him. Mac Intyre would then write a second rehearsal script and that was the script which would be given to the actors. Often his works were inspired by actual texts; Patrick Kavanagh's poem for *The Great Hunger*, the works of Jonathan Swift for *The Bearded Lady*, the legend of the seventh century Ulster king Suibhne Geilt for *Rise Up Lovely Sweeney*, *Dance for your Daddy* and *Snow White*[5] were not based on previously existing texts but were explorations of much more personal themes, the relationships between father and daughter and between mother and daughter, for instance.

SJS. One of the areas that interested me was the notion of what can be considered text-based and what may be considered as physical theatre. Even though Mac Intyre's work during the 1980s may be described as image based and physically based theatre, it now seems to me that this work was still predominately governed by the writer's script. What I mean by this is that although Mac Intyre's script for *Snow White* consists of physical gesture, lexical text and descriptions of images and movement scores, it is still scripted, written down as a script. The question is, however, was this script moveable or fixed, and did the performers have the agency to change the actual script in any significant way? Michele explains how this worked in her overall experience of working on Mac Intyre's plays of the 1980s.

MF. The rehearsal script was a very comprehensive draft – encompassing text, description of images, linguistic notation of physical gestures. Each scene in the play would already have been given a title by Tom Mac Intyre to act as a guide to what he saw as the essential energy of the scene. During the first two or three days of rehearsal each scene would be broken down to even smaller units. Some of these would be obvious and suggest themselves, they could be a certain block of text or a contained physical description of the actor/actors moving in space. Others would be less obvious, pared back in size, for instance, to become more manageable to work with in rehearsal. Breaking the scenes down like this in the initial stages of the read-throughs was a very important part of the process. Each smaller section of each scene would be given its own title, agreed by the whole company. In this sense the company were already codifying and interpreting the play, as one would with a more naturalistic or traditional piece of theatre, breaking it down in order to establish a common footing, a common ground from which to explore it.

SJS. I asked Michele to give me an example of this.

MF. For instance, in *The Bearded Lady* we named one of the sections where the Yahoos appear 'The kids take over'. This gave us as performers a very concrete hook, a palpable and understandable sense of the performance energy which was required of us moving onto the rehearsal floor. We were able to, individually, have a clearer sense of what we could play with in improvising the scene.

Mac Intyre's text would outline what he thought could happen: 'The Yahoos are now active in the space ... They're up the tree, jeering at him (Swift) and shitting on him from a height'.[6] But inevitably, the theatre directions would include 'work from the following suggestions' or 'explore' (and how do you theatrically shit on someone from a height?!). There was also discussion on a more general level about the subject matter of particular plays. In some we looked at the historical background in which the play was set, the Augustan Age of the eighteenth century for *The Bearded Lady*, the political background existing in Northern Ireland for *Rise Up Lovely Sweeney* or, as was mentioned earlier, the original text on which the play was based.

SJS. In *Snow White* although I played four characters I could not really say that I played 'characters' in the conventional sense; it was more like performing an image or even a costume to a certain extent. I wondered how Michele had approached this as she seemed to have a very keen sense of how to play her part of Snow White.

MF. Once we had linguistically/intellectually/analytically defined our parameters within the text our function as performers was to bring what Tom Mac Intyre had written and what had been discussed within the group to the floor, to physically and vocally explore the ideas. Lifting the ideas from the page and from the realm of verbal discussion to something physical was always challenging and exciting and nearly always frightening! Well, then it becomes an exploration of interaction and a whole new element emerges – how is the actor on the rehearsal floor with me going to react to what I'm doing, and how am I going to react to them? How do we begin to physically and vocally clarify what we've just been discussing around a table?

SJS. So, for Michele and the other actors it became a process of making the idea represented by the image or physical/verbal score come to life. They worked together to try and embody both physically and vocally what Mac Intyre was trying to express through the script. But, as I had always started from the idea and progressed through the physical to an image, I asked her how much, if at all, the initial scripts changed during the process.

MF. To ask how much the scripts changed from the original second draft I would have to say not a great deal on the page but, as the actors rehearsed more and more together, the fluidity of performance would increase and nuances would grow and gestures become more robust, verbal refrains more layered. As actors we were fleshing out the central ideas of the scripts and trying to communicate them to an audience. Mac Intyre's impulse was always to avoid the declarative, to not make it too accessible to the audience – as in, for example, the interpretation of dreams where the subconscious does not always make it easy or obvious and therefore you have to dig for association, for meaning. Mason's instinct was to try to clarify theatrically what was going on so that in fact the images and words could resonate in a more direct way.

SJS. For me at that time I took my body to be clay or, perhaps, a clean slate. I suppose my idea was that the body, my body, was the site wherein the ideas and energy that were to be explored would find physical expression. I tried not to have a plan of what might happen and to just let go and let the training that I had undergone speak through my movement. However, I found that this did not work for me at all and I was lost; I didn't know what to do. I thought that this was how everyone else was working so when Michele and I started talking about the process I asked her how she had coped with this aspect and also how she felt the 'characters' functioned in terms of the overall play.

MF. In order to find my own route as an actor through what would be considered an unconventional script I would often have worked through various ideas, in a general sense, in my own head before stepping out onto the rehearsal floor – what would I like to play with in this scene? – How do I play a character whose every word and gesture on stage is infused with anger without becoming boring? For instance, the Angry Boy or Snow White, how do I physically play the part of a yappy little Jack Russell? And even if this remained unused or unusable it gave me a personal angle to connect me to the part I was playing, but this is what all actors do anyway in a more conventional play – isn't it?

SJS. As far as the definition 'character' is concerned, there was a recognition in rehearsal of the dilemma this term created in relation to the kind of imagistic theatre we were presenting. We were conscious of that. We were not portraying a character in the traditional sense, with a history and background supported by the script, a time and a place defined for them, obvious likes and dislikes, realistic connections with other people on stage. We could have considered ourselves as 'cyphers' rather than as characters, giving flesh to the idea of something, Mac Intyre's ideas of mother, wife, schoolgirl, were defined in relation to the central figure of the play. For me, the approach to playing a 'cypher' as opposed to a 'character' wasn't significantly different in that I still had to ask myself the question – will the audience be interested? I still approached 'the schoolgirl', 'the dark daughter', 'the angry boy', 'the Yahoo', 'Snow White', 'the nurse', in the same way that I approached my roles in more conventional theatre, film and television. I had to personalize it for myself. For me to take on the idea that I was playing a construct/construction of any sort would not have been helpful as a performer – how does one play a construct? Whether they were seen as constructs is a different matter I think, an academic judgement, but as a performer I wouldn't know how to take that on.

Scripting the body

So, from my rereading of the scripts and from the above discussions with Michele it appears that these plays *seem* very elusive and improvisational, but that they were in fact following a very clear blueprint given firstly by Mac Intyre and then solidified in collaboration with both Mason and Hickey. There is an important distinction to be made concerning the method of improvisation involved. The images and movement/vocal scores were actually scripted from the outset and the process for the performers was to improvise around these already conceived movement and vocal scores. They were to *embody* the text rather than create a new one; in this case text had to be taken as both verbal and physical. The actors took those very precise gestural and lexical scores and embodied them in as meaningful a way as they could. This was important for me to identify in retrospect, in that it highlighted Mac Intyre's background as a writer. Although his texts involve movement and visual imagery they are still coming from the idea of the written text. A Mac Intyre text includes gestural and movement scores but it is still text as written creatively from a particular perspective.

The body as script writer

If for Mac Intyre you could say he *scripted* the body, then for Niedzialkowski, Hawkins and Odo, you could say that the body was the *script writer*. By that I mean that I was trained, throughout all these various movement disciplines, in a process of *identification*. This is in one way a very simple concept and in another very complex. *Identification* can be with a character, its physicality, gestures, psychological profile, how the character identifies with time, space, atmosphere and other characters on stage. Basically, the use of the body with its movement in space is how the performer communicates everything, and he/she should not move unless he/she has a reason to. In this sense, in training, Niedzialkowski always distinguished what we were doing from *pure dance*. Nowadays the boundaries have become more and more blurred between physical theatre and dance. The idea with the kind of performance Niedzialkowski was promoting was that you use your own body to create feelings, thoughts, sensations within the individual bodies of the audience. I suppose it is a kind of manipulation of the senses and aesthetic responses of the audience. The training and technique undergone to achieve this is very rigorous but the audience should be unaware of 'the technique' and the actor should not be consciously using it. *Identification* as such does not have to be applied on a 'realistic' level. It can refer to *identification* with cold, wind, autumn, water, air, fear, memory etc., so it is not used as a substitute in physical theatre for a Stanislavskian approach in text-based theatre. Butoh uses *identification* with images to find the way to move. In this case the body is moving not consciously but through the application of the creative use of imagery. For instance, you might imagine clouds under your armpits, or smoke passing through your body, to find the energy you are looking for to move but all the time you are using your trained body/mind to actually create the image.

This is the kind of approach to improvisation that I experienced in the various movement disciplines I had been trained in and worked with whilst in New York and later in Greece. First there was the idea, a reason to move, what you were trying to communicate to the audience. Then would come the work, the physical improvising around the idea. We worked with our bodies to create the language and images for the piece. If we used words they were as part of this creative process that would lead us on occasion to some place very different from where we had thought we would end up. We were always consciously shaping not just our individual bodies but sculpting the stage space itself with our bodies. We played with the audiences' perceptions of time and space and all the time we needed to be lost in the moment, but also consciously creating the moment through the use of our physical performance.

I had spent four years of very intense training in this area and found difficulty in finding a way into the improvisation process that had already been established within the Mac Intyre group. In this particular process the image or score was already scripted. Even the way into each day of rehearsal was one that the actors were all very comfortable with, but that I started to feel very disconnected from. At the time I thought it was a skill that I just didn't have, but later realized that the group had their own established improvisational language and that I just couldn't speak it. Raymond Keane talks about the lack of a 'shared language' among theatre practitioners at the time in Ireland, of a form of 'separation' between the 'movers' and the 'actors'. [7] Some of us had gone abroad to try and learn deeper ways of performing but came back to Ireland feeling very much out of place because there was no one else trained in a similar way. At that stage 'training' was almost a dirty word. Sometimes I found it very easy to connect in rehearsals, especially at times when we were very physical. One such situation was in an improvisation between my sisters Briar Rose, Rose Red and myself Goose Girl. We burst on to the stage and the instructions were to freak out physically when there was silence, then when this deafening, crazy, musical sound came on we were to go in on ourselves, without moving. This felt great as a performer, being physically unleashed and restricted alternately in opposition to the normal tendency, which is to move when there is music and stop when there is silence.[8] Another particularly exciting memory is watching Michele improvise the scene where Snow White eats the apple. Although when I re-read the script I realized that Mac Intyre had scripted this scene in terms of what Snow White actually did, at the time I would lie on the floor at the edge of the stage watching in awe at how she interpreted those directions as if for the first time. She is such a marvellously instinctive actress. Every time she ate the apple I thought she was actually choking until she would start laughing at the audience as she revealed her joke. 'Thought I was for the glass coffin, didn't you? That display case. Not a bit of it. I'm not into glass coffins.'[9] It was fascinating to watch her in action, embodying the physical text, bringing the script to life.

One of the main areas of difficulty arose by my constant need to know *why?* Every time myself and my sisters came on stage I needed to know why. I played a daughter in a ball gown, a schoolgirl, a mermaid in a wetsuit, a nurse and an egg and for each one I wanted to know what was meant and what the scene was trying to achieve. I realize now how frustrating that must have been given the non-declarative[10] element of what Mac Intyre was trying to achieve but because of my intensity and my training and possibly my own belligerence I could not just keep it to myself. It was a scorching June and we were in the basement of the Peacock, which had no kind of air-conditioning and was absolutely stifling. I had contracted shingles during the rehearsals and was dosed up to the hilt on painkillers. We had five costume changes. I can vividly remember getting help peeling off the wetsuit in the little space that was used as a green room. Yet despite the fact that the audiences weren't coming[11] and we were pretty isolated within the Abbey there was a very positive attitude among the cast and everyone gave it their total concentration every performance. There was a sense of solidarity about the process of experimentation that we had been involved in.

In considering the thesis of this article, 'Performing Women in Mac Intyre's Drama', there are a few elements to be addressed. Firstly, in a Mac Intyre play one doesn't perform character as such but as Michele said it is more that we were performing 'cyphers, giving flesh to the idea of something, Mac Intyre's idea of mother, wife, schoolgirl, and defined in relation to the central figure of the play'. *Dance for your Daddy* and *Snow White* represented departures from the other scripts that were based on objective narratives, within the public domain. In the worlds of Swift, Kavanagh's Ireland, Sweeney in the Badlands between North and South, the audience and actors were all operating in the context of a recognizable framework. Mac Intyre could 'avoid the declarative' with his imagery and gestural/vocal scores as there was a shared understanding of what was *not said*. *Rise Up Lovely Sweeney* is a great example of this and it reads so well in terms of its imagery. An Irish audience would have been able to read the imagistic text in a very sophisticated manner. However, in *Snow White* this recognizable framework becomes much more complex, as we need to establish what exactly is the common understanding of the notion of the feminine and if there even is one; the subject matter here being the relationship between the mother and the daughter, with the psychoanalytical implications of this relationship being rooted in the fairy tale of *Snow White*. This is as much a difficulty for the actor as for the audience.

Laura Mulvey writes in her essay, 'Visual Pleasure and Narrative Cinema':

> Woman then stands in patriarchal culture as signifier for the
> male other, bound by a symbolic order in which man can live
> out his phantasies and obsessions through linguistic command
> by imposing them on the silent image of woman still tied to
> her place as bearer of meaning, not maker of meaning.[12]

It is this notion of woman as the 'bearer of meaning, not maker
of meaning' that I will now address with regard to *Snow White*.

For me as a woman there was something unsettling about
reading the play again and seeing how my memory of the Seventh
Dwarf was accurate in terms of his role of voyeur. Bruno Bettelheim
writes of *Snow White* as a fairy tale that has deeply
psychoanalytical readings for children, when dealing with their
growth from a pre-oedipal child to a fully mature and healthy adult.
He argues:

> The story of *Snow White* warns of the evil consequences of
> narcissism for both parent and child. Snow White's narcissism
> nearly undoes her as she gives in twice to the disguised
> queen's enticements to make her look more beautiful, whilst
> the queen is destroyed by her own narcissism.[13]

Bettelheim also speaks about the sexual jealousy between the
mother and the daughter and the Oedipal conflicts represented
within the story. He says that dwarves have different connotations
in different fairy tales but in *Snow White* they are of the helpful
variety. He writes 'In *Snow White* it is the years Snow White spends
with the dwarves which stand for her time of troubles, of working
through problems, her period of growth'.[14] However, in Mac
Intyre's *Snow White* the Seventh Dwarf is seen as the character who
orchestrates her development and who orchestrates the mother's
coming to self awareness both sexually and otherwise. The females
in the play are all in various ways conducted by him, controlled by
him which creates a *male gaze* over the piece from within the
narrative itself. He even introduces the play by way of the telling of
the story before the 'play' begins. The Seventh Dwarf takes control
of the action of the play by telling the story directly to the audience
at the beginning of the performance. This gives him the authority of
the omniscient narrator of the piece.

Mulvey speaks of the various ways in which the human form can
be *looked at*. She uses Freud's notion of 'scopophilia' to analyse
ways of looking in cinema. She writes of Freud:

> At this point he associated scopophilia as taking other people
> as objects, subjecting them to a controlling and curious gaze ...

At the extreme, it can become fixated into a perversion, producing obsessive voyeurs and Peeping Toms whose only sexual satisfaction can come from watching, in an active controlling sense, an objectified other.[15]

In this regard, it becomes unclear whether the Seventh Dwarf is himself a part of the action. Does the spectator adopt his gaze as that of the omniscient narrator, or is he to be seen in terms of the overall psychoanalytical interpretation of the play itself? He is always present, orchestrating the action in an ironic and mischievous way. At one point he watches the mother as she masturbates on the swing, but she thinks she is alone. *'The Seventh Dwarf is now a viewer of her activity. The Seventh Dwarf from far stage left watching the undulations of her buttocks, her back ...expressionless ...'.*[16] When she realizes he is there she gets mad and takes the infants (props) and hurls them at him in an hysterical state. The description of her is 'she's approaching wild fury', of him that he is, 'serene'.[17] What does this character represent within a play about women? It presents the female as hysterical needing the balance of the watcher, the Seventh Dwarf, to help her express what is deep inside her. In Michele's rehearsal notebook she has written down the following after discussion on her relationship with the Seventh Dwarf:

> He (the Seventh Dwarf) represents everything that is possible for Snow White. He is the dream in which she confronts the things she cannot confront in ordinary life – her sexual side, the tender unembarrassed love for her mother. It is through the willingness to meet him that she will find these things out.[18]

I played the parts of four aspects of the feminine, a Daughter/Egg, Mermaid, Schoolgirl and Goose Girl. I realize that these were cyphers and not to be considered characters as such but in a play dealing with the subconscious it is of particular interest. For me the question is what is a 'Schoolgirl' in the scheme of things? How does one begin to decide what the performative aspects of 'Schoolgirl' are? Throughout the piece it seemed that the women were manifestations of the perceptions of a male world. Mulvey writes 'In a world ordered by sexual imbalance, pleasure in looking has been split between active/male and passive/female.'[19] Although the play was looking at uncovering the problems inherent in the mother/daughter relationship and the performers who played them were two of the strongest and most talented female actors, this objective did not succeed.

For me the Seventh Dwarf's constant presence and controlling part in the play, no matter how playfully rendered, put the whole performative experience very firmly within the *gaze of the male* and as such could not possibly raise questions of a probing or real nature for the women either within the piece, or in the audience. The Seventh Dwarf seems to be *directing* the process of *looking* for the audience. It is ironic then that one of the problems that Fintan O'Toole had with *Snow White* was that Hickey was not present enough. He writes:

> The crucial factor in *Snow White* is the reduced role of Tom Hickey, with his extraordinary ability to include both the naturalistic and the gestural in his acting, who has been the embodiment of Mac Intyre and Mason's vision, who has made it concrete.[20]

O'Toole goes on to point to what he perceives as the problem inherent in Mac Intyre's work: 'Mac Intyre is trying to do with non-dancers what in America and Europe would be the prerogative of avant-garde theatre-dance companies'.[21] He feels that the problem lies in Hickey's reduced presence and the absence of choreography, which he attributes to O'Neill now being absent from the core group.

As was noted earlier, in the Ireland of the 1980s 'physical theatre' and 'image-based theatre' were terms that covered a multitude, basically anything that didn't have the primacy of words as a starting point. Now we can look at these terms and analyse them in greater detail. What makes a text *physical* or *image-based* as opposed to *literary* or *text-based*? Is the text itself scripted *by* the body or *on* the body? Does the image arise from the physical or is it created by the writer?

For me, ultimately, *Snow White* was problematic for two reasons, both of which affected my analysis of performing women in Mac Intyre's drama. The first was my own particular understanding of physical theatre when I went in to the rehearsal process. The second was the problem of the *male gaze* which came primarily from the use of the Seventh Dwarf and which infiltrated the psychoanalytical aspects of the play in an unhealthy manner. Although I could see how successfully the non-declarative approach[22] worked in *The Great Hunger* and I could read how well it must have worked in *Rise Up Lovely Sweeney*,[23] it did not work in *Snow White* for me. This was due in part to the extremely complex theme that *Snow White* was exploring and also the path that that exploration took. I would love to be taking part in this play now at this period of my life. I feel that now that I am older and have gone through both the experience of being a mother and a daughter I can realize how complex this whole relationship really is. It is a shame that there was not an older woman cast, like Joan O'Hara for instance, who could have brought the wealth of her experience as a woman and a mother to the process. In a play about women I feel that this relationship needs to be viewed from a woman's perspective. That might sound sexist but it is what I feel.

It was very disappointing as a performer never to have had a chance to revisit this experience in any way. Experimentation in this area seemed to have stopped at the end of Mac Intyre's ensemble work at the Peacock in the 1980s. This ensemble group had pushed boundaries in many ways that have never really been followed through. I wonder why? Are we afraid of the whole dictum of experimentation in art, in that you should be allowed to fail? How can we create in a fresh way if we cannot afford to fail? As Michele Forbes said in an address to Trinity College students, after the run of *Snow White*:

> The environment of the University is very important for exploration and experimentation – it allows us to make mistakes. That is probably one of the most important things we can do and also it reminds us that we must not be afraid. Hopefully that energy can find its feet alongside mainstream theatre.[24]

Works Cited

Primary Sources

Forbes, Michele, Rehearsal notebook for *Snow White*, 1988.
-- Speech for Trinity Students, AGM in defence of the Mac Intyre work, 1988.
Mac Intyre, Tom, *Rise Up Lovely Sweeney*, Rehearsal Script, 1985.
-- *Dance for your Daddy*, Rehearsal Script, 1987.
Mac Intyre, Tom, *Snow White*, Rehearsal Script, 1988.
Scaife, SarahJane, in conversation with actor Michele Forbes, 2007.
Scaife, SarahJane, interview with Raymond Keane (actor and director) Barrabas Theatre Company, interview 10 June, 2004.

Secondary Sources

Bettelheim, Bruno, *The Uses of Enchantment; the Meaning and Importance of Fairy Tales* (London: Penguin Books, 1991).

Mulvey, Laura, 'Visual Pleasure and Narrative Cinema', *Screen* 16:3 pp.6-18.

O'Toole, Fintan, 'Love and Death in the Decade of Quiet Despair', review from *The Sunday Tribune*, 10 July 1988.

---

[1] Mary Harron 'Edinburgh Fringe; Stuck in The Slot of Sterility' *The Observer*, 17 August 1986.

[2] I refer here to Bruno Bettelheim, *The Uses of Enchantment: The Meaning and Importance of Fairy Tales* (Penguin Books, London, 1991) and Laura Mulvey, 'Visual Pleasure and Narrative Cinema', *Screen* 16, 3: 6-18.

[3] The Mac Intyre group here refers to the collaboration of playwright, director Patrick Mason, designer Bronwen Casson, and actors led by Tom Hickey, Michele Forbes, Olwen Fouéré, Conal Kearney, Fiona McAnna, Dermod Moore, Bríd Ní Neachtain, Joan O'Hara, Vincent O'Neill, SarahJane Scaife, Martina Stanley, who worked on Mac Intyre's work variously throughout the 1980s at the Abbey (Peacock) Theatre, Dublin. Other actors who appeared during this period include: Graham Boland, Catherine Byrne, Geoffrey Golden, Michael Grennell, Ciaran Grey, and Sian Maguire.

[4] Here, and in the following sections marked MF, Michele Forbes in conversation with SarahJane Scaife, Spring, 2007.

[5] *Snow White*, however, references the fairytale of the same name.

[6] Tom Mac Intyre, *The Bearded Lady*, Rehearsal Script, (1984), p. 17.

[7] Interview with Raymond Keane, Barrabas, 10 June 2004.

[8] Although we improvised around this scene, it wasn't used in the final piece.

[9] Tom Mac Intyre *Snow White* Rehearsal Script, p.75.

[10] This refers to Michele's comments on Mac Intyre's wish to 'avoid the declarative'.

[11] The audiences for *Snow White* were very small and the play had to be pulled [withdrawn] before the end of its scheduled run.

[12] Laura Mulvey 'Visual Pleasure and Narrative Cinema' (1975), p. 586, *Screen* 16, 3: 6-18

[13] Bruno Bettelheim, *The Uses of Enchantment*, p. 203.

[14] Ibid.

[15] Laura Mulvey, 'Visual Pleasure and Narrative Cinema', p. 587.

[16] Tom Mac Intyre, *Snow White*, Rehearsal Script, (1988), p.63.

[17] Ibid, p. 64.

[18] Michele Forbes, Rehearsal Notebook, *Snow White*, 1988.

[19] Laura Mulvey, 'Visual Pleasure and Narrative Cinema', p. 589.

[20] Fintan O'Toole, 'Love and Death in the Decade of Quiet Despair', *The Sunday Tribune* 10 July, 1988.

[21] Ibid.

[22] The term 'non-declarative' refers to Michele Forbes's description of Mac Intyre's impulse 'to avoid the declarative'.

[23] Tom Mac Intyre, Rehearsal Script, *Rise Up Lovely Sweeney*, 1985.

[24] Michele Forbes, taken from the script for her talk to an AGM in Trinity College in defence of the innovative work the Mac Intyre group had been producing, 1988.

Theatre of the Image and Tom Mac Intyre
Daniel Shea

Labels like 'Theatre of the Image' and 'imagistic' have repeatedly been applied to Tom Mac Intyre's plays of the mid-1980s, *The Great Hunger* (1983, 1986), *The Bearded Lady* (1984), *Rise Up Lovely Sweeney* (1985), *Dance for your Daddy* (1987), and *Snow White* (1988).[1] But are these plays 'Theatre of the Image'? If so, how exactly does this label describe them? What is the relation between theatre and image? Are they independent of one another? Or can one be regarded as subordinate or integral to the other? In this essay I will use the published and unpublished texts of Mac Intyre's mid-1980s plays to give initial answers to these questions. When the thought, the associations, and the practices surrounding the words *image* and *theatre* are rigorously applied to Mac Intyre's Peacock collaborations, rich possibilities open for the understanding of these unusual Irish plays.

I focus this article on five plays by Tom Mac Intyre, but I do so in order to find out more both about image as it relates to theatre and about theatre as it relates to image. I hope to uncover much as yet unnoticed in Mac Intyre's plays by explaining much more about the connections between or even the integral relationship of image and theatre. Although the combination of theatre and image presents me with various aspects, I will approach it first by examining theatre through image (i.e. theatre as an activity done in images) and then by examining images through theatre (i.e. a kind of theatre which makes particular use of images).

In order to begin examining image as something integral to theatre, I direct critical attention to the audience. In two books, *Theatre and Everyday Life* (1993) and *Theatre, Intimacy & Engagement* (2008), Alan Read has worked to give place to the audience beyond their hackneyed conception as the other half of the show.

The audience is vital to the act of theatre because audience members take part in those practices which constitute the characters, the time, and the space of a performance. Read argues that since the essence of theatre lies in appearances in the place of performance, that is, since it happens through its images, 'theatre no longer resides as an object of study, separated from its audience, for it is in their imagination that images occur'.[2] Imagination here refers to the creative imagination, that mental faculty which Read cites Gaston Bachelard and Richard Kearney as declaring originative of reality as we perceive it through our senses and our minds. And it is just this same reality which image refers to. From a phenomenology of the poetic image, such as Bachelard delineates in his *Poetics of Space*,[3] Read deduces a phenomenology of the theatre image, so that the ambivalent roles of poet and reader in literary creation become the parts of performer and spectators in performative creation. When Read claims that 'the audience as critic always must concede the act of theatre as one they might have made',[4] he finds words to express that active reciprocity about the affects of a performance which, for example, Dermot Healy experienced at *Rise Up Lovely Sweeney*. For Healy, appreciating this play meant coming at it 'from the inside' and not, in an effort to make sense of it, encircling it with some narrative or other schema which the performance might be fit to.[5] One of the collaborators' stated aims had been the arousal of just such affects in the audience. 'It is essential,' Tom Hickey has said, on acting Maguire:

> that the spectator should feel a deep sense of recognition, and that the image should draw the spectator into the experience of the play. The actor must enable the spectator, to some degree, to see the experience of the play as his own experience.[6]

So, the people watching a performance just as much as the people putting it on are in the act of creating from the material of a stage production the immaterialities of performed characters, performed time, and performed space.

Here language use is, as always, a good indicator of ideological code because even just by using the word 'immaterial' I run the risk of being misunderstood to mean 'unimportant' when I want to say 'not consisting of matter'. Despite the work of any number of theorists and theatre practitioners from Gernot Böhme to Bert O. States and Roland Barthes to Michael Chekhov, whose writings on images Englhart briefly reports,[7] the metaphysics of performance have so often been overlooked and ignored because, as Peggy Phelan duly notes, we are programmed to lose sight of the immaterial by a culture which lays no store by it.[8] But Mac Intyre has aimed directly at sequences of movements as well as positioning in the set that, as he has said of Maguire 'sitting on a wooden gate,' exude 'more than a whiff of the metaphysical'.[9] In a scene like the one where Maguire masturbates over the coals, many an audience let voyeuristic fantasies get the better of their imaginations and, as in New York and Philadelphia, took offense at a pornography of their own making.

Throughout the chapter 'Regarding Theatre' in *Theatre and Everyday Life*, Read makes the following case for regarding images as that often felt but rarely understood 'something more' of theatre performance. When images are regarded as something happening and not as something merely seen, their study as well as the study of theatre will 'challenge the persistent and detrimental division of intelligence and feeling'.[10] Experience as well as documentation of acts of performance will then be shifted toward the centre of the field of Theatre Studies, and so the kinds of knowledge to be had from theatre become marked by those means capable of rendering theatre images 'without losing a sense of their incidental glories'.[11] In this way, theory of theatre, after turning from a 'diagnostic' criticism which objectifies such surface appearances as what happens onstage and what is spoken or visibly performed, can attain a 'responsive attention' which grasps the metaphysical qualities of the theatre image.[12]

In his remarks on the masturbation scene in *The Great Hunger*, Tom Hickey captures its impact brilliantly when he describes how some nights 'you could feel a wave in the audience, the way crows fly off a tree'.[13] Not only do his words prove that in theatre the experience of performance is two-way, but also his vivid expression demonstrates the affinity between image and image. No matter what the medium or quality, images seem best suited to describing other images, and it would be hard for anyone who hadn't been to this particular run of *The Great Hunger* to top Hickey's rendition of what it was like to experience Maguire masturbating, Hickey miming with bellows, onstage, in Dublin in 1983. And this is because the theatre image is something much greater than visual perception.

The act of theatre occurs in images not because it hinges on such contested binaries as liveness and mediatization, body and word, experimental and mainstream, but because it hinges on the perspective we take on it. Theatre is a surface art: if one scratches the surface, the image that was there fades because it never actually was there but was in the imaginations of those in attendance and those performing. The theatre image forms and is lost sight of again and again because an act of performance is less an act of appearance/disappearance or showing/hiding than it is a way people can show showing and a position from which people, things, and events are appearing to appear.[14] To account for this experience of performance and to turn it to good critical use, Read adopts in *Theatre, Intimacy & Engagement* a parallax view on the relations between theatre and politics, between the human and the animal, and between theory and practice, and his findings and conclusions on a wide range of performance-related matters are astonishing. Parallax constitutes what we witness at a performance not only because it determines what we see, hear, and otherwise perceive, but also because it determines how we imagine that witness, how experience of a performance becomes, in that same performance, our images of that performance. Mac Intyre has shown through his theatre work as well as through his reflections on it just how well he grasps the essentiality of parallax to performance. He knows, for example, that an image rich enough to lay claim to the largest number of people's attentions, like the image of a dream, is likewise the product of parallax: 'Every slightly altered angle the viewer gives it sets new reverberations loose'.[15]

Read's parallax view focuses critical attention on what he calls the 'remainders' of critical theory and performance practice. Much critical work on identity, Read argues, has been arranging and ordering the differences of class, gender, nation, and race but, in the process, is missing a difference not even considered, a difference which forms a remainder in opposition to 'this humanist agenda':[16] the inhuman. When examining the basics of performance, Read wants not to extrapolate from a definitive statement like 'Performance's only life is in the present'[17] concepts such as 'liveness' and 'presence,' but he wants to take life itself as the starting point. So doing, he concludes from a wealth of sources and various lines of inquiry that humans must constantly recognize the difference between themselves and other animals in order to be human at all, and this ongoing task requires an ongoing show (in both senses of the word) of self-definition. Read's abundant illustrations of how we are constantly going about the task of distinguishing ourselves from the inhuman – e.g. the motives behind and the reactions to jihad manoeuvres in New York, London, and Madrid[18] – demonstrate how this same task is the act of being human. We are not the only animals who perform – just think of the variety of species that play dead – 'but the human is able to receive a remarkable variety of forms and faces upon its evacuated identity',[19] and this makes us the only animals forced to perform if we are still to choose who we would be. Unlike other animals who see either self or other, either sameness or difference, we perceive likeness,[20] and so we must expend an exorbitant amount of energy on play if we are to know ourselves for who we'd be: humans.

In the company of inanimate objects or other animals, we know who we are through our, and not their acts of association and separation. In all five of Mac Intyre's plays of this period, things normally inanimate as well as the objects of everyday life come alive to fret or to help, to worry or to ease the characters: for example, the dummy in *Rise Up Lovely Sweeney* or in *Snow White*, the stag's head on the back wall for *Dance for your Daddy*, and a fridge (*Rise Up Lovely Sweeney*), a shower (*Dance for your Daddy*), and a swing (*Snow White*). When Snow White 2, the name of the mannequin in the play, is served half the apple by Snow White herself (scene 11), identities blur so that this thing begins appearing like the young woman. Snow White plays on this confusion when, after indicating through her reactions that the mannequin hasn't gotten the poisoned half, she pretends pangs of death before enjoying her good fake at the audience's expense: 'Thought I was for the glass coffin, didn't you? That display case. Not a bit of it'.[21] The uncertainty which she's caused, not to mention the expectations raised by the fairy tale, makes 'Not a bit of it' sound overconfident. Besides, something is on display here, and that something is the display of displaying or, in theatre vocabulary, the performance of performing. It is not just in the talk, onstage, of a display case for death (i.e. the glass coffin) that death is shown being shown, but most efficaciously in Snow White's mock pangs as well as in the mannequin's vicariously conveyed healthiness. Both these acts are acts of deception just frisky enough that only a character possessed of the human could have carried them off, and so it is that we glimpse the human in this character only to lose sight of it until her next exchange with the things around her.

In Mac Intyre's works, character and action and their performance sometimes coincide in such ways that contact with the inhuman as well as play at being human become all one show. One such moment occurs in *The Bearded Lady* when Swift must undergo, by order of The Master Horse, clinical examination as to whether or not he is a Yahoo (Act 2, scene 5). Another such moment occurs during the closing scenes of *The Great Hunger*. The last to leave Maguire is the School-Girl, who glances back at him '*as if remembering*'.[22] Acting during this scene in a capacity other than that of a schoolgirl, she adopts the role of Poet with her action here, just as she has with her lines in scene 8: 'The poor peasant talking to himself in a stable door, an ignorant peasant deep in dung ...'.[23] Since the School-Girl's memories are most likely of Maguire's life and, by extension, the life of the peasant, the transition to the last scene must derive from section XIII of Kavanagh's poem, where are the lines:

> The girls pass along the roads
> And he can remember what man is,
> But there is nothing he can do.[24]

The peasant, at once wellspring of civilization and 'only one remove from the beasts he drives',[25] remembers his sex and remembers his humanity, but he can't act them because he's originary or, in psychoanalytical parlance, regressive. He must die alone, without people or animals to keep him company, without mother, sister, or wife:

> That was how his life happened.
> No mad hooves galloping in the sky,
> But the weak, washy way of true tragedy –
> A sick horse nosing around the meadow for a clean place to die.[26]

In the play, Maguire imitates this movement (as indicated through the quotation in the stage directions) after the School-Girl leaves, and then:

> *His foot paws the ground searchingly – here, there, elsewhere. Soon enough he's satisfied – or he abandons the search. He lies down, gives himself to the ground. MAGUIRE is still.*[27]

What is he searching for? Or what has he found? Himself, maybe. But the animal steals any fugitive show of the human, while the peasant, anyway 'half a vegetable,'[28] his foot pawing the ground, dissolves into clay where all beginnings are – even the poem's ('Clay is the word').[29] During the closing moments of *The Great Hunger*, the audience watch for what Maguire will do now. But he does as the peasant does, as the horse does. So the audience may glimpse Maguire in this series of acts, but what they see is the similarity between human and animal tragedy.

In our acts of self-definition we must admit the similarities between ourselves and other animals, but it is by discerning further differences in these very similarities that we come to know the human. The differences which we need to perceive if we are to distinguish the human from the inhuman are often locked away in images, images like that of the peasant half wild and half civilized, half man and half beast. W.J.T. Mitchell notes how our interaction with images evinces the very consciousness that helps make us human. We are capable of perceiving images in the first place only because we have mastered 'a paradoxical trick of consciousness, an ability to see something as "there" and "not there" at the same time,' while ducks, for example, are not so much taken in by hunters' decoys as they are unfortunate in being incapable of distinguishing between duck and duck-like.[30] Mitchell also notes, in his acutely perceptive essay 'What Do Pictures "Really" Want?', that we may have been going about studying images from the wrong perspective completely and that, instead of searching them for what they mean to us or for us, we should be asking what they want. Mitchell's proposal is no simple anthropomorphizing, but precisely the kind which Read considers valuable to the study of theatre, that is, anthropomorphizing 'with due regard for both partners in the odd couple'.[31] Since Mitchell here is pursuing 'an idea of visuality' adequate to the ontology of the image, he proposes granting images desires of their own, whether those desires turn out to be human, inhuman, or even nonhuman.[32]

When Mitchell's thought is applied to the theatre image, we find ourselves relating differently to performance. We begin taking the 'something more' of theatre to be also 'some thing' or 'some body' more than ourselves, and so we begin positioning ourselves differently from the theatre image, a position from which the reality of this image comes into view. 'The theatre image is taking on a life of its own!' comes the anxious cry. But that's just the point. Read considers the possibility that it is not a particular example of life or the representation of human life that finally may emerge from acts of performance, rather it is the flaring of a life.[33] A life is one indefinite instantiation of living which belongs to neither me nor you, neither him nor her but is noticeable and notable just the same and is there for everyone to feel. In theatre, a life is like an image because for either to take shape a group of people must be attendant. The phenomenology inherent to theatre images makes it impossible for me to claim this or that image for myself because these images only come about through performance. With theatre images, there is no mine and yours, only a. Ultimately, the image of theatre, being mine and yours and theirs, is our images of ourselves, of our humanity each time it slips our notice. It is as if, after all our attempts at identifying ourselves as human, all we were privy to was an image that's passed, but this image is potent enough to motivate the next attempt and the next attempt and the next.

For any theatre image there will be a difference in the similarity, for example, between Tom Hickey before a spectator and their (i.e., Hickey's and that spectator's and the audience's) image of Maguire as Maguire would be. In short, Tom Hickey can only move and gesture with his body and hold a prop, but in the masturbation scene, for example, what he's after and what may be seen is masturbation, dearth of sexuality, guilt. In the theatre, appearance may be reality, but material reality never disappears, and any audience will be aware, at least on some level, that what they see is not what they get or, in this example, that a posture and a bellows are not really masturbation. But by making it look like masturbation, Hickey tunes audience response to an image, and such an image, when performed, is nothing more than the knotty combination of what they see but don't get and what they get but don't see.

The team of Mac Intyre's Peacock collaborations have, in general, shown themselves especially adept at bringing to the fore the images at work in all theatre. For example, behind the decision to cut the intermission from *The Great Hunger* for its re-staging in 1986 lies both shrewd dramaturgy and, even at a studio theatre, venturesome production tactics for a play this long. But whatever may have been lost to the shorter performance time or to any reduction in structural complexity was regained tenfold by focusing the unbroken span of audience attention on intermittent images of desire, mystery, ecstasy, and death. Also, Mac Intyre's organization of each scene or each phase within a scene around the tripartite structure pre-climax/climax/post-climax heightens what Andreas Englhart calls the *Anziehungskraft* (force of attraction) which the theatre image anyway exerts by progressively closing in on and moving away from that which it would express.[34] When the meeting between Swift and the Female Yahoo climaxes with each gesturing markedly toward their genitals[35] or when at the closing of 'The Park Races' (*Dance for your Daddy*) the characters exit 'in a post-coital dusk',[36] I begin to suspect that Mac Intyre had been modelling his tripartite structure on the foreplay, coitus, and post-coitus of sex. Climaxing his plays' images in steady cycles of anticipation and consummation – a technique in tune with Mac Intyre's thoughts on and practice of his art – taps the potential of these images by redoubling the efficacy of their force of attraction. But such intense performance must also afford all participants relief of some sort or other if fatigue, irritation, and surfeit are not to set in. Of this, too, the collaborators were aware. Mac Intyre calls this relief 'the element of *jeu d'esprit*',[37] and in the performance texts its instances are often referred to as 'interpolations.' Spectator to three showings of *Rise Up Lovely Sweeney*, Dermot Healy had seen how '[e]verything depends on striking the right note between events,' and in his review he attests to the actors' skilful achievement of comic relief between phases of very strong emotion.[38]

While above I have been focusing on the elemental part which the image has in theatre performance, I will now refocus on the word 'image' in order to show how theatre uses the image as one of the many instruments at its disposal, next to speech, the body, or lighting, machinery, and sound. This reading of Theatre of the Image makes it just one particular kind of theatre amongst others, for example, Mac Intyre's Theatre of the Image contrasts a Shavian Drama of Ideas. So, if one play can have more or fewer images than the next, theatre can be more or less imagistic, and any Theatre of the Image will have definitive features by which it lives up to its name.

What, then, is so especially imagistic about Mac Intyre's Peacock collaborations during the 1980s?

For one, the salient effect which Theatre of the Image has on a performance is to order speech, the dominant component in conventional drama productions, not above but beside the other means of performance. Against the conventional relation of much dialogue to little description, the texts of *The Great Hunger*, *The Bearded Lady*, *Rise Up Lovely Sweeney*, *Dance for your Daddy*, and *Snow White* run for pages with few or no spoken lines. Before the start of rehearsals for *The Great Hunger*, Tom Hickey remembers wondering how they were going to meet the 'unusual demands' of this 'very strange' script.[39] On the page these plays give seem strange because the conventions for reading them as well as the tools for analyzing them reside, as Read notes for performance texts of this kind, partly outside the field of literary criticism.[40] The bias against nonconventional forms of theatre among literary critics and theatre reviewers alike is plain to see, for example, in Robert Hogan's dismissal of Mac Intyre's performance texts as 'outlines for theatre performances' which 'have little to do with the drama as literature or indeed with literature itself'.[41] Not only does this ask of theatre (which is a performing art) that it be literature (which is a written art), but it also misses how Mac Intyre accomplishes in these texts a rigorous notation for a kind of theatre that is both difficult to direct – how to read text meant to be done, not spoken? – and resistant to documentation – how to write down movement, not words? Mac Intyre not only accounts equally for speech, positioning, and movement through a 'verbal score' and a 'gestural score,' but he also deploys an arsenal of sense vocabulary to capture the images of performance by describing them as 'blasts,' 'echoes,' 'flavours,' 'radiation,' 'reprises,' 'rhythms,' 'textures,' 'vignettes,' and 'whiffs.' One particularly dense illustration of his notation is the opening of 'The Park Races' in *Dance for your Daddy* (scene 4):

> *The din and light and colour of the meeting, the gloss of the members' enclosure, the haze of opulence and the sensual or dubiously sensual ... Dad (as Elderly Roué), Homme Fatal and Romeo are onstage ... The flavour is of the parade ring, parading in the parade ring, waiting for the talent to appear in the parade ring.*[42]

A passage like this is not meant to direct the positions and movements of the actors or the employment of props and scenery, but to make possible the creation of an image in performance.

The way Mac Intyre writes characters also makes for more images in each of the five plays than in the average theatre performance. Mac Intyre's characters are not constructed in a narrative/psychological frame. The distinguish themeselves through a repetitive set of gestures, routines, positions, and lines. In contrast to the conventional characters of theatre who speak in their idiolects about their pasts, presents, and futures, who reason in their own peculiar ways about their circumstances, and who respond in comprehensible language to others' conversation, Mac Intyre's characters are less what we hear them say and more what we see them do. In *Snow White*, this technique of characterization is most clearly illustrated when one character imitates another, as when the Mother becomes like the Seventh Dwarf by *'quoting'* his *'cancellation geste'*[43] or when Dad, Romeo, and Homme Fatal become *'The Males as Females'* during 'Reversals' (scene 10), which is itself the reprise of 'The Park Races' (scene 4) when Dau, Dark Dau, and Girl Child each plays racehorse to the male characters' bettors. In the *Rise Up Lovely Sweeney* rehearsal script, Sweeney and the Interrogator even play a *'transformation game'* in which Sweeney wears the Interrogator's coat, while the Interrogator does *'his Sweeney/fugitive cameo,'* which involves being *'murky in the spiral staircase zone, peering from its whorls,'* and imitating Sweeney's voice.[44] In a play that airs the perennial Stage-Irish question 'What ish my nayshun?',[45] this exchange of characteristics between the terrorist and his interrogator show the identity crisis which, in part, all the fighting has been based on. And when Sweeney and the Interrogator, again themselves, then stand back to back in order each to cooperate on the other's *'archetypal "affliction" story from their side of the conflict'*,[46] Mac Intyre's physical brand of theatre shakes the ideological foundations of The Troubles.

The last and most important thing making especially imagistic Mac Intyre's Peacock work of this period is its basis in collaboration. Collaboration need not produce imagistic work, but collaboration can be exceptionally imagistic because, as an activity which a group of theatre practitioners do to come up with and to test out what they will do in a play, it is itself integral to and active in the creation of theatre imagery. At the simplest level during rehearsals, writes Andreas Englhart, the writer, director, actors, and other artists and technicians will be engaged in a continuous process where they form and formulate their images of the final production and where those images are compared to what has so far been done and matched to what is deemed still practicable.[47] Practitioner such as Tom Mac Intyre,[48] and researchers/-practitioners such as Bernadette Sweeney[49] attest to the creative activity of collaboration.And it is this creativity which Mac Intyre and other practitioners of image-rich theatre draw on from the earliest rehearsals. Images devised and practiced in collaboration don't need to be translated or carried into the actual performance because they are already what they should be. This explains the powerful resonance of the images in Theatre-of-the-Image plays: collective production of a collective product. The bias against unconventional theatrical forms appears, again, in scepticism about Mac Intyre's contribution, as writer, to such highly collaborative theatre work. Such doubt Patrick Mason answers by explaining how the Abbey's collaboration with Mac Intyre first was made possible and then thrived both because Mac Intyre had initiated it with detailed, illuminative scripts and because, after that, he was completely prepared to let rehearsals, and not the scripts, determine content and shape of the plays. Not clinging to what is written nor calling on the authority of the text, Mac Intyre is in Mason's opinion a great exception among playwrights.[50]

Much remains to be researched in the relations between image and theatre. Alan Read has staked out a field of investigation where questions like 'What comprises theatre?' and 'How do performer and spectators interact?' are given ample room. The centrepiece of this article has been to broach the matter of the image as a vital element of theatre performance, on a par with other such radicals of the art of theatre as human performers and spectators, a place to perform, and proxemic and kinesic relations in the theatre space. Using the example of Tom Mac Intyre's Peacock work of the 1980s, I have wanted not only to present Read's thought on the theatre image, but also to show how Tom Mac Intyre, his collaborators, and his audiences prove Read's theory both in their reflections on theatre and in their reactions to performances. In the next section I stepped off Read's theoretical standpoint to view theatre not as it is, but as it seems to be; in other words, I have shifted perspectives on the image from one on the deep, essential qualities of the image of theatre to one on the surface, adventitious features of images in a theatre. For this step, Mac Intyre's five plays have served well as a backdrop to the question 'What makes a play imagistic?'

I can conclude that *The Great Hunger*, *The Bearded Lady*, *Rise Up Lovely Sweeney*, *Dance for your Daddy*, and *Snow White* – five Irish plays too seldom researched critically – are a wealth of material for the combined study of image and theatre.

Works Cited

Bachelard, Gaston, *The Poetics of Space*, translated by Maria Jolas (Boston: Beacon Press, 1969).

Englhart, Andreas, '*Was ist ein Theater-Bild?: Anmerkungen zur aktuellen Diskussion über den iconic turn und zum Phänomen des Bildes im Theater*' (What Is a Theater-Image?: Notes on the Current Discussion about the Icon Turn and about the Phenomenon of the Image in Theatre), *Forum Modernes Theater* 19.1 (2004), pp. 3-25.

Etherton, Michael, *Contemporary Irish Dramatists* (Houndmills: Macmillan, 1989).

Göler, Hans von, *Streets Apart from Abbey Street: The Search for an Alternative National Theatre in Ireland since 1980* (Trier: Wissenschaftlicher Verlag Trier, 2000).

Grene, Nicholas, 'Tom Mac Intyre', *The Oxford Encyclopedia of Theatre and Performance*, ed. Dennis Kennedy, 2 vols (Oxford: OUP, 2003) pp. 780-781.

Healy, Dermot, 'Let the Hare Sit', *Theatre Ireland* 11 (1985) pp. 9-10.

Hogan, Robert, 'Mac Intyre, Tom (1931-), man of letters', *Dictionary of Irish Literature*, ed. Robert Hogan, 2nd edn (Westport: Greenwood Press, 1996) pp. 772-74.

Holmquist, Kathryn, 'In the Beginning Was ... the Image ...', *Theatre Ireland* 6 (1984) pp. 150-152.

Hurley, Vincent, '*The Great Hunger*: A Reading', *The Great Hunger: Poem into Play*, by Patrick Kavanagh and Tom Mac Intyre (Westmeath, Ireland: Lilliput Press, 1988) pp. 73-82.

Kavanagh, Patrick (& Tom Mac Intyre), *The Great Hunger: Poem into Play* (Westmeath, Ireland: Lilliput Press, 1988) pp. 3-25.

Llewellyn-Jones, Margaret, *Contemporary Irish Drama and Cultural Identity* (Bristol: Intellect Books, 2002).

Mac Intyre, Tom, *The Bearded Lady*, rehearsal script (The Abbey Theatre, no date).

---, *Dance for your Daddy* (The Abbey Theatre, March 1987).

---, *The Great Hunger*, rehearsal script (The Abbey Theatre, no date).

---, *The Great Hunger* (The Abbey Theatre, [1983]).

---, *The Great Hunger: Poem into Play* (Westmeath, Ireland: Lilliput Press, 1988) pp. 29-68.

---, *Rise Up Lovely Sweeney*, rehearsal script 2 (The Abbey Theatre, 1985).

---, *Snow White*, rehearsal script 1 (The Abbey Theatre, no date).

Mason, Patrick, Director's Note, *The Great Hunger: Poem into Play*, by Patrick Kavanagh and Tom Mac Intyre (Westmeath, Ireland: Lilliput Press, 1988) pp. 69-70.

Meyer-Dinkgräfe, Daniel, *Who's Who in Contemporary World Theatre*, ed. Daniel Meyer-Dinkgräfe (London: Routledge, 2000) pp. 183-184.

Mitchell, W. J. T., *Iconology: Image, Text, Ideology* (Chicago: U. of Chicago Press, 1986).

---, 'What Do Pictures "Really" Want?', *October* 77 (Summer 1996) pp. 71-82.

Morash, Christopher, *A History of Irish Theatre 1601-2000* (Cambridge: CUP, 2002).

Mulrooney, Deirdre, *Irish Moves: An Illustrated History of Dance and Physical Theatre in Ireland* (Dublin: The Liffey Press, 2006).

O'Toole, Fintan, 'Tom Mac Intyre', *Continuum Companion to Twentieth Century Theatre*, ed. Colin Chambers (London: Continuum, 2002) pp. 465.

Phelan, Peggy, *Unmarked: The Politics of Performance* (London: Routledge, 1993).

Playwrights in Profile – Series 1, presented by Sean Rocks, RTÉ Radio, Radio 1, Dublin, February-April 2007
<http://www.rte.ie/radio1/playwrights/1160140.html>

Read, Alan, *Theatre and Everyday Life: An Ethics of Performance* (London: Routledge, 1993).

---, *Theatre, Intimacy & Engagement: The Last Human Venue* (Houndmills: Palgrave Macmillan, 2008).

Sweeney, Bernadette, *Performing the Body in Irish Theatre* (Basingstoke: Palgrave Macmillan, 2008).

---, 'Tom Mac Intyre', *Dictionary of Literary Biography*, vol. 245, 3rd series.

Welch, Robert, 'Tom Mac Intyre', ed. Robert Welch, *The Oxford Companion to Irish Literature* (Oxford: Clarendon Press, 1996), pp. 339.

---

[1] Michael Etherton, *Contemporary Irish Dramatists* (Houndmills: Macmillan, 1989), pp. 45-47.

[2] Alan Read, *Theatre and Everyday Life: An Ethics of Performance* (London: Routledge, 1993), p. 63.

[3] Gaston Bachelard, *The Poetics of Space*, translated by Maria Jolas (Boston: Beacon Press, 1969).

[4] Read, *Theatre and Everyday Life*, p. 84.

[5] Dermot Healy, 'Let the Hare Sit', *Theatre Ireland* 11 (1985), pp. 9-10.

[6] quoted in Holmquist, pp. 151-152.

[7] Andreas Englhart, '*Was ist ein Theater-Bild?: Anmerkungen zur aktuellen Diskussion über den iconic turn und zum Phänomen des Bildes im Theater*' (What Is a Theater-Image?: Notes on the Current Discussion about the Icon Turn and about the Phenomenon of the Image in Theatre), *Forum Modernes Theater* 19.1 (2004), pp. 15-16.

[8] Peggy Phelan, *Unmarked: The Politics of Performance* (London: Routledge, 1993), p. 5.

[9] quoted in Holmquist, p. 152.

[10] Read, *Theatre and Everyday Life*, p. 65.

[11] Ibid., p. 70.

[12] Ibid., p. 83.

[13] quoted in Holmquist, p. 152.

[14] compare Alan Read, *Theatre, Intimacy & Engagement: The Last Human Venue* (Houndmills: Palgrave Macmillan, 2008), pp. 16-17.

[15] quoted in Holmquist, p. 152.

[16] Read, *Theatre, Intimacy & Engagement*, p. 85.

[17] Phelan, 146.

[18] Read, *Theatre, Intimacy & Engagement*, pp. 71-73.

[19] Ibid., p. 93.

[20] W. J. T. Mitchell, *Iconology: Image, Text, Ideology* (Chicago: U. of Chicago Press, 1986), p. 17.

[21] Tom Mac Intyre, *Snow White*, rehearsal script 1 (The Abbey Theatre, no date), p. 75.

[22] Tom Mac Intyre, *The Great Hunger: Poem into Play* (Westmeath, Ireland: Lilliput Press, 1988) p. 67.

[23] Patrick Kavanagh, *The Great Hunger: Poem into Play* (Westmeath, Ireland: Lilliput Press, 1988): 14 and Mac Intyre, *Great Hunger*, 1988, 51. At two other moments the School-Girl adopts the role of Poet, which had been included in the earliest rehearsal script (Tom Mac Intyre, *The Great Hunger*, rehearsal script (The Abbey Theatre, no date)) but was, according to Patrick Mason (Director's Note, *The Great Hunger: Poem into Play* (Westmeath, Ireland: Lilliput Press, 1988): 69-70), absorbed also by the new part of Packy: when she says, 'Holy Spirit is the rising sap ...' (Mac Intyre, *Great Hunger*, 1988, 42 and Kavanagh, *Great Hunger*, 7) and when she says, 'Oh to be wise...' (Mac Intyre, *Great Hunger*, 1988, 62 and Kavanagh, *Great Hunger*, 3 and 5). In act 2, scene 7 of the 1983 performance text, the part of the School-Girl is explicitly directed to adopt the role of Poet: '*The School-Girl*, eyes on the house, speaks – her tone is recitation – but with an undertow of more than that' (Tom Mac Intyre, *The Great Hunger* (The Abbey Theatre, [1983]): 52-53).

[24] Kavanagh, *Great Hunger*, p. 22.

[25] Ibid.

[26] Ibid., p. 23.

[27] Mac Intyre, *Great Hunger*, 1988, p. 67.

[28] Kavanagh, *Great Hunger*, p. 22.

[29] Ibid., p. 3.

[30] Mitchell, *Iconology*, p. 17.

[31] Read, *Theatre, Intimacy & Engagement,* p. 76.

[32] W.J.T. Mitchell, 'What Do Pictures "Really" Want?', *October* 77 (Summer 1996), p. 82.

[33] Read, *Theatre, Intimacy & Engagement*, p. 96.

[34] Englhart, pp. 16-17.

[35] Tom Mac Intyre, *The Bearded Lady*, rehearsal script (The Abbey Theatre, no date) p 45.

[36] Tom Mac Intyre, *Dance for your Daddy* (The Abbey Theatre, March 1987) p. 33.

[37] quoted in Holmquist, p. 152.

[38] Healy, pp. 9-10.

[39] Playwrights in Profile – Series 1, RTÉ Radio.

[40] Read, *Theatre and Everyday Life*, pp. 63-65 and 83-84.

[41] Hogan, Robert, 'Mac Intyre, Tom (1931-), Man of Letters', *Dictionary of Irish Literature*, ed. Robert Hogan, 2nd edn (Westport: Greenwood Press, 1996), p. 773.

[42] Mac Intyre, *Dance for your Daddy*, pp. 22-23.

[43] Mac Intyre, *Snow White*, p. 84.

[44] Tom Mac Intyre, *Rise Up Lovely Sweeney*, rehearsal script 2 (The Abbey Theatre, 1985), pp. 57-58.

[45] Mac Intyre, *Rise Up Lovely Sweeney*, p. 88.

[46] Ibid., p. 61.
[47] Englhart, p. 14.
[48] Mulrooney, p. 179.
[49] Sweeney, *Performing the Body in Irish Theatre*, p. 76.
[50] Playwrights in Profile, Series 1, RTÉ Radio.

CHAPTER 5: 'A GRADLE O' STORIES'[1]

Programme Note: *Kitty O'Shea* by Tom Mac Intyre

(Peacock Theatre, October 1990)
'Dear Tom'
A Letter from Medbh McGuckian

I don't know much about Kitty O'Shea herself and all I remember about her and Parnell is what we were taught at school, that his relationship with her caused a scandal which ruined him and any hope of Home Rule for Ireland, that the people's love of him turned to hatred and he died of a broken heart. Nobody heard what happened to her. Your play tells us how she lived on, afterwards. I don't know if it is authentic or not. I think it might be how a woman like her might feel about a man like him. There was a woman on the radio today being interviewed about how she felt about her husband having an affair with a younger woman, and the interviewer was surprised to hear that she could understand how the other woman could have fallen in love with him since she herself, after twenty-four years of marriage, still adored him. She used the word 'idol', and the interviewer remarked, not greatly to the woman's comfort, that it was a rare thing for women to use that word about their husbands, even if they were faithful to them. I think your play analyses this 'rare', perhaps not so rare, capacity or tendency in some women, even nowadays, 'to select their own society, then shut the door' as Emily Dickinson puts it. The idol remains an idol whether it is there or not, simply by having been chosen.

Irish history gives us many such noble and swashbuckling heroes. What was it about Parnell that gave him such mastery and caused his downfall? I heard this week about George Best's

exhibition of himself on the *Terry Wogan Show* – is there
something shared in this repeated pattern, the man of genius, the
moment of opportunity and triumph, the first low, the fatal flaw, the
debasement? Last summer I happened to be in an upper room in
Navan, from whose front window Parnell had delivered one of his
speeches, and to visit a nearby house in which he stayed. Those
places held a little still of his glory and his tragedy, as the bare fields
of Tara still shimmer with a power not dead, as the grey trees and
twisting paths of Murlough Bay are sweet with the lamenting and
unburied ghost of Roger Casement, similarly maligned for sexual
and private reasons, similarly destroyed. I like the sense your play
gives of this mysterious, indefinable force – perhaps it is manhood,
or manliness itself – though the times they lived through were no
less full of courage than our own. Other plays I've been to seem to be
trying to contribute positively to healing divisions by
demythologizing our idealized martyrs, cutting them down to size,
making them mock-heroic or real. I don't doubt that fear is reduced
by laughter, but in an age of anti-heroes Kitty's commitment to her
image here strikes me as traditional or regressive. Her intensity is as
exaggerated as that of Yeats's *Countess Cathleen*, she's as vociferous
as Mauyra in *Riders to the Sea*. Your setting is typical of the early
and most popular O'Casey, all of which is going back to the
beginning of things in the Abbey Theatre, although the form, with
its difficult monologue, is more akin to Beckett and the theatre of
the absurd. But it is no mere Irish female protagonist your Kitty
resembles most – indeed she is most assertively not Irish, has never
and will never even set foot in the abhorred place; the universal
madness of her depiction is the morbid derangement of a Lady
Macbeth, or the demented, lovesick despair of a Cleopatra. She
reminds me most of Cosima Wagner, who was fated to outlive her
life in the same way, who would rather have died like Dido on the
pyre.

   A play about a woman should contribute something new, if
possible, to an understanding of the workings of the female mind
and what we have here is an insight into feminine role-playing itself,
the comfort of self-dramatization for women, where they relive the
moment of ecstacy and agony with themselves, the Scarlet O'Hara.
The most poignant realization of this is the scene where the ageing,
aged, long-past childbearing figure, relives, re-enacts the walk of a
young and pregnant self, a concept you describe accurately as both
fragile and monstrous. Perhaps that's what we are, ultimately,

beautiful, misshapen, change-ridden. The play offers also an intellectual satisfaction in the taut contrast between spiritual and worldly values, symbolized in the balance between the two acts, the two photographs, the two deaths, the two daughters. The positive crescendo of the ending is well worth waiting for. And its theme should be of vital current interest to anyone involved in the ever-increasing syndrome of what to do with the energy of the obsolete, the crisis of the nursing-home. Needless to say, it points up the nightmare, both physical and mental, of bereavement in the Irish situation, the suffering of each girlfriend or widow we see fleetingly stagger through our newsreels.

With admiration and best wishes, Medbh

---

[1] Tom Mac Intyre *Sheep's Milk on the Boil*, p.93.

Theatre Review: *Kitty O'Shea* by Tom Mac Intyre

Victoria White
(*Theatre Ireland*, October 1990)

This is an excellent example of the dramatic monologue form. Its language is rich and poetic, its cadences exquisite, as it traces the life of Katherine O'Shea, the Englishwoman who married an Irish Captain and then seduced Charles Stewart Parnell. A woman quite different from the Kitty of popular folklore emerges. She is not Kitty O'Shay but Kitty O'Shee. She was a snob and she hated the Irish. Something which both Mac Intyre and popular folklore agree on, however, is that she was very sensual. And Mac Intyre adds a twist by making her a woman obsessed with self-dramatization.

In the first half, Kitty is in an off-the-shoulder nightdress, shimmying around a bedroom peopled with the men of her past and visited periodically by Norah, the one daughter who has stayed by her. Norah is a young woman as repelled by sex as her mother is propelled by it. Dave Nolan's beautiful wave sounds filter through and play with the language, for it is in Brighton that Kitty ended her days. Suddenly, dramatically, Kitty is pulled back into the past and, as a storm rips through the room, she remembers the day Parnell suggested they jump into the sea and end it all.

The second half of the piece has her an older, poorer woman, her sensuality lost in horsiness. But she still remembers the moments of real passion she has lived through and Mac Intyre seems to affirm that it was worth it for this.

The play is deeply reminiscent of Beckett – of Krapp looking back over his life and remembering his few significant moments; of the radio play *Embers*, set to the sound of waves. The poetry of the language is often as intense as that of Beckett. But the intellectual content isn't there. Mac Intyre gestures towards themes – the importance of passion, the ability of womankind to look back and dramatize the self – but can't follow the themes well because he is also telling us the story of Kitty O'Shea. We have the strange sensation we had with Aodhan Madden's *Josephine in the Night*, of watching someone whose life has influenced history, having exactly the same sort of problems and thoughts as trouble all of us. There's nothing wrong with that ... except two things: why make it Kitty

O'Shea; and, if it must be she, why pass up on the drama of a full-scale historical bash?

Why pass up on the drama? Although Fiona Victory's performance was spell-binding, directed with obvious sensitivity by Ben Barnes; and although Kathy Strachan's wood-panelled set was beautiful, it's really only just about enough to justify bringing us out of our warm homes and into the theatre. It would be over-prescriptive to suggest that one-man or one-woman shows (although Orla Charlton appears, the play is really a monologue) shouldn't be done or should be done sparingly. But they have to be so good to stop us, or at least to stop me, yearning for drama. *Kitty O'Shea* is just about good enough but with *The Misogynist* playing upstairs and *High Germany* at the Gate, I was simply sick and tired of one-character shows. They really constitute a separate genre, often as near to poetry and prose as to drama – and let me stick my neck out and say – they are usually easier to write. They are also cheaper and easier to stage and I came out of this year's Festival with a certain sense of having been cheated out of something.

There is, I feel, something wrong when a woman is standing alone on the Peacock stage discussing woman's lot, with a man on the Abbey stage, discussing man's lot. Will one of these talented playwrights – and on this showing the adjective applies particularly to Mac Intyre – please bring them together and let us see what happens.

Theatre Review: *Fine Day for a Hunt* by Tom Mac Intyre
'Mac Intyre's Powerful and Unsettling Hunt'

Jeff O'Connell
(*The Galway Advertiser*, 23 July 1992)

Tom Mac Intyre's *Fine Day for a Hunt*, Punchbag's Arts Festival play, is a powerful and unsettling piece of theatre. Like some mysterious tableau glimpsed by flashes of light, it intrigues and frustrates in almost equal measure. Dramatically, it is light years removed from the world of, for example, Druid's *Gaslight* or even Punchbag's previous production, *Eclipsed*. But for anyone interested in seeing what happens when a highly gifted playwright decides to toss out the normal theatrical conventions, this play is a rich and rewarding experience.

Fine Day for a Hunt is located in an Ireland that seems a deliberate blend of fantasy and reality. It is the world of the 'Big House' and the peasant's cottage, of the idleness and seediness of the feckless gentry and the grinding, hopeless poverty of the ordinary Irish. The Major (Brendan Murray in a fine, sneering performance that chillingly portrays the underlying brutality of his class) summons a peasant girl (Nicole Rourke in a very difficult role) and tells her to strip. As she stands naked and humiliated, he uncorks a bottle and anoints her limbs with the liquid it contains, a 'scent', the purpose of which gradually becomes evident.

An old couple (Shay Rooney and Theresa Evers) are brought before the Major – they may be the girl's parents but this is not made very clear – and are offered work on the estate. Another young woman (Margaret O'Sullivan) encounters the peasant girl and during their fragmented conversation it becomes clear that the girl has been selected – she is 'ripe for the plucking' – to take part in the forthcoming hunt, that she is to be the 'hunted', the equivalent of the fox and that the older woman is herself a previous 'prey'.

The hunt begins. Dicky Paget (Tommy Tiernan as a comical racing commentator) describes its progress. Packy (Dermot Arrigan, once again showing what a versatile actor he is) arrives on a bicycle to provide his own breathless commentary on the action. A pack of braying beagles (played by several of the actors who also take other parts) rushes across the stage, sniffing and searching for the prey. Meanwhile Miss Betty (Theresa Evers), the grand lady of the house

– the Major's mother or aunt? – and Monique (Carol Hunt with a nearly incomprehensible French accent), a visiting Frenchwoman excited by the action of the hunt, wait back at the house for news.

It is a very strange play. Although the reference points are all Irish, it has the logic and sense of inevitability of a dream or a nightmare. The hunt, which has as its focus the hunting down and rape of the young peasant girl, has the formality of a ritual. And the references to previous 'hunts' (one girl got as far as Cobh, we are told) lend it the quality of myth. I found myself thinking of American writer Shirley Jackson's short story 'The Lottery' where a festive New England picnic culminates in the ritual stoning of a young woman in order to ensure the fertility of the coming year's crops.

Sean Evers directs his very talented cast with great pace and the only sections that drag slightly are those involving Miss Betty and Monique and this would seem to be the fault of the author who – so far as I was concerned – did not make clear enough their function in the play. There are scenes of almost hallucinatory beauty, such as that where two hunters are searching for the girl in a glade. Naked except for body paint that imitates the dappled greens and browns of the wood, she moves out of sight with a sinuous grace that perfectly captures the innocence and cunning of a hunted woodland creature.

The original score by Gan Ainm provides a brilliant musical counterpart to the action, and the lighting design by Eamon Fox is most effective.

Fine Day for a Hunt is a powerful theatrical experience, even allowing for the sometimes irritating obscurity it displays. Disturbing and occasionally brutal, its mesmerizing images will remain in the mind long after you leave the theatre.

Theatre Review: *Chickadee* by Tom Mac Intyre 'Love Lost and Love Eternal'

Jocelyn Clarke
(*The Sunday Tribune*, 23 May 1993)

The older man falling for the younger woman, and she falling after him, blissfully drowning together as friends and family throw life belts, ignored and unwanted, is a familiar story. In Red Kettle's production of Tom Mac Intyre's new play *Chickadee*, the telling of the story is different, with devices many and styles various. The style is the thing of it, not the substance.

Hubert is the older and wiser man in pursuit of that elusive something, younger and more vital. Julie is the pursued younger and more vital, wise in her youth and innocent in her years. Their relationship, tender and uncertain from within, is subject to the disapproval of Mom and the resigned acceptance of Dad. Both are concerned about their baby doll. Bonzo, Hubert's friend, is the voice of indifferent reason, bemused by Hubert's folly. Julie's friend, Daphne, the vamp with a heart, and Sunniva, forlorn and alone, offer advice and support as Julie is torn by jealousy of the past and uncertainty of the future.

The telling of the story is self-conscious and theatrical. Each of the acts is punctuated by bird song, and the scenes by predominantly Willie Nelson songs of love lost and love eternal. The set design (Bláithín Sheerin and lighting by Stephen McManus) is a deep sky blue backdrop with bright yellow stars, with a raised circular dais, crowned by a scarlet aureolar love seat. Characters walk and leave through brightly coloured entrances, play golf, prune flowers and hold parties on the green carpet. It's a day-glo bright state of mind, archetypal and self-referential.

Character becomes cypher, slightly pixillated and laconic, and conversations become increasingly gnomic and meditative. Emotionally charged encounters and situations (Hubert encountering Mom and Dad, the ghosts of former lovers, parent concerned about daughter), replete with psycho sexual and mythic undertones, are transformed into witty and self-reflexive pastiches.

Though fun filled and playful, amusing and occasionally provoking, *Chickadee* is a self-reflexive manipulation of surfaces and fancies, undermined by a deliberate hesitancy to explore and investigate the substance beneath. It is more the appearance of emotions rather than the emotions themselves.

Garrett Keogh as Hubert is fluid and robust and Bongi MacDermott as Julie is uncertain and occasionally over emphatic. The rest of the cast (Des Nealon, Joan Sheehy, Michael Grennell, Deirdre Molloy (excellent), Sian Quill and Simon Manahan) give vigorous performances full of energy and verve, and Tom Hickey directs with flair and style.

**Programme Note: *Sheep's Milk on the Boil*
by Tom Mac Intyre**

'The Night Before, the Morning After'
(Peacock Theatre, February 1994)
Ciaran Carson

Some years ago my wife and I were invited to a musical wedding on Inishbofin island. Rather than going from A to B, we went by way of X: a circuitous route that took in Fermanagh, Sligo and Galway, where we learned that we could get a lift to Inishbofin on a Galway hooker owned by Bruce Du Ve, the Australian uilleann piper. We were to sail from *Cill Chiarain*, and the night before we hoisted sail we visited the local Galway hooker genius, for guidance and crack. The talk was in Irish and English, a macaronic colloquy that spoke of ebbs and tides, wind directions, compass points, concealing reefs, bearings, mearings; language itself articulating how to get there.

Reading Tom Mac Intyre's *Sheep's Milk on the Boil*, I was reminded of that time, of English coming from an underlying skein of Irish, becoming bright and new in its engagement with the old. I was reminded of tunes and songs, of celebrations that went on to the morning after the night before, till time became a continuous present marked by musical time. Mac Intyre's language comes from the grit and rasp of speech and the backlog of stuff embedded in it: proverbs, spakes, pronouncements, jokes, tags, song-fragments, references, yarns. It is a language, that for all that it is embedded in a *Locus*, refers constantly to another, wider world; the world of past action, the other world, the World that is to be. The characters are bound by language, but they revel in it.

The play is set on an island. At the heart of the play is a looking-glass; not a mirror, but a looking-glass as if the glass enables you to see something that you didn't glimpse before. The island is a kind of looking-glass in which people are tranformed by talk and action. You can conceal the looking-glass in a pocket or a purse. You can carry a whole language in one brain.

The morning after the night before, your brain is swarming with bits and pieces of Last Night's Fun – song-fragments, snatches of speech, bars of tunes and dances – 'in swithers and swives', as Mac Intyre has it. Now that I think of it, I remember spending an evening with Tom Mac Intyre many years ago in Belfast. Some of the talk was of the Russian story writer Isaac Babel, and I am reminded how Mac Intyre himself has some of his precision and joyful violence. I am reminded of Babel, and the complicated tower from which language emerges.

'Between two languages ...'

Olwen Fouéré

[With the kind permission of RTÉ we present the following extract from Olwen Fouéré's interview with Sean Rocks as part of the first series of *Playwrights in Profile* (RTÉ Radio 1, Dublin, 11 Feb 2007.)]

I first met Tom Mac Intyre walking a road on Inishbofin and I remember saying hello to him, so we've known each other since then. I was 17 at the time. Then I bumped into him occasionally in Dublin in the 1980s, when he was working with Patrick Mason at the Abbey. I'd done a workshop with Patrick and we talked about the possibility of my being involved in their work at that time but I think I was committed to other work with Jim and Peter Sheridan at The Project Arts Centre so it never really happened. However, I saw a lot of Tom's early work and I was very excited by the way he was shifting the emphasis of playwriting away from the written word and into the body. This is very much an area of interest for me, not least because I was brought up in between two languages (French and English) and I realized that the place I existed was in between both of them, and not speaking! So, the kind of theatre I was interested in was rooted in the body and Tom's work really appealed to me. I am also, of course, very excited by theatre based in language, but in Ireland of the 1980s there was such a huge emphasis on the written word as opposed to theatre as a language in itself, or as a form in itself.

I could also see, and was very interested in, the highly collaborative nature of Mac Intyre's work, and the way in which Patrick, and all of the actors in the company, were as involved in the creation of the piece as the writer. As far as I remember Tom would provide a basic score, which would then be thrown upside down and inside out and backwards and forwards, and what emerged would be almost unrecognizable from the script that was originally presented.

Over the years we kept missing opportunities to work together, that is up until *Snow White* (Peacock Theatre, 1988) when Tom asked me to play the roles of 'The Woman' and 'The Mother'. I accepted, of course, and it was great to finally work with Tom and

Patrick. In fact the whole process was terrific because Patrick is such a brilliant midwife of plays. The whole working environment was one in which the material was explored physically. It was almost like working in a dance piece but with theatrically based intentions. So it was a fantastic situation where, as an actor, you were speaking and improvising with your body yet leaving language out of it, although sometimes you would have language there too.

In *Sheep's Milk on the Boil* (Peacock Theatre, 1994) I played 'The Inspector of Wrack' and probably had the best entrance that any actor in Irish theatre could ever hope for: the walls of a cottage at the centre of the play shake and crack open and I walk in on the couple who live there. It was a pretty dramatic entrance. I had this fantastic costume, a sort of fur coat with a gorgeous red silk dress underneath it. Every aspect of my costume represented some aspect of heightened female sexuality, or conjured up all of the fantasies you've ever had about playing every female icon from the movie screen. When 'The Inspector of Wrack' comes in through this cottage wall her male counterpart, 'The Visitor' (played by Owen Roe) appears more or less at the same time. They are archetypal energies or male/female opposition figures, but they are also there to create chaos and to throw the established order upside down, to unleash all the repressed aspects of the domestic situation. In the course of the action various things happen to the couple in question, Matt and Biddy, which present challenges or temptations. For me, 'The Inspector of Wrack' was very much the embodiment of the female energy in all its aspects, particularly the trickster aspect.

Tom's later work, of course, has moved much more towards spoken language and the written word. He is such an extraordinary poet. I remember people in the 1980s asking why he wasn't using more of that in the theatre and so I think in the later work there is a greater emphasis on spoken language. I believe, however, that the earlier work has informed this move. What was really magical about all of that work in the 1980s was its ensemble quality. Tom recognizes that. He is a great fan of Pina Bausch and various other companies who work in an ensemble way. The power of that early work, then, came out of the ensemble, the joint creative, and the multiple creative inputs.

Images of *Sheep's Milk on the Boil*

(Peacock Theatre, February 1994)
Amelia Stein

Fig 5.1 *Sheep's Milk on the Boil*. (From left) Pat Kinevane and Olwen Fouéré. Set design: Monica Frawley. Photographer: Amelia Stein. Courtesy of Amelia Stein.

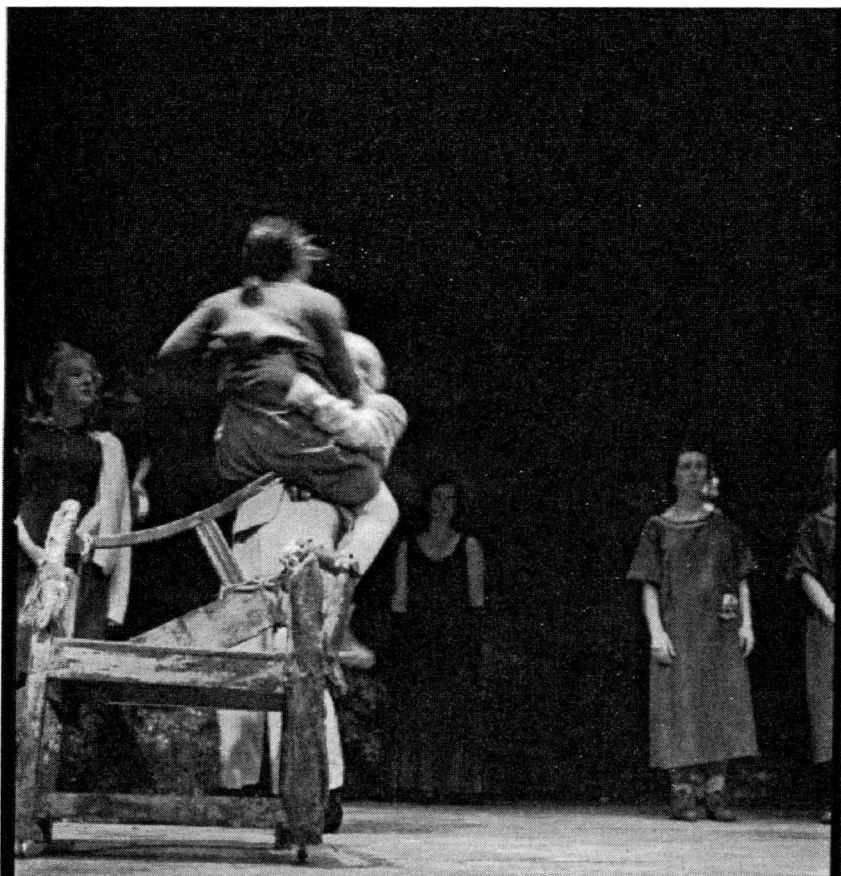

Fig 5.2 *Sheep's Milk on the Boil.* (From left) Joan Sheehy, Deirdre Molloy, Owen Roe, Bongi MacDermott, Kathryn O'Boyle, Jasmine Russell. Set design: Monica Frawley. Photographer: Amelia Stein. Courtesy of Amelia Stein.

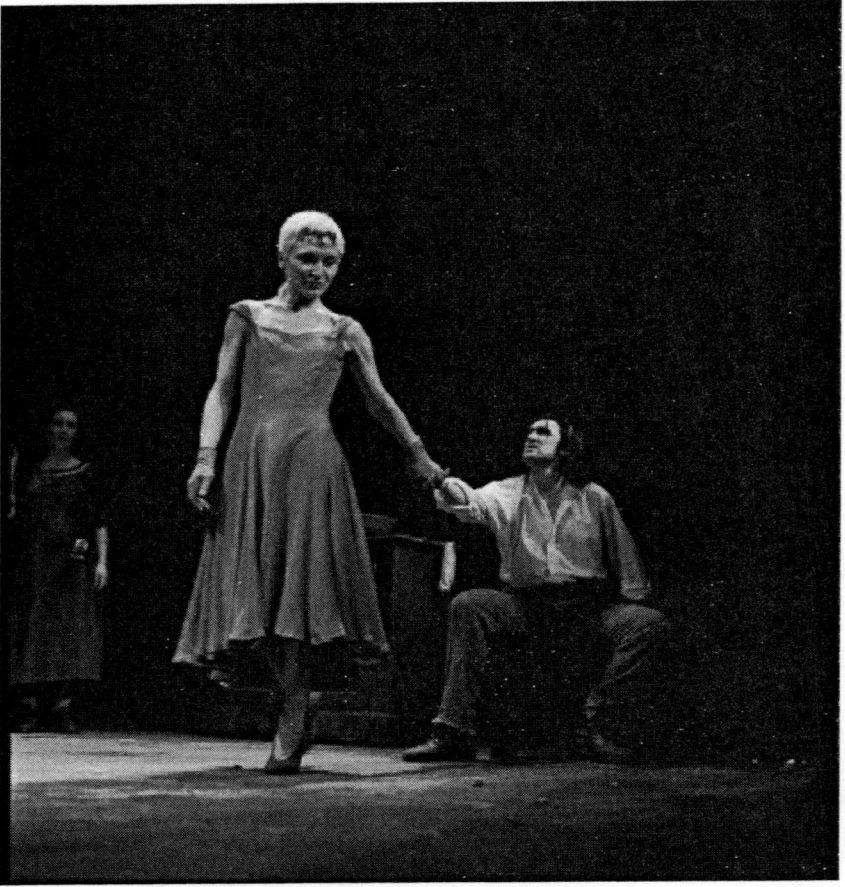

Fig 5.3 *Sheep's Milk on the Boil*. (From left) Olwen Fouéré and Pat Kinevane. Set design: Monica Frawley. Photographer: Amelia Stein. Courtesy of Amelia Stein.

Fig 5.4 *Sheep's Milk on the Boil*. Olwen Fouéré. Set design: Monica Frawley. Photographer: Amelia Stein. Courtesy of Amelia Stein.

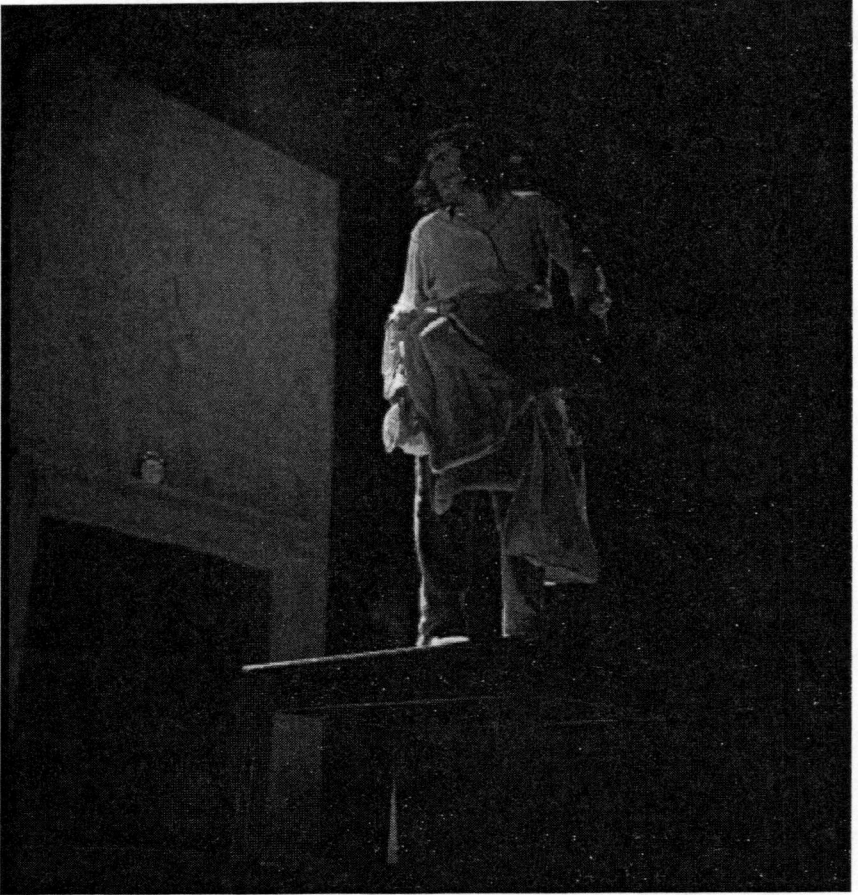

Fig 5.5 *Sheep's Milk on the Boil*. Pat Kinevane. Set design: Monica Frawley. Photographer: Amelia Stein. Courtesy of Amelia Stein.

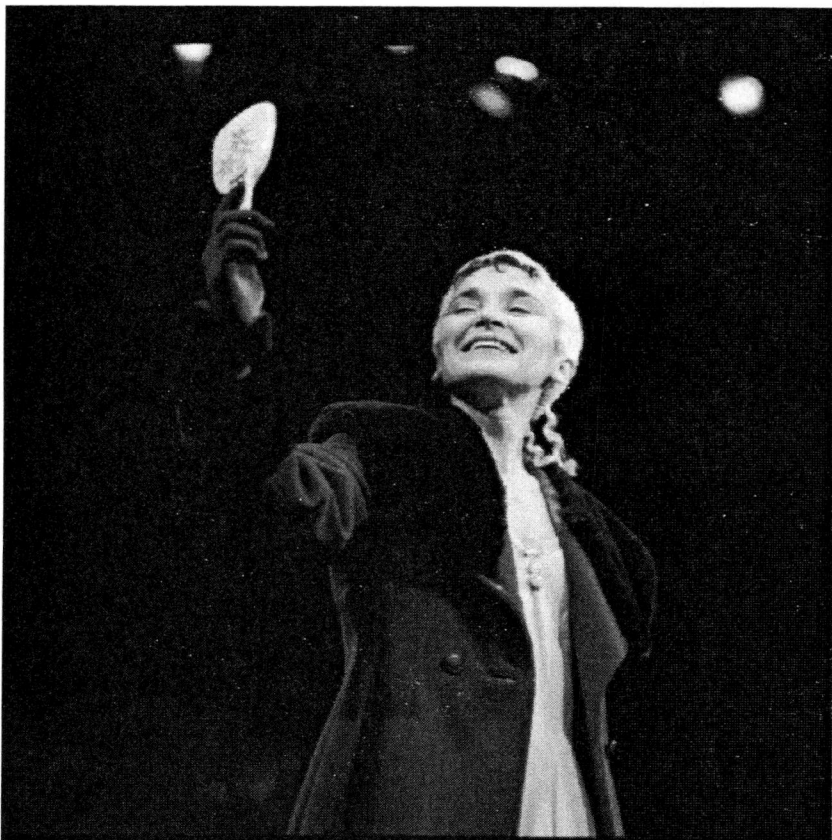

Fig 5.6 *Sheep's Milk on the Boil*. Olwen Fouéré. Set design: Monica Frawley. Photographer: Amelia Stein. Courtesy of Amelia Stein.

Fig 5.7 *Sheep's Milk on the Boil*. Owen Roe and Joan Sheehy. Set design: Monica Frawley. Photographer: Amelia Stein. Courtesy of Amelia Stein.

Fig 5.8 *Sheep's Milk on the Boil*. (From left) Jasmine Russell, Kathryn O'Boyle, Pat Kinevane and Olwen Fouéré. Set design: Monica Frawley. Photographer: Amelia Stein. Courtesy of Amelia Stein.

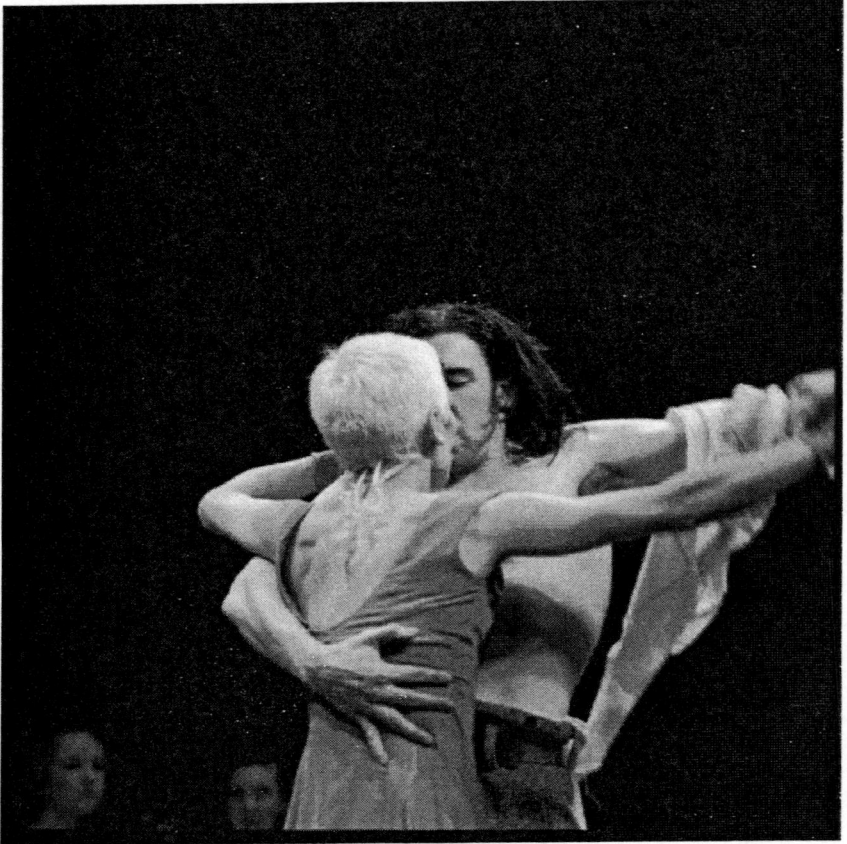

Fig 5.9 *Sheep's Milk on the Boil*. (From left) Olwen Fouéré and Pat Kinevane. Set design: Monica Frawley. Photographer: Amelia Stein. Courtesy of Amelia Stein.

Fig 5.10 *Sheep's Milk on the Boil*. (From left) Olwen Fouéré and Pat Kinevane. Set design: Monica Frawley. Photographer: Amelia Stein. Courtesy of Amelia Stein.

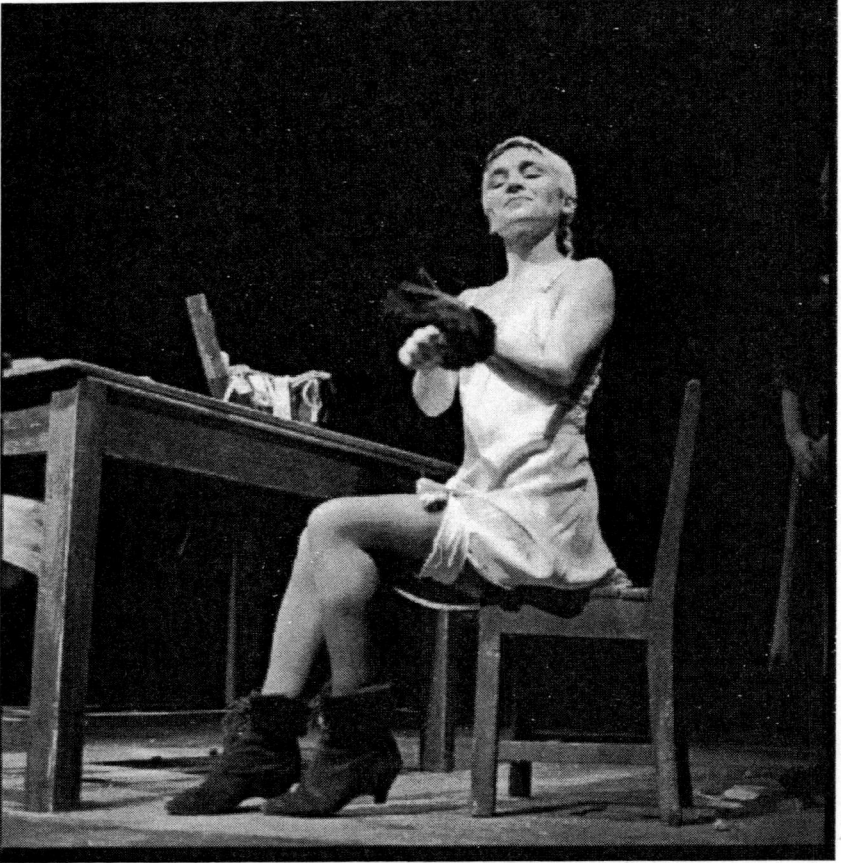

Fig 5.11 *Sheep's Milk on the Boil*. Olwen Fouéré. Set design: Monica Frawley. Photographer: Amelia Stein. Courtesy of Amelia Stein.

Second opinion: *Sheep's Milk on the Boil* 'Tom Mac Intyre off the Boil'

Fintan O'Toole

(*The Irish Times*, 2 March 1994)

In the folklore of island and fishing communities, there is always the sense of being at the border between two worlds. The people of the sea and the people of the land, try as they might to remain aloof from each other, find themselves drawn, by malice or desire, into each other's lives. The watery world, the shifting, mysterious, aquatic universe, draws men and women into its bosom, or seeps into their homes and lives. Women creep from men's beds at night, put their seal-skins back on and slip beneath the waves. Children with webbed feet and scaly skin walk the roads.

These stories, always sad and haunting, have great power. They speak of the limits of the human life, of the need to embrace what we are not and the impossibility of doing so. But they have found few echoes in contemporary Irish theatre. Macnas gave us its Tír Faoi Thoinn spectacular, and Eamon Kelly brought his incomparable artistry to bear on some of the stories for his theatre shows. But only Tom Mac Intyre has come close to a full engagement with their strangeness.

In Mac Intyre's splendid book of (very) short stories, *The Harper's Turn* (published by Gallery Press in 1982), a number of the pieces – *Cliodhna's Wave, Sionnan, Lovers of the Island* – come out of that engagement. That book, in turn, has been a rich source for Mac Intyre's plays, and *Lovers of the Island* is clearly discernible in the background of his latest theatre piece, *Sheep's Milk on the Boil*, at the Peacock. The story of a man who throws his knife at a wave which is about to drown him and is later called to remove it from the heart of a sea-woman, is repeated almost to the word in the play by the Visitor (Owen Roe), a mysterious figure who comes, with his female accomplice, the Inspector of Wrack, (Olwen Fouéré) to seduce the simple island couple, Biddy and Matt.

The play, therefore, comes out of something rich and deeply rooted. If it is strange, so are the stories from which it takes shape. It is more a re-working of tradition than a piece of flagrant avant-gardism. And, indeed, its problems come out of its failure to really re-work that tradition in theatrical terms, rather than from the 'experimental' nature of the forms with which Mac Intyre works.

In one sense, the disappointments of the piece merely illustrate the old saw that nothing dates faster than the avant garde.

Mac Intyre's collaborations with Tom Hickey and Patrick Mason in the early 1980s were hugely liberating for Irish theatre in their move away from verbal texts, their insistence on the communicative power of visual images and their experiments with disconnected narratives. Those innovations, however, are now mainstream. The most popular Irish play of recent years, *Dancing at Lughnasa*, also directed by Patrick Mason, had a wordless dance sequence at its core. Many of Garry Hynes's mainstage productions at the Abbey in the last three years were much more extreme in their visual starkness than anything attempted in the Mac Intyre project. And every late-night comedian now uses disconnected narratives. *Sheep's Milk* therefore abandons the verbal and visual minimalism of the 1980s Mac Intyre plays and, with Tom Hickey as director and Pat Kinevane replacing him, brilliantly, as the lead actor, strikes out for further shores. Perhaps because of its folkloric elements, the direction the piece takes is backwards, not forwards, back to Synge, Yeats and Lady Gregory. The kitchen table, the painted set of Monica Frawley's design, the footlights of Tony Wakefield's lighting, the Synge-song of the language, all signal a very conscious turn towards the look and forms of the early Abbey.

Thus, to the plain texture of *Lovers of the Island*, Mac Intyre adds the image of Christy Mahon gawping at himself in the mirror from *The Playboy of the Western World* and the puppet-show devils of Yeats's *The Countess Cathleen*. Matt, on a trip to the mainland, buys a mirror and falls for it. Biddy (Deirdre Molloy) assumes that the object of his desires is a mainland floozy. (The myth of Narcissus and Echo is somewhere at the bottom of the pot, too.) The Visitor and the Inspector of Wrack, devils of some description, set out to exploit their dispute by seducing them and luring away their souls.

Unfortunately, the theatrical texture is much closer to the gauche whimsicality of *The Countess Cathleen* than it is to the rich weave of *The Playboy*. We are brought back, not to the burgeoning energies of the early Abbey, but to the underdeveloped shadow-play of the early Yeats. The great power of the stories with which the play tries to connect – the profound sense of otherness in human intercourse with the natural world – is never attained. The sense of the other-world embodied in the Visitor and the Inspector of Wrack is clichéd both as an imagining of devils and as an embodiment of sexual desire. A man in a cravat and a woman in red tights are hardly, in the late twentieth century, convincing images of the darkly attractive forces at play in the universe. Without a way of tapping into the dark forces of the sea, the play can only dip its toes in the water.

Good Evening, Mr Collins

Christina Hunt Mahony

[The following is an extract from *Contemporary Irish Literature: Transforming Tradition* by Christina Hunt Mahony (Basingstoke UK: MacMillan, 1998)].

Tom Mac Intyre, a prolific writer, has experimented in many genres, often simultaneously. Mac Intyre approaches historical subjects from a highly experimental and at times surrealistic point of view. *Eye-Winker, Tom-Tinker*, staged at the Peacock in 1972, deals caustically with a nervous IRA man called Shooks. *The Bearded Lady* (1984) is an irreverent but probing play that explores the contradictory personality of Jonathan Swift through sexual means. *Rise Up Lovely Sweeney* (1985) takes an absurdist view of the familiar tale of the king condemned to live like a bird, never lighting on the ground, as punishment for having been disrespectful to a saint. Although this myth has attracted many fine Irish writers, Mac Intyre's *Sweeney* is remarkably original. (Another version of *Buile Suibhne*, or *The Madness of Sweeney*, appeared on the Dublin stage in 1997 in the form of Paula Meehan's *Mrs Sweeney*, which approached the myth from a feminist perspective.)

Good Evening, Mr Collins (1995), a play more conventionally scripted than many of Mac Intyre's works, provides another idiosyncratic and perceptive treatment of Irish history. Rather than shining a spotlight on his subject, Mac Intyre turns a strobe light on a twentieth-century Irish icon, sometimes to grotesque effect.

Michael Collins, an historical figure who has appeared in much recent fiction and is also the subject of a controversial film by Irish director Neil Jordan, was a charismatic soldier/statesman in the early days of Irish independence. He was assassinated when he was thirty-two years old, and had become an iconic hero. Called 'The Big Fella' because of his size and athleticism, Collins stood in vivid physical and psychological contrast to Éamon de Valéra, with whom he was allied in the Anglo-Irish War and against whom he fought in the Irish Civil War (1919-1923 inclusive). De Valéra, an ectomorphic mathematician, brilliantly outmanoeuvred Collins, and though he never captured the imagination of the people as Collins had, he went on to become the prime architect of the Irish constitution, served both as *Taoiseach* (Prime Minister) and *Uachtarán na hÉireann* (President of Ireland) and died peacefully in old age. The two men's roles in modern Irish life have always provoked heated partisan debates in life and, as now, in art.

Good Evening, Mr Collins has three female characters, all of whom are played by one actress. The rest of the characters are male, some of the actors doubling roles as called for, especially for minor parts. The play is constructed in two acts with many short scenes in each. The sets are 'minimalist,' as indicated in Mac Intyre's stage direction, and the pacing, as in his other plays, is fast, if not frenetic. By using rapid lighting changes, Mac Intyre aims to provide the audience with cameos, glimpses, epiphanies, and bits of illumination. Thus, he crystallizes character and dominant personality traits, both positive and negative. Mac Intyre wishes to exhibit complexity, but this method can also risk reinforcing simple stereotype as well.

One of Collins's lovers, Moya Llewelyn Davies, an Anglo-Welsh socialite, appears first to engage Collins in a sexually tinged exchange. The dialogue reveals the political infighting of the day and a preoccupation with the Irish language, which was typical of the era. The political scene that follows the rather coquettish curtain raiser with Moya is markedly different, in that its dialogue is delivered in much longer and more fully developed passages. Collins is portrayed as ruthless in his avenging of sectarian deaths, and devoted to his men, who are in turn fiercely loyal to him. This sequence is then balanced with a duet between Collins and Kitty Kiernan, the Irish woman to whom he was engaged at the time of his death. Their exchanges are in part delivered as an imaginary tennis volley, which gives them a playful innocence, and undercuts the more serious aspect of their relationship.

The first prolonged exchange between de Valéra and Collins takes the significant, but comically rendered, form of a classroom lesson, with 'Dev' as teacher and Collins as cheeky pupil. The ostensible subject is Macchiavelli's *The Prince*, a pragmatic text on how to rule. Here the fantasy element is quickly replaced by a realistic argument between the two men on how the new Ireland needs to be governed. This segment is then reinforced by a dialogue on fair fighting versus incipient terrorism and retaliation, conducted by Collins with Cathal Brugha, another minister in the government of the day.

Throughout *Good Evening, Mr Collins* there are portents of Michael Collins's impending premature death. Collins, alone on the stage, recounts a miraculous escape from death he experienced as a child. Talk of death and assassination or the threat of same is constant. Even talk of love with women is truncated and notable for its sense of being tenuous and fleeting. The character of Collins is restless throughout.

As the play continues, the insertion of surreal and fantastic episodes increases. Oddly matched couples sing and dance, lending an incongruous vaudevillian element to the proceedings. Such episodes link well with Mac Intyre's representation of a historically accurate, but equally bizarre, incident that features Collins, a wanted man, dining brazenly in the Gresham Hotel among British Army officers. It is Christmas and the British have put a price on his head. Collins, reckless and secure in the knowledge of his anonymity, was noted for such acts of foolhardiness and panache. A later speech by one of the officers emphasizes and attempts to analyze this quality:

> **IO (INTELLIGENCE OFFICER).** ... curious thing Counter Intelligence – there was that moment when I knew – and he knew – it was this thing of shared knowledge in a hot situation – it was even sexy, don't mind saying that, it really was – something in a phrase he used brushed me – I've forgotten the phrase – but it brushed off me – and there we were, knowing – and next thing I'd let him go ... Why? I don't know – you can't answer questions like that ... In a riddly sort of way, you're given leave to thus behave ... By whom?[1]

In Act 2 Collins' military side is emphasized from the start as he appears in his commander-in-chief uniform. Also introduced is Collins' third love, the beautiful Hazel Lavery, wife of painter Sir John Lavery. (Lady Lavery, the American-born Hazel Martyn, is an iconic figure, and for many years was the figure in the watermark in Irish bank notes.) This knowing encounter with the accomplished and socially secure Hazel Lavery contrasts with a later scene featuring Kitty Kiernan once more. Kitty, insecure before going to bed with Collins, models various lingerie before finding one that suits her mood, and she hopes, his. This and other exchanges, however, always include extraneous or intermittent stage appearances. Dev plays something of a voyeuristic role, and a British army Captain, a potential sexual rival, skirts the edges of the drama.

Collins's distress mounts in his new thankless role as negotiator of the treaty for Ireland with the British government. He is haunted by the recent dead, for whose deaths he feels in part responsible. Similarly his torn allegiances to the women in his life intensify. The innocent Kitty at home cannot compete at times with his infatuation for Hazel, and Moya becomes his confidante. The intensity of this part of the play is then narrowly focused in a long debate with Dev in which the likelihood of Collins's impending death is discussed with an element of second-sight. The exasperated and exasperating dialogue with Dev is matched in a farewell scene with Hazel, in what is Collins's desperate attempt to escape what he has come to view as a fatal attraction.

The final scene of *Good Evening, Mr Collins* introduces Sir John Lavery, here 'Wee Johnny Lavery' (a reference to Lavery's small stature in reality) as a cartoon figure of a painter. The scene also recreates briefly a cameo by George Bernard Shaw (who dined with Collins two days before he died). That Collins is being turned into myth even before his death is apparent, but this is of no comfort to Collins himself. The play closes with a mixed sequence of Collins lying in state, undercut jarringly by comic turns by Dev, Kitty, and Wee Johnny Lavery.

Tom Mac Intyre's afterword to *Good Evening, Mr Collins* discusses both Collins and Dev as looming figures in his boyhood. The former was remembered as a mere biography on the family bookshelf; Dev a real and 'cheerless tyrant'. Mac Intyre's illicit relationship with 'the Cavalier' dead hero began as an adolescent act of rebellion, with no knowledge of Collins's reputation as a lover. Eventually the combined traits of the man would engage the playwright to undertake this work for the stage, a suitably public art for this public figure of great contradiction and perhaps unrealized potential.

Good Evening, Mr Collins, perhaps more than Mac Intyre's other dramas, is typified by fellow playwright Frank Mc Guinness thus:

Behind all the diversity of Mac Intyre's writing lies a terrific sense of play, an imaginative disturbance, and a darkly creative obsession with Ireland's past ...[2]

---

[1] Tom Mac Intyre *Good Evening, Mr Collins* in *The Dazzling Dark: New Irish Plays*, ed. Frank McGuinness (London: Faber & Faber, 1996) p. 219.

[2] Frank McGuinness *Good Evening, Mr Collins* in *The Dazzling Dark: New Irish Plays*, ed. Frank McGuinness (London: Faber & Faber, 1996) p.193.

Theatre Review: *Good Evening, Mr Collins*
by Tom Mac Intyre.
'Dev Has All the Best Lines'

David Nowlan
(*The Irish Times* October 12 1995)

It might as readily have been titled *Bad Luck to You Devious Dev*, for the dominant presence in Tom Mac Intyre's new work (which turns out in performance to be an hilarious comedy), is not Michael Collins but Eamon De Valera in a variety of guises. The extent to which this dominance results from the author having given Dev most of the best lines or from Pat Kinevane's gorgeously under-stated, straight-faced, convulsively comic performance is not immediately apparent. But funny and irreverently and subversively pervasive it certainly is.

The action starts with Dev strolling around the audience incanting repeatedly: "The good news is the majority have no rights whatsoever. Ponder that. Ponder that now." It continues with the acknowledgement by Collins – a sturdy but fraught Corkonian Brían F. O'Byrne – that all the further action will take place within the confines (the mind frame?) of the house occupied by Moya Llewelyn Davies, also known as Kitty Kiernan, also known as Lady Hazel Lavery, the women in Collins's life. And it is punctuated thereafter by Dev, in mortar board and gown urging the study of Machiavelli, with shaven head playing piano, now at the Christmas party in the Gresham where Collins is interrogated by British intelligence, later as a concert pianist accepting international applause for himself while Collins is trying to stop the killing.

The verbal anachronism demonstrates the level of irreverence for a history which, were the audience better versed in its detail, might prove even more hilarious. Here is a vision of Collins driven primarily by his sexual drives and De Valera spurred on by the acclaim of the crowds: not quite the version of this State's official account of how it came into being. And, as usual, Mac Intyre is butting his head against the accepted means of theatrical communication, here mixing imagination with reality, words with images, certainty with fantasy, and the nation with a tatty damaged Georgian Dublin room with holes in the walls and a piano in the corner.

Kathy McArdle has managed to impose a directorial cohesion within Barbara Bradshaw's detailed yet enigmatic setting, excellently lit by Nick McCall. Karen Ardiff embodies all the women who, in the author's analysis, give primal shape and motive to Collins's life. Mal Whyte, Sean Campion and Sean O'Neill provide a variety of characters from Arthur Griffith through G.B. Shaw and Dick McKee, with Charlie Bonner and Tim Ruddy filling more generic roles, while Conor Guilfoyle accompanies the whole with telling and effective percussion. It may all amount to not much more than an ephemeral, inventive, provocative and entertaining night of theatre, but this reviewer enjoyed it a lot.

Programme Note: *Good Evening, Mr Collins* by Tom Mac Intyre

'The Bandit Pen'
(Peacock Theatre, October 1995)

Marina Carr

There is something about Tom Mac Intyre that exudes The Monarch in exile. What is it? Is it the purple clothing? The King Lear hairstyle? The imperious voice? The commanding gaze? The Bandit Pen? Most of all it's The Bandit Pen.

Mac Intyre's territory is the crossroads between the worlds and his large body of work, poems, plays, short stories, attest to this. He's a poet of the undertow, of the basement dark, of night visions. He chats up ghosts and records for us what they've said to him. His facility for language, his large and exotic vocabulary, his use of Latin, Greek, Irish, French, Hiberno English – not a usual occurrence these days. He points back to an era when writers had several languages at their disposal. He points to a time when pursuit of writing was synonymous with learning. He points to a banished civilization where writers were highly literate. In other words he possesses The Old Mind.

There is writing out of love and there is writing out of hatred, in my book anyway. Mac Intyre belongs to the first category, and so too do Emily Dickinson, Virginia Woolf, T.S. Eliot to name but a few. And for a writer to attain that sort of writing, writing motored by Love, by understanding, by compassion, is in my view the highest form of writing. *Good Evening, Mr Collins* is writing out of love and shows Mac Intyre at his most fluent, his bravest, his most innovative. The Bandit Pen is singing its rebel heart out.

There's the way he plays with Time in the piece. He moves it over and back with due irreverence. Like Blake, he knows that Time as we understand it, with all its imposing logic, is merely a construct of The Fallen World and therefore to be treated with suspicion. So Mac Intyre plays with it – you've Collins, the living man, trapped inside time and you've Collins outside time, watching himself, commenting on himself. And then you've both merging, the living man and the ghost. Indeed the whole play is peopled with ghosts. It is what Mac Intyre himself calls 'A Ghost Sonata'. You've one actress playing the three women – Moya, Kitty and Hazel. Another piece of banditry but it works a dream. The women merge into one another, separate, merge again. They're ghosts, Collins's own private ghosts. They're what keep him awake at night. They're the vital connection between Collins and his fate. Mac Intyre juxtaposes them with Collins the public man. The piece takes on a haunting logic of its own.

Mac Intyre's interpretation of Collins is one I warmed to instantly. He's there in all his greatness and fragility. He's the archetypal hero – a warrior, storyteller, a lover of women, but we also see through Mac Intyre's eyes the undertow Michael Collins. We see the hurts, the losses, the vanities, the childishness, the dark, we see the road not taken. Subtle craftsman that he is, detail by detail, Mac Intyre expands, shapes, shadows Collins to give us a comprehensive view of a complicated man. One of the things I love best about *Good Evening, Mr Collins* is the abundance of storytelling in the script. Above all, 'The Lap of Hay' story blows me away. Firstly it's the lyricism of it, then it's the simplicity. Finally it's how Mac Intyre uses the story, how it resonates through the whole piece, how all of Collins's life and death is in that story. This is craftsmanship at its best. This is The Bandit Eye focusing on a detail, shaping it, growing it until it becomes the cornerstone of the piece.

And what of Dev? Dev has been relegated to the position of Court Jester, with this difference, he's the Court Jester who has his eye on the throne. Again we see Mac Intyre's deftness of touch in his portrayal of Dev in the feathers, smoking the pipe of peace. It's absurd, its hilarious, but it's also spot on and only Mac Intyre could come up with it.

Another aspect of Mac Intyre's work that fascinates me is the courage of it and it's here in abundance in *Good Evening, Mr*

Collins. He is never afraid to show us how he sees, how he feels, how he thinks. It is apparent he hasn't much time for prose, his journey is through poetry. Neither has he much truck with realism, favouring what he calls 'Tilted Reality'. He comes at you from the diagonal with sometimes soaring lyricism, sometimes quieter music, but he always touches a chord and usually a chord you didn't know you had.

Towards the end of her life Emily Dickinson (another monarch in exile, another bandit pen) wrote 'Consider the lilies, was the only commandment I ever obeyed'. It always reminds me of Mac Intyre. Thank God for monarchs in exile, for Bandit Pens, let us cherish those whose only dictum is to consider the lilies of the field.

Stories Happen to Storytellers

Karen Ardiff

I don't remember when Tom Mac Intyre used these words over the three rehearsal periods I spent with him, but I do know that these words have continued to resonate with me in many different ways over the subsequent years. It's a statement that unpacks itself with a kick: 'Stories happen to storytellers, and only to storytellers'. Knowing a story does not make you a storyteller, it is the ability to experience and recognize stories that counts.

Tom Mac Intyre's plays happen in the rehearsal room as much as they do through the printed text. The script that sits in front of each person – actor, designer, director, stage manager – on the first day of rehearsal is like a map. The territory is known and understood beforehand by Tom, but the landscape is yet to be discovered.

I can't think of any other writer for whom it is impossible to imagine a production of their work without them actually being present in the rehearsal room. Certainly in the three productions that I was part of he was a constant presence either in person or through his close working with the director. Tom initially writes a verbal score. What he oversees during the rehearsal process is the creation of another set of scores: physical, aural, emotional, musical and visual.

My experience of working with Tom Mac Intyre stems from three plays of his that I appeared in the late nineties: *Good Evening, Mr Collins, Caoineadh Airt Uí Laoghaire* and *Cúirt an Mheán Oíche*, all of which originated in the Peacock Theatre and all of which toured the length and breadth of the country. In the case of the last two plays the tours encompassed every major Gaeltacht – including Inis Meáin in the Aran islands and the wild and wondrous Ceathrú Thaidhg in deepest Mayo. It was a magical time. When you work with Mac Intyre you work with heightened senses and the stakes are high.

⧂⧂⧂

In his afterword to the published version of *Good Evening, Mr Collins* which appeared in the 1996 collection, *The Dazzling Dark*, Mac Intyre tells the following story:

> My last *Collins* story – for the moment – goes like this. In the deeps of writing the play, I was roused from sleep one night by a clap of thunder. Every stone in the house turned over, settled. Stillness again. Next morning, I enquired. My companion had heard nothing. No one in the townland had heard anything. Fine. What I'd heard, I'd heard. And it didn't surprise me. Collins was – is – the *coup de tonnerre*, the *coup de foudre*. If you're dealing with that kind of energy, expect a visitation. A nod in your direction, yours to interpret.[1]

Reading back over this recently, while preparing this piece, I was struck by just how fantastically 'other' this way of seeing the world is. Of course, whilst I was rehearsing and performing in Mac Intyre's work it very quickly became absolutely normal to be in the company of one who viewed the world poetically, viscerally. It was contagious. But re-reading and remembering the language of creativity that Mac Intyre uses, drives home the passionate strangeness of his outlook. A man who believes that a violent clap of thunder is a creative visitation is no mere wordsmith.

⧂⧂⧂

Speaking on the RTÉ series *Playwrights in Profile* (to the actor Sean Rocks, the second incarnation of 'Collins' in *Good Evening, Mr Collins*) Mac Intyre proffered the following when asked for his legacy:

> This writer believed intransigently in the unconscious, believed in writing as a spirit journey, that he wrote under the direction of the powers and that if he didn't his strong awareness was that he couldn't write a syllable.[2]

There are no qualifiers with Mac Intyre. You will never hear him speak of *a kind* of spirit journey. There are no apologies and it strikes me that it is very rare indeed in this age for people to speak unapologetically about matters spiritual or indeed any articles of belief. I fell in love with Mary Robinson at the start of her presidency when she was asked in a television interview whether she was a feminist. She replied simply: 'Yes'. Both the interviewer and the television viewing public waited for qualification or explanation but none came. Mac Intyre is like that.

Indeed, in the same interview he talks of his own relationship with the feminine. This is in the context of discussing his play *Sheep's Milk on the Boil*:

> I'm forever interested in the female inside me, who's concerned with making the next mad jump, while the conservative male inside me is freckened out of his wits.[3]

It seems to me that Mac Intyre honours the female inside himself in myriad ways, not least by concerning himself dramatically and poetically with the feminine muse. In the three Mac Intyre plays I worked on women were thematically fore and centre. He writes of women with profound respect, and he speaks and writes about female sexuality in a way which – in my experience – no other male writer approaches. There is a robustness about Mac Intyre's women. They are ineluctably there.

Of the women I have played in Mac Intyre plays, four are ostensibly 'partners' – to use the current inelegant phrase – of a male historical figure: Michael Collins in the case of Kitty Kiernan, Moya Llewelyn Davies and Hazel Lavery (also wife of Sir John Lavery), and Airt Uí Laoghaire in the case of Eibhlín Dubh Ní Chonnaill. But that is not how they feel to play.

As an actor, it was a great gift to play three women as differentiated as Kitty, Moya and Hazel within the one play. They are nuanced, full-blooded individuals, and if that sounds like it should go without saying I would regretfully offer that it does not. In every form of modern storytelling there is still a tendency to sideline women. It is so ingrained that it has become barely noticeable. Any actress of any age will tell you that their character description will often begin with 'X's wife/lover/daughter/muse/mother/P.A.' An old hackneyed complaint? Well, to echo Mary Robinson: 'Yes.' The problem here is not one person's connection to another, we are all so connected, but that that is the entirety of their having been imagined and called into being.

Mac Intyre's use of the words of love and sex and womanhood are primal, ancient and visceral. In an age of political correctness this leaves him open to being lazily misunderstood. He is in the grip of an old, old muse, it seems to me – Grave's White Goddess perhaps – and he speaks the language of that religion. We are so used to the language about women being debased or diluted in meaning that Mac Intyre's profoundly respectful and resonant use of it is shockingly fresh. It seems in hindsight that it was almost inevitable that he would gravitate towards Brian Merriman's *Cúirt an Mheán Oíche*, for a more subversive piece of woman-centric writing there never was. The *Bean Álainn* (whom I played) piqued by the blindness and idiocy of men who fail to satisfy her sexually or even appreciate her lusciousness, pleads her case to the highest court:

> **BEAN.** Is deas mo bhéal, mo dhéad 's mo gháire ...
> Is glas mo shúil, tá m'urla scáinneach ...
> Mo phíob, mo bhráid, mo lámha 's mo mhéaraibh
> Ag síorbhreith barr na háille ó chéile.
> Féach mo chom, nách leabhair mo cnámha ...
> Seo toll is cosa agus colann nách nár liom
> Is an togha go socair fá cover ná tráchtaim.[4]

Sir Henry (a character of Mac Intyre's invention played by the actor Barry Barnes) at a later point in the play gives the male point of view:

> **SIR HENRY.** I saw her through a hawthorn hedge one day. It was the haymaking. One look and I was caught. A bit more sensitivity and I'd have fainted. We met. We ate and drank together. I sent her away two or three times. I don't know why. Because she was out of my understanding, perhaps.[5]

৵৵৵

Rehearsing with Mac Intyre is exhilarating. Perhaps it is precisely because he believes that bringing a piece to fruition is a spirit journey no less than the act of writing the verbal score in the first place. He is keenly alive to the thunderclaps and like all passionate people his ardour is infectious.

Rehearsing a Mac Intyre play is far from being a free-for-all, but he is a great respecter of the people with whom he works. Just because you are not scripted into a scene is no bar to ultimately appearing in it, because neither he nor his characters inhabit a literal universe.

For me, the most satisfying part of performing in his plays was that the process led to a liberating on-stage consensus. The moments which made up a scene were complex and, for the audience, often demanding, but they were precise. Indeed, every Tom Mac Intyre piece I have seen has that quality of precision. As an audience member you know that what you are witnessing is full and complete even if it tantalizingly eludes your conscious understanding. As Patrick Mason said to an audience member during a post show discussion of a Mac Intyre play: 'I know you don't understand it, but do you recognize it?'[6]

There was a scene in *Good Evening, Mr Collins* where Kitty Kiernan speaks to Collins as if writing him a letter. She speaks in that fractured, chatty manner of one whose mind races, and as she speaks she tries on different nightwear against his arrival. Through the play of rehearsal, a wooden table – one of our playthings – upturned and became a mirror. Collins (Brían F. O'Byrne) who was a taciturn participant in the scene used the reverse of the prop to settle in, and Mac Intyre and Kathy McArdle, the director, had a new context for the scene. For the company, the scene was always understood to be taking place both in a musty attic in Kitty's home in Granard and in a rainy bothán[7] in some besieged spot elsewhere in the midlands. The lugubrious Dev (played by the actor Pat Kinevane) occupied both worlds, favouring, though, the coziness of Kitty's domain.

This duality in the scene allowed the worlds to crash together at the end of the scene where Kitty's mind is invaded by the reality of the murderous conflict outside. The scene as written ends with a delicate and broken speech of rage by Kitty against the bloody conflict and the wasted lives of the young men who were killed:

> **KITTY.** ... Cathal Brugha dead in O'Connell Street, and Harry Boland gone and two young fellas from here shot in Dundalk and everywhere shooting and killing and nobody knows and nobody cares which side is which ...[8]

This monologue became a pair of scenes, one with words and one without. The story shifted from the words being spoken by Kitty to a much more complex and revealing story that was created fresh in the minds of the audience. That's how he works.

It is not necessary for the audience to know precisely where each character is located in time and space, but it is essential for the company to do so.

Tom Mac Intyre respects his audience. The storytellers to whom stories happen include his audience. Mac Intyre's plays leave synapses across which electricity may travel: the 'tzzz!' of recognition, the circuit completed in the mind of the watcher. This, of course, is true of all great writers, but Mac Intyre is not just a writer, he is a theatre practitioner and he trusts the mechanisms of the theatrical rehearsal process to such an extent that he allows the work to mature and come to fruition through them. Naturally this makes rehearsing a Mac Intyre play a rewarding and scarifying process.

The images that Mac Intyre and his companies draw forth from his texts are not glosses or offshoots from them, they are supportive of a story that he has already imagined. He is interested in the most minute details of theatrical storytelling. As *An Breitheamh* says in Mac Intyre's play *Caoineadh Airt Uí Laoghaire*:

> **AN BREITHEAMH.** silence has its own resonance ... and at least one ancient writer − was it Tacitus? − has pointed this out, it's not sufficient to be silent, one must attend to the nature of one's silence.[9]

There is, for example, a myriad of ways to touch a glass of 'curds and whey' as Moya Llewelyn Davies does in *Collins*, but there seems to be only one which carries what has come before in the story and anticipates and amplifies what comes after. Mac Intyre knows what this is, recognizes it when he sees it and communicates it in his own inimitable way. I've often thought that it is a shame that Tom's utterances when he sees something in rehearsal which delights him go unrecorded. Throughout my copy of the text are scribbled tantalizing fragments: 'swimming bucket', 'phantasmogoria', 'painter gauging perspective'.

Sometimes the discoveries are bolder. In *Cúirt an Mheán Oíche* a scene in which the harassed Irish censor (*an Cinsire*) repeatedly takes phonecalls from an angry Taoiseach about a problem concerning a 'filthy' poem, developed through rehearsals into a witty and resonant comment on the connection between art and censorship. The end of the wire from the prop phone ended up between the legs of the 'Bean' where it pleasured her intensely every time it rang.

When audience members experience the results of these explorations and choices they, I think, recognize that there is purpose and meaning in that caress, that character's isolation, that held note. Mac Intyre's plays reverberate, they cast forth ripples and they are particular in the way that a voice heard in a swimming pool is different from a voice heard in a car. He requires specific intention.

However, divining what that specific intention is can, on occasion, be immensely challenging. Whilst rehearsing for *Cúirt an Mheán Oíche* he asked me to pour libations from a bottle. Fair enough. He and the director Michael Harding – another poet/shaman – spoke at length about the bottle and its life giving qualities and how the liquid from it would affect and change each character on stage. Harding understood him perfectly and the two of them expounded on said receptacle for a good half hour. I think it was about half five in the evening and the cast it must be said were feeling pretty prosaic and bewildered, eventually we meekly enquired if this was a bottle of the imagination (cast problem) or an actual bottle (stage management problem). After a further half hour's discourse we called it a day. As we were packing up I saw our stage manager make a note on her notepad: 'Bottle?'

For then again, sometimes in rehearsals, I remember being struck by the raw power of the words. In *Caoineadh Airt Uí Laoghaire* the character of Morris (played by actor Tom Hickey) utters the following:

> **MORRIS.** The last time I saw my mother what struck me was how bald she was – a bald little woman, nothing left of her there in the coffin. I kissed her on the forehead – or was it the lips? Lips. I didn't know I was her son until then. My head was sober – family around, prayers, whimperings – but, as our lips met, my body suddenly drunk, from nowhere the blood roared and the lungs filled – air, air, air – head out, into the world, I got the smell of being born. I've never spoken of it. To anyone.[10]

And the stage direction which follows in this Irish language piece is:

'Níonn sé a aghaidh' (he washes his face). [11]

⊱⊰⊱

'You can't go wrong with sex and death' Mac Intyre has said, 'There is no other story.'[12]

About a year ago I met Tom by chance walking past the Mansion House and I proudly told him that I had just published my first novel. 'It's a love story, of course!' he said, vehemently. I was a little taken aback. 'Well. Not really,' I said, fearful of him thinking me a hackneyed or weedy writer.

'Of course it is!' he said, eyes glinting.
Naturally, he was right.

ꝏꝏꝏ

I remember, above all, from working with Mac Intyre, a sense of freedom. Controlled freedom. It is a little like the sense you have in writing when you have got to a point (that wonderful point) when the story is enough of an independent entity that your options are still limitless but your parameters defined.

One of the pleasures of almost any rehearsal process is the nature of the kinds of dialogue in which you engage to explore the piece. It is often intimate, not (God forbid!) in a 'spilling' kind of way, but from the fact that you need to trawl quite deeply to engage with experiences that are never precisely your own.

Rehearsing a Mac Intyre play, in my experience, pushes the actors into exploring seldom used areas of the psyche. This was never more the case than when we were rehearsing *Cúirt an Mheán Oíche* under the direction of Michael Harding. I had at this time a bit of a horror of 'theatre games' as a rehearsal tool, which was not very big or clever of me – it was just a personal inclination towards the text and a distrust of 'off text' meanderings.

However, one of the most resonant rehearsal experiences I have ever had was during the rehearsals for *Cúirt*. The rehearsal room was filled with costumes, shoes, material, playthings, and Michael and Tom asked us to each build a 'shrine'. This, it must be said, seemed an entirely natural request.

Wandering around the shrines some hours later was enchanting and illuminating. And relevant to the work which had much to do with ideas of the sacred. I remember particularly following a winding trail of little shoes that led to a tiny space where dancer Rianach Ní Neill lay curled. At least that is what I think I remember.

That's the kind of space in which Tom, and those who work with Tom, find themselves.

Another way to put it is that in the world of Mac Intyre, where everything from object to shaft of light to silence has meaning, you too have meaning. And that is the freedom which the fullness of his imaginings of the world in the theatre space gives to an actor.

Works Cited

Mac Intyre, Tom, *Good Evening, Mr Collins* in *The Dazzling Dark: New Irish Plays Selected and Introduced by Frank McGuinness* (London: Faber and Faber, 1996).

---, *Cúirt an Mheán Oíche,* (Baile Átha Cliath: Cois Life Teoranta, 1999).

---, *Caoineadh Airt Uí Laoghaire,* (Baile Átha Cliath: Cois Life Teoranta 1999).

---, *Playwrights in Profile* (Series 1) Presenter: Sean Rocks (RTÉ Radio 1, Dublin 11 Feb 2007).

---

[1] Tom Mac Intyre in *The Dazzling Dark: New Irish Plays Selected and Introduced by Frank McGuinness* (London: Faber and Faber, 1996), p. 233.

[2] Tom Mac Intyre in *Playwrights in Profile* (Series 1) Presenter: Sean Rocks (RTÉ Radio 1, Dublin 11 Feb 2007).

[3] Ibid.

[4] Tom Mac Intyre *Cúirt an Mheán Óiche,* (Baile Átha Cliath: Cios Life Teoranta, 1999), p. 11.

[5] Ibid. p. 47.

[6] Patrick Mason in *Playwrights in Profile* (Series 1) Presenter: Sean Rocks (RTÉ Radio 1, Dublin 11 Feb 2007).

[7] Outhouse, hut or shed.

[8] Tom Mac Intyre *Good Evening, Mr Collins* in *The Dazzling Dark: New Irish Plays* (ed. Frank McGuinness) (London: Faber and Faber, 1996), p. 212.

[9] Tom Mac Intyre *Caoineadh Airt Uí Laoghaire* (Baile Átha Cliath: Cois Life Teoranta, 1999) p. 32.

[10] Ibid. p.42.

[11] Ibid.

[12] Tom Mac Intyre *Playwrights in Profile* (Series 1) Presenter: Sean Rocks (RTÉ Radio 1, Dublin 11 Feb 2007).

You Must Tell the Bees: An interview with Tom Mac Intyre, Carolyn Swift and John Scott

Deirdre Mulrooney

[This interview was first published on the UCD website
Irish Theatre Forum 1.1 (Summer 1997)
http://www.ucd.ie/irthfrm/morforum.htm]

In October 1996 writer Tom Mac Intyre and choreographer John Scott of the Irish Modern Dance Theatre presented their collaboration *You Must Tell the Bees* at the Peacock Theatre. This innovative collaboration comes in a line of experimental theatre pieces from Tom Mac Intyre, including his groundbreaking 1980s collaborations with Patrick Mason and Tom Hickey, *The Great Hunger*, *The Bearded Lady*, *Rise Up Lovely Sweeney*, *Dance for your Daddy*, and *Snow White*. More recently his theatrical endeavours have embraced figures who loomed large in Irish history, *Kitty O'Shea*, and *Good Evening, Mr. Collins*, as well as non-historical subjects like *Sheep's Milk on the Boil*.

John Scott and the Irish Modern Dance Theatre also have an impressive track record of experimentation and collaboration, most notably in their 1995 production at the RHA Gallagher gallery, *Macalla*, part inspired by the poetry of Liam O'Muirthealla, and early Celtic Christian texts.

Below John Scott (JS) and Tom Mac Intyre (TMacI) elaborate on their collaboration, and dance critic Carolyn Swift (CS) gives her opinion on this exciting departure from the more traditionally text-bound canon of Irish theatre, and the ripples or tidal waves this type of hybrid and imaginative work is unleashing in our pond.

Deirdre Mulrooney

JS. *You Must Tell the Bees* is a collaboration with the writer Tom Mac Intyre. It's for five dancers, and a musician/performer. We have been discussing it for the last two years. Tom Mac Intyre has attended many of our dance productions. We like to experiment in Modern Irish Dance Theatre in different forms. It's not just pure dance. It's a mixture of theatre, of visual art, of many different elements, and this piece is no exception. Tom and I discussed themes that were close to both of us, and that we had in common. Tom told me a story about his grandfather who was a beekeeper. He wrote a poem about him, because there is a kind of a folklore among beekeepers that when someone dies in the family, you must tell the bees that they have died, or they won't come out of the hive anymore. We rely on bees not just for honey, but for pollination of crops and of everything. If we didn't have bees we wouldn't have fruit and vegetation in the same way. They are a very crucial part of the whole chain of our existence.

It started with the whole idea of the beekeeper's widow going to tell the bees in an orchard that the beekeeper was dead. He wrote this beautiful poem called *Widda*, and Tom is from Cavan and the piece is very much based in that whole area and in a rural Irish background. He then developed a piece. Now Tom is a writer, so writers are writers of words and of text but he also wrote a type of a screenplay, which is a mixture of text, spoken text, in Irish, and in English, and French. It's combined with images, and some movement descriptions, which he gave to me as a very loose suggestion, really a choreographic suggestive screenplay as opposed to a direct text. I then worked with the text for about two months, and then we went into rehearsal with the dancers.

It's a combination of pure dance, the performance of the text, the interpretation of his images, and our own meditations on the whole thing. It's a collaboration between all of us, where I do the choreography, and do the overall directing.

What Tom did with this was he wrote about love, it's the notion of love, and the notion of bees and honey, and if love is the honey, love is also the sting. There are two couples of young lovers, so-called young lovers, so it's the archetypical couple. And there is this older woman who is like the widow of the beekeeper; she is known as the Chatelaine. She is a very powerful figure, almost like a witch, and she in a sense directs the whole piece, and the piece is her. And the other people are her past in a way; they are part of her imagination. I have used text in a few other pieces, I did a big environmental piece in the RHA Gallagher gallery in 1995, called *Macalla*, which had poetry by Liam O'Muirthealla, it also had some texts from a very early Celtic Christian psalter of some prayers, some incantations. But this piece was different. As performers, we all develop our own characters, which stem from movement qualities, they stem from things that happen. Of course you make abstract dancers moving in space, but no matter how abstract there is an emotion, there is a character coming out. Tom studied all our work, he studied the performers, he wrote these parts very specifically for this company, and he did not impose character that, this is the younger sister, this is the older brother, this is the ex-boyfriend, he didn't create characters that strictly. Working with the text while we weren't having to interpret the text, when everyone sees the piece they think 'Tom wrote the words', and I did all the rest, but in fact Tom gave a lot of imagery. The work is my response to what Tom gave us.

Widda

> *You must tell the bees*
> *the bee-keeper is dead ...*
>
> She waited a few days
> to catch breath, hold
> while she might, his step,
> Sunday, an ass's heat,
> she approached the orchard,
> found her way to the hives.
>
> Low din of the business;
> she watched the smart bundles
> arrive loaded, enter, un-
> load, leave on the wind
> that was no wind, a wave,
> suspended, knew again
> the honey, comb, way
> he'd present it – *Yours, Mary,*
> let her taste-buds travel
> heather-honey, clover-honey,
> honey warbling the rose ...
>
> She'd shut eyes to pray,
> sip tea from a saucer,
> bring word to the bees –
> *Thomas, your keeper is dead.*
>
> She stood there, she looked,
> was aware of the bees'
> to-and-fro, and next
> she saw him, head veiled,
> move through the trees –
> he moved bolder than life –
> her chest thumped good-bye,
> the light bee-keeper stride
> became one with the haze.[1]

DM. The theme of the piece seems very much about the environment, and recreation?

TMacI. Well the interior environment, and transformation, yes. I think it aims to be about love and the sensual, and therefore death, and therefore about the only stories that are around us.

DM. Do you start with images already in your mind before you start working with the dancers?

TMacI. Well I start with the bees, and the honey, and therefore I have naturally a whole computer full of related images, and I let them hit the page. But the fun, the challenge is to let them hit the page from the unconscious without interfering with them on the way.

DM. What about the music?

TMacI. It seems to me that Rossa O'Snodaigh is a genius; the music he has composed has an extraordinary texture, full of surprise, full of today. Marvellous edge to it. I'd go anywhere with him. I think he is quite extraordinary.

DM. Would you ever consider returning to plot-based theatre, or does this type of imagistic theatre transmit something more that you would like to put across to an audience?

TMacI. I thought the Collins piece [*Good Evening, Mr Collins*] relies strongly on the imagistic, the visual, and movement but also relies very strongly on a verbal score and a quite discernible story. I suppose the essence of the storytelling for me is that I should always be surprised in the composition of it. And my experience is if I allow that to be the case then the actors, and the audience, and all involved are constantly on the edge of surprise, and that's what makes the magic.

DM. There is definitely a script, but there isn't that sense of a beginning, middle and an end...

TMacI. Not on an overt level but people who see it, including critics, would say that the narrative line is overt enough. That it moves to a zone of tension, and then quasi-resolution. I see it that way.

DM. It seems to me that it is quite like poetry actually.

TMacI. It certainly wanted to have the intensity and the edge of poetry. Above all, in any of the verbal scores for which I am primarily responsible, there's where the entire collaborative venture comes into focus. You're asking musician, choreographer, writer, dancer to combine – it's awfully challenging and exciting – so that you have four or five strong energies producing a moment on the stage which has the audience spellbound. That is to say, aware of poetry loose in the theatre. That is what one works for.

DM. It's extremely original in the canon of Irish theatre. Is there any movement outside of Ireland which you might see yourself being a part of, or having an affinity with?

TMacI. You reach a certain stage on highway 99 when you are perfectly happy to sit down on your own hills and your own metropolis and work from the travels you have been on, and work from what's inside you, and what's happening in the field outside your window.

DM. I think it was very interesting. Tom Mac Intyre has a long history of working with visual theatre, both mime and dance. Some time ago he collaborated with the Calck Hook Dance company, and John Scott is very much dance-drama rather than pure dance. So it is very logical that the two should collaborate. And I think it does succeed to a certain extent. There is room for improvement. And indeed throughout the tour, since the first time I saw it, and reviewed it, which was in Cork, since then it has been to Limerick, and Galway, and Drogheda and Derry and Monaghan, and Cavan, and all sorts of places. And it has suffered considerable sea-change, both in the score, and in the choreography. All the time it has been tightening up and improving. I think it is an ongoing thing. I think if it was revived again that it would probably continue to evolve.

Carolyn Swift, do you consider 'Dance Theatre' a new category? To what extent is it dance, and to what extent is it theatre?

CS. I think that perhaps here in Ireland we have a limited sense of dance. We put things into boxes. We say this is ballet, this is drama, this is contemporary dance. I don't see why all these things can't overlap. There is no reason why these things cannot be combined, and indeed always have. Martha Graham's contemporary dance uses drama very strongly. Personally, my own taste is for the dramatic. I do like dance just for dance, but I suppose it is because I have worked in theatre for most of my life, I very much like allying dance to drama.

DM. Do you think that there is a 'way' to watch the pieces? Tom Mac Intyre referred to it yesterday as 'watching with the eyes of a child', which is quite different from a strong narrative theatre ...

CS. I think it is a matter just of being open-minded, not putting things into boxes and just reacting to what you see. It's full of symbolism and this is something that dance does very well. For example, at the end of the piece, Joanna Banks who plays the widow is imprisoned, trapped inside the hive, which is obviously a sort of metaphor for being trapped within her memories, since the whole piece in a way could be seen to be her memory. There are all sorts of little symbolic things like that. But I think you just let it wash over you. You don't just sit there looking frantically for meanings. I can't bear that. A lot of people did that with *Waiting for Godot*. People were so busy going in with lists of what everything meant. You should just let these things wash over you and react to them.

DM: Yes, it's quite a personal experience. Do you think the image tells its own story?

CS. Oh I do, but I think this applies to all theatre. I think everything is what it says to you. I hate this idea of what you are supposed to think.

DM. Where do you think that Irish Modern Dance Theatre and this imagistic work of Tom Mac Intyre, now in his collaboration with John Scott, fits into a wider global context, or does it?

CS. Well I think there has been a big movement; it has been very noticeable in Ireland recently, ever since *Els Comediants* went to the Galway Arts Festival some years ago, and ever since street theatre and Macnas hit us, generally, I think there has been a movement now to bridge this gap. Interestingly, a lot of the works in the Dublin Theatre Festival that were not dance as such, or billed as dance, still had a large movement and mime content. Some of them indeed had no words at all. We are more and more beginning to incorporate the visual in drama. Because I suppose it was possibly Yeats influenced. But Irish drama has always been particularly word-bound, but there has been a big change. And in this festival this was particularly noticeable. Only a very small percentage of the items in it were text-bound.

DM. So do you think that the audiences are now more ready to have their preconceptions challenged in the theatre?

CS. Yes, I would say that younger audiences respond more easily. I would say perhaps that older audiences still expect, when they go to the theatre, that it will be a traditional play, the ready-made play that they can follow with a beginning, middle, and an end and a text, but I don't think that young people do. And I think that the influence of film too is very noticeable. The flashback technique spread from film into theatre a long time ago. Television again influenced the fact that you almost intercut between scenes now in theatre. Nobody has really noticed this, but the whole technique has been very influenced by film and television.

DM: Do you think that *You Must Tell the Bees* is quite different from *Good Evening, Mr Collins*?

CS. *Good Evening, Mr Collins* is much closer to a play, even though it does use this very free technique that is modern theatre. But this is more movement based. It is after all done by Irish Modern Dance Theatre. Basically, it begins and ends with dance, even though dance is really only a part of it. But it is a major part of it.

DM. In the context of the canon of Irish Modern Dance Theatre, do you see this as a radical new departure?

CS. Well, *Macalla* I think was the first move, as far as Irish Modern Dance Theatre is concerned, that was an extraordinary piece, moving around the galleries, from one gallery to another, and it almost reminded me of a German expressionist film. I think that Tom Mac Intyre saw that piece and that that is what made him feel he wanted to collaborate with John Scott on this piece. But certainly I do think it is extremely interesting, and I do think that there will be more work of this sort in the future.

DM. Where do you see the work of the Irish Modern Dance Theatre going?

CS. Well I think it will remain very drama based because I think that John Scott is a man of the theatre. He is very strong on ideas, he is well versed in music and literature, and he is essentially a man of the theatre with great feeling for drama, and he achieves great dramatic effects. On pure choreography he is not as strong. He is not one of our strongest choreographers. He is a little bit limited in his vocabulary, but he makes up for this in his extraordinary sense of theatre.

---

[1] Tom Mac Intyre, *ABC New Poems* (Dublin: New Island, 2006), p. 3.

The Magic of Dissonance

Helen Meany
(*The Irish Times*, 24 September 1996)

A triangular skeletal structure, vaguely reminiscent of an electricity pylon, crashes to the floor of Digges Lane Studio. 'Wonderful' cries John Scott. 'Yes, yes, I like that.' The wooden pylon evokes the structure of a bee hive and is the central prop in the new dance piece devised by choreographer John Scott and playwright, novelist and poet, Tom Mac Intyre called *You Must Tell the Bees*. Performed by Irish Modern Dance Theatre with live music composed by Rossa O'Snodaigh, the show goes on tour next Thursday before playing at the Peacock during the Dublin Theatre Festival.

'You could say', Tom Mac Intyre observes as we walk out in search of lunch 'that knocking over a bee hive is the essence of what theatre is all about'. You could say that, certainly, in fact what emerges from a conversation with Mac Intyre and Scott is a sense that all statements are admissible, particularly if they are allusive, symbolic and elastically ambiguous. Over lunch John Scott is breathlessly expansive, while Mac Intyre only occasionally interjects, to emphasize certain key terms which have a mantra-like resonance, such as 'play', 'magic', and 'explore'.

He is committed to fluidity and spontaneity in the creation of a piece of theatre, and in this he has found his counterpart in John Scott, who says with some pride that 'on a bad day, our rehearsals are anarchistic and chaotic looking.' In rehearsal, Scott develops a series of movements with the dancers, discards them and begins again, always remembering that 'the body doesn't lie'.

'We start,' he says, 'with the basic bones and then we layer.' In this case, the basic bones are the words provided by Mac Intyre's text, a compressed, fragmented dialogue, which is spoken by the dancers. The work is loosely derived from his own poem, *Widda*, in which a bee-keeper's widow goes to tell the bees that her husband has died. Using the images of bees, hives and honey, the dance becomes a sensual mediation on love and desire, on 'love's honey and love's sting'.

The dancers – Aisling Doyle, Justine Doswell, Daryn Crosbie and James Hosty – take the roles of four young lovers who are learning 'the language of love' under the tutelage of chatelaine (the English ballerina, Joanna Banks). For Scott, working with a text has been 'a liberation rather than a limitation', and says that 'the dancers' approach to the words, and what they do with the words, is what the piece is.'

The script, too, has evolved in rehearsal: Mac Intyre describes it as 'a map, which, of course, has to be torn up. One of the most seductive things in theatre is the way that stories and ideas are always supple; scripts are made for infidelity'.

This collaboration has been in the two men's minds for some years, alluded to wistfully during snatched meetings. Setting aside the time to make it happen was the problem, but both knew that it made sense in terms of their individual work. Since its foundation in 1991, Scott's company, Irish Modern Dance Theatre, has been blending dance and theatre in various ways, using music, language, lighting, costume and props such as buckets, panes of glass and metal cones to striking visual and dramatic effect, particularly in *Ruby Red* and *Macalla*. He hopes that *You Must Tell the Bees* will extend the company's audience, attracting theatre fans and is excited about playing in the Peacock.

Mac Intyre has followed the work of Irish Modern Dance Theatre keenly. For him words are just one of the languages available to theatre, and he is still as fascinated by 'the poetry of gesture and of images' as he was when he and Patrick Mason created the plays in the late 1970s and early 1980s – *Rise Up Lovely Sweeney, Dance for your Daddy,* and *The Great Hunger* – which, in their emphasis on elements of physical and visual theatre, have been hugely influential.

While it could be frustrating for the dancers to have to answer to two directors, Mac Intyre and Scott say that the basic necessities are agreed between them, although the emphasis is always on open-ended work-in-progress, on creative chaos. 'We wait for the magic to come, rather than forcing it,' Mac Intyre says. 'It's fluidity at the mercy of jagged incursions. It's play, play – exploring the magic of dissonance.'

The dancers, Mac Intyre says, have 'a proper reverence' for the words. To use actors would 'unbalance the general innocence'. Having encouraged actors, over the years, to develop gesture, movement and even dance, it is 'a joy' for him to work with professional dancers. 'I've always been fascinated by the magic of movement, so this is an enhanced climate as far as that delectable poetry is concerned. To see them create a dance paragraph, the way

I can dash off a verbal paragraph, has been an education and a delight.'

Theatre Review: *The Chirpaun* by Tom Mac Intyre

Victoria White
(*The Irish Times*, 4 December 1997)

She is a young and very beautiful girl and she has a miracle in her belly – a little sprog they call 'the chirpaun'. It is a mystery which has bewitched through the centuries, from long before the first apple-cheeked Madonna appeared in an Italian fresco.

It really is not that mysterious a mystery, however, just nature taking its course.

Tom Mac Intyre's cast of old, broken men are spellbound, just as Sharon Rabbitte's father was spellbound in *The Snapper* – because natural as the condition is, in the past its implications were removed as far as possible from the lives of men.

Picking up some of the themes of Mac Intyre's mid 1980s play, *Dance for your Daddy*, *The Chirpaun* is concerned with the distance between this generation and the young, independent girl Jacinta. It is a distance which causes hurt, anger and desire.

The men also desire the girl – it is chilling that Eva Birthistle, who plays the mother of the Chirpaun, appeared most recently in Alan Gilsenan's film *All Soul's Day*, and in that was also desired by her father's generation, and also spent time in a lunatic asylum.

Perhaps that says something very telling about the position of very beautiful young girls.

However, the mother of the Chirpaun is dedicated to finding her own, mystical path, and leaves behind the men, who seem to have strayed into her world from an old Abbey play, or she into theirs.

Whether or not these men feel the mystery of the girl is immaterial, however, if the audience does not; this writer felt irritated by the iconic status she is given.

This was not helped by Birthistle being ill-cast. She never masters the north-midlands lilt, and so the sense of her having strayed in from another play is intensified.

This judgement – and if it was not made by her she should not have stuck with it – unhinged Kathy Mc Ardle's direction of what was always going to be a difficult and static piece.

The other characters are essentially bit players: Pat Kinevane is a class of a hypnotist, Dolores and Pauline (Renee Weldon and Pauline Hutton), Jacinta's cronettes, Granpa and Bossman (Des Keogh and Bosco Hogan), Jacinta's father, John Joe Concannon's cronies.

The saving grace of the night is a wonderful performance by Tom Hickey as John Joe, full of ill-channelled affection.

Theatre Review: *Caoineadh Airt Uí Laoghaire* by Tom Mac Intyre

Diarmuid Johnson
(*The Irish Times*, 20 April 1998)

A play of strong women, Tom Mac Intyre's lament for Art O'Leary provides an antithesis to feminist reading of Gaelic literature and reminds us that notions of the subjugation of the matriarch may be coloured by Victorianism.

Eibhlín Dubh (Karen Ardiff), author of the lament, widow of Art O'Leary, is passionate, sensuous and uncompromising. The old woman (Máire Ní Ghráinne) lends the events her wit and coaxes fate to avenge Art's killing as in Gabriel Garcia Marquez's *Crónica de una muerte anunciada*.

Set amongst a Gaelic Munster aristocracy, the dress and eloquence of the Irish set them above the churlish English soldier and the contemptuous judge (Tom Hickey). On the note of national characteristics, Art O'Leary (Liam Heffernan) is fiery and impetuous, as much an archetype as the imperial sheriff (Tom Hickey).

Visits by a professional company are a fillip to the Gaeltacht and regional drama will learn much of stage presence, characterization and timing.

The visitors' diction, however, was imperfect: compare Moliére played in Paris by learners of French. More realistic was the use of English where appropriate. This co-existence of the two national languages is too rarely met in dramatic writing, be it for stage, print or television.

Packed into a parish school hall in Carraroe on Saturday night, many would have asked themselves when will Connemara be able to welcome its visitors to the comfort of a modern theatre? And the performances of local Síle Nic Chonaonaigh and Bríd Treasa Ní Ghaoithín lend weight to argument in favour of such an amenity.

Programme Note: *Caoineadh Airt Uí Laoghaire* by Tom Mac Intyre

(Peacock Theatre, April 1998)
Alan Titley

Níor dhóigh leat gur scéal é scéal Airt Uí Laoghaire agus Eibhlín Dhuibh Ní Chonaill ar gá drámú ar bith a dhéanamh air. Is é atá drámata go smior. An grá mór paíseanta, an choimhlint leis na húdaráis, an teannas aicmeach agus creídimh, an spiadóireacht, an dúnharú agus an dán dochreidte a lean. Tá siad go léir san imirt cheana. Ach is amhlaidh go dtugann na gnéithe sin go léir scóp do bhua faoi leith Tom Mac Intyre an rud atá fairsing a chuimriú, an rud atá scaoilte a chur faoi smacht, agus an rud atá ceilte a thabhairt chun solais.

Ní foláir nó bhain sé ardtaítneamh as an eachtra chorraitheach seo a láimhsiú, a chóiriú agus, go deimhin, a chruthú as an nua, mar sin é atá le tuiscint as gach mír is radharc de. Leideanna amháin atá againn faoi charachar Airt sa *Caoineadh*. Duine lándéanta spórtúil, maíteach, mustrach, poimpéiseach anseo é ag tabhairt dúshlán an tsaoil agus na Sasanach. Mar a chéile le hEibhlín Dubh. Déarfá gur soitheach í a líonfadh an traigéide agus a chuirfeadh thar maoil le dubhrón i gcás an dáin de – duine fulangach nach mór ar snámh ar a dúchínniúint. Pearsa bheartach, sheiftiúil, ghníomhach anseo í i lár an aicsin istigh, bean diongbhála Airt agus i bhfad thairis. Ach, dá éamais sin, samhlaíonn tú an dráma ag brúchtaíl le beatha an ochtú haois déag, agus le gach cineál duine arbh ann dó lena línn: meabhlairí, bithiúnaigh, alfraitsí, spiairí, mná feasa, leannáin, uaisle nár thuig an saol. Tá seo ar fad déanta ag Tom Mac Intyre sa tslí is duai dó, nod a thabhairt dúinn anseo, leid ansúid, macalla a dhúiseacht anseo, ár gcuid samhlaíochta a spreagadh abhus. Is cuma nó nath anois é go mbaineann sé leas as trealamh uile na drámaíochta idir cheol agus mhím agus fhilíocht agus shoilsiú agus uile. Ach ní móide go bhféadfadh, le hinsint réalaíoch chúng ar bith saibhreas iomlán *Caoineadh Airt Uí Laoghaire* a ghabháil nó a nochtadh choíche.

Mar is amhlaidh go músclaíonn scéal an chaointe seo dúinn í bhfad níos mó ná cibé lomthuairisc is féidir a thabhairt air.

Tarraingíonn sé ar théadracha na staire, dúisíonn na mothúcháin is doimhne timpeall ar an ngrá, ar an mbás, ar an ealaín. Tá an chruinne go léir mar a ritheann laistigh den aon scéal gairid seo amháin. Ní haon iontas nach foláir tarraingt ar an mbéaloideas, ar an bhfilíocht, ar seanbhailéid is rabhcáin, ar cheol, ar chleasaíocht, ar thaibhisí, ar thaispeántaí ón alltar, ar ghreann dubh. Féasta léiriúcháin é seo a mheallann isteach ina chraos sinn.

Ach i ndeíreadh báire *scéal* is ea an drámaíocht i gcónaí. Caithfear tochas an lucht féachana a shásamh maidir le cad a thárla is cén fáth. Ní leasc leis an dráma an gnáthréalaíochas nuair is gá – Gaeilge á labhairt nuair is í a labhraítí, Bearla nuair ba Bhéarla. Mar éagsúlacht bhreise in athchruthú seo Tom Mac Intyre, áfach, tá, go ndíritear freisin ar ar tharla tar éis an dúnmharaithe agus tar éis a bhfuil ar eolas againn ó fhianaíse an dáin. Éiríonn leis é seo a nascadh leis a mbuneachtra chéanna leis an díamhaireacht agus leis an draíocht is gá chun aonad iomlán ealaíonta a dhéanamh. Tugtar carachtair nua isteach, nó daoine nach raibh ach a scáil le fáil san insint thraidisiúnta. Méadaítear agus cuirtear feoil na drámaíochta orthu ionas go luíonn siad isteach go nádúrtha síothóilte leis na príomhcharachtair. Duine díobh seo is ea dearthair Airt ar cruthú uathúil é ionas go n-áitíear ort go gcaithfidh gur mar seo a bhí.

Ceann de mhórdhánta na Gaeilge é *Caoineadh Airt Uí Laoghaire*. Tá ag dul dó go ndéanfaí síor-athleamh agus síor-athchruthú air i bhfoirmeacha éagsúla. Tá seo déanta go hálainn sa leagan seo ag Tom Mac Intyre. Fairis sin, áfach, más é an dán a spreag an dráma, is fíor a rá freisin go saibhríonn is go n-uaíslíonn an dráma seo an dán ar ais.

Programme Note: *Caoineadh Airt Uí Laoghaire* by Tom Mac Intyre

(Peacock Theatre, April 1998)
Alan Titley

The story of Art Ó Laoghaire and Eibhlín Dubh Ní Chonaill hardly needs to be dramatized – it's dramatic enough as it is, including a passionate love, conflict with the authorities, class and religious tensions, spying, murder. An extraordinary poem is the result. But it is as if these themes give scope to Tom Mac Intyre's exceptional gift to restrict that which is extensive, to control that which is unconstrained, to uncover that which is hidden.

Each scene of *Caoineadh Airt Uí Laoghaire* suggests that Mac Intyre must have thoroughly enjoyed shaping, arranging, and indeed creating this moving event. We only get hints of Art's character in the Caoineadh: a pompous, boastful, ostentatious, playful and complete person who challenges life as much as he does the English. As for Eibhlín Dubh – throughout the poem she is depicted as a vessel filled with tragedy and overflowing with mourning – a person suffering, barely able to float on her dark fate. Mac Intyre highlights that she is also a resourceful, active, and cunning personality in the centre of the action, Art's steadfast woman and much more besides. He draws for us a drama bursting with the life of the eighteenth century, and with every sort of character of that time: deceivers, villains, scoundrels, spies, fortune-tellers, lovers, nobles who don't understand life.

Tom Mac Intyre achieves all this in *Caoineadh Airt Uí Laoghaire* in his own inimitable way, a nod here, a hint there, awakening an echo here, inciting our imagination there. Needless to say, he utilizes every theatrical tool – music, mime, poetry and lighting and much more. This is fitting, as mere realism could hardly capture or expose the richness of *Caoineadh Airt Uí Laoghaire*.

The story of this lament awakens us far more than any other unadorned narrative. Drawing on the threads of history, our deepest feelings on love, death and art are invoked. The entire world is represented in this short story and so it's no wonder it draws on folklore, on poetry, on old ballads and tunes, on music, on trickery, on ghosts, on appearances from the other world, on black humour. This production entices us into its gut.

But at the end of the day, a drama is a story which must satisfy the audience's curiosity about what happened and why. Mac Intyre's drama isn't reluctant to use everyday reality when there is a need – to speak Irish when it was spoken or English when it was spoken. Also, in an extension of his source material, Mac Intyre focuses on what happened after the murder and on what we know from the evidence of the poem. He ties this to the central action with mystery and magic to achieve a complete artistic product. New characters, or people who barely registered in the traditional story, are introduced, developed and fleshed out so that they complement the main characters. One example of this is Art's brother, who is such a compelling creation here we are persuaded that this is how he must have been in real life.

Caoineadh Airt Uí Laoghaire is one of the major poems in the Irish language, and it is adapted and reimagined in different forms again and again. Tom Mac Intyre has done this beautifully in this adaptation. However, if the poem inspired Mac Intyre's play, it is fair to say that the play enriches and inspires the original poem also.

Choreographing *Cúirt an Mheán Oíche*

Finola Cronin

I first met Tom Mac Intyre in Wuppertal Germany, in the Lichtburg, the converted cinema that houses Pina Bausch's rehearsal studio. Early in my first season with the company (Tanztheater Wuppertal), my new colleagues joked about my apparent alacrity in organizing a writer all the way from Ireland to record my progress. Mac Intyre was, of course, only interested in Pina, an acknowledged source of influence on his work in theatre since the 1970s.

I worked on Mac Intyre's *The Chirpaun* (1997), but dance and choreography promised to be more integral elements of *Cúirt an Mheán Oíche* in 1999, as Mac Intyre and director Michael Harding made clear in the pre-production meetings that the work was to have a 'rhythmical and bacchanalian sense of intoxication and excess'[1] and thus offer myriad opportunities for choreographic investigation and invention.

As it turned out, the first two weeks of rehearsals devoted entire mornings to physical investigation and material gathering for the play. Each morning began with a warm-up, and, following the process used by Bausch to gather material for her dance theatre pieces – the performers were set tasks or questions which they responded to either individually or in groups, with dance, text, song or scene making. In keeping with another Bauschian rehearsal device, performers had at their disposal rows of costumes – some everyday and others wildly extravagant, along with boots, shoes and an array of props, all of which were chosen to stimulate the imagination and encourage a sense of play.

The tasks were intended to help develop distinct physical scores and establish the performers' sense of ownership of their characters. My introductory notes to the cast include:

> physical memory is key – do it [task] twice and then write it down – a general character build up – material gestural – some

specific – some open to be modified – quality can be played with – don't think about your character – but about you – what you do/imagine – look for things easy – familiar –[2]

The idea was that the performers' responses to the tasks produce an array of possibilities that can be manoeuvered to provide spatial, visual and movement maps. These maps then are used to stage transitions and scenes in an organic way and encourage a sense of fluidity and flow in the whole performance.

Dance sequences were choreographed for both the ensemble and dancer Ríonach Ní Néill, who played the *Leannán Sí*, and were accompanied, live in performance, to an original score by Steve Wickham. Initial discussion of the *Leannán Sí* with Tom, teased out the notion that she was not visible to any of the others [performers], but was '*the* fresh and startling current in the space'.[3]

Shortly before the piece opened Tom accused me of being a sensationalist. I *am* interested in creating material in rehearsal that prepares the way for text, movement and image to become superimposed and interwoven in performance and 'escape from their original meaning to the point of becoming indistinguishable from each other'.[4] I am also drawn to work that enables a sensory engagement for the spectator, such as you find with Bausch, and it may be that this aspect of her work, her so called 'theatre of experience'[5] which is hugely emotionally charged, is also what Tom Mac Intyre finds appealing.

The accompanying notes include: tasks (Aufgaben) lists, sketches of the presentation of the task: 'Sun Sun Sun', and notes of the entrance of the *Leannán Sí* (Prologue Act 2). (See figs 5.15-5.17).

---

[1] Meeting 17 August 1999.
[2] Finola Cronin, Choreographic Notebook 21 September 1999.
[3] Stage direction from early draft of the play.
[4] Simone Benmussa, *The Singular Life of Albert Nobbs* (London: John Calder, 1984), p. 22.
[5] Norbert Servos, *Pina Bausch Wuppertaler Tanztheater. The Art of Training a Goldfish* (Verlag: Ballett Bühnen, 1984).

Fig 5.12 *The Chirpaun*. Actor: Tom Hickey. Set design: Barbara Bradshaw. Photographer: Amelia Stein. Courtesy of the Abbey Theatre Archive.

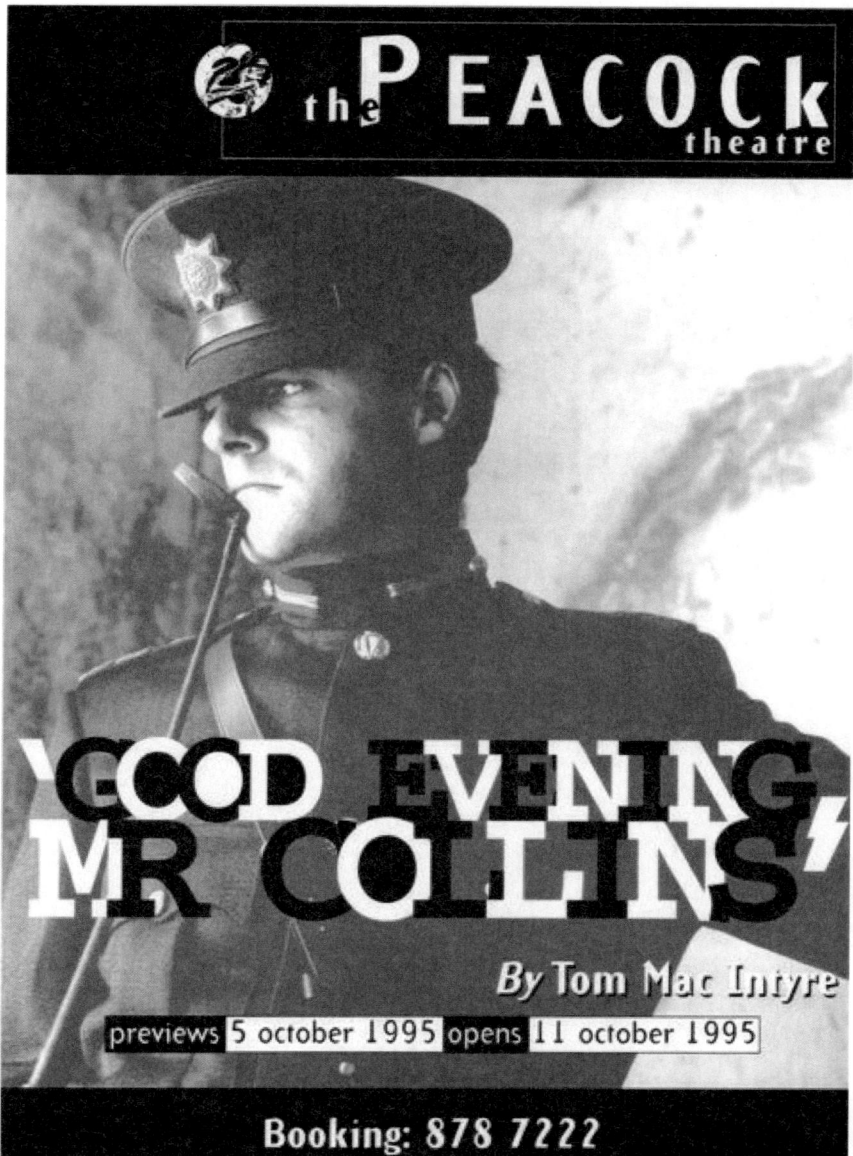

Fig 5.13 *Good Evening, Mr Collins* (poster). Actor: Brían F. O'Byrne. Poster: Abbey Theatre Archive. Photographer: Amelia Stein. Courtesy of the Abbey Theatre Archive.

Fig 5.14 *Good Evening, Mr Collins*. Actors: Brían F. O'Byrne / Karen Ardiff (with backs to audience). Set design: Barbara Bradshaw. Photographer: Amelia Stein. Courtesy of the Abbey Theatre Archive.

Aufgaben 21/9/99

Sun Sun Sun Bathing positions x 3 — 22/9
Bathroom Rituals FOR Animals — (?) 23/9
Sleeping Positions x 3 21/9

Belly Dancing -teaching someone

Fidgeting positions x 6 23/9

Find ways to bounce all the body or a part x 3 21/9

Rian na laimhe (hand prints /hand trace on someone) 23/9

The Fox Hunt — 22/9.

Carnival in Rio 21/9

Loosing your Shoes 21/9

Sheelagh na Gig — 23/9 —

Partnering -Die Ansatz 21/9

Carry someone as high as possible

✳ Mexican Night of the Dead   Fashing Reverse -Roles —

A Rite of Passage   Gender divide ? 22/9

A Brutal Frolic / TRICK in pairs — 22/9

Take Someone for a Ride — 23/

Walking the walls 23/

Measuring 23/

A Nest of Herons — Clumps- Still —

— Mal Barry Bread Pead —
— Niall Thomas — Han

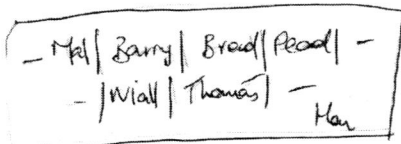

← Deadly Sins →
Dance → FORWARDS Ka Ri, -niall Reader back WARDS FORWARDS Thomas
BACKWARDS

sideways left   Side ways Right

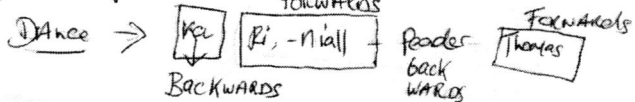
Sile -Brenda- Jodie/ Brid - Mal -Barry

Fig 5.15 *Cúirt an Mheán Oíche*. Choreographer's rehearsal notes. Courtesy of Finola Cronin.

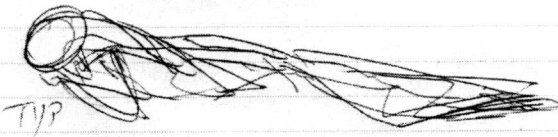

Fig 5.16 *Cúirt an Mheán Oíche*. Choreographer's rehearsal notes. Courtesy of Finola Cronin.

Sun Sun Sun   22/9/99 –

Thomas :

Hands over eyes – to tummy – hand on knee – fanning –

Malachi – head up stage – turned around – The Leader paused – Sun on neck – ← Re

Beid – Face on Floor – Twist → Mid-Rib bare – On Back –

Karen – sitting up – Vertical Fast –

Peadar → Takes Pants – Fiddles with underpants – Bare & Hairy chest head up –

Brendan → Music good in pain – Panting a little – mouth open Collapse to floor – To head down –

Barry – feet waving – Roll to Back – sand – have gloss – Wipes hands clean

Fig 5.17 *Cúirt an Mheán Oíche*. Choreographer's sketch of scene arrangement. Courtesy of Finola Cronin.

CHAPTER 6: 'BETWEEN THE WORLDS'

Theatre Review: *The Gallant John-Joe* by Tom Mac Intyre

Fintan O'Toole
(*The Irish Times*, 29 November 2001)

What is it about Tom Hickey that makes him such a unique presence on the Irish stage? There's his courage, of course. Hickey is one of the few established actors who will go into the uncharted realms beyond embarrassment, glamour and convention. There's also his physical energy, that extraordinary repertoire of gestures and expressions through which his whole body speaks to an audience.

More than either, though, is the fact that Hickey's presence is not mediated through an established system of performance. His roots are in the Stanislavsky school at the Focus, where he is recreating his one-man performance of Tom Mac Intyre's play. But he is no method actor. His courage and physicality seem to link him to the European avant-garde. But there's no trace of its self-conscious formality, either.

What *The Gallant John-Joe* reveals is the secret of how Hickey manages to be such a coherent actor while remaining so apparently instinctive and individual. He inhabits the words. In the tiny Focus space, the audience gets something very special: an almost tangible sense of language on stage, of the audible made visible.

The Gallant John-Joe is, at one level, a recognisable literary text. There is a strong central character, the old Cavan widower John-Joe Concannon. There is a vivid plot, concerning the mysterious pregnancy of Jacinta, John-Joe's teenage daughter, and the suspected fathers that haunt his obsessive imagination. There is a strong sense of locality, bound together by the mythic presence of John-Joe O'Reilly, the great Cavan footballer of the 1940s.

Much more than any of this, though, the play is a skein of words. Leaving behind the increasingly problematic Hickey-Mac Intyre collaborations after the triumph of *The Great Hunger*, in the 1980s, it gives full rein to the exuberance of Mac Intyre's prose. John-Joe's baroque monologue is a torrent of mumblings and malapropisms, of mediaeval dialect and pop slang, of yearning tenderness and murderous xenophobic rantings.

Hickey conveys the feeling that these words are speaking the character rather than the other way round. The line between what may be true and what must be the ravings of a hurt mind disappears. Hickey conveys the sense that truth and lies are both just words, and that the only available reality is the sound he makes.

It is a performance of rare virtuosity, in which there is not a hair's breadth between author, actor and text. Though the play is an act of mourning for the individuality lost in a blander Ireland, it is itself a fierce vindication of a lingering uniqueness.

Ballet in the Bog

John O'Mahony
(*The Guardian*, 23 February 2005)[1]

On a bleak hill in the Irish midlands, Michael Keegan-Dolan, one of the most talented choreographers ever to emerge from Ireland, has spent the past six months building a house with his bare hands. The skeleton of the structure is a derelict two-room schoolhouse. 'It hadn't been used since 1963,' he says. 'And even in '63, they only had two lightbulbs, no water, no toilet. So we knocked it down, just to the stone walls. We had to break it down so we could start again'.

The view is even less heartening. To the front is a windswept road, while a peaty scrubland stretches away to the rear. Every morning, the field is strewn with dead sheep, the handiwork of a crazed local dog. It's a barren landscape that might have been plucked straight from the bog-gothic novels of Pat McCabe, or from the anarchic settings of Keegan-Dolan's own shows. 'Some people like looking at icebergs, some people like looking at lakes,' the choreographer says defensively. 'I like looking at the Irish midlands'.

Though he would object to any use of tidy symbolism, there can be little doubt his building project mirrors his quixotic crusade to establish an internationally renowned company in the desolation otherwise known as Irish modern dance. Ireland has never produced a choreographer of any international renown. There is no national ballet, and just a handful of contemporary companies. 'There was nothing I saw here that made me want to become a dancer,' he says. 'Anyone who was good left and didn't come back. It was a wasteland'.

The main reason for Ireland's historical disregard for dance is that this is a country where literature, poetry and theatre maintain an absolute hegemony at the expense of non-verbal art forms. But equally to blame is Catholicism, which led to dance being regarded as immoral, sinful and degenerate. 'There was a potent cocktail of puritan Catholicism and fanatic nationalism', says dance historian Deirdre Mulrooney. 'Only after all the scandals, and an erosion of the church, are we now becoming a little more comfortable with the idea of dance'.

The final impediment was Irish folk dance, enshrined as the only public form permissible by the Dance Halls Act of 1935. This was a form of dance bondage where the arms are immobile; dancers have been known to stitch down the sleeves of their costumes to radically strip away expression above the waist. 'The whole technique of step dance is down in the feet', says Colin Dunne, former lead dancer with *Riverdance*, now a student of modern dance. 'The more emotional or intelligent parts of the body – your gut, your stomach, your heart, your lungs, your head, your brain, even the face – were just disconnected from the dance form'.

In this unfertile ground, modern-dance schools and companies did sporadically and briefly manage to rise up, often disappearing again just as quickly. But the first truly experimental dance-theatre movement didn't come until the 1980s, courtesy of wild-man poet and playwright Tom Mac Intyre, who (not coincidentally) lives just an hour's drive north of Keegan-Dolan in the even more rugged environment of Co. Cavan.

After a trip to the US in the 1970s, where he hung out at La Mama and stumbled on the work of Richard Foreman and the Living Theatre, Mac Intyre managed to persuade the Abbey to put on his adaptation of Patrick Kavanagh's poem *The Great Hunger*, in 1983. An uproarious riot of movement, it baffled and outraged Irish audiences with its indulgent experimentalism (at one stage the central character hangs upside-down from a gatepost hollering and cursing for what seemed like an eternity) and its masturbatory references. But what made the work quintessentially Irish was the way it retained the word as the central element.

'The Irish believe in the magic of language', says Mac Intyre. 'We believe that magic can break a bottle, or smash a glass. So if we have the words and we know the words are magic then they must have an effect on the way we move. So, in the theatre I was making, language was pushed to an incantatory level, where it had a direct effect on the body'.

Despite often being compared to Mac Intyre, Keegan-Dolan had never seen any of his work: 'I never even heard of him until people started making the references.' In fact, when Keegan-Dolan decided as a teenager to become a dancer, the only dance he had seen was on television. 'I remember on the *Late Late Show*, they were interviewing a Russian ballet dancer and they had a chart of a Russian person's spine and an Irish person's spine, demonstrating how the Irish spine is not right for ballet. And I remember thinking: 'I'm not going to be restricted by my DNA. Just because I'm Irish doesn't mean I can't be a ballet dancer'.

In the early 1990s, Keegan-Dolan joined the Irish 'muscle-drain' and took up a place at the Central School of Ballet in London. On graduation, he worked as a jobbing choreographer with everyone from English National Opera to Peter Hall on the Oedipus plays. He had given up dance and become a bicycle courier when, in 1997, the call came from a regional Irish dance institute in Limerick to set up his company, Fabulous Beast [this call actually came from the Institute for Choreography and Dance in Cork[2]]. The first work he created for the company was a domestic dance-theatre piece called *Sunday Lunch*, followed by *Fragile*, a powerfully visual work involving startling images of corpse-like dancers immersed in bath-tubs of flour and based on the cynic's maxim: 'Conception is Sinful, Birth a Punishment, Life Hard Labour, Death Inevitable'.

However, it was *Giselle*, premiered at the Dublin Theatre Festival in 2003, that displayed the true scope of his talent. The action is transplanted to the fictional Irish small town of Ballyfeeny. For the traditional flouncy, immaculately coiffed peasants, he has substituted disturbingly authentic Irish gombeenmen, transplanted from the same midlands where he spent childhood summers and is now building his home. Employing brutal physical and sexual abuse, much of it directed at his asthmatic Giselle, the choreographer's dark and dangerously anarchic vision transforms the superficial original beyond recognition. 'There is still a prince,' Keegan-Dolan protests. 'OK, so he's not a prince. He's really a Slovakian bisexual line-dancing teacher'.

The movement palette is almost primordial in its intensity, as if these simple steps were being discovered for the first time by the inhibited characters. 'I'm personally very 'tied up' physically and not good with touching and being too close to people', he says. 'That creates all sorts of tension in the body. A lot of the work I do is based on the huge levels of tension you find in Irish people because of that fear of intimacy and fear of sensuality and sexuality'.

Uniquely among modern choreographers, Keegan-Dolan begins with an old-fashioned script. 'It takes me months', he says. 'I'd just get an idea of a guy sitting in a bath covered in flour or a woman being covered by a bucket of red paint or a section of dialogue. It would come from nowhere but I would just write it all down'. Much of this has to do with the practicality of an underfunded art form: 'When rehearsals start, I have to get it up there in a matter of weeks'.

But most of it can be attributed to the same archetypal verbal impulse that moved other Irish dance-theatre pioneers. 'My primary instinct is story-telling', he admits. 'It's just part of me. Language is functional. It all has to be functional for movement to be functional – it has to create a character, it has to create a feeling, it has to lend itself to some other bigger thing, it can't be purely movement.'

If anything, Keegan-Dolan feels he benefits from the lack of any kind of dance tradition in Ireland. 'I'm lucky in that I've no pedigree – I had to work it out myself'. In the past year, thanks largely to the ecstatic reviews of *Giselle*, he has achieved extraordinary success. But despite accolades abroad, Keegan-Dolan will continue to be driven by that glorious sense of insecurity that only an Irish dance practitioner can truly appreciate. 'I've already had flirtations with that kind of promise of mega-stardom. It doesn't actually mean anything', he says, as the tour of his midlands hillside comes to an end. 'Dead sheep are real. The wind cutting into you half-way up a ladder, that's real. Getting into the rehearsal room for the first time, that's real. All the rest is just bollocks'.

---

[1] This correction was printed in *The Guardian*'s corrections and clarifications column, Saturday 5 March 2005: 'In the article [...] we said Michael Keegan-Dolan had given up dance and become a bicycle courier when, in 1997, the call came from a regional dance institute in Limerick to set up his

company, Fabulous Beast. That is incorrect. It was the Institute for Choreography and Dance in Cork, not Limerick, that commissioned Michael Keegan-Dolan to create his first work, *Sunday Lunch*, and second work, *The Good People*, for Fabulous Beast'.

[2] Ibid.

Mapping the World of Bridgie Cleary

Joe Vaněk

Cheerless ... sepia tinted ... atmosphere of a prison ...(1) [1]
Walls ... canvas curtains ... flimsy ... stir and flap ...(1)
Bedraggled chairs [and a] *makeshift table ...*(1)
Apertures in the curtain flaps that pass for doors ...(13)
[*The Void* – ointment hurled into it ...] *hurls the ointment box into the void* (93)
[The Space] *the storm flings* [*Mikey*] *back into the space ...* (90)
scarcely visible ... trapped in their habitual stations on the margins ... (94)
everyone is pale in this climate ... (1)

Tom Mac Intyre, with typically restrained eloquence, gives the designer a tantalizing array of clues as to the enigmatic world that his characters inhabit. Staging directions from authors can veer between the pedantic hyperbole of Shaw to the arid functionalism of Beckett and all the stops in between. But Tom's unique style is to map out the 'lie of the land' (as it were) with haunting and subtle nuances. And, then his characters speak:

There's no clocks here – but there is *time*, funny enough (Bridgie, 6)
Are we here forever? (Mikey, 30).
What, what's it like – in this place? What goes on? (*Beat.*) Does anything – *happen*? (William, 59)

On my very first reading of the script, and before I met with director Alan Gilsenan, there formed in my mind an image of a place suspended somewhere between wakefulness and sleep. Essentially, this place seemed to me to be some form of transitional chamber, and, whilst the three characters sensed they were 'on the head of a journey' as the play progresses, their real journey is gradually revealed to be internal. Through reverie, remembrance and recrimination within themselves and then each other, they are seemingly held in a state of questioning limbo.

Alan and I started to investigate a mass of visual references from ancient Celtic mysticism to contemporary art in order to fathom exactly what constitutes a visualization of this state. I was also struck by the parallels that this play had with Jean-Paul Sartre's *Huis Clos* where three characters enter an anonymous room – are locked in by a valet and discover during the course of the encounter that 'hell is other people'. The English title *No Exit*, has a particular resonance for *Bridgie Cleary*, as much of this text throws emphasis on a 'lack of doors', and it soon became apparent that one of our first tasks in the design process was to find a way of conjuring them into the space without the usual exits and entrances ... and this space that they find themselves in? Well, a considerable amount of time is spent contemplating it and what it is, or is not, and what lies beyond.

What's (*he tilts his head*) outside there? (Mikey, 10)
Nuthin'. Everythin'. Have a luk. You won't get far. (Bridgie, 10)

The sense that their actions are circumscribed is very much borne out by Bridgie's observations: 'I've, this long while, me own circles drawn te steady me balance in these dominions', (Bridgie, 23) and, as to the scale of these dominions? 'Yer in a great chasm o' space here, as ye'll discover', (Bridgie, 12).

The Peacock Theatre stage is wide, and the proscenium line low giving it an almost widescreen feel. This was a distinct advantage in creating a space in which the characters could find distance and a sense of isolation from each other. We felt a need to channel them into this space through a small, focused 'aperture', the main playing area then spread out to the left and right as they emerged. Also this aperture would need (from the audience's point of view) to seem to have no visible means of access. An image of a viewing room in a US prison with low horizontal windows looking onto an execution chamber seemed apposite. It was clinical and remote, lit with stark, fluorescent tubes, and, reimagined in the form of a long corridor, it seemed an ideal conduit for their arrival. Its upstage end was truncated by a featureless, wooden slatted box but this in fact had hidden doors through which the actors passed in lighting changes.

What Happened Bridgie Cleary
By Tom MacIntyre

as BRIDGIE

Comprises —
Corset
Red Petticoat
White over petticoat
Blouse
Jacket
Skirt			optional —
Boots —		HAT - Shawl - gloves

Joel Vaněk — March 2005

Fig 6.4 *What Happened Bridgie Cleary*. **Costume sketch (for the character of Bridgie Cleary) by Joe Vaněk. Courtesy of Joe Vaněk.**

What Happened Bridge Cleary
by Tom MacIntyre

Declan Conlon
as William

joevanek
march 2005

Fig 6.5 *What Happened Bridgie Cleary.* **Costume sketch (for the character of Mikey Cleary) by Joe Vaněk. Courtesy of Joe Vaněk.**

What happened Bridgie Cleary.
by Tom MacIntyre

Tom Hickey
as Mickey

Fig 6.6 What Happened Bridgie Cleary. Costume sketch (for the character of William Simpson) by Joe Vaněk. Courtesy of Joe Vaněk.

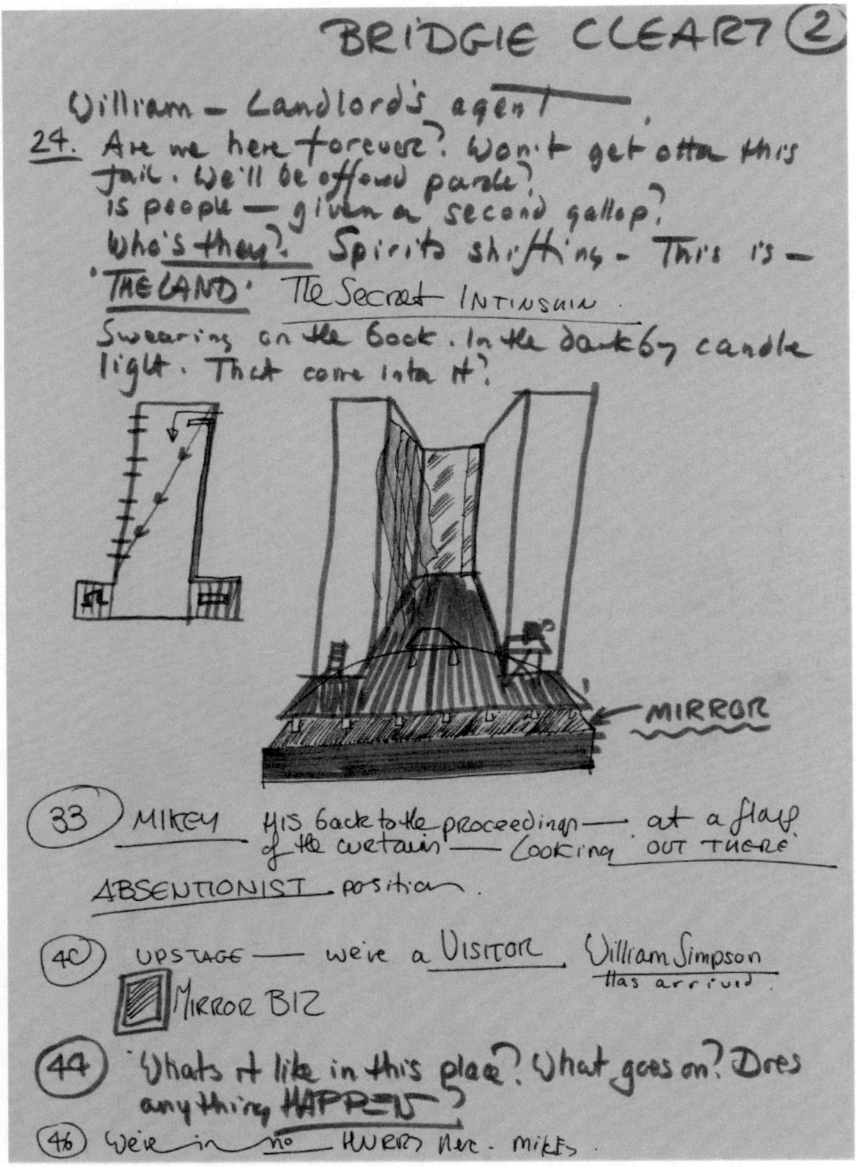

Fig 6.7 *What Happened Bridgie Cleary*. Designer's notes (Joe Vaněk). Courtesy of Joe Vaněk.

Fig 6.8 *What Happened Bridgie Cleary*. The set at get-in for Peacock Theatre. Photographer: Joe Vaněk. Courtesy of Joe Vaněk.

Fig 6.9 *What Happened Bridgie Cleary*. Actors: (from left) Catherine Walker and Declan Conlon. Set design: Joe Vaněk. Photographer: Pat Redmond. Courtesy of Pat Redmond.

The presence of curtains within the space is referred to ambiguously in the text on several occasions. Sometimes there is a sense that the space itself is entirely curtained, at other times these curtains would seem to be hanging in the spaces created by more solid forms. What would appear to be a constant, however, is a sense of confinement and that an element within this is soft and pliable. Allied to Bridgie's obsessive love of fabrics (hardly surprising as she was in fact, a dress-maker) we pondered how best to evoke this 'material world'. Alan had the notion of the space being initially shrouded by fabric, so that on entering the theatre, the audience would only dimly perceive what lay before them. The theatre of Brecht famously used the half curtain, traversing the stage on steel wire, to effect scene changes or sub-divide the stage. Alan felt that a similar device could offer an intriguing opening to the play. With the use of a high-powered wind machine, we hung across the full width of the stage mottled cotton curtains. Initially these floated and eddied until, without warning, they billowed ferociously out into the auditorium as Bridgie's sewing machine whirled into action. With the judicious use of smoke and lighting amidst the mayhem, Bridgie seemed to mysteriously appear. Thus, the entire first scene was staged with Bridgie slowly and hypnotically taking down and folding the curtains into neat piles as she addressed the audience.

Throughout the play, she returns again and again to her beloved fabrics – at the beginning – 'magickin' gossamer stuff, silks, satins, and so on, the smooth feel of – *downey* items' (14) ... And, at the end – 'Gossamer ... Gossamer ... Silk ... Raw silk ... Slubbed silk, slubbed silk' (103). These litanies, often repeated, were very powerful and affecting, and would provide a wealth of insights into her own costuming later.

We devised an entry into the space and created an opening sequence, but where was this space that these three inhabited? Perhaps they were in some place of 'fairy lore'? (for after all, the house at Ballyvadlea had, according to legend, been built on a fairy fort!). Perhaps it should have the aura of a penitentiary (as a place of abjection) – which would continue the prison metaphor? Maybe a softer, holy site, such as a well (for its redemptive qualities)? A fourth possibility came from a photo of the Catacombs at Domitilla, but the image that finally 'nailed' it was to come from a book called – *fishstonewater* – which brought us back to the world of the wells. A photo of Tober na Molt in Co. Kerry, showed a minute cottage – or 'dressing house'. Ordered benches lined its two whitewashed walls as in a waiting room and debris of holy water bottles, feathers, dead leaves and candle holders littered the floor and window sills. A sense of people passing through and on was palpable. This seemed to be the key. Another photo of blackened footprints in snow seemed to add more resonance, but we agreed that the final space needed to have about it a touch more of the charnel house than the devotional.

> Sometimes, sometimes I wonder is people ... given a second gallop, lek books goes on about (Bridgie, 30).

We decided that maybe some people had been given a second chance ... but not our threesome. As the set design emerged, we decided to create one vast back wall parallel to the stage front, with benches running its full length. Through this wall at its centre would thrust the sealed corridor with fluorescent tubes and industrial hanging lights. It became a place for the displaced and the dispossessed. In replicating the debris that we had seen in the dressing house, this became magnified with the scattering of boots and shoes, and hats and scarves hung high on hooks, and abandoned piles of clothing. Dusted with snow, the final look took on a further connotation with the world of the internment camps, which whilst commented on by observers, had not been intentional.

> That silence out there ... if it wasn't for a colour in the silence out there, I believe I'd say good-bye te me moorin's. (Bridgie, 97).

> Out there (Bridgie, 97) ... *the void* (93) ... *the margins* (94)

The script repeatedly conjures their particular world suspended in a greater cosmos. How to represent this? Obviously, characters moving to the front of the stage – the fourth wall – and looking out solves this problem to some extent, and yet, for the audience, looking in, it expects to see some evidence of this world beyond. This is where lighting comes to the fore, and utilizing chiaroscuro effects as seen in the paintings of Caravaggio and Joseph Wright of Derby, we devised with Kevin McFadden, the lighting designer, two black side walls to the set with hidden lighting slots. To one side they were the full height of the set, to the other, simply small rectangular openings high up. These enabled us to isolate the characters with intense, full length side light from one direction, throwing them into a dramatic positive and negative relief. From the other high angle we were able to float heads and shoulders achieving a disembodied effect that made figures appear insubstantial. The large back wall – a dusty blue/grey – faded into these black side walls as the floor faded too. With the characters stepping out of the centre playing area they moved into the 'margins' and beyond the light sources that illuminated them we hoped there was a sense of the 'void'. We also chose to highlight the back wall at key moments and I designed the floor to curve up under the benches and debris to conceal lighting battens. These gave an unearthly glow to the walls festooned with their detritus of hats and scarves, heightening the drama at significant moments. The floor fading away was conceived as an icy, central area with a vague, foetus like shape, veined and in rusty colours and where the body would have been sited we placed a small glinting pool. When Bridgie's body was discovered in its shallow grave, it was described as a 'marshy hole' and a photograph showed its surface puddled with water. Her illness was variously attributed to pneumonia and later TB, but the more feverish and hallucinatory she became, the more the family and friends gathered at her bedside came to believe that she was a 'changeling', and that the burned body that was later to be unearthed was not in fact her at all. Superstitions surrounding the world of fairy lore, included the belief that women in labour were often spirited away, and whilst the post-mortem found no signs of pregnancy there was a rumour that with her several lovers (in particular the egg man – Phildy Redden and William Simpson – the land agent) her 'state' could have been caused by a condition that her family was unaware of.

we're here te do sums, make discovrees, clarify gloom –
(Bridgie, 3).

Bridgie has her own realm set up for her in the play, and it is anchored by her sewing machine, an ancient Singer. The mechanics of springing this machine unaided into life called for some quite complex mechanics under the stage floor, but it brought a frisson of 'otherworldliness' to the action at pivotal moments. When first we meet her she is shredding a shirt, preparing for business later in the play when she will disperse the pieces around the space as one would devotional objects at a holy site.

Yes – there's a hat, remember, we called a 'gossamer' –
(Bridgie, 103).

When discussing the 'look' of Bridgie herself, Alan was quite clear about the fact that she should look translucent. There was an image I recall him finding of a girl in a long white layered dress, of no particular period but with a high buttoned bodice, (it could have come from a slightly off the wall production of *Giselle*). Gossamer seemed to be the watchword and he felt that whatever she wore there was to be about it a sense that if you looked at her long enough you might just be able to see through it. (She was, after all, essentially a ghost, or at least a restless spirit). In her local community she had always been considered well dressed and superior. As she says herself: 'Always a step or two above buttermilk' (Bridgie, 2). We conceived her 'look' in layers – and found an amazing sepia/grey shot taffeta that was semi transparent. This became the outer layer of a long, boned period jacket and a flared skirt, beneath which lurked layers of similar petticoats until we finally reached one of red flannel. Under the jacket was a similarly transparent blouse of dusty pink flowers through which one could see the stern lines of her corset.

> Maybe I'm a class of a wanderin' Jew that flung the boot at Christ an' had te travel roads ever after (Bridgie, 17).

Following his release from prison, Mikey Cleary took off for Canada and continued his work as a barrel maker. Tom sees him very much as still the image of this working man and describes his look as 'peasant tradesman garb'. During the early part of the play he spends much time on his knees in absent minded rituals with his carpentry tools that he carries with him in a sack.

> A trade is what gives a man dignity (Mikey, 15).

He wore a three-quarter length, flared greatcoat – grimy and stained from a period more mid-nineteenth century than the late 1890's when the atrocity occurred. This was complemented by huge scuffed work boots, thick woollen trousers, a heavy waistcoat, collarless shirt, mittens and copious ragged scarves. Despite his demeanour being otherwise, a leather cap added a jaunty air and also the look of a sea captain (which given his travels, both actual and metaphysical) seemed apt. Colours again, as with Bridgie, were greys and steel blues, charcoal and black, and when his clothes were finally put together they were broken down so that they seemed as if bound together with dust.

> The bit of style, applied with the bit of style. Poor world without the bit o' style, don't ye think? (William, 54).

As if to reinforce this air of dandyism about him, stage directions dictate that William ...'*busies himself combing his hair, his moustache, fixing his collar*' – and later ... '*is brushing his spats with a wire brush*' (63). From their earliest encounter, we are left in no doubt as to Mikey's opinion of him ... 'Simpson, Esquire, of the trained moustache, an' the curry-combed spats an' the ramblin' fingers itchy for the rumps o' the lonesome ladies' (Mikey, 60) yet, it is suggested, he too exudes a 'sepia pallor' despite being a 'fancy dresser'.

Fabrics were sampled for a dapper, slimline, two-piece suit with a contrasted waistcoat. We found a dun coloured, minutely checked wool cloth with a fine wine red line on it forming a grid that resembled the veins on the back of a hand. We matched that red to an identical, solid cloth which became a striking waistcoat with broad revers, and a gold filigree fabric became an ostentatious tie. This whole look was topped off with a spectacular and square shouldered brown double breasted top coat. William Simpson cut quite a dash when his hatted and spatted silhouette first materialized in the white corridor.

'The Powers' that Be (Bridgie, 2).

Bridgie, Mikey and William were not alone – the play is underscored with sounds that amplify their melancholy rites. The tinkling of a piano, the distant cry of a heron, a softly moaning wind and the discordant braying of an ass! At one point Mikey attempts to leave and a sudden storm forces him back. William, however, has no such difficulties in leaving, yet quickly returns having experienced his own dark night of the soul.

To create the storm we placed a large fan to the rear and above the end of the corridor and leaves were dropped by way of a simple release mechanism. On cue, Mikey tumbled into the ensuing maelstrom amidst flickering lights and howling winds, and, that this was the work of unseen hands, teasing and tormenting them, was commented on, adding to a pervasive sense of helplessness.

Tek care, Bridgie, tek care the minit passin' – an'–' not returnin' (Bridgie, 99).

Despite her youth and her love of life, when the chance came to make a clean break of it and run away with William Simpson, her courage failed her and the repercussions were to be truly horrific. The country was shocked at the savagery of her killing and the subsequent callous disposal of her body. In a country barely five years away from the dawn of the twentieth century, it seemed inconceivable that there were still places in Ireland subject to superstitions involving the powers of the 'beyond crowd' as they are referred to by Mikey. Their cottage in the townland of Ballyvadlea is to be found in the shadow of Slievenamon, a solitary hill famed for its place in fairy lore and a constant brooding presence in Bridgie's dreamy incantations.

Tom's elegiac play was awarded the Irish Times Best Play of the Year in 2005, and for her mesmeric and heartbreaking performance as Bridgie, Catherine Walker won Best Actress.

As a designer for the stage working in Ireland since the mid 1980s, it has been my fortune to originate designs for some of the finest new plays of the last two decades and of course, in doing so, to work with such leading playwrights as Brian Friel, Frank McGuinness, Tom Kilroy, Stewart Parker, Sebastian Barry, Tom Murphy and Tom Mac Intyre. Each of their distinctive voices has brought a continuing challenge to my visualization of their writings and to them and all the directors that I have collaborated with, I am eternally grateful.

What Happened Bridgie Cleary was a unique work that by virtue of its poetic, almost musical form, spoke with an unexpected resonance and power from the very first sighting. Teasing out the route that this production would take visually with Alan and Kevin was a fascinating and memorable journey – but then, after all, we did have a master map-maker guiding us.

---

[1] Tom Mac Intyre *What Happened Bridgie Cleary*, (Dublin: New Island Drama, 2005). All quotations in this essay are taken from this edition of the play. References to this play are incorporated in parenthesis in the text.

**Theatre Review: *What Happened Bridgie Cleary*
by Tom Mac Intyre**

Fintan O'Toole
(*The Irish Times*, 29 May 2005)

In 1938, when his play *Purgatory* was first staged at the Abbey, William Butler Yeats told an interviewer, 'I think the dead suffer remorse and re-create their old lives'. Since then, most major Irish playwrights have written their own versions of *Purgatory*, but few have followed Yeats as literally as Tom Mac Intyre does in his intriguing new play, *What Happened Bridgie Cleary*.

Set in the realm between earth and heaven, it evokes the remorse of three of the protagonists in one of the most infamous of Irish murders, as they re-create their old lives. In its densely poetic language, its use of the stage as a sacred space and its air of repeated ritual, this is perhaps the most Yeatsian play the Abbey has staged since its co-founder's death.

The first thing to be said is that, in spite of its title, the play is not about Bridget Cleary. If it were, it would be a wild, violent epic. Cleary, a strong and attractive young dressmaker in rural Tipperary, was murdered in 1895. At the trial of her husband, father, aunt and cousins, it emerged that she had been tortured and burned in the apparent belief that the real Bridget had been taken away by the fairies and a changeling left in her place. The trial, which coincided with the arrest of Oscar Wilde, became a paradigm of the clash between tradition and modernity, and the whole episode would make a great Brechtian drama. But anyone expecting a big, vivid, violent play will be taken aback by what they find here.

Mac Intyre's piece is emphatically *not* about what happened Bridgie Cleary. His real interest is in stray suggestions in two brilliant accounts of the case. In her dazzling book, *The Burning of Bridget Cleary*, Angela Bourke briefly mentions rumours that Cleary and the landlord's agent William Simpson were lovers. In his essay *The Eggman and the Fairies*, Hubert Butler mentions that Bridget's husband Michael made mention of the fact that his wife 'used to be meeting' a man who bought eggs from her. Mac Intyre transforms these possibilities into facts. Butler's suggestion that people 'thrust upon the fairies the guilt for desires and jealousies whose crudities they shrank from facing' is his template. His Bridgie was the lover of William Simpson and the Eggman, and it is the jealousies generated by her desires that hover now in Purgatory.

The play, then, is very much more a thing of shades and shadows than its title might suggest. It is low-key, slow-burning, evocative, not a symphony but a string quartet. And rather a lovely one, too. In the text of the play, published by New Island, Mac Intyre refers to it as being 'scored', and its great strength is its coiled, bittersweet music. If anything, indeed, the whole business of Bridget Cleary is an unnecessary background noise that can only distract from Mac Intyre's real business – an exploration of the language of love, desire, regret and remorse.

Fortunately, director Alan Gilsenan and the superb cast of Catherine Walker as Bridgie, Tom Hickey as Michael and Declan Conlon as William Simpson, are not distracted for a moment. On Joe Vaněk 's wonderfully misty blue-grey set, whose ghostly quality is enhanced by Kevin McFadden's dim-toned lighting, Gilsenan creates a quietly compelling spectacle that is utterly attuned to the modulations of Mac Intyre's language.

Rich as a Christmas pudding but with an earthy, salty tang, Mac Intyre's dialogue is a strange but forceful confection of archaic rural speech and angular, modernist sounds. Gilsenan and the actors are smart enough to know that the drama is in the lift and swoop of the language, and to trust themselves to its flow.

It is Walker, alone on stage for the first scene, who has to get the surge of words running, and though at first her accent seems almost like a Hollywood brogue, she quickly reaches a perfect, mesmerizing pitch. She achieves, too, a calm dignity that balances both Hickey's raw-boned anguish and Conlon's suave but sorrowful bemusement. Marvellously alert to every shift in tone, the trio describe a graceful arc from anger to guilt to resignation. Raising as it does the mundane viciousness of humanity to a hard, unearthly beauty, this is a piece that Yeats would have been glad to see in his theatre.

Theatre Review: *What Happened Bridgie Cleary* by Tom Mac Intyre

Patrick Lonergan
(*Irish Theatre Magazine*, 19 May 2005)

In 1886, W.B. Yeats published 'The Stolen Child', a romanticized presentation of the west of Ireland, in which a child is stolen by the fairies, a changeling left in his place. Nine years later Michael Cleary, together with his neighbours, burned his wife Bridget alive – believing that she too had been kidnapped by the fairies, a changeling left in *her* place. It's an interesting distinction, this. For Yeats, the changeling was a legend that allowed him to create a beautifully poetic celebration of the Irish landscape. But for Cleary it was a terrible reality – one grounded in ignorance, poverty, and violence. What's disturbing about Tom Mac Intyre's dramatization of Bridget Cleary's murder is that he seems aware of the tragic brutality of his source material, but surrenders to a Yeatsian impulse towards poeticization – beautifying and therefore sanitizing the violence at the heart of this story.

What Happened Bridgie Cleary is a meditation on love and forgiveness, stuffed to the brim with intertextual references to other Irish plays. The action is set in a purgatorial space where Bridgie (Catherine Walker) confronts both her husband (Tom Hickey) and her supposed lover (Declan Conlon) about what was done to her. This arrangement immediately calls to mind Beckett's *Play*, but it's also reminiscent of Yeats's own *Purgatory*.

The style of performance chosen by director Alan Gilsenan is also reminiscent of those works. In *Play*, Beckett had his characters trapped in urns, only their heads visible; while Yeats often wished that he could immobilize the Abbey actors from the neck downwards. Movement here is similarly restricted: each actor works within a limited zone of the stage, rarely moving out of it – and there is little movement or physical interaction between characters. Things aren't helped much by Joe Vaněk's set, which locates events somewhere between a moonscape and a gothic castle, incongruously filling the backdrop with hats resting on stands.

This means that the success of the play is almost entirely dependent on the actors' ability to carry Mac Intyre's language, a homogenized Hiberno-English that sounds like Synge being filtered through Marina Carr – there's plenty of beauty in the carefully modulated lines, but there's a harshness of tone too.

A few problems arise from this. The first is that Mac Intyre is presenting us with what could be called a poetics of destitution and ignorance. We quickly forget that there is a relationship between the conditions that gave rise to Michael Cleary's murder of his wife, and his and Bridget's romanticized use of speech, which is full of twee malapropisms, infelicities, and mispronunciations. The second difficulty is that each member of the cast seems to have adopted a different approach to speech and enunciation. Walker attempts – not always successfully – to perform in an 'authentic' Irish accent, but doesn't seem comfortable with the rhythms and tones of the script. Conlon on the other hand performs the language without ornamentation, but seems uncomfortable with his rather underwritten character. Hickey gives us his usual blend of energy and conviction, and shows an affinity with Mac Intyre's work that undoubtedly results from their many collaborations with each other. But the performances don't cohere: these characters are supposed to be from different worlds, but at times it feels as if they are performing in different plays.

In the end, the greatest difficulty with this play lies in trying to establish who exactly is being addressed by this work – and what exactly it's trying to say. I don't think the intention is to cause us to reinterpret the story of Bridget Cleary, but instead to use it as a springboard for a celebration of female individualism, sexuality, and love. That celebration is weighted down by its relationship to the source material, however: what's tragic about the burning of Bridget Cleary is not that she was heroic or individualistic, but that she died with such an utter lack of dignity. Any attempt to re-present that disgraceful incident in a positive or transcendent light risks eliding what actually did happen to Bridget Cleary – I found myself wondering during the performance how we'd feel if, in another hundred years, the Abbey was hosting plays set in purgatory about the Kerry Babies Case or the killing of Robert McCartney. Mac Intyre's play is beautifully written, elegantly performed, and often very interesting – but this production doesn't seem sufficiently aware that Bridget Cleary was not a character in a play, or a symbol of anyone's ideals – but a real person.

Theatre Review: *What Happened Bridgie Cleary* by Tom Mac Intyre

Karen Fricker
(*The Guardian*, 29 April 2005)

The title's fractured syntax is the first clue that Tom Mac Intyre's play will not be a straightforward retelling of the story of Bridget Cleary, a Tipperary woman who was burned to death by her husband in 1895 for suspected witchcraft.

The second hint that we are in for an unusual evening is Joe Vaněk's odd but lovely setting: a series of five gossamer panels hanging before an open space, with hats hanging from the walls, piles of shoes on the ground and a tall panelled doorway centre stage. But the most compelling evidence of this production's strange beauty appears when the radiant young actor Catherine Walker pulls down the panels one by one and speaks directly to the audience: 'You're thinkin', She's a prisoner ... Bridgie's a prisoner ... And you're not, I suppose?' The setting, we realize, is the afterlife, where Bridgie sits at her Singer sewing machine, listens to distant heron cries, and tells stories with a compelling combination of intensity and matter-of-factness: 'Bridgie Cleary, who made weskits for the gentry, hats for the quality. Bridgie Cleary, always the step or two above buttermilk ...'. She is joined by her husband Mikey (Tom Hickey), now an old man because he outlived her. Indirectly and allusively, they exchange stories and information, working their way towards an inevitable reckoning. A third party then appears, their snooty neighbour William (Declan Conlon), who was previously Bridgie's lover.

Director Alan Gilsenan keeps the focus on Bridgie's emotional and sexual life: the high point is Bridgie's soliloquy to the man she truly loved, Phildy Reddon. Exceptional production values, including Kevin McFadden's lights and Cormac Carroll's sound design, superb ensemble acting, and Mac Intyre's dense and colloquial prose-poetry combine to create a haunting event.

Anarchic and Strange: *Only an Apple*

Bernadette Sweeney and Marie Kelly
with interview material from Selina Cartmell.

In advance of the 2009 opening of *Only an Apple*, *The Irish Times* published 'Born with Storytelling in his Blood', a feature article on Tom Mac Intyre by Sara Keating. Keating contextualized Mac Intyre at this point in his career:

> Mac Intyre is one of the lesser-known playwrights of a particular generation who, writing in the 1960s and 1970s, used the theatre to challenge the legacies of de Valera's Ireland. Where Brian Friel, Thomas Kilroy and Tom Murphy put alternative Irish realities onto the stage, Mac Intyre was interested in looking beyond reality altogether, in seeking a

symbolic space in which the unconscious desires and needs of those repressed and repressive years might be explored and maybe satisfied.[1]

This description by Keating prefigured *Only an Apple*'s exploration of a world where the real and the unreal meet and merge. The play opened on 21 April 2009, and featured Taoiseach, a modern-day political figure trying to hold onto his power during a (much-relished) visitation by Elizabeth (I) and legendary pirate Grace (O'Malley). The two women are matched by a third, described in the character listings of the published script as 'The Wife ...'.[2]. The Wife is a character who is 'playing at' invalid, a role to which she's accustomed and which she can assume or discard as she pleases' (47). These women are offset by the three men who surround the Taoiseach, butler Sheridan, press secretary Hislop and Cultural Attaché Arkins, while on the margins lurks would-be political usurper McPhrunty. Mac Intyre's Taoiseach references the former Irish political leader Charles Haughey, whose extravagance and corruption generated much controversy at the end of his career. The Taoiseach of Mac Intyre's play resides in Taraford – a culturally-recognizable reference to Haughey's home Abbeville in Kinsealy. Mac Intyre's Taoiseach is a broader reference too, to Irish politics, to the preponderance of corruption and the seductive powers of extravagance, be it material, sexual or political.

Mac Intyre has always given his audiences something familiar – a place, a person, a myth or story – on which to ground their experiences in the theatre. It is from the depths of the audience's own associations with these historical, mythological or iconic figures that the live performance springs. How deep can you go with Adam and Eve in the Garden of Eden? And how deep can you go with an infamously corrupt political leader at a time of economic recession and government scandal?

Mac Intyre has spoken about what he strives for as a playwright:

> In my experience of the theatre I know there's only one note that would give you what I call 'an edible silence' and it's what the playwright works for: 'an edible silence'. How do you get that note? You can only get it from the themes of sex and death, and that's what I work for in the theatre'.[3]

The Taoiseach of *Only an Apple* is balanced precariously between Mac Intyre's favourite themes of sex and death, and in one of his final speeches he references jockey Mornington Wing to describe his own gamble:

TAOISEACH. Any gamblers among you? I keep a few race-horses. The father a close friend of Morny Wing, the great jockey. Mornington Wing – what a name for a jockey! Had I been named Mornington Wing I'd have been fine. Or if I'd a child – girl-child – called Morning. A girl-child called Morning – whom I could have watched playing. Or picking primroses in March. Or staring astonished, at a white horse. *(Long pause)* Tell you something, and for free: I'm minded to gamble – just go for it – y'know, like closin' your eyes and walking over a cliff. Donegal. Or Clare. Aran Islands. Am I going mad? I feel in balance. I think. [...] I want the trip. Am I ready to pay the price? Will there be a price? Always a price. For coming. Going. Pray for me (98).

Much excitement was generated by the Abbey's choice of director Selina Cartmell for this production. Of a younger generation of directors, Cartmell is renowned for her visual sensibility and her experimentation with imagery and theatricality, and seemed the perfect match for Mac Intyre's latest play. *Only an Apple* lived up to Cartmell's reputation on all of these fronts with an audacious staging of the female and a vibrant and playful sense of the performative. The play projects make-believe on the characters and us as the audience by staging barely-concealed political commentary through farce, musical and the surreal.

From the director

Cartmell spoke about her involvement in the project and her experience working with Mac Intyre in response to a series of questions:

MK/BS. How did you become involved in this project and what is it about the work of Tom Mac Intyre that interested you?

SC. Tom called me about another play he had written that he wanted to discuss with me after he had seen some of my previous work. I remember it very clearly – I met him for breakfast at Elephant and Castle in Temple Bar and we just hit it off. I enjoyed his company and the way he spoke about the world and theatre and why we do the work we do. He was also a good friend of Marina Carr's and I remember leaving breakfast thinking he was certainly one of the tribe if not the leader of the tribe.

A few months later I was asked by Aideen Howard if I would read his latest play, *Only an Apple* that the Abbey had commissioned. I then met with Fiach MacConghail to discuss directing the project.

I had seen very little of Tom's previous work but remember hearing a diverse array of responses, some cult-like in the intensity of the following of the stories he told and the way he told them. The first time I read *Only an Apple* I remember thinking this is one of the most anarchic and strangest plays I had ever read. I was inspired by the imaginative leaps of the language and haunted by the visitation of Elizabeth (I) and Grace O'Malley at Taraford. I also remember finding the story outrageously funny and entertaining.

MK/BS. How do you feel that Mac Intyre's use of imagery matches the visual aesthetics of your own work as a director?

SC. When reading *Only an Apple* it was clear here was a writer and poet who loved images, dance and physical language as much as the written text. It is rare to find a writer who is so willing to experiment with different styles and bold forms of theatrical language and I found this challenging and inspiring in equal measure.

As a director it is important to create a safe environment where the actors and creative team feel free to 'play', and this is the word I most associate with the visual aesthetic of the Mac Intyre world. I found when directing *Only an Apple* that it is only by 'playing' that you can fully unlock the true spirit of Tom's vision.

MK/BS. Can you give an outline of your approach to the rehearsal process and how the work developed? (How did Mac Intyre contribute to the work in the rehearsal room, for instance? What particular hurdles were overcome? How did the actors respond to the complexity of the text?)

SC. *Only an Apple* is an ensemble piece of work and this is where the challenge lies for both actor and director. I was blessed when directing this production by being given an inspiring and immensely talented company.

I feel the Mac Intyre actor needs not just intelligence but strong physical skills and energy that transcend the spoken word. I also feel a Mac Intyre actor needs to be fearless as what he demands and asks of the actor sometimes pushes you beyond any logical understanding of the world.

We had a five-week rehearsal process for *Only an Apple*. This consisted of mostly scene rehearsals, with a few weekly dance and singing rehearsals for the madcap 'Pussy Drives the Train' that ends Acts 1. For the first three weeks of rehearsals most communication was done over the telephone between Tom and myself or via e-mail if new scenes were being written. In the last two weeks he was more present in the rehearsal room looking at sections of the play that he would then respond to with new scenes or ideas.

The text of *Only an Apple* is dense and complex and has multi-layered meanings. As we discovered during rehearsals Tom sometimes wrote phrases or words because he likes the sound of them or it gives a speech a certain musical pulse. I think the actors found it helped to find a physical score for speeches or sections of the play that lifted the language to a more heightened style of presentation. I hoped the actors found his world in which to play a liberating experience where anything is possible and where anything can happen.

Staging Strange

It is clear from Cartmell's comments that many of the defining features of Mac Intyre's other work were present here too – a need for the actors to be playful and indeed brave, an ensemble approach to the work and its 'physical score', and a willingness to go beyond 'any logical understanding of the world'. Mac Intyre was working once again in the realm of the unreal. He himself described *Only an Apple* as 'surely a dream play. And as such it is choc-a-bloc with the energies and motifs and symbols of my dreams. But if you call the whole thing surreal, you have to admit that it is as real as the cup in your hand as well'.[4] In fact, in a talk at the Abbey theatre as part of the 'Meet the Makers' series, Mac Intyre advised young writers to 'start dreaming fast' as this is the 'most immediately available door' to them.'[5] He continued: 'there's only one story – are you going to wake up or are you going to stay asleep? Are you interested in becoming conscious?'[6] Mac Intyre's latest play gives evidence of this process of dreaming, and stages a world where the dream and the reality are hard to distinguish. This allows for exuberant political satire, free from the ties of historical exactitude or documented record. It also allows for an overt theatricality, well staged by Cartmell's visual response to the play, as captured by stage photographer Ros Kavanagh.

Dick Bird's startling setting brings the audience directly into the classic splendour of a Georgian drawing room with its imposing bay window, floor to ceiling bookcases, and large framed portraits which extend out along the auditorium walls. Kavanagh's images (see figs 6.1-6.3 included here) document the production's staging of the ostentatious lifestyle of the political leader which houses the iconic and incongruous images of the two historical figures Elizabeth (I) and Grace O'Malley. They also highlight Matthew Richardson's brilliantly garish lighting which further disrupts any naturalist response to the piece.

In Ros Kavanagh's photographic images there is no mistaking the atmosphere of this shared space and its tantalizing extravagance. Somewhere between *Alice in Wonderland* and Taraford/Kinsealy there is the playful and then the foreboding. Kavanagh's three images capture this movement in the darkening sky and the narrowing or tunneling from three panels of the bay windows to one as the play comes to a close.

Cartmell emphasized the theatricality of the play through her use of half-mask, allowing the 'contemporary' characters to become other for the musical number 'Pussy Drives the Train' at the end of Act 1, and for the end of the play as the characters gather around the fated Taoiseach. Arkins also dons the mask when in conversation with the Taoiseach towards the end of the play, see below and fig. 6.2.

Figure 6.3 shows Fiona Bell as Elizabeth with apple, (standing), Michael McElhatton as Hislop, seated, Marty Rea as Arkins, (seated), and Cathy Belton as Grace (seated on one arm of the sofa, with her head up). Here we see the imagery of the apple staged overtly as Elizabeth teases and tantalizes in a suggestion of Eve, to the smiling fascination of Hislop. Arkins, meanwhile, in the luxurious setting of 'Taraford', gazes raptly at the unlikely figure of Grace O'Malley, perched at the other end of the sofa.

Figure 6.2 depicts Marty Rea as Arkins in mask opposite Don Wycherley as Taoiseach. Here the men are seated on the arms of the leather sofa involved in an intense conversation. The real is disrupted here again, however, as the Taoiseach is in everyday shorts and tennis shoes while Arkins is wearing an Elizabethan ruff and halfmask, with a heavy beak giving it a bird-like profile. Here we see the Taoiseach perched across from his shadow self, between them one panel of the great bay window, a symbol of the entrance to that unknown place, the place for 'closin' your eyes and walking over a cliff'(98).

Figure 6.1 shows Cathy Belton as Grace (at door left), Michael McElhatton as Hislop, Don Wycherley as Taoiseach, Marty Rea as Arkins, (at table centre) and Fiona Bell as Elizabeth (at door right). This image documents the stage picture and shows how the design encroached on the audience's space by extending the décor of

Taraford out onto the walls of the auditorium. This both drew the eye of the viewer to the stage and implicated the audience – making us somehow complicit in this corrupt and distorted world.

In Mac Intyre's plays we have become accustomed to an element of consciousness in the material object – the effigy in *The Great Hunger* as mentioned earlier, the refrigerator in *Rise Up Lovely Sweeney*, more recently, the Singer sewing machine in *What Happened Bridgie Cleary*. In *Only an Apple* this is carried through to the architecture, as the drawingroom itself represents consciousness as interrupted by the unconscious. This is not entirely a haunted house, but a haunted self. Throughout the play doors fly open of their own accord and secret compartments magically slide open to reveal the repressed, the forbidden, the carnal. The action takes place on a red chequerboard tiled floor, the game of life underfoot. The relentlessness of such powerful images throughout this magical play speaks volumes. Together with the dramatic weight of Mac Intyre's beautifully poetic yet symbol-laden text, there is little room for the audience to breathe, to have time to luxuriate in either of these vibrant aspects of the piece. *Only an Apple* exposes the competition between this poetic text and the strong visual and physical aesthetic that is well underway in the later plays of Tom Mac Intyre.

... the males: unsure of what's next ... the women: altogether commanding ... (29)

In *Only an Apple* Taoiseach and his male colleagues are like putty in the hands of three voracious women. *Only an Apple* stages archetypal women, and as such it follows a tradition established by Mac Intyre: in his staging of The Mother as an effigy in *The Great Hunger*; as iconic in the character of Jacinta (present onstage in *The Chirpaun* and central, though absent, in *The Gallant John-Joe*); through the merging of characters' subjectivity in *Good Evening, Mr Collins* with the device of three female characters as played by one actor (Karen Ardiff); and the female as purgatorial and ethereal in *What Happened Bridgie Cleary*.

While extremely effective this tradition of Mac Intyre's begs the question, are his female characters empowered as figures, or disempowered as they are robbed of individuality, or, in some cases, agency? Do they serve simply as objects onto which the male characters project their desire(s)?[7] This is an especially apt question in relation to *Only an Apple*, which is overt in its staging of the female and sexuality, from the staging of The Wife to the voraciousness of the two historical women to the, in the words of the director, 'madcap' musical number 'Pussy Drives the Train'. The sexual power of the female as threatening is indicated by the final stage directions for this musical number, as included in the published text. Here Mac Intyre stipulates that 'As soon as the celebratory thrust has been established, the colour of the proceedings should take a turn towards the troubling, the menacing, the chasm, i.e. sure pussy drives the train, but pussy, by the same token, is high octane, and the mere lighting of a match has blown many away' (46).

Elizabeth (I) and Grace O'Malley are described as 'succubi' (demons who take female form to have sexual intercourse with men in their sleep) variously throughout the text, and the male characters are simultaneously wary and in thrall:

> ELIZABETH/HISLOP. *She takes him by the hand, leads him downstage left. Next she positions him so that the two are standing together in conversational mode,* ELIZABETH *brimming with seduction,* HISLOP en garde *and then some. Locking eyes with her prey,* ELIZABETH *lets her beautiful upstage hand drift to her cleavage, dally there, and, from that sweet nest, she fetches a lime-green apple. She admires the apple, kisses it, listens to it.*
>
> ELISABETH. *(to the apple)* Vraiment?
> *She glances at* HISLOP, *apple now resting on her palm, extends her palm with its precious cargo.*
> ELISABETH. Touch it (29).

By locating extreme female sexuality in these two historical figures Mac Intyre clearly draws these women as fetish objects as well as agents of another world. Thus Mac Intyre adroitly removes them from the everyday and they become projections of Taoiseach's desire rather than characters in their own right. The only 'real' female figure then is 'The Wife' who, in her position in the Taoiseach's reality, does not merit a name of her own, and mirrors Taoiseach's sexual games with one of her own, an ongoing affair with the butler Sheridan.

> TAOISEACH *on. Decidedly on edge. Snaps out of that, tours the room, sniffing, sniffing ...*
>
> TAOISEACH. My wife and my ever-obliging butler are now in bed together – the ravenous two-backed beast! Well, I suppose

they could be at worse. What she sees in him – perhaps he has a big cock? Does size matter? If they tell you it doesn't, they're lying (55)

These three women, then, are unabashedly staged as cyphers, functioning as different elements of the Taoiseach's sexual life, rather than as independent characters.

The male characters fare little better. Taoiseach is of course the centre of this world and is, as such, the architect of all we see. The characters that surround him – male and female, contemporary and historic – are there to serve in one capacity or another. Mac Intyre draws a very unflattering picture of Irish politics (including sexual politics) with very broad strokes, which conversely allows him to make some very fine points. Sheridan the butler is obsequious but knowing, McPhrunty is the 'inflated-in-waiting' a political rival treated with contempt, Hislop the press secretary has a dubious level of power which is swiftly compromised by his fascination with Elizabeth, and Arkins the Cultural Attaché is the token (and gay) artist:

> **TAOISEACH.** It's the poet in you understands, that's why I've always said 'Have a poet on the premises' (23).

Thus Taoiseach is surrounded by a group of sycophants and enablers, unchallenged and indulged. The visiting *succubi* herald a change in his circumstances, which the action moves us towards inexorably.

Script in process and performance

There are significant differences between the published script and the performance of the play at The Peacock in 2009. One of these Mac Intyre commented on: 'the snake vanished in the whirligig of rehearsals', as it was 'deemed a biteen too literal'. Mac Intyre went on to state that, for him, the snake is invisibly there, and that the afflicted Taoiseach, driven to a clifftop, must concede 'a lot of terrifying, beautiful truths that he has excluded from his breathing and his bloodstream all his life, the snake among them.'(23). However much Mac Intyre might still see the edited snake, such differences raise an interesting issue about the performance life of a piece, when it becomes definitive, if ever, and whether or not the published text, when published before performance, can claim any kind of authority. Of the writers of his generation, Mac Intyre's work is the most responsive to the processes of rehearsal and performance, and therefore the least likely to remain unaffected by the collaborative journey that an ensemble production can be. The traditional rules of production and publication don't apply so easily here as Mac Intyre's work, in its performativity, resists such typical transactions.[8]

Critical Response

Only an Apple, like so much of Mac Intyre's work, prompted mixed responses from critics. Mick Heaney of *The Sunday Times* felt that, as in previous works by Mac Intyre

> the fate of the protagonist is bound up with his libido, though in this case the problem is a surfeit of sensuality. But the playwright's latest gambit is an unwise move. The drama is idiosyncratic, daring and, in a flawed way, entertaining, but it lacks the earthily mythical quality that marks his best work.[9]

However, Emer O'Kelly of *The Sunday Independent* argued that

> Mac Intyre inhabits a magical world where it's possible to right wrongs if you have faith and courage. But he then transfers it to the real world, where such moral alchemy is far more difficult.'[10]

Patrick Lonergan reviewed the play for *Irish Theatre Magazine* [reprinted here, see next article]. Like O'Kelly, he is supportive of the play's political ambition, and identifies Mac Intyre's use of form as key to realizing this. Lonergan concludes his review with the following provocative overview:

> *Only an Apple,* then, is vacuous, crude, and infantile. It is consistently sexist and occasionally homophobic. It is incoherent and self-regarding. And because it is all of those things, it is a stunningly appropriate and stimulating portrait of our political system – one that allows us to imagine what the world looks like from the perspective of a mediocre man with serious responsibilities. So many recent Abbey plays have suffered from trying too hard to be topical; *Only an Apple* is relevant and absorbing precisely because it chooses to leave itself open to interpretation, trusting audiences to relate what they are seeing to their own lives, and their own situations.[11]
> (*Irish Theatre Magazine* 6 May 2009)

If *Only an Apple* has anything to say about the development of Tom Mac Intyre's theatre craft over the last forty years it is that here is a relentlessly daring risk-taker, a writer who fears nothing when it comes to trying something new or exposing his own funny, fantastical and often dark or alternative side. Of course, it is just this alternative side that compels us to go back again and again to see what it is that Mac Intyre is up to this time. It is this alternative side, moreover, that speaks to the very place in us that recognizes the darkness and alterity that exist within ourselves.

Works Cited

Cartmell, Selina, Unpublished Director's Notebook, 2009.
Heaney, Mick, *The Sunday Times* 04 May 2009.
Keating, Sara, *The Irish Times* 25 April 2009.
Lonergan, Patrick, *Irish Theatre Magazine* 6 May 2009.
Mac Intyre, Tom, *Meet the Makers* talkback series, Abbey Theatre, 26 May 2009.
---, *Only an Apple*, (Dublin: New Island, 2009).
O'Kelly, Emer, *The Sunday Independent* 04 May 2009.

---

[1] *The Irish* Times, 25 April 2009.
[2] Tom Mac Intyre *Only an Apple*, (Dublin: New Island, 2009), unnumbered. All quotations in this essay are taken from this edition of the play. References to the play will be incorporated in parenthesis in the text.
[3] Tom Mac Intyre speaking at the *Meet the Makers* talkback series, Abbey Theatre, 26 May 2009.
[4] *The Irish Times*, 25 April 2009.
[5] Tom Mac Intyre speaking at the *Meet the Makers* talkback series, Abbey Theatre, 26 May 2009.
[6] Ibid.
[7] As mentioned in the introduction to this book, *Only an Apple* shares some themes with Mac Intyre's *Fine Day for a Hunt* (first produced as a full-length play in 1992), such as the presence of the Big House, the symbol of a pack of hounds and a merging of the real and the unreal. *Fine Day for a Hunt*, however, staged a much darker fate for the female protagonist – not so much an archetype as a timeless victim.
[8] It must be acknowledged that his work also resists, to some extent at least, the project that is this publication.
[9] *The Sunday Times*, 4 May 2009.
[10] *The Sunday Independent*, 4 May 2009.
[11] *Irish Theatre Magazine*, 6 May 2009.

Fig 6.1 *Only an Apple*. Actors: (from left) Cathy Belton, Michael McElhatton, Don Wycherley, Marty Rea, Fiona Bell. Set design: Dick Bird. Photographer: Ros Kavanagh. Courtesy of Ros Kavanagh.

Fig 6.2 *Only an Apple*. Actors: (from left) Marty Rea and Don Wycherley. Set design: Dick Bird. Photographer: Ros Kavanagh. Courtesy of Ros Kavanagh.

Fig 6.3 *Only an Apple*. Actors: (from left) Fiona Bell, Michael McElhatton, Marty Rea, Cathy Belton. Set design: Dick Bird. Photographer: Ros Kavanagh. Courtesy of Ros Kavanagh.

Theatre Review: *Only an Apple* by Tom Mac Intyre

Patrick Lonergan
(*Irish Theatre Magazine*, 6 May 2009)

You have to wonder why Irish dramatists keep writing plays about politicians. In 1969, Brian Friel's *The Mundy Scheme* brilliantly satirized the political life of that period, while anticipating much that would follow. Yet that play is never revived, has been out of print for years, and is rarely written about. In 2001, Sebastian Barry premiered *Hinterland*, another grossly underrated drama about a fictitious Taoiseach, who in this case resembled Charles Haughey. Barry's play was accused of being 'moronic' in the press; he later said that the critical response in Ireland was like something out of Stalin's Russia. Marina Carr's 2002 *Ariel* had as its protagonist a midlands politician who sells his soul for political power. That work was greeted not with hostility, but with indifference and snide contempt – and Carr has not written a play set in the midlands since.

One of the reasons that such plays have been poorly received is that our politicians are so mediocre as to defy dramatization. When

Irish playwrights present such figures in tragic mode, their work seems overblown and pretentious. Yet to write about them in a comical way seems facile: politicians do a perfectly good job at making themselves seem ridiculous, after all. Nevertheless, Irish dramatists continue to write about politicians – and continue to face problems when they do so.

As is so often the case in Irish theatre, Tom Mac Intyre is an exception to this rule. In his 1995 play *Good Evening, Mr Collins*, he showed an ability to sidestep the risks inherent in presenting political figures – in that case, Michael Collins and Eamon De Valera. He did so by making clear that he wasn't attempting to present a convincing biographical portrait of anyone, but was instead exploring how Ireland's understanding of his two characters has developed through time. His play was deliberately fantastical, often self-contradictory, and overwhelmingly confused – just like the collective Irish memory of Collins and Dev themselves.

Mac Intyre repeats this trick successfully with *Only an Apple*, a play that is – yet at the same time most definitely is not – about Charles Haughey.

As the lights come up, Don Wycherley – only called 'Taoiseach' during the play – appears centre stage, standing in an impressively regal pose, in an impressively regal drawing room. This set, designed by Dick Bird, matches perfectly the play's tone, being full of pretty objects that are revealed to be hollow when we look beneath their surfaces. There is a packed bookcase and a gorgeous old globe that suggest their owner is very learned – but the real function of both is to hide a generous stash of booze. There are impressive portraits on the walls, showing the Taoiseach skiing, golfing, and on horseback – achieving physical rather than intellectual excellence, and acting in pursuit of pleasure rather than power. At the end of the play, Wycherley himself strips away his clothes, showing that beneath his expensively clad exterior, he is little more than a clown, mooning at the audience like a disgraced toddler. The play seems constantly to recall *The School for Scandal*, that other Irish satire of a society obsessed with surface appearances – as may be indicated by Mac Intyre's decision to name the Taoiseach's trusty servant 'Sheridan' (played by Malcolm Adams, who is hilarious but in danger of being typecast in the role of comic subordinate).

The play succeeds mainly because the action is mediated through the consciousness of the Taoiseach – we see the world not as it is, but as it appears to him. He is being haunted by Grace O'Malley and Queen Elizabeth (Cathy Belton and Fiona Bell respectively), two succubi whose characterization is used to reveal the Taoiseach's attitude towards women in general. *Only an Apple* quickly becomes a domination fantasy in which virgin and whore come together to fuck with the play's male characters (that crude expression, with all its connotations, is really the only way to describe it). So we get to enjoy Belton and Bell's torment of the Taoiseach's press secretary (McElhatton), his stereotypically gay national poet (Rea), and his political rival (Blount, in a performance that was received by the audience as a cheap send-up of Brian Cowen, though it's not clear if it was intended as such).

The visual imagery employed by Selina Cartmell recalls the tone and aesthetic of pre-Revolutionary France – a surprising but effective choice that complements Mac Intyre's style without overwhelming it. By broadening the frame of reference, Cartmell universalizes the play's treatment of political power, shifting our attention away from the parochial – away, that is, from Haughey and our own sorry state. As always with Cartmell, one constantly senses that the action could spill at any moment from the stage and into the auditorium.

Only an Apple, then, is vacuous, crude, and infantile. It is consistently sexist and occasionally homophobic. It is incoherent and self-regarding. And because it is all of those things, it is a stunningly appropriate and stimulating portrait of our political system – one that allows us to imagine what the world looks like from the perspective of a mediocre man with serious responsibilities. So many recent Abbey plays have suffered from trying too hard to be topical; *Only an Apple* is relevant and absorbing precisely because it chooses to leave itself open to interpretation, trusting audiences to relate what they are seeing to their own lives, and their own situations.

Letters to the Editor ....

[As Fiach Mac Conghail says in the preface to this anthology, 'The plays of Tom Mac Intyre have continually probed awkward questions, provoked discussion and stimulated controversy.' From a survey of the newspapers of the day here are just a few prominent reactions from Mac Intyre's fellow writers:]

Hibernia, Friday 24 June 1977
Find The Lady
Eilish MacCurtain Pearce (Lismore, Co. Waterford).

Sir,

It looks as if Mary Manning has started something with her letter about *Find the Lady*, Tom Mac Intyre's recently produced play at the Peacock.

Poor play reviewing, lacking a modicum of perception, has, regrettably, become prevalent – for me a growing irritant.

Only a respect for the Sheridan brothers and what they are doing for contemporary Irish theatre prevented me from writing about Peter Sheridan's thin understanding of Mac Intyre's outstanding play. But with other pens and voices raised, I now have courage to contribute more.

Firstly, permit me to bore your readers, maybe, with my interpretation of Tom Mac Intyre's *cherchez la femme* theme. I saw the play as within a play. The actors, circus people or strolling players, were once again interpreting *à la* 'Peg O My Heart', the story of Salome and John the Baptist. This gave the play just the edge of alienation needed.

Then we were shown the theme of the private world with its personal values in which John found himself, because of his imprisonment, played against the public world with its community values represented by the corporate role John had committed himself to. This was interpreted for us by the 'John' player acting out his 'nightmares' i.e. fantasies and doubts. And once he had 'overcome' them, how greatly he destroyed Salome's innocence, who in turn, released her introverted emotion into the strange revenge of taking his head.

Mac Intyre laughs at us poor humans all the time, or laughs with us as he places himself unequivocally within the framework of the human condition.

All sorts of interesting sidelights make *Find the Lady* rich and amusing (*cherchez* Beckett, Ionesco, Brecht). Herod's temptation to become a good man, goaded by John into contemplating his release; the clowns interpreting our frustrations by comic fetishes and offers of crutches/crotches – a favourite Mac Intyre symbol – and the whole implication of liberty and the extent of one's capacity to experience it (see also *Jack Be Nimble*, Mac Intyre, Peacock, 1976). There is also, to my mind, in Mac Intyre's work the classical theme of the mask and its mythical origins. A private theatrical joke, one suspects, like many of his asides.

Tom Mac Intyre is not the only Irish playwright now writing to suffer at the hands of the journeyman critic. Tom Kilroy, Tom Murphy, Brian Friel, M. J. Molloy, are all wasting their spirits in a desert of misunderstanding and uncaring market-places. Brian Moore's recent adaptation got little showing; neither did I see a serious review of Peter Sheridan's fine production of Gallivan's *Dev*.

I must make my points as briefly as I can. Irish drama is needed very badly, mainly because we are dependent on it as a means of seeing ourselves in truth; not just as a way of confirming what we already know or suspect about ourselves. Lacking as we do, a post-war *cinema verite*, we cannot expect RTÉ to provide a major diet of art in life.

In Ireland, all too easily, we invalidate the intangible; the theatre can provide the antidote to this. (For example: the world not only belongs to the strong, it also belongs to the weak.)

There are splendid writers, playwrights, such as Hugh Leonard, Denis Johnston, John B. Keane, Fergus Linehan who supply other needs. Our need for rationality, for irony and the *mondaire*. But our most pressing need is for a reflecting art form.

Like the Swiss who are good at making watches and growing Alpine flowers, the Irish are in tune with the theatre. Let us not brush aside our natural assets.

For these reasons I call on newspaper trustees and proprietors who (we hope, and in some cases know) make a profit, to give, in all conscience, the public full-time theatre critics, proven in their understanding and love of the drama.

Press barons and broadcast moguls can afford full-time political and economic correspondents – so why not full-time correspondents of the arts?

James McKenna was right to stand for election.

Yours etc.,

Eilish MacCurtain Pearce.

The Irish Times, 30 May 1983
'Great Hunger'
Augustine Martin (Dublin 6).

Sir,

Though the critical response to Tom Mac Intyre's *Great Hunger* at the Peacock has been enlightened and favourable, full justice has not been done to its uniqueness as total theatre. What we see at the Peacock might be called the 'Ur-version' of Kavanagh's poem. By a remarkable leap – or more likely an arduous pilgrimage – Mac Intyre has gone back to the experience out of which *The Great Hunger* was born, the aboriginal, pre-reflective almost pre-verbal emotions, drives, longings and inhibitions of 'Maguire and his men'. The idiom of grunt, sigh, gesture, exhalation, embodies a human crisis that has not yet found release and articulation in Kavanagh's poetry.

The cast, directed by Patrick Mason and led by Tom Hickey in one of the greatest individual performances I have ever seen – its only rival in recent times is Donal McCann's in *Faith Healer* – create a world best summed up by Yeats's remark on the peasants in Carleton's fiction, 'like the animals in Milton, half emerged only from the earth and its brooding.'

It is no coincidence that Mac Intyre, Kavanagh and Carleton come from the same drumlin country – I do myself. Its quintessence is embodied in this production, and the universality of its comedy, tragedy and pathos. This is one of the best things the Abbey has done in recent years: the sort of play Synge might have written in *The Well of the Saints* if he had not been infatuated with language and its dangerous liabilities.

Yours etc.,
Augustine Martin

The Irish Times, 20 September 1985
Rise Up Lovely Sweeney
Sebastian Barry (Monkstown, Co. Dublin).
Sir,

David Nowlan, in his interestingly rustic review of Tom Mac Intyre's new play, sings (with anapaest and amphibrach, to an old tune): 'But we do not lift off with Sweeney.' This reminds one of a possible and rhythmic monk being faced with the *fait accompli* of (even, anciently) Thomas Stearns, Eliot, and silvering, agreeably: 'But there is no assonance in this glory.'

Could David Nowlan not see that he has given Tom Mac Intyre's machines, but for two or three faint-hearted riders, what is popularly called a 'rave review'; that what he misses in it is not there because Tom Mac Intyre is *urbanus* in relation to our present alarmed *urbs*; that no man identifies with no man when the ships and the proconsuls are down; that empires are inconveniently over and Charles Dickens has done his work, as have his theatrical equals; and something other is now appropriate, sirens and torches and video and all?

David Nowlan's last remark, a bone through his nose to spite his face, is: 'It does not come to dramatical life.' Dramatical life is the imaging of liturgical life on the stage; when liturgical life has been so long threatened, and challenged, images of death and defiance must start to aid it. David Nowlan is too cozy in the shroud of his baptismal robes: he should look to his guts, not his Victorian heart, for information – or else be assigned kindly, and kindness is stressed, to a perpetual reviewing of the next 4,500 performances of *The King and I*.

Yours etc.,
Sebastian Barry

The Hurt Mind

Tom Mac Intyre

[With the kind permission of Tom Mac Intyre we reproduce here Sweeney's monologue from the 1985 play *Rise Up Lovely Sweeney*. This text also appeared in verse form as 'Appalachia' in the collection of poems entitled *I Bailed Out at Ardee*, (Dublin: Dedalus Press, 1987)]

SWEENEY. What do I want? I want to know. What ish my nayshun? What ish my nayshun? My nayshun is Appalachia, Appalachia, Appalachia – the worn trail of eye for hand, tooth for claw, scalp for cup and saucer ... busted telly in the bog-hole, washing-machine sneezing rust on the uninsurable bargain line – listen to the wind through the nuts and bolts, excuse me! We keep the baby in the fridge, a cool clear sound when she jingles, her eyes – believe it – a snow sky. Not a hyacinth, not a tint, tall blue of the garlic, never no more. And in the towns – into the banger and give her stick – in the towns I see, marooned mum-to-be lamenting last year's laughter, look at her, belle of the local, perched before the one-armed sweepstake, cloud of peanuts her only prayer. While the arcades spit and stutter like The Sea of Tranquility inside a poxy equinoctal moon and the crouched young put their heads away with galactic zippity-dooh-dah ... It's too long a war ... *it's too long* ... it's too long ... SHE GROWS OLD ... I'm wrecked. A bush in the gap, please – she's cratered, the scenic route, she's cratered and all the bridges smithereened ... christ, I *love* this country. All right – please – wash me in the water where you wash your dirty daughter – but you won't – you won't – you will not do it ... The what? *What?* The heart's needle. We have met. Right, she knows the know, she knows the reason, she knows the cause of the reason – But I'm talking of the hurt mind, hurt mind in wait and knowing as the hurt mind knows ... lift that baby out of the fridge ... air the house, fumigate the floors ... hold your simple tongues, will you? I ask why have they hidden trust? And where may I find it? The white of an egg? The shoe-box smell? Under the ash-tray? Can *you* tell *me*? Cable collect, benefactor out there, and American papers please stop-press and banner till the type melts ... *ego te baptizo. Ego te exorciso.* 'Appalachia', scalp for scalp and cup for saucer, broken road of we leaf-people – broken road of we leaf-people – how much do you

weigh? You? You? You? – State your weight – leaf-people number-
less as autumn, and the whine, oh that whine in the chair when
night comes ... You do not perhaps credit the hurt mind? I
remember one morning a disc in the sky ... Is that sun or moon? I
can't tell sun from moon ... I can't tell sun from moon ... .

Notes on Contributors[1]

Karen Ardiff trained at the Samuel Beckett Centre at Trinity College Dublin and has appeared regularly on stage in Dublin, on television and film. She played Moya/Kitty/Hazel in *Good Evening, Mr Collins* (1995) Bean Álainn in *Cúirt an Mheán Óiche* (1999) and Eibhlín Dubh Ní Chonnaill in *Caoineadh Airt Uí Laoghaire* (1998) by Tom Mac Intyre. Karen's first novel *The Secret of My Face* was published by New Island Books in 2007.

Selina Cartmell holds post-graduate degrees in Advanced Theatre Practice (Directing) from Central School of Speech & Drama, and History of Art and Drama from Trinity College, Dublin, and Glasgow University. For Siren Productions she directed *Titus Andronicus, Macbeth* and *La Musica* (Project Arts Centre). Other productions: *Here Lies* and *Passades* (Operating Theatre), *Catastrophe, Festen* and *Sweeney Todd* (Gate), *Woman and Scarecrow* by Marina Carr (Peacock), *Big Love* by Charles Mee (Abbey), Tom Mac Intyre's *Only an Apple (Abbey) and The Cordelia Dream* by Marina Carr (RSC).

Bronwen Casson was Set and Costume Designer at the Abbey Theatre for twenty-five years. During this time she designed sets and costumes for both the Abbey and Peacock stages including Tom Mac Intyre's *The Great Hunger* (1983), *The Bearded Lady* (1984), *Rise Up Lovely Sweeney* (1985) and *Dance for your Daddy* (1987). She now works as a photographer and a visual artist. Her most recent media/installation works include, *No Man's Land* (2004) *Moonscapes* and *Ebb and Tide* (2006) and *The Sun Rising Over The Sea* (2008).

Finola Cronin trained in both classical ballet and contemporary dance in London and was a member of Pina Bausch's Tanztheater Wuppertal. At The Peacock Theatre she was Movement Director on Tom Mac Intyre's *The Chirpaun* (1997) and *Cúirt an Mheán Oíche* (1999). Finola was Dance Specialist at the Arts Council from 2003 to 2007 and currently lectures in the School of English, Drama and Film at University College Dublin.

Ben Francombe is principal lecturer in Performing Arts at the University of Chichester. His PhD (Glasgow University, 1993) was on the development of performance strategies for new writing at the Abbey Theatre. He has worked as a freelance theatre director and taught at the Royal Scottish Academy of Music and Drama, Liverpool, John Moores University, Bretton Hall and the University of Leeds. His recent research has been on the Scottish National Theatre, Practice as Research in Performance, British Actor Training and on playwrights Friel, Murphy and McGuinness.

Marie Kelly worked at The Abbey Theatre from 1993 to 2006, firstly as an Executive Assistant and subsequently as Casting Director. She has an MA in Modern Drama and Performance and is currently working on a PhD on the work of Tom Mac Intyre at the School of English, Drama and Film at University College Dublin. Her research is funded by the Irish Research Council for the Humanities and Social Sciences.

Fiach MacConghail has been Director/CEO of the Abbey Theatre since May 2005. Prior to this Fiach was Arts Adviser to John O'Donoghue, Minister for Arts, Sport and Tourism (2002-2005) and Artistic Director of Project Arts Centre (1992-1999). Fiach was also one of the founders and, subsequently, Chairman of the International Dance Festival of Ireland. He has also produced several award winning dramas for RTÉ, TG4 and with Brothers Films.

Dermod Moore was an actor in *The Bearded Lady, Rise Up Lovely Sweeney,* the first revival and subsequent tours of *The Great Hunger, Dance for your Daddy,* and *Snow White,* all by Tom Mac Intyre. He also appeared in Marina Carr's first play, *Low in the Dark,* and at one point he realized he had played on every stage in Dublin. He's now a writer, documentary film-maker, teacher and, God forgive him, a psychotherapist.

Bríd Ní Neachtain is a native of Galway, a native Irish speaker, and was a member of the Abbey Theatre Company until 1999. Abbey performances include *Translations, The Mai, Riders to the Sea, The Playboy of the Western World, The Well of the Saints, Dancing at Lughnasa* and *Woman and Scarecrow* and Mac Intyre's *The Great Hunger, Dance for your Daddy* and *Rise Up Lovely Sweeney*. She has worked with Taidhbhearc Na Gaillimhe and was nominated for an Irish Times/ESB Award for *Cre Na Cille* (2003).

Catriona Ryan is from County Mayo. She is currently in the finishing stages of her Phd in English at Swansea University: 'The Poetics of Tom Mac Intyre: A Multi-Generic Perspective'. She is a published poet and has been published in six anthologies of poetry in Ireland.

SarahJane Scaife received her M.Phil. in Irish film and theatre from Trinity College, Dublin. She has been an actor, director, and scholar of theatre for over 20 years. She specializes in the visual and physical approach to theatre, specifically in relation to the works of Samuel Beckett, W. B. Yeats, and Marina Carr. She has directed Beckett's plays in Europe and many countries in Asia. She is currently a doctoral candidate at Queen's University Belfast.

Daniel Shea is from Worcester, Massachusetts. He wrote 'Stage Irishman, Stereotype, Performance: A Perspective on Irish Drama of the Second Half of the Twentieth Century' as his doctoral thesis and received his PhD in English and German at the University of Heidelberg. He now lives in Germany and works at the University of Heidelberg teaching language and literature courses. His contribution to *The Methuen Drama Guide to Contemporary Irish Playwrights* (2010) is on Tom Mac Intyre.

Amelia Stein lives and works in Dublin. Over the past 25 years Amelia Stein has established herself as a singularly exacting photographer. Her area of expertise has been portraiture, working with actors, performers, playwrights, poets, authors and musicians on commissioned images and on production photography in the Irish theatre. Personal exhibitions which have been seen in selected galleries throughout Ireland: *In Loving Memory* (1989), *Triúr Ban* (1995), *Palm House* (2001) and *Loss + Memory* (2002). In 2003 she was the first photographer to be elected a member of the Royal Hibernian Academy, Ireland. In 2006 Amelia Stein was elected a member of Aosdána.

Bernadette Sweeney lectures in Drama and Theatre Studies at University College Cork. She undertook her doctoral research at the School of Drama, Trinity College Dublin and published *Performing the Body in Irish Theatre* with Palgrave Macmillan in 2008. She is a theatre practitioner and is currently in rehearsal with Beckett's *Krapp's Last Tape* and *Play*. She is currently visiting faculty at the University of Montana. She is a founder member of the Irish Society for Theatre Research.

Joe Vaněk has been designing extensively for the Irish stage since 1984 and his work has covered drama, opera and contemporary dance. He was Director of Design for The Abbey Theatre from 1994 to 1997 and Design Associate for the Wexford Festival Opera during the 2006/7/8 seasons. He is principally known for designing several premieres of Brian Friel plays between 1990 and 2003. For *Dancing at Lughnasa* (seen in Dublin, London and New York) he was nominated for two Tony Awards on Broadway.

---

[1] Many other writers have contributed to this book by allowing us to reprint previously published material. This list includes commissioned writers only.

Index

A

Abbey Theatre, The, *passim*
Almost Free Theatre, London, 89
Appia, Adolphe, 67, 69, 71, 117
Ardiff, Karen, xiv, xvii, xix, 16, 31, 33, 245, 247, 266, 274, 308, 322
Artaud, Antonin, 6, 100, 114, 116f., 122, 124, 145

B

Bachelard, Gaston, 199, 209, 211
Banks, Joanna, 260, 264
Barnes, Barry, 250
Barnes, Ben, 27, 29, 37, 219
Barrett, John, 6, 87ff.
Barry, Sebastian, 20, 297, 314, 319, 320
Hinterland, 314
Barthes, Roland, 157, 161, 199
Bausch, Pina, 18, 24, 40, 57, 67, 69, 71, 76, 110, 139, 145, 225, 270f., 324
Beckett, Samuel, 19, 46f., 109, 123, 165, 216, 218, 285, 300, 317, 323-26
Bell, Fiona, 35, 307, 316

Belton, Cathy, 35, 307, 316
Benmussa, Simone, 271
Berman, Ed, 90
Bettelheim, Bruno, 12, 183, 192, 196
Billington, Michael, 6, 95
Bird, Dick, 35, 306, 315
Birthistle, Eva, 32, 265
Blount, Steve, 35, 316
Boland, Graham, 159, 196, 251
Bonner, Charlie, 245
Bosmajian, Hamida, 122
Bourke, Fergus, 1
Bradshaw, Barbara, 90, 245
Brook, Peter, 6, 72, 100, 114, 122, 124, 145
Brown, Terence, 148, 159
Bruce, Fink, 122
Byrne, Catherine, 159, 196
Byrne, Mairead, 41, 124

C

Calck Hook Dance Theatre, 24, 31, 37, 76ff., 82, 260
Calvert, David, 11, 179
Campion, Sean, 245
Carr, Marina, 16, 30, 36-42, 50, 245, 300, 304, 314, 323ff.

Carysfort Press was formed in the summer of 1998. It receives annual funding from the Arts Council.

The directors believe that drama is playing an ever-increasing role in today's society and that enjoyment of the theatre, both professional and amateur, currently plays a central part in Irish culture.

The Press aims to produce high quality publications which, though written and/or edited by academics, will be made accessible to a general readership. The organisation would also like to provide a forum for critical thinking in the Arts in Ireland, again keeping the needs and interests of the general public in view.

The company publishes contemporary Irish writing for and about the theatre.

Editorial and publishing inquiries to:
Carysfort Press Ltd.,
58 Woodfield,
Scholarstown Road,
Rathfarnham,
Dublin 16,
Republic of Ireland.

T (353 1) 493 7383
F (353 1) 406 9815
E: info@carysfortpress.com
www.carysfortpress.com

HOW TO ORDER

TRADE ORDERS DIRECTLY TO:
Irish Book Distribution
Unit 12, North Park, North Road,
Finglas, Dublin 11.

T: (353 1) 8239580
F: (353 1) 8239599
E: mary@argosybooks.ie
www.argosybooks.ie

INDIVIDUAL ORDERS DIRECTLY TO:
eprint Ltd.
35 Coolmine Industrial Estate,
Blanchardstown, Dublin 15.
T: (353 1) 827 8860
F: (353 1) 827 8804 Order online @
E: books@eprint.ie
www.eprint.ie

FOR SALES IN NORTH AMERICA AND CANADA:
Dufour Editions Inc.,
124 Byers Road,
PO Box 7,
Chester Springs,
PA 19425,
USA

T: 1-610-458-5005
F: 1-610-458-7103

Irish Appropriation Of Greek Tragedy

Brian Arkins

This book presents an analysis of more than 30 plays written by Irish dramatists and poets that are based on the tragedies of Sophocles, Euripides and Aeschylus. These plays proceed from the time of Yeats and Synge through MacNeice and the Longfords on to many of today's leading writers.

ISBN 978-1-904505-47-1 €20

Alive in Time: The Enduring Drama of Tom Murphy

Ed. Christopher Murray

Almost 50 years after he first hit the headlines as Ireland's most challenging playwright, the 'angry young man' of those times Tom Murphy still commands his place at the pinnacle of Irish theatre. Here 17 new essays by prominent critics and academics, with an introduction by Christopher Murray, survey Murphy's dramatic oeuvre in a concerted attempt to define his greatness and enduring appeal, making this book a significant study of a unique genius.

ISBN 978-1-904505-45-7 €25

Performing Violence in Contemporary Ireland

Ed. Lisa Fitzpatrick

This interdisciplinary collection of fifteen new essays by scholars of theatre, Irish studies, music, design and politics explores aspects of the performance of violence in contemporary Ireland. With chapters on the work of playwrights Martin McDonagh, Martin Lynch, Conor McPherson and Gary Mitchell, on Republican commemorations and the 90th anniversary ceremonies for the Battle of the Somme and the Easter Rising, this book aims to contribute to the ongoing international debate on the performance of violence in contemporary societies.

ISBN 978-1-904505-44-0 (2009) €20

Ireland's Economic Crisis - Time to Act. Essays from over 40 leading Irish thinkers at the MacGill Summer School 2009

Eds. Joe Mulholland and Finbarr Bradley

Ireland's economic crisis requires a radical transformation in policymaking. In this volume, political, industrial, academic, trade union and business leaders and commentators tell the story of the Irish economy and its rise and fall. Contributions at Glenties range from policy, vision and context to practical suggestions on how the country can emerge from its crisis.

ISBN 978-1-904505-43-3 (2009) €20

Deviant Acts: Essays on Queer Performance

Ed. David Cregan

This book contains an exciting collection of essays focusing on a variety of alternative performances happening in contemporary Ireland. While it highlights the particular representations of gay and lesbian identity it also brings to light how diversity has always been a part of Irish culture and is, in fact, shaping what it means to be Irish today.

ISBN 978-1-904505-42-6 (2009) €20

Seán Keating in Context: Responses to Culture and Politics in Post-Civil War Ireland

Compiled, edited and introduced by Éimear O'Connor

Irish artist Seán Keating has been judged by his critics as the personification of old-fashioned traditionalist values. This book presents a different view. The story reveals Keating's early determination to attain government support for the visual arts. It also illustrates his socialist leanings, his disappointment with capitalism, and his attitude to cultural snobbery, to art critics, and to the Academy. Given the national and global circumstances nowadays, Keating's critical and wry observations are prophetic – and highly amusing.

ISBN 978-1-904505-41-9 €25

Dialogue of the Ancients of Ireland: A new translation of Acallam na Senorach

Translated with introduction and notes by Maurice Harmon

One of Ireland's greatest collections of stories and poems, The Dialogue of the Ancients of Ireland is a new translation by Maurice Harmon of the 12th century *Acallam na Senorach*. Retold in a refreshing modern idiom, the *Dialogue* is an extraordinary account of journeys to the four provinces by St. Patrick and the pagan Cailte, one of the surviving Fian. Within the frame story are over 200 other stories reflecting many genres – wonder tales, sea journeys, romances, stories of revenge, tales of monsters and magic. The poems are equally varied – lyrics, nature poems, eulogies, prophecies, laments, genealogical poems. After the *Tain Bo Cuailnge*, the *Acallam* is the largest surviving prose work in Old and Middle Irish.

ISBN: 978-1-904505-39-6 (2009) €20

Literary and Cultural Relations between Ireland and Hungary and Central and Eastern Europe

Ed. Maria Kurdi

This lively, informative and incisive collection of essays sheds fascinating new light on the literary interrelations between Ireland, Hungary, Poland, Romania and the Czech Republic. It charts a hitherto under-explored history of the reception of modern Irish culture in Central and Eastern Europe and also investigates how key authors have been translated, performed and adapted. The revealing explorations undertaken in this volume of a wide array of Irish dramatic and literary texts, ranging from *Gulliver's Travels* to *Translations* and *The Pillowman*, tease out the subtly altered nuances that they acquire in a Central European context.

ISBN: 978-1-904505-40-2 (2009) €20

Plays and Controversies: Abbey Theatre Diaries 2000-2005

Ben Barnes

In diaries covering the period of his artistic directorship of the Abbey, Ben Barnes offers a frank, honest, and probing account of a much commented upon and controversial period in the history of the national theatre. These diaries also provide fascinating personal insights into the day-to- day pressures, joys, and frustrations of running one of Ireland's most iconic institutions.

ISBN: 978-1-904505-38-9 (2008) €35

Interactions: Dublin Theatre Festival 1957-2007. Irish Theatrical Diaspora Series: 3

Eds. Nicholas Grene and Patrick Lonergan with Lilian Chambers

For over 50 years the Dublin Theatre Festival has been one of Ireland's most important cultural events, bringing countless new Irish plays to the world stage, while introducing Irish audiences to the most important international theatre companies and artists. Interactions explores and celebrates the achievements of the renowned Festival since 1957 and includes specially commissioned memoirs from past organizers, offering a unique perspective on the controversies and successes that have marked the event's history. An especially valuable feature of the volume, also, is a complete listing of the shows that have appeared at the Festival from 1957 to 2008.

ISBN: 978-1-904505-36-5 €25

The Informer: A play by Tom Murphy based on the novel by Liam O'Flaherty

The Informer, Tom Murphy's stage adaptation of Liam O'Flaherty's novel, was produced in the 1981 Dublin Theatre Festival, directed by the playwright himself, with Liam Neeson in the leading role. The central subject of the play is the quest of a character at the point of emotional and moral breakdown for some source of meaning or identity. In the case of Gypo Nolan, the informer of the title, this involves a nightmarish progress through a Dublin underworld in which he changes from a Judas figure to a scapegoat surrogate for Jesus, taking upon himself the sins of the world. A cinematic style, with flash-back and intercut scenes, is used rather than a conventional theatrical structure to catch the fevered and phantasmagoric progression of Gypo's mind. The language, characteristically for Murphy, mixes graphically colloquial Dublin slang with the haunted intricacies of the central character groping for the meaning of his own actions. The dynamic rhythm of the action builds towards an inevitable but theatrically satisfying tragic catastrophe. ' [The Informer] is, in many ways closer to being an original Murphy play than it is to O'Flaherty...' Fintan O'Toole.

ISBN: 978-1-904505-37-2 (2008) €10

Shifting Scenes: Irish theatre-going 1955-1985

Eds. Nicholas Grene and Chris Morash

Transcript of conversations with John Devitt, academic and reviewer, about his lifelong passion for the theatre. A fascinating and entertaining insight into Dublin theatre over the course of thirty years provided by Devitt's vivid reminiscences and astute observations.

ISBN: 978-1-904505-33-4 (2008) €10

Irish Literature: Feminist Perspectives

Eds. Patricia Coughlan and Tina O'Toole

The collection discusses texts from the early 18th century to the present. A central theme of the book is the need to renegotiate the relations of feminism with nationalism and to transact the potential contest of these two important narratives, each possessing powerful emancipatory force. Irish Literature: Feminist Perspectives contributes incisively to contemporary debates about Irish culture, gender and ideology.

ISBN: 978-1-904505-35-8 (2008) €25

Silenced Voices: Hungarian Plays from Transylvania

Selected and translated by Csilla Bertha and Donald E. Morse

The five plays are wonderfully theatrical, moving fluidly from absurdism to tragedy, and from satire to the darkly comic. Donald Morse and Csilla Bertha's translations capture these qualities perfectly, giving voice to the 'forgotten playwrights of Central Europe'. They also deeply enrich our understanding of the relationship between art, ethics, and politics in Europe.

ISBN: 978-1-904505-34-1 (2008) €25

A Hazardous Melody of Being:
Seóirse Bodley's Song Cycles on the poems of Micheal O'Siadhail

Ed. Lorraine Byrne Bodley

This apograph is the first publication of Bodley's O'Siadhail song cycles and is the first book to explore the composer's lyrical modernity from a number of perspectives. Lorraine Byrne Bodley's insightful introduction describes in detail the development and essence of Bodley's musical thinking, the European influences he absorbed which linger in these cycles, and the importance of his work as a composer of the Irish art song.

ISBN: 978-1-904505-31-0 (2008) €25

Irish Theatre in England: Irish Theatrical Diaspora Series: 2

Eds. Richard Cave and Ben Levitas

Irish theatre in England has frequently illustrated the complex relations between two distinct cultures. How English reviewers and audiences interpret Irish plays is often decidedly different from how the plays were read in performance in Ireland. How certain Irish performers have chosen to be understood in Dublin is not necessarily how audiences in London have perceived their constructed stage personae. Though a collection by diverse authors, the twelve essays in this volume investigate these issues from a variety of perspectives that together chart the trajectory of Irish performance in England from the mid-nineteenth century till today.

ISBN: 978-1-904505-26-6 (2007) €20

Goethe and Anna Amalia: A Forbidden Love?

Ettore Ghibellino, Trans. Dan Farrelly

In this study Ghibellino sets out to show that the platonic relationship between Goethe and Charlotte von Stein – lady-in-waiting to Anna Amalia, the Dowager Duchess of Weimar – was used as part of a cover-up for Goethe's intense and prolonged love relationship with the Duchess Anna Amalia herself. The book attempts to uncover a hitherto closely-kept state secret. Readers convinced by the evidence supporting Ghibellino's hypothesis will see in it one of the very great love stories in European history – to rank with that of Dante and Beatrice, and Petrarch and Laura.

ISBN: 978-1-904505-24-2 €20

Ireland on Stage: Beckett and After

Eds. Hiroko Mikami, Minako Okamuro, Naoko Yagi

The collection focuses primarily on Irish playwrights and their work, both in text and on the stage during the latter half of the twentieth century. The central figure is Samuel Beckett, but the contributors freely draw on Beckett and his work provides a springboard to discuss contemporary playwrights such as Brian Friel, Frank McGuinness, Marina Carr and Conor McPherson amongst others. Contributors include: Anthony Roche, Hiroko Mikami, Naoko Yagi, Cathy Leeney, Joseph Long, Noreem Doody, Minako Okamuro, Christopher Murray, Futoshi Sakauchi and Declan Kiberd

ISBN: 978-1-904505-23-5 (2007) €20

'Echoes Down the Corridor': Irish Theatre - Past, Present and Future

Eds. Patrick Lonergan and Riana O'Dwyer

This collection of fourteen new essays explores Irish theatre from exciting new perspectives. How has Irish theatre been received internationally - and, as the country becomes more multicultural, how will international theatre influence the development of drama in Ireland? These and many other important questions.

ISBN: 978-1-904505-25-9 (2007) €20

Musics of Belonging: The Poetry of Micheal O'Siadhail

Eds. Marc Caball & David F. Ford

An overall account is given of O'Siadhail's life, his work and the reception of his poetry so far. There are close readings of some poems, analyses of his artistry in matching diverse content with both classical and innovative forms, and studies of recurrent themes such as love, death, language, music, and the shifts of modern life.

ISBN: 978-1-904505-22-8 (2007) €25 (Paperback)
ISBN: 978-1-904505-21-1 (2007) €50 (Casebound)

Brian Friel's Dramatic Artistry: 'The Work has Value'

Eds. Donald E. Morse, Csilla Bertha and Maria Kurdi

Brian Friel's Dramatic Artistry presents a refreshingly broad range of voices: new work from some of the leading English-speaking authorities on Friel, and fascinating essays from scholars in Germany, Italy, Portugal, and Hungary. This book will deepen our knowledge and enjoyment of Friel's work.

ISBN: 978-1-904505-17-4 (2006) €30

The Theatre of Martin McDonagh: 'A World of Savage Stories'

Eds. Lilian Chambers and Eamonn Jordan

The book is a vital response to the many challenges set by McDonagh for those involved in the production and reception of his work. Critics and commentators from around the world offer a diverse range of often provocative approaches. What is not surprising is the focus and commitment of the engagement, given the controversial and stimulating nature of the work.

ISBN: 978-1-904505-19-8 (2006) €35

Edna O'Brien: New Critical Perspectives

Eds. Kathryn Laing, Sinead Mooney and Maureen O'Connor

The essays collected here illustrate some of the range, complexity, and interest of Edna O'Brien as a fiction writer and dramatist. They will contribute to a broader appreciation of her work and to an evolution of new critical approaches, as well as igniting more interest in the many unexplored areas of her considerable oeuvre.

ISBN: 978-1-904505-20-4 (2006) €20

Irish Theatre on Tour

Eds. Nicholas Grene and Chris Morash

'Touring has been at the strategic heart of Druid's artistic policy since the early eighties. Everyone has the right to see professional theatre in their own communities. Irish theatre on tour is a crucial part of Irish theatre as a whole'. Garry Hynes

ISBN 978-1-904505-13-6 (2005) €20

Poems 2000-2005 by Hugh Maxton

Poems 2000-2005 is a transitional collection written while the author – also known to be W.J. Mc Cormack, literary historian – was in the process of moving back from London to settle in rural Ireland.

ISBN 978-1-904505-12-9 (2005) €10

Synge: A Celebration

Ed. Colm Tóibín

A collection of essays by some of Ireland's most creative writers on the work of John Millington Synge, featuring Sebastian Barry, Marina Carr, Anthony Cronin, Roddy Doyle, Anne Enright, Hugo Hamilton, Joseph O'Connor, Mary O'Malley, Fintan O'Toole, Colm Toibin, Vincent Woods.

ISBN 978-1-904505-14-3 (2005) €15

East of Eden: New Romanian Plays

Ed. Andrei Marinescu

Four of the most promising Romanian playwrights, young and very young, are in this collection, each one with a specific way of seeing the Romanian reality, each one with a style of communicating an articulated artistic vision of the society we are living in. Ion Caramitru, General Director Romanian National Theatre Bucharest.
ISBN 978-1-904505-15-0 (2005) €10

George Fitzmaurice: 'Wild in His Own Way', Biography of an Irish Playwright

Fiona Brennan

'Fiona Brennan's introduction to his considerable output allows us a much greater appreciation and understanding of Fitzmaurice, the one remaining under-celebrated genius of twentieth-century Irish drama'. Conall Morrison

ISBN 978-1-904505-16-7 (2005) €20

Out of History: Essays on the Writings of Sebastian Barry

Ed. Christina Hunt Mahony

The essays address Barry's engagement with the contemporary cultural debate in Ireland and also with issues that inform postcolonial critical theory. The range and selection of contributors has ensured a high level of critical expression and an insightful assessment of Barry and his works.

ISBN: 978-1-904505-18-1 (2005) €20

Three Congregational Masses

Seoirse Bodley

'From the simpler congregational settings in the Mass of Peace and the Mass of Joy to the richer textures of the Mass of Glory, they are immediately attractive and accessible, and with a distinctively Irish melodic quality.' Barra Boydell

ISBN: 978-1-904505-11-2 (2005) €15

Georg Büchner's Woyzeck,

A new translation by Dan Farrelly

The most up-to-date German scholarship of Thomas Michael Mayer and Burghard Dedner has finally made it possible to establish an authentic sequence of scenes. The wide-spread view that this play is a prime example of loose, open theatre is no longer sustainable. Directors and teachers are challenged to "read it again".

ISBN: 978-1-904505-02-0 (2004) €10

Playboys of the Western World: Production Histories

Ed. Adrian Frazier

'The book is remarkably well-focused: half is a series of production histories of Playboy performances through the twentieth century in the UK, Northern Ireland, the USA, and Ireland. The remainder focuses on one contemporary performance, that of Druid Theatre, as directed by Garry Hynes. The various contemporary social issues that are addressed in relation to Synge's play and this performance of it give the volume an additional interest: it shows how the arts matter.' Kevin Barry

ISBN: 978-1-904505-06-8 (2004) €20

The Power of Laughter: Comedy and Contemporary Irish Theatre

Ed. Eric Weitz

The collection draws on a wide range of perspectives and voices including critics, playwrights, directors and performers. The result is a series of fascinating and provocative debates about the myriad functions of comedy in contemporary Irish theatre. Anna McMullan

As Stan Laurel said, 'it takes only an onion to cry. Peel it and weep. Comedy is harder'. 'These essays listen to the power of laughter. They hear the tough heart of Irish theatre – hard and wicked and funny'. Frank McGuinness

ISBN: 978-1-904505-05-1 (2004) €20

Sacred Play: Soul-Journeys in contemporary Irish Theatre

Anne F. O'Reilly

'Theatre as a space or container for sacred play allows audiences to glimpse mystery and to experience transformation. This book charts how Irish playwrights negotiate the labyrinth of the Irish soul and shows how their plays contribute to a poetics of Irish culture that enables a new imagining. Playwrights discussed are: McGuinness, Murphy, Friel, Le Marquand Hartigan, Burke Brogan, Harding, Meehan, Carr, Parker, Devlin, and Barry.'

ISBN: 978-1-904505-07-5 (2004) €25

The Irish Harp Book

Sheila Larchet Cuthbert

This is a facsimile of the edition originally published by Mercier Press in 1993. There is a new preface by Sheila Larchet Cuthbert, and the biographical material has been updated. It is a collection of studies and exercises for the use of teachers and pupils of the Irish harp.
ISBN: 978-1-904505-08-2 (2004) €35

The Drunkard

Tom Murphy

'The Drunkard is a wonderfully eloquent play. Murphy's ear is finely attuned to the glories and absurdities of melodramatic exclamation, and even while he is wringing out its ludicrous overstatement, he is also making it sing.' The Irish Times

ISBN: 978-1-90 05-09-9 (2004) €10

Goethe: Musical Poet, Musical Catalyst

Ed. Lorraine Byrne

'Goethe was interested in, and acutely aware of, the place of music in human experience generally - and of its particular role in modern culture. Moreover, his own literary work - especially the poetry and Faust - inspired some of the major composers of the European tradition to produce some of their finest works.' Martin Swales

ISBN: 978-1-9045-10-5 (2004) €40

The Theatre of Marina Carr: "Before rules was made"

Eds. Anna McMullan & Cathy Leeney

As the first published collection of articles on the theatre of Marina Carr, this volume explores the world of Carr's theatrical imagination, the place of her plays in contemporary theatre in Ireland and abroad and the significance of her highly individual voice.

ISBN: 978-0-9534257-7-8 (2003) €20

Critical Moments: Fintan O'Toole on Modern Irish Theatre

Eds. Julia Furay & Redmond O'Hanlon

This new book on the work of Fintan O'Toole, the internationally acclaimed theatre critic and cultural commentator, offers percussive analyses and assessments of the major plays and playwrights in the canon of modern Irish theatre. Fearless and provocative in his judgements, O'Toole is essential reading for anyone interested in criticism or in the current state of Irish theatre.

ISBN: 978-1-904505-03-7 (2003) €20

Goethe and Schubert: Across the Divide

Eds. Lorraine Byrne & Dan Farrelly

Proceedings of the International Conference, 'Goethe and Schubert in Perspective and Performance', Trinity College Dublin, 2003. This volume includes essays by leading scholars – Barkhoff, Boyle, Byrne, Canisius, Dürr, Fischer, Hill, Kramer, Lamport, Lund, Meikle, Newbould, Norman McKay, White, Whitton, Wright, Youens – on Goethe's musicality and his relationship to Schubert; Schubert's contribution to sacred music and the Lied and his setting of Goethe's Singspiel, Claudine. A companion volume of this Singspiel (with piano reduction and English translation) is also available.

ISBN: 978-1-904505-04-4 (2003)   €25

Goethe's Singspiel, 'Claudine von Villa Bella'

Set by Franz Schubert

Goethe's Singspiel in three acts was set to music by Schubert in 1815. Only Act One of Schuberts's Claudine score is extant. The present volume makes Act One available for performance in English and German. It comprises both a piano reduction by Lorraine Byrne of the original Schubert orchestral score and a bilingual text translated for the modern stage by Dan Farrelly. This is a tale, wittily told, of lovers and vagabonds, romance, reconciliation, and resolution of family conflict.

ISBN: 978-0-9544290-0-3 (2002)   €20

Theatre of Sound, Radio and the Dramatic Imagination

Dermot Rattigan

An innovative study of the challenges that radio drama poses to the creative imagination of the writer, the production team, and the listener.
"A remarkably fine study of radio drama – everywhere informed by the writer's professional experience of such drama in the making…A new theoretical and analytical approach – informative, illuminating and at all times readable." Richard Allen Cave

ISBN: 978- 0-9534-257-5-4 (2002)   €20

Talking about Tom Murphy

Ed. Nicholas Grene

Talking About Tom Murphy is shaped around the six plays in the landmark Abbey Theatre Murphy Season of 2001, assembling some of the best-known commentators on his work: Fintan O'Toole, Chris Morash, Lionel Pilkington, Alexandra Poulain, Shaun Richards, Nicholas Grene and Declan Kiberd.

ISBN: 978-0-9534-257-9-2 (2002)   €15

Hamlet: The Shakespearean Director

Mike Wilcock

"This study of the Shakespearean director as viewed through various interpretations of HAMLET is a welcome addition to our understanding of how essential it is for a director to have a clear vision of a great play. It is an important study from which all of us who love Shakespeare and who understand the importance of continuing contemporary exploration may gain new insights." From the Foreword, by Joe Dowling, Artistic Director, The Guthrie Theater, Minneapolis, MN

ISBN: 978-1-904505-00-6 (2002) €20

The Theatre of Frank Mc Guinness: Stages of Mutability

Ed. Helen Lojek

The first edited collection of essays about internationally renowned Irish playwright Frank McGuinness focuses on both performance and text. Interpreters come to diverse conclusions, creating a vigorous dialogue that enriches understanding and reflects a strong consensus about the value of McGuinness's complex work.

ISBN: 978-1904505-01-3. (2002) €20

Theatre Talk: Voices of Irish Theatre Practitioners

Eds Lilian Chambers, Ger Fitzgibbon and Eamonn Jordan

"This book is the right approach - asking practitioners what they feel." Sebastian Barry, Playwright "... an invaluable and informative collection of interviews with those who make and shape the landscape of Irish Theatre." Ben Barnes, Artistic Director of the Abbey Theatre

ISBN: 978-0-9534-257-6-1 (2001) €20

In Search of the South African Iphigenie

Erika von Wietersheim and Dan Farrelly

Discussions of Goethe's "Iphigenie auf Tauris" (Under the Curse) as relevant to women's issues in modern South Africa: women in family and public life; the force of women's spirituality; experience of personal relationships; attitudes to parents and ancestors; involvement with religion.

ISBN: 978-0-9534257-8-5 (2001) €10

'The Starving' and 'October Song':

Two contemporary Irish plays by Andrew Hinds

The Starving, set during and after the siege of Derry in 1689, is a moving and engrossing drama of the emotional journey of two men.

October Song, a superbly written family drama set in real time in pre-ceasefire Derry.

ISBN: 978-0-9534-257-4-7 (2001) €10

Seen and Heard: Six new plays by Irish women

Ed. Cathy Leeney

A rich and funny, moving and theatrically exciting collection of plays by Mary Elizabeth Burke-Kennedy, Síofra Campbell, Emma Donoghue, Anne Le Marquand Hartigan, Michelle Read and Dolores Walshe.

ISBN: 978-0-9534-257-3-0 (2001) €20

Theatre Stuff: Critical essays on contemporary Irish theatre

Ed. Eamonn Jordan

Best selling essays on the successes and debates of contemporary Irish theatre at home and abroad. Contributors include: Thomas Kilroy, Declan Hughes, Anna McMullan, Declan Kiberd, Deirdre Mulrooney, Fintan O'Toole, Christopher Murray, Caoimhe McAvinchey and Terry Eagleton.

ISBN: 978-0-9534-2571-1-6 (2000) €20

Under the Curse. Goethe's "Iphigenie Auf Tauris", A New Version

Dan Farrelly

The Greek myth of Iphigenie grappling with the curse on the house of Atreus is brought vividly to life. This version is currently being used in Johannesburg to explore problems of ancestry, religion, and Black African women's spirituality.

ISBN: 978-09534-257-8-5 (2000) €10

Urfaust, A New Version of Goethe's early "Faust" in Brechtian Mode

Dan Farrelly

This version is based on Brecht's irreverent and daring re-interpretation of the German classic. "Urfaust is a kind of well-spring for German theatre… The love-story is the most daring and the most profound in German dramatic literature." Brecht

ISBN: 978-0-9534-257-0-9 (1998) €20